# WORLD-BUILDING IN THE GRAND TRADITION BY *NEW YORK TIMES BESTSELLING*

## KEVIN J. ANDERSON

### RAVES FOR KEVIN J. ANDERSON'S *CLIMBING OLYMPUS*

# KEVIN J. ANDERSON

# BLINDFOLD

ASPECT ®

WARNER BOOKS

A Time Warner Company

WARNER BOOKS EDITION

Copyright © 1995 by Kevin J. Anderson
All rights reserved.

Aspect is a registered trademark of Warner Books, Inc.

Cover design by Don Puckey
Cover illustration by Stephen Youll
Interior design and typesetting by Kevin J. Anderson

Warner Books, Inc.
1271 Avenue of the Americas
New York, NY 10020

Ⓦ A Time Warner Company

Printed in the United States of America

First Printing: November, 1995

10 9 8 7 6 5 4 3 2 1

This book is for

KRISTINE KATHRYN RUSCH

for all of the help and love she has shared over the years in
helping me become a better writer

## ACKNOWLEDGMENTS

Special thanks to Mark Budz, Marina Fitch, Leslie Lauderdale, and Kathy Dyer for their detailed comments and suggestions to improve this book, Lillie Mitchell for her transcribing skills, Dr. Henry Stratman for medical and biological advice, Betsy Mitchell for her whizbang editing expertise, Wayne Chang for keeping the trains running on time, and Rebecca Moesta Anderson for her love and support during the writing of my most ambitious novel to date.

"Our conscience is not the vessel of eternal verities. It grows with our social life, and a new social condition means a radical change in conscience."

—Walter Lippmann

"The way of paradoxes is the way of truth. To test reality we must see it on the tight-rope. When the Verities become acrobats we can judge them."

—Oscar Wilde

ACCUSED

to think of reporting to yet another timid Master set because you fell off and bruise your rear. You've outgrown that is more.

# CHAPTER

## II

### i

Outside the Truthsayers Guild, the crowd had already started to gather. Kalliana could hear the murmur of voices, feel the press of their excited thoughts even through the shielded walls of Guild Headquarters.

They were waiting.

She looked through the stained glass windows of her quarters on the third deck. She brushed pale fingers across the smooth, cool glass panes—brilliant shards of crimson, green, and blue epoxied into dull alloy tracks—as if to rub away the shadows of milling people anticipating the trial. But they would not leave, not until Kalliana had made her judgment.

The people of First Landing waited in the plaza for the Truthsayer to come out, to face the accused murderer, to read the guilt or innocence directly from his thoughts.

Perhaps it was the spectacle the colonists wanted, a bright entertainment, or just relief from their strenuous jobs for an hour or so. Kalliana knew they all had hard lives out there; she wouldn't have traded with them for anything.

Officially, the Truthsayers Guild believed the citizens longed for a reaffirming lesson in morality, a demonstration of what would happen if they slipped from the narrow but clearly defined path of the law. . . . Then again, after spending so much time descending into the minds of criminals, Kalliana wondered if maybe the spectators were just thirsty for blood.

The accused—a man named Eli Strone—had supposedly spilled enough blood.

Raw sunlight filtered through her window to spill rainbows

across the rugs that covered the cold deck plates. Her quarters, once the cabin of a high-ranking officer on the scuttled spaceship that had been converted into the Guild building, seemed safe and warm to her, a shelter from the evil thoughts of the populace at large. Every day she and the eleven other telepathic Truthsayers had to face the sins of the people, but today would be worse. Today, if the accused was indeed guilty, she would be forced to confront his memory of slaughtering twenty-three people.

Kalliana wrapped herself in her white robe, clean and pure, made of bleached cotton grown here on the planet Atlas, then tied it with the emerald sash of a Truthsayer. Her petite body, fine blond hair, and translucent skin made her look like a pale angel. The cloth rustled like hushed whispers as she moved. She completed her ceremonial costume with a wide, ornate gold collar that added extra weight to her shoulders, as if her burden wasn't already heavy enough. But the formal spectacle required all the trappings of a mystical ritual.

The crowd was growing restless in the plaza. Her reluctance had already made her late. She would have to face the people soon, face Eli Strone.

## ii

She had read the proclamation a dozen times over, but Kalliana picked up the discolored sheets and stared at the words again. Documents printed on genuine paper made from kenaf fibers, because a physical document implied a permanence that electronic records could not convey.

The Strone Case. The brutal murders had occurred in the isolated wastelands between the landholdings of Carsus and Bondalar, out in the construction camps for the new mag-lev rail that would link the two holdings. An efficient mag-lev network already connected each of the nineteen scattered landholdings with the hub city of First Landing, but in an unprecedented alliance, Carsus and Bondalar had decided to join their holdings directly, without passing through the central point.

The construction work had proceeded for three years, plagued by disasters, sabotage, defective materials. And now this: Three separate labor gangs, twenty-three people, had been murdered. The bodies hadn't been discovered for days, since the crews reported to their overseers only once a week. The killings had gotten progressively more monstrous down the line.

A man named Eli Strone had shown up on the roster of each slaughtered crew. Up until two years ago, Strone had been a member of the elite guard working in the Guild Headquarters, steadfast and ready to defend the Truthsayers against any sort of disturbance—but he had abandoned his post suddenly, without explanation, after years of service. Strone had then bounced between minor jobs in First Landing's hydroponic greenhouses or loading docks, eventually heading out to the wilderness and a more rugged life.

Three months ago Strone had volunteered for the backbreaking work of laying inductance coils and alloy rails for the transportation link between Bondalar and Carsus holdings. Such work had generally been assigned as slave labor to criminals convicted of minor offenses, or even the religious fanatics, the Pilgrims, but crew bosses would not turn down a willing worker.

Then the murders had occurred.

Eli Strone had survived; no one else had. He had applied for labor on a fourth crew shortly after the massacres were discovered, and the soldier-police had apprehended him.

Strone insisted he was innocent. But then, most guilty people did. Only a Truthsayer could tell. . . .

Finally ready to face the accused, Kalliana stepped toward her cabin door. Her stomach knotted, and she felt the frosty electricity of nervous sweat, but she did not hesitate. She had been raised in the Guild since the embryo stage, developed for this duty. It was the way she paid for the comfortable life she lived.

As she stepped into the corridor, she saw Guild Master Tharion striding toward her: a tall man with sunlight-yellow hair and eyebrows, granite-gray eyes, and a long white robe cinched with a royal blue sash. He was thirty-four, thirteen years her senior; only two years ago he had found himself suddenly saddled with leadership of the Truthsayers Guild.

"I'm ready, Guild Master," Kalliana said, averting her eyes, certain Tharion had come in impatience.

"A moment, Kalliana," he said, gesturing back into her quarters. "The people can wait. They enjoy the anticipation."

Kalliana retreated into her quarters, glad for the delay but worried about what Tharion would ask. She detected no anger in his expression, no stiffness in his movements. He had a pleasant face, calm but firm, just beginning to show the lines of responsibility that came with middle age.

With her own residual telepathic enhancement, Kalliana was tempted to reach out and pluck the concerns directly from Tharion's mind, to prepare herself—but after her years of rigorous ethical training, she would never do such a thing.

Guild Master Tharion lowered his voice, commanding her attention. "There may be more to this case than the murders, Kalliana," he said. "It troubles me deeply. You know that Strone used to be one of our elite guards, but he left us just after I became Guild Master. Very mysterious. He always seemed a bit of an odd sort, but reliable. He escorted me many times when I was younger. I got the impression he revered the Truthsayers, looked up to us as great dispensers of truth, wielding the sword of justice." He laughed, then frowned, letting his thoughts come through.

"I've done a lot of thinking . . . and I cannot help but wonder if he may be a pawn in a larger, older plot against . . . us? Against some of the landholders? I don't know."

Kalliana frowned, not sure what he wanted from her. "What makes you say that? Murders were committed, and this man was implicated. It's up to me to declare whether he is guilty or innocent."

"There may be more," Tharion said. "Given the constant delays and frequent setbacks on the rail-construction project, Hektor Carsus has informally petitioned me for some answers. If any information comes to light during your reading of Strone . . ."

"What kind of information?" Kalliana asked, suddenly wary. She knew clearly, from her years of ethical training, exactly how far she was expected to go inside the criminal mind. "I am not required to read any deeper than necessary to determine his guilt or innocence."

"Just be watchful. Perhaps his motivations will be plain enough," Tharion said, a pair of small creases forming between his pale brows. "We all know Hektor Carsus is a suspicious hothead, but he does have certain valid points. From the day he and Janine Bondalar announced their plans to form a marriage alliance, the mag-lev project connecting their holdings has been beset with unreasonable problems. Cursed, some people might say."

Tharion wove his long fingers together. "I have privately brought some of his concerns to Guild Mediators. There's a distinct possibility these murders might be another attempt by some rival landholder to destroy the direct rail link. Strone may just be a hired killer—or a patsy who hasn't really done anything."

Kalliana considered this and nodded uneasily. Tharion looked at her with an open expression, not quite a plea. "When you're inside Strone's head, try to determine whether he was acting under orders from someone else. Is this just a random act of violence, or is there a deeper plan?"

"If he is guilty at all," Kalliana pointed out.

"True," Tharion said, embarrassed. "We need that answer too, of course."

She could hear the continued droning of the crowd in the plaza, rising and falling in irregular waves. "Why should Truthsayers worry about more landholder rivalries? They always squabble with each other—but we are independent, and have been for a hundred years. Let them do their own investigations, their own snooping. I won't be a spy for Carsus or Bondalar or Dokken or any other landholder —"

Tharion held up his hand. "Not for the landholders. For *us*. Because if another landholder is working this plot, then *we* are being manipulated."

Kalliana finally saw his logic and could not think of an excuse to deny his request, despite her reluctance. She nodded and followed him out the door. "All right, let's get this over with."

### iii

The huge ground level opening of the half-buried spaceship, the *SkySword*, had originally been designed for loading cargo and launching military assault vehicles, but the Truthsayers had replaced the doors with ornate slabs of metal cast in the foundries of one of the mountain holdings. The regal portals were inlaid with beautiful and complex mosaics of bright polished rock. Grandeur to impress the masses.

A cascade of sunlight spilled into the main corridor as the doors swung open. Kalliana walked down the ramp beside the Guild Master, her petite form dwarfed by the immense size of the Guild Headquarters.

Outside, a group of elite guards flanked the door, ready to escort her through the crowd to the speaking platform in the center of the plaza. Kalliana raised her chin and walked forward, her feet bare on the shadowed flagstones, her white robe fluttering around her in the breeze. The air outside smelled dry and flat, like rock dust, without the enriching moisturizers and perfumes that circulated through the Guild's confined chambers. She felt instantly uncomfortable, but she would be back inside soon, as soon as she finished her duty.

The elite guard fell silently into ranks beside her, their scarlet gauntlets and boots, deep blue uniforms, and goggled helmets setting them apart from the citizens. Kalliana ascended the granite steps to the speaking platform.

Overhead, the skies turned gray with an approaching cloud front, one of the fast-moving storms that cruised over the surface of Atlas. The orbital Platform had not issued a weather warning, but she wondered if it would rain soon. The water would probably make a big difference to those living in the outer landholdings, though it wouldn't matter to the Truthsayers inside their Headquarters. Often, she found it soothing to listen to the raindrops beating an irregular rhythm against the hull plates and watch them stream and ripple over the stained glass windows.

Kalliana would need some forced relaxation after this ordeal in front of so many people. She hated murder cases.

The crowd was larger than usual. Eli Strone's alleged crimes were so heinous that many had come even from the far landholdings to witness her pronouncement. Guild Master Tharion seemed pleased at the turnout.

As she walked among them, Kalliana felt the surge of anticipation from the audience, a maelstrom of conflicting thoughts that forced her to put up mental barriers. Though she had not taken a booster dose of the mind-enhancing drug Veritas in days, she still felt the backwash of their thoughts—disjointed hopes, bitterness, frustration, new love, anticipation, even physical thoughts of muscle aches and noontime hunger.

She shook her head to clear her mind, pushing back the psychic babble. While she was required to experience the sins— if any—of Eli Strone, these other citizens could keep their weary lives to themselves.

Kalliana didn't comprehend how all these people lived, what their dreams were, how they coped with such a bleak and difficult existence. The colonists often seemed happy, though she could not understand it. She had seen so much anger and misery in the minds she had truth-read. Nervously, she glanced behind her at the polished hull of the Guild Headquarters, her landmark of safety and shelter.

In the front row of spectators, sitting in canvas chairs covered with sun shades, swarthy Hektor Carsus sat beside his betrothed, landholder Janine Bondalar, who was at least fifteen years the man's senior. The two held hands and stared woodenly ahead, waiting to hear Kalliana's judgment about the man accused of killing so many of their workers.

Kalliana wondered what they wanted to hear—did the allied landholders wish to find a scapegoat so they could start another feud with somebody? Hadn't Atlas already suffered enough bloody civil wars during its two centuries of colonial history?

But it didn't matter what Carsus and Bondalar *wanted* to hear. Kalliana would speak the truth of the case. The consequences were not her concern.

The Guild's other eleven Truthsayers sat on shaded stone benches to the side of the stage; many of the crimson-sashed Guild Mediators, those who had lesser telepathic powers but greater skills as negotiators and politicians, had also come to watch Kalliana's pronouncement, though they were not required to witness the spectacle.

From the height of the raised platform, Kalliana looked down at the intimidating sea of faces, all strangers to her. The citizens gazed up at their Truthsayer. They did not know her, because their names were not divulged. To them, all Truthsayers were identical, equally trained, equally capable.

And they were right.

The Guild Master took the center of the stage, raising his arms so that the wide white sleeves of his robe pooled around his elbows. His bright blue sash made him look regal; his sun-yellow hair blew in the breeze.

"The Truthsayers Guild does everything in its power to see that you remain safe," Tharion said, thrusting his voice into the hush of the crowd. As he grew more accustomed to his position as Guild Master, his voice seemed to grow stronger, Kalliana thought. "Your lives are difficult enough, trying to wring an existence from our untamed world, and we do all we can so that you may go about your business without fear of violent crime or war.

"But sometimes we fail. Here, the Guild has failed twenty-three citizens, now dead, found murdered as they worked to construct a new mag-lev rail line that would have benefited the holdings of Carsus and Bondalar." Tharion drew a deep breath, and paused meaningfully.

"When the Guild fails to protect the people, the best thing we can do is to make certain that justice is done, that a criminal does not escape punishment—and that an innocent person is not convicted of someone else's crime. Today, the Truthsayer will determine the guilt or innocence of the man accused of these murders. The dead cannot be brought back to life, but your safety can be assured."

Tharion swept his pale gaze over the gathered people, hesitating on the calm figures of Hektor Carsus and Janine Bondalar, then moved on to glance at the other landholders, each standing separate from their rivals in the crowd. Kalliana noted that Tharion's friend and mentor, the landholder Franz Dokken, had not bothered to attend the trial.

"Over the years," Tharion continued, "despite the best efforts of the Council, some landholders have still attempted to settle disputes through violence, or to usurp lands or resources that have not been distributed to them. For generations, under the authority of the Truthsayers Guild, regiments of soldier-police have been stationed at each holding to deter such hostilities. In the wake of these new murders, I have asked that the sol-pols step up their patrols, keep a more diligent watch for violence brewing in outlying lands as well as here in First Landing. Until we can all work together, Atlas will never become the Eden we were promised it would be."

Looking satisfied, Tharion took a step backward until he stood next to Kalliana again. "Now let us determine the truth about Eli Strone, and learn whether or not we can sleep safely tonight."

Guild Master Tharion gestured, and one of the white-sashed Guild children came up to Kalliana bearing an ornate brass and copper case that held a booster dose of the precious Veritas drug. Kalliana took the case without smiling, and the white-robed child ran back to her companions.

From the gilded, fingerprint-locked cache, Kalliana withdrew one of the sky-blue Veritas capsules. She rolled its smooth shape in her palm. Then, turning her back to the crowd and looking up at the towering metal curves of the Guild Headquarters, she popped the pill into her mouth.

Drawing a long breath, she cracked down on the capsule to make it work faster. The bitter syrup spilled along her tongue, down her throat. She swallowed repeatedly as she gazed up at the motto of the Truthsayers Guild emblazoned on the metal bulkhead over the arching structure of the derelict starship. She stared at it hypnotically, concentrating, focusing.

*Truth Holds No Secrets.*

Kalliana straightened her white robe, swallowed, and let the Veritas boil within her mind. She closed her dusty blue eyes, nodded, then opened them again. One of the elite guards gestured. From the detention decks beneath the Guild Headquarters, Eli Strone emerged.

Already feeling the psychic rush building in her mind, Kalliana turned to look as the accused murderer was brought before her.

iv

When Strone walked forward, a mental hush fell over the crowd. Kalliana detected a faint, indescribable change in the smell of the air, like ozone. A cool breeze rippled across her white robes, as if presaging a storm from the gunmetal gray clouds. She stiffened.

Tall and angular, Eli Strone seemed incredibly placid. His face showed nothing but peace, and he presented a totally cooperative demeanor—but the sol-pol guards had shackled his ankles and chained his wrists, nonetheless. These were primarily symbolic bonds, because if Kalliana pronounced him innocent, she would remove the chains herself, freeing Strone in front of all the spectators. But the bonds also kept the prisoner under control on the off chance that he turned violent.

Kalliana looked down at the accused, bracing herself, but not yet releasing her telepathic abilities. She wasn't ready, but she couldn't show it. She rubbed sweaty palms against her white robe. The weight of the golden collar on her shoulders seemed to increase as she studied the man before her.

The big man wore a gray jumpsuit, barefoot, bare-handed. His knuckles were large and bony, his wide hands callused as if he was accustomed to heavy labor. His hair was a rich, chocolate brown, cut short, but with an unruliness that implied wild curls. What did his thoughts hold?

If Strone had actually committed the killings, Kalliana would find out the moment she looked into his mind—and he knew it. The entire justice system depended on the infallibility of the Veritas drug. No one on Atlas could get away with a crime if brought before a telepathic Truthsayer. The guilty ones often confessed and accepted a lighter punishment rather than be taken before a Truthsayer. Therefore, since Strone insisted he was innocent, Guild Master Tharion's suggested conspiracy might indeed be true. And that would mean the real murderer remained out in society, uncaught.

Eli Strone stood directly before her, gazing into the bright wash of translucent sky. Something about him made Kalliana's skin crawl: an inhuman quality that made him seem aloof from his own circumstances. His eyes, the color of rusty water, were wide, almost circular with unblinking detachment. Guilty or not, he was a strange one, no question about that.

Strone gave her a thin-lipped smile and raised his chin. Kalliana focused her mind. The sol-pol guards placed their hands on their weapons. The gathered audience in the plaza held its breath.

Kalliana touched Eli Strone's temples with her short delicate fingers. She closed her eyes —

*And entered a chamber of horrors.*

v

The first work gang of eight: he had shot them all in the middle of the night as they slept huddled for warmth under their tents in the wasteland. The blood was black as oil in the starlight.

Strone cleared his thoughts to make it easy for Kalliana. Proud, he wanted the Truthsayer to see, to understand. He thought of nothing but what he had done to those abominably guilty human beings. He expected some sort of reward for what he had done.

Strone had been with the team only three days—but that was enough for him to see their sins, the guilt written all over their faces, their expressions, their manners. They coveted things that didn't belong to them, they fantasized about other men's wives, they thought of violence toward one another. They were so twisted. Their evil ran so very deep. In these outlying lands there was no one to dispense justice . . . no one but himself.

Sick with revulsion at their guilt, Strone had crept out of his own tent, blinking his eyes in the watery light of the silent greenish aurora overhead. The mag-lev rail under construction stood like a sentinel, a silver line drawn by a hooked claw across the rocky landscape, raised up on boxlike pedestals with induction coils, transformers, and magnetic boosters. Dust blew across the open desert like a lost sigh.

Strone had killed the sentry first, lulling the man by distracting him, volunteering to take night watch for a few hours since he couldn't sleep anyway. Then, Strone had balled his fist and punched like a sledgehammer into the side of the man's head, cracking the eggshell-thin temple bone. As the sentry slumped, Strone wrapped his forearm around the man's neck, settling the chin into the crook of his elbow. He knelt, using his knee and his back muscles to snap the sentry's neck so thoroughly that Strone could have ripped his entire head off if he had pulled just a little harder. That wouldn't be necessary, though.

He took the sentry's weapon and with fast, cold efficiency, walked from tent to tent, firing into the seven flimsy shelters. A few workers, awakened by the sound of gunfire but still groggy, staggered out, fumbling with the flap zippers even as he shot them. They sprawled on the ground, half out of their tents. Some of them groaned in pain. And he shot them again.

They had continued thinking evil thoughts even in their last moments of life. Strone could tell. He could read their sins.

Eli Strone had been brought up believing that the Truthsayers were dispensers of justice, that the white-robed telepaths kept all crime and sin in abeyance. But he had learned that not even the Truthsayers were perfect. And though they worked diligently, evil still ran rampant among the citizenry. Even in First Landing the Guild couldn't possibly handle it all. There was just too much.

In rare and secret instances, Strone had seen others peripherally able to read thoughts, common people given a brief and illegal rush of telepathy, not the long-standing ability of a Truthsayer, but enough to know the *truth*. He had heard rumors about black market availability of the Veritas drug, normally held in such tight control by the Guild.

Strone, though, had his own access to the truth. He was a vigilante, who could sense the evil lurking inside the other colonists. And he would quietly assist the Truthsayers in their quest for justice. It was his mission. . . .

Leaving the bodies behind at the first site, Strone had walked along the path of the mag-lev rail until he found another group of seven workers and offered them his services.

The second group were all Pilgrims, the quiet religious order who wore dark woolen clothes despite the heat. The Pilgrim crew gladly accepted the help of Eli Strone, then set about attempting to convert him to their religion, but Strone had no interest. His secret powers revealed the hypocrisy in their facial expressions. He could see the hidden desires they harbored within themselves, the evil thoughts, the twisted dreams.

His killing was quieter and more efficient this time. Strone slipped from tent to tent in the deepness of the night. With a knife blade, he made no sound, and neither did the cooling bodies as they twitched and spilled their blood on the ground while Strone held a broad callused hand across their mouths and noses. A few Pilgrims thrashed and fought even after he had slit their throats, but their struggles soon faded.

He was drenched with blood when he finished punishing the second camp, his clothes sticky, his skin painted copper red. He stripped himself naked and scoured his body with handfuls of sand until his flesh felt tingly and raw, and he was cleansed, inside and out, with the purging fire of justice. He was like the Truthsayers he so greatly revered. He didn't need the Veritas drug, because the power of rightness was on his side. . . .

As Kalliana touched his forehead, Strone's thoughts continued to hammer her, cold and impersonal, a simple recitation of factual memories, like a sol-pol incident report. Despite her revulsion, she was forced to view all the flashbacks through *his* eyes. Strone's lack of emotion nauseated her just as much as the vivid slaughter. He continued to pour out his thoughts eagerly, as if offering her a gift:

The members of the third camp looked at him with greater suspicion when he offered to join their detail. These were exiles guarded by two sol-pols, people convicted of crimes and put to hard work for Carsus Holding, blasting and leveling the grade for the mag-lev rail.

Strone wore a rough, ill-fitting robe stolen from one of the Pilgrims. The guards looked strangely at his tattered clothing. They asked him his name, and he gave it freely. He had nothing to hide, since no one had yet learned of the previous murders. As a former member of the esteemed elite guard, he had no blot on his record. He was a righteous man.

Warily, they accepted him because the work team had fallen behind schedule. They had several more kilometers of rail to lay down before they could take furlough back at the main village.

Within three nights it was Strone's turn to help with the cooking, a heavily spiced rice dish. He drugged them all with a small supply of *stenn*, often used by sol-pols to quell disturbances.

Before leaving the Guild, Strone had kept the *stenn* given to him as an elite guard. He put it to good use now. No one tasted the paralysis drug mingled with the pungent spices.

All the victims lay helpless as darkness fell. A line of scarlet clouds clumped on the flat desert horizon. Strone withdrew his most prized equipment, scalpels and pliers. He had planned ahead, dreaming of this day. They all deserved it.

He was in no hurry, so he took his time with this group. They were paralyzed and could not run—but they could still scream. He made one incision with the scalpel in exchange for every outcry they made, continuing his tally until they could make no more sound.

It took him all night long. These people were very evil. . . .

Kalliana tore herself away, reeling backward. More darkness lay deeper, more secrets, a tangled labyrinth of shock and betrayal—information Kalliana did not dare to witness. She fled, coming back to herself.

Eli Strone looked up at her with an open eagerness, like a pet waiting to be praised by its master.

"Guilty," Kalliana choked. "Guilty!" She staggered away and fell to her knees. The sol-pols rushed forward to grab the shackled Strone as he stood gaping at her in shock, too surprised even to struggle.

"But you saw," he said. "You saw my reasons! You know!"

In answer Kalliana felt revulsion rush upward inside her, as if a fist had plunged into her stomach, and she vomited onto the speaking platform. The thoughts of all the crowded people sliced at the edges of her mind like a whirlwind of razor blades.

"But how can you call me guilty?" Strone wailed.

Kalliana couldn't bear to open her eyes as the elite guard caught her, supporting her by the shoulders and arms as she slumped. They rushed her back to the sanctuary of Guild Headquarters.

# CHAPTER

## 2

i

Craning his neck to gaze up into a sky that had been threatening rain for days, Troy Boren watched the space elevator car come down through the clouds. It hung from a braided diamond-fiber thread like fine spider silk thousands of kilometers long.

Sol-pol guards opened the chain-link security fence around the anchor point as the space elevator glided down, silently propelled by motivators along the unseverable cable. Troy squinted at the approaching shape, an artifact of old Earth technology: its armored walls were streaked with tarnish and ionization scars from daily trips to orbit and back over two centuries.

Troy imagined what it must have been like so long ago, when conditions were even more rugged than now. Upon their arrival at the raw, new planet, the original colonists had lived in orbit aboard a platform detached from the main shell of the ship. After several years they had dropped the elevator cable and anchored it at the place that would become First Landing, then they had begun their mass exodus down to the surface. . . .

Now the cylindrical elevator car thrummed as it decelerated on the sturdy cable. A complicated network of servomotors, impellers, tension sensors, docking attachments, and control apparatus crowned its roof, looking as if someone had hammered random scrap components into place without prior planning. But the elevator worked, and it had always worked, and Troy had no doubt that it would continue to work for as long as he lived.

He hadn't grown tired of the sight yet, not in his three weeks at the new job in First Landing. The space elevator seemed so . . . majestic. He squinted his bright, hazel eyes and watched the car descend. A wonder-filled smile crossed his face.

"All right, everybody, prepare for arrival," Cren shouted. Troy's boss worked with a feverish intensity that exhausted him just to watch. "Got it this time, Boren? Don't screw up again. Training period is over. I don't care who your father paid off."

"Yes, sir!" Troy nodded, then glanced upward again, unable to tear his gaze from the elevator car's final descent toward the anchor point.

"Oh, stop gawking," Cren said. "You make me sick. It's embarrassing to have such a starstruck kid on my crew. Go over there and get ready. You got the cargo manifests?"

"Uh, yes sir!" Troy waved the four paper cards printed with itemized lists of supplies, as if his boss might not believe him. He wondered how long it would take for Cren to believe in his competence.

"Be sure you get the damned numbers right this time. I don't think it'll stretch your mental capacity." With a disgusted look, Cren went off to harass someone else. He clapped his hands as he flitted like a sand flea from worker to worker, double-checking, issuing orders, reinforcing his control.

Troy stared nervously down at the manifest cards in his hands, as if that could prevent him from making another mistake. Only two weeks ago he had transposed some digits in two shipments, which sent valuable cargo off to a pair of landholders who had not paid for it—and who refused, even on threat of sol-pol intervention, to return the precious resources that had arrived at their cargo stations. The Landholders Council and the Guild Mediators had been brought in and were even now working to settle the dispute. Cren had never let Troy forget just how much trouble his incompetence had caused.

"Never again," Cren had said, leaning close enough to Troy that the young man could count the bloodshot lines on his boss's eyeballs. Troy knew Cren got more enjoyment out of intimidating his workers than in getting the job done well. "Don't you ever even dream of putting me through this another time."

Troy was of medium height and thin, fidgety as he moved from one task to another. His family had been frustrated with his distractibility, unable to comprehend why he couldn't just work hard and be content with his lot in life like the rest of them were. He just wasn't cut out for a life as a miner, though.

He had done a brief stint on an ore hauler in one of the mine shafts, but he simply could not handle the strenuous physical toil.

He had been transferred to one of the chemical leaching plants, and finally to an inventory shop, where he had received some of his training on computers. He had been reprimanded twice for letting his thoughts wander, for doodling, for letting the paperwork pile up. His mother had lectured him, making everything worse. Though he loved them, like a dutiful son, Troy couldn't understand his family, why they were blind to dreams and possibilities, why they saw no further into the future than the next day—until it involved them directly.

Once the elevator car docked, Troy's job was to go through the manifests and inspect every item as it came off the ramp, tallying it with the orders from various landholders, the Council, the Truthsayers Guild, merchants, or wealthy private citizens. When all the shipments had been removed and stored in the low holding warehouse for later distribution, and their totals entered into the computer systems, Troy would hand the double-checked manifests to Cren, who would then determine an equivalent amount of supplies to be sent back up to the Platform in exchange: water, canisters of air, craftwork, and hydroponically grown food or actual agricultural produce.

Under the overcast sky Troy and a dozen coworkers marched into the fenced area as the car settled onto its toroidal supports and padded bumpers. Chain links rattled as the fence gates moved apart. Two sol-pols stood at their station, looking bored; they had seen the car come and go hundreds of times.

Stalls lined the streets around the anchor point. First Landing's marketplace bustled with merchants selling oddities, from desperately needed supplies to valueless trinkets: new fossils dug up in the mountain holdings, gaudy gemstones, exotic plants grown in private greenhouses.

The mag-lev lines from each landholding ran straight into First Landing at the large supply hub and boarding station. Single-passenger cars whistled in from the outlying areas, and cargo haulers trundled along the rails delivering supplies and resources: sweet-smelling pine lumber from Toth Holding, fish and kelp and bricks from Sardili Shores, salt and processed chemicals from the dry lakebeds of Dokken Holding.

As the other workers plodded through the elevator arrival procedures, Troy watched a big ore hauler come in from Koman Holding. As the cargo hauler locked itself down, burly miners sprang out, reminding him of his home and family up in the

Mining District . . . how his father's skin was always grimy from work in the ore shafts, his fingernails black no matter how much scrubbing he did. His squat mother had developed sloped shoulders and biceps as large as hams from her own backbreaking labor.

Troy's family knew full well he could not have handled such a life. His little sister Rissbeth belittled him incessantly about being a weakling. His older sister Leisa understood and loved him unconditionally, though she had no idea what advice to give him. But Troy's gruff father Rambra had unexpectedly rescued him. Paying a large bonus out of their family savings—all the credits he had set aside from his years of work—Rambra had petitioned their landholder, Victoria Koman herself, and she had found Troy a job in First Landing.

His job at the anchor point had been a godsend, and he knew his family had pinned all their hopes on the slim chance of his success. They gambled on him working his way up in the world, and finding a spot for them, too, so that *they* could escape from the mines.

If he could only establish a foothold here, perhaps Troy could find jobs for his sisters, a new position for his father, anything to free them from their cramped quarters and daily drudgery. Troy had vowed to do his best, but the way Cren treated him, he didn't think his chances were too great.

On one of the first days, the boss had yanked him aside for a lecture. Cren jabbed a finger at Troy, keeping his voice low. "I don't like being ordered to hire a redneck yokel from dirt-digger Koman Holding," he said. "I don't care who your father is or what he did, but this isn't a free ride for you. I'm going to watch you closer than any of my other team members—because if you don't *deserve* to keep your job here, there are plenty of others who do. Don't think your father is going to get you out of trouble again."

Troy swallowed and shook his head. "No, sir. He can't—he has no money left. He spent it all just to get me this job."

Now, Troy looked around him, wide eyed at the big city, where citizens went about their jobs as if everyone on Atlas was so blessed. Sol-pol guards stood at the corners, keeping order. Pilgrims in hooded robes moved about, muttering to themselves. Representatives from the outer landholdings met to make deals, trade supplies, and increase their own power. The space elevator landed with a thunking sound of locks and stabilizers.

Cren yelled at Troy again. "Hey, Boren—I've got a suggestion. *Quit daydreaming!* Come help us unload. Do your work, dammit! The car is down."

Troy snapped out of his reverie and ran to do his job.

ii

When the tall elevator car opened its bottom level, two passengers disembarked, stepping carefully onto the ramp the workers had rolled up and clamped into position by the access hatch. Troy was fascinated by the two Guild Mediators, in their white robes and crimson sashes, who had gone up to inspect operations on the Platform. A pair of elite guards also emerged from the elevator, escorting the Mediators.

When the passengers were clear and checked through security, Troy and his coworkers entered the cramped main chamber of the elevator, bumping shoulders as they wrestled with the containers lashed down in the lower storage bay.

Troy held the manifest cards, shuffling them as he tried to keep track of everything that came out of the elevator. He was especially careful not to get distracted and miss an item. Everything had its place on his list and in the storage warehouse.

Over by the chain-link fences Cren stood watching, checking each activity around him as if he could somehow keep control through the intensity of his scrutiny. Troy worked with greater diligence, trying not to reveal that he knew he was being watched.

Men in cargo hauler jumpsuits unloaded the sealed packages of replacement computerware: perfectly sandwiched circuits grown in orbit, sapphire films laid down in impedance paths on wafers, then sliced into specially patterned chips that followed old templates from Earth.

The man in charge of the Platform, Kareem Sondheim, whose property and power rested in orbit, was called the "landholder without land." The ancient man was said to be one of the original occupants of the first colony ship that had arrived 231 years earlier. Sondheim had never set foot on Atlas. He had remained alive by staying in zero gravity and indulging in sophisticated geriatric treatments that were not available on the surface.

Sondheim kept control of the Platform's genetic library of embryos and cloning sequences the colonists had brought from Earth; its vast array of species, a veritable Noah's ark, would provide the foundation of an Earthlike ecosystem on a new world.

Unfortunately, Atlas had proved more inhospitable than they had expected.

The planet's atmosphere and climate were tolerable, with the right temperature range and an amenable mix of component gases. But Atlas was just at the very cusp of bringing forth life of its own. Its fledgling ecosystem was shallow and undiversified, with only a few primitive species, most of them in the cradle of the sea. The soil was utterly barren, forcing the colonists to begin their work several steps farther down the chain than they had hoped.

The native biochemistry was incompatible with human systems, but for a very few exceptions, such as the Veritas drug. The planetary ecology and the new Terran organic matrix were two independent and parallel paths.

Unable to turn back to Earth across the gulf of a fifty-year voyage, the colonists had to start from scratch, and they had held on by their fingernails, gradually using up what supplies they had brought with them. Separated from assistance by half a century, they could not simply send home for a new batch of supplies. The colony's technical resources had been only marginally replenished by the four other ships that had arrived in the intervening years.

Landholders continued to claim swaths of land, bombarding them with fertilizers, fixing nitrogen, irrigating deserts, and plowing under grasses, mosses, algae they had planted to lay down a nutritive soil matrix. New life forms were introduced experimentally and with great caution once they were carefully selected from the genetic library on the Platform. . . .

As the packages were unloaded from the elevator, Troy documented the computer chips, finding their notation on his manifests, then moved on to log a series of insulated fish tanks for Dokken Holding. The tanks were filled with thousands of trout and salmon fry that might find enough to eat among the strands of algae and the dragonfly larvae Franz Dokken had previously introduced into his warm artificial ponds.

Toth Holding had ordered cages and cages of live chicks grown from embryos aboard the Platform, and the birds were now ready to be turned loose in the grain debris in the fields.

Muttering to himself to verify his own markings, Troy moved about to inspect the cargo with loose manifest pages fluttering in his hand. He found a trio of cages holding three water buffalo calves, small and fragile and bleating. The beasts had knobby knees and large wet nostrils. Their dark eyes flicked around in confusion. According to the manifest, the water buffalo would be put to work in the rice fields in the river delta at Sardili Shores.

When someone called for a new species—such as these water buffalo, or the chickens—biological technicians on the Platform took the stored embryos from their precious library, cloned them, and grew the new animals to their birth age. The offspring were then shipped down on the space elevator.

The cargo haulers heaved the water buffalo cages out of the elevator car, bumping into each other and wrestling the beasts onto the concrete receiving area. Troy followed them briskly, needing to verify the serial numbers tattooed in the animals' ears and scribbling on his manifest sheets.

The calves shifted awkwardly in their cages, trying to maintain their footing. Suddenly, one of the handlers slipped and let loose his corner of the cage. It crashed to the ground with a loud noise that triggered a panicked reaction. The female handler shouted and scolded her partner. The water buffalo bleated a pitiful sound.

On the pad the handlers roughly set down their wire mesh cages containing thousands of cheeping chicks, not noticing that one door had not been fastened properly. Suddenly the front of the cage sprang open, spilling a chaotic flock of fuzzy yellow chicks that scattered chirping across the landing area. Some ran toward the toroidal supports and padded bumpers around the anchor point where the elevator had come to rest.

"Hey!" Cren shouted. The handlers dropped what they were doing and rushed to help. "Get those chicks! They're all accountable."

Already unbalanced, the water buffalo cage tipped over as the calf tried to move. The metal crashing on the concrete sounded like thunder, which further startled the already-panicked chicks. The pathetic calf lowed as if bemoaning its fate, and the other two calves set up a similar racket. The two handlers yelled at each other, voices raised over the din.

Troy had been shuffling through his manifest sheets, but now he stuffed the papers in his various pockets as he ran to help out.

The burly handlers seemed to think the best way to catch chicks was to lunge after them, large hands outspread. But the fuzzy birds simmered across the area, rushing toward the chain-link fence.

The four sol-pols leaped into action, pointing their weapons at the escaped birds, as if their threatening posture could help.

Troy crept toward some of the chicks, whistling cheerily at

them, extending his hands and trying to coax them nearer. He nabbed one, which squirmed and pecked at him, peeping comically, but Troy didn't let go until he had stuffed it back in its cage.

The people in the merchant district paused to observe the spectacle. Apparently, the frantic action of workers scrambling about was worth giving up a few minutes of business. Troy shook his head, muttering to himself that this was the most spectacular entertainment the citizens had seen since the grim judgment of Eli Strone several days earlier. He wondered what might come next— a comet striking the planet and obliterating all life?

One of the handlers managed to find a shovel and used it unceremoniously to scoop up five chicks at a time, depositing them back in the wire cage. Downy feathers flew in the air like a seed storm in one of the kenaf fields.

On the other side of the fence Cren used his palms to rattle the chain link, which frightened away the chicks that were trying to work their way through the openings in the wire. They ran around in circles, cheeping in terror.

It took the better part of an hour to recapture the birds. But the victory was not without casualties. Three of the delicate chicks had been killed in the roundup, and another had a broken leg.

Troy sighed, knowing he had done a good enough job, even as Cren used a low tone of voice to rail at the handlers for their stupidity and clumsiness. Cren checked out the water buffalo calves, then sent them to the big holding warehouse. The following morning they would be whisked off on the mag-lev to Sardili Shores.

At the end of his shift, Troy handed in his crumpled manifest sheets listing his tally of the computer chips, pharmaceuticals, supplies of the Truthsayers' precious Veritas drug, and live animal cargo.

He shook his head, thinking again of the frantic escape attempt by the baby chickens, the mishandling of the water buffalo calves. This wasn't exactly what he had expected when he left the Mining District to take a respectable job as a documenter for First Landing.

Oh, well. All in a day's work.

### iii

As evening gathered around the city, and the glass-and-steel buildings lit up with hydroelectric power, Troy settled in to his small rooms. The new place in the multiple-dwelling complex was still unfamiliar to him, and he reveled in the delicious privacy. He could think and breathe and not bump into anybody else when he decided to daydream. It seemed like heaven.

For too long Troy had been cramped in the same apartment with his mother and father and sisters, listening to loud arguments, tedious conversations about the day's events (which always sounded the same to him, though his mother and father went through the same dialog every evening, as if it were a ritual). He smelled Rissbeth's acrid homemade perfume, endured entire days without five minutes of privacy or quiet. For release, he dabbled with painting, strictly for his own enjoyment, though his mother resented the expenditure on useless items and his little sister criticized his work.

Their quarters had become even more crowded when Leisa married and brought her husband to live with them; he had lost much of his older sister's attention as well, one of the few tolerable aspects of his life there. No doubt Leisa and her husband would soon wish to start a family—a large one, as most colonists preferred—and that would take up even more space. But these new rooms were Troy's own space, and he had already begun to think of it as his "home."

After preparing a meal of hydroponic vegetables and a few small morsels of cultured turkey and setting it to cook, he settled back to unwind and to begin painting. What a luxury to indulge himself with a hobby. He had been experimenting with new paints available from First Landing vendors, vibrant colors he had never before seen in the small merchant shops up in Koman Holding. Brilliant blues, reds, and yellows made from cobalt and cinnabar and uranium oxide.

He dabbed designs with his paint. Some of his fresh work hung on the walls, like trophies. Nothing very good, he knew, but Troy enjoyed the soothing yet exhilarating act of painting. He'd experimented with different techniques, different styles. His abstract imitations were complete failures—but then, he wasn't quite sure how to tell when an abstract painting "failed."

He preferred painting imaginary landscapes, looking out upon the vastness of Atlas with his mind's eye. He had already drawn the low, rocky hills of Koman Holding, honeycombed with mine shafts. He swirled the colors, sketching out another barren landscape—but this time adding forests, swamps, beautiful birds spreading their wings to display remarkable plumage in the sunlight as they glided across the air . . . pure fantasy.

Troy hummed to himself, scratching his curly, light brown hair. Muffled noises came through the thin walls, his neighbors arguing, the children crying. He had lived his life among the sounds of other people, so it didn't bother him, but he would have preferred to overhear a happy family.

He painted part of a granite outcropping, adding fanciful wind-bent cypress trees in the crannies of the rock . . . and then on impulse he sketched in some stylized mountain sheep. He recognized that he was mixing a great many ecosystems here— accuracy was not his goal at the moment. He looked at the mountain sheep and smiled.

He went to change his clothes, pulling on a wool sweater Leisa had made for him (though her new husband grumbled that it was a waste of expensive Bondalar yarn). As he folded up his work pants, Troy heard a faint and unexpected crinkling sound. He reached into his back pocket to find one of the wayward manifest sheets. He must have thrust it there during the chaos of the escaping chicks.

Then the implications struck him. He blinked rapidly, and his throat tightened like a piece of gnarled wood. He had recorded all of the deliveries from the elevator car, but without this last sheet he had missed several items. The logs wouldn't match—and that meant big trouble.

Troy sighed and sank into a seat beside the bed, wearing the pullover sweater but leaving his pants crumpled on the floor. He looked at the manifest sheet and groaned. Cren would have his hide for this—he just knew it! After his previous mistake of the transposed shipments, his boss would be utterly unforgiving. No more chances. After only three weeks, Cren would have an excuse to send him whipped back home, no doubt imagining a preposterous chain of disastrous effects.

Red-faced, Cren would yell, "This error could set up echoes throughout the entire system, mistake upon mistake, leading to misdirected supplies, unreported shipments, and major upheavals in the economy of Atlas itself!"

Troy sighed. "Or more likely Cren will be the only one to notice, and I'll still be on the next mag-lev car back to Koman Holding." He would spend the rest of his life down in the shafts, coming home to a crowded apartment no bigger than a cargo container, with his own family glaring at him because he failed them in their one opportunity to get a foothold in the city.

He didn't want to go back to the Mining District.

Troy ran his fingers over the rough scrap of paper in his hands. He knew exactly how he could fix this mixup, if he could get back to the holding warehouse and the inventory terminals before anyone noticed. Troy knew the appropriate passwords to access the records computers—he had been so proud when Cren had grudgingly given him the access codes the week before.

The idea caught hold, and he clutched it like a drowning man clutched a twig. If he could log in these receipts before the space elevator began its return journey up to the Platform, no one would be the wiser. Sondheim would get his expected shipment, and First Landing's records would accurately reflect the supplies that had come down.

Troy felt so stupid. Abruptly, the smell of his dinner overheating on the stove unit penetrated his melancholy, and he dashed into the kitchenette to remove his now soggy and overcooked vegetables.

He would wait a few hours yet, go in much later that night and make a few quick adjustments on the computer. Simple enough. No one would ever know. His stomach was already tied into a knot of nervousness, but this would be the quickest and safest solution.

Simple, he thought. Simple.

# CHAPTER
# 3

i

The storm front finally rolled in just after dark, pelting down clean fresh rain that gave the air a metallic tang, slicking down the streets with muddy runoff that gurgled in the gutters. Breezes tore the clouds to shreds, and the tattered remnants scudded across the sky, clearing patches of night flecked with stars.

The wet cobblestones of First Landing's thoroughfares looked oily under the wavering aurora, and silted runoff curled through drainage channels. Because of the heavy weather, most streets were deserted. Only a few vendors of fried vegetables, sweet desserts, and warm beverages remained open to catch brave customers. The smell of hot oil, burned honey, and watery coffee mixed with the scent of rain.

Four figures moved through the wet shadows, keeping to narrow alleys when possible. Two sol-pols took the point, wearing deep blue uniforms that turned them into silhouettes in the falling darkness.

A tall bald man with a craggy face, his features seemingly carved out of stone with a blunt chisel, strode confidently behind the guards, taking long steps in his loose gray jalaba. The fourth man betrayed the greatest eagerness, but he hung back behind the bald man, glancing furtively about. "Maximillian—"

The bald man cut him off with a quick gesture of his broad hand. "Don't worry, Cialben. We have everything we need."

"But what if we're stopped?" Cialben pressed.

"We won't be stopped. We're obviously going about official business. We're accompanied by two sol-pols."

"Sol-pols assigned to Dokken Holding, not First Landing—"

"Who's going to stop us?" Maximillian asked in a sharp tone.

Cialben swallowed and looked ahead to the stadium-sized lit area where the space elevator car sat docked, ready for resupply in the morning. "I've just never picked up a shipment myself, that's all. Is this the way it's always done?"

"It's different every time," Maximillian answered. "Dokken insisted you come along this time."

"He's never done that before either, not in ten years of this kind of scut work. You don't think that's unusual?"

"You must learn to trust people," Maximillian said.

"Dokken's the one who taught me *not* to trust anybody," Cialben said in exasperation.

"Stop asking questions," Maximillian said.

Cialben muttered. The sol-pols said nothing—they rarely did.

The guards led the way through the streets with no indication of uneasiness. Cialben and Maximillian had an excuse if they were stopped and questioned . . . but Dokken had made it clear that he preferred they not be questioned.

The Veritas drug was rigidly controlled by the Truthsayers Guild, but Cialben managed to distribute a small fraction of it to the black market. He had never dared to ask what sort of arrangement the powerful landholder Franz Dokken had made with Kareem Sondheim up on the Platform, how he obtained capsules skimmed from the supplies allotted only to Truthsayers. By Atlas law—established by the Guild itself, of course—no one but a designated Truthsayer was allowed to use the mind-boosting drug.

That didn't mean there was no demand elsewhere, though. Cialben fed that demand.

True, only Truthsayers could use the Veritas to maximum effect. Their bodies had built up a tolerance from a lifelong exposure to the drug. For them the psychic boost lasted hours or days, whereas in a regular human the Veritas rush was good for only a few seconds.

But, oh, those seconds! Like having a dozen minds at once, lifetimes of memories, experiences right at his mental fingertips . . . though they faded as fast as the drug did in his nonacclimated system. Short-term memories, like vanishing dreams.

Cialben had taken Veritas himself back in the early days, when Dokken had used him as a spy numerous times to get an edge in the constant power struggle for land. Cialben had performed admirably each time, though Dokken had been miserly with his rewards.

But Dokken had flown into a rage when Cialben had once dared to carry Veritas in his presence, intending to use it later for enjoyment among the servants . . . possibly even dipping into the mind of Dokken's beautiful lover Schandra. He hadn't anticipated Dokken's violent reaction. In a terrifying instant Maximillian, Dokken's faithful and powerful manservant, had locked Cialben's arms behind his back, driving him to his knees in the private drawing room of the villa. Franz Dokken had glared down at him, his teeth bared in anger that transformed him into a beast.

"I do like secrets, Cialben," Dokken had whispered, "especially when they belong to someone else." His voice was low and cold. "But I want to keep my own secrets. You are *never* to use Veritas in my presence. Is that understood?"

Cialben, his neck aching from staring up at the landholder, tried to nod. Maximillian's powerful fist clutched Cialben's short graying hair, yanking his head up so that he gazed directly into Dokken's tanned face.

"I understand," Cialben said. "Really, I do."

"No one on Dokken Holding is to use this drug, but you're free to sell it to all the other landholders. I know how destabilizing Veritas can be. Let my rivals tear themselves apart."

Since that time, they had indeed kept their understanding—but now, tonight, he and Maximillian had been sent all the way in to First Landing to obtain a large shipment of Veritas capsules, the largest delivery ever. If Guild Master Tharion found out about it, he would probably have a cerebral hemorrhage.

The group of four splashed through the darkening streets. The air jealously held on to its damp coolness, and Cialben felt his hands growing numb. He stepped in a puddle, which made his ankle cold and wet. Cialben shook his foot. Maximillian gestured for him to hurry. Faint steam curled from his breath.

The bright lights of the elevator anchor point stood in front of them. A squad of First Landing sol-pols stood around the chain-link fence, huddled together to keep warm. But Cialben knew the shipment wasn't on the elevator. It remained in the inventory warehouse, where the computers and shipping manifests were kept, along with the supplies waiting to be distributed to the outer holdings.

The inventory warehouse was a low, one-story building made of steel supports, darkened glass windows, and adobe bricks, only one building in a district of similar warehouses. The group approached from the rear. Maximillian showed not the slightest tension.

While the regular night shift sol-pols had established a firm presence at the anchor point, the inventory warehouse had been locked and left alone. Their two sol-pols slipped toward the building. The shorter of them withdrew an access key card and slid it in to the sealed door.

The door opened silently, letting Maximillian and Cialben enter. Lined with pale bricks, the entrance yawned like a cave. Faint lights burned inside, tiny illumination resisting complete darkness and leaving only murk.

"How can you be sure the warehouse is empty?" Cialben said.

Maximillian looked down at him with scorn, his craggy face creasing in distaste. "Look how dark it is."

They crouched inside, using their hand illuminators to send bright spears of light into the shadows. "Shouldn't be hard to find," Cialben whispered, moving forward, still reluctant to take the lead. One of the sol-pols remained stationed at the door while Cialben, Maximillian, and the second guard went past administrative cubicles equipped with old computer systems and paper files, to the chill warehouse section.

"This way." Maximillian's pale gray outfit made him look like a ghost in the dimness.

A clutter of canisters, supply crates, and cages waited in the rear. The boxes of computer chips and sterilized pharmaceuticals had been placed in neatly ordered bins along one wall. The cold concrete floor made flat echoes of their footsteps as they walked.

Cialben flashed his light around. Segmented metal doors rolled up for loading heavy transports; beside them stood bins of metal sheeting, girders, and other supplies. Sweet, resinous lumber had been stacked in the middle of the concrete pad. Outside in separate storage barns were further shipments, bulky items brought in from one holding and marked for commercial distribution to the highest bidders.

In the livestock section Cialben went to a wire cage filled with hopping, cheeping chicks. The stupid birds had spilled their water and dumped feed all over the bottom of their cages. They looked filthy.

"Here," Maximillian said, squatting by one of the large cages. "Shine the light over here."

Inside, the black water buffalo calf seemed eager for attention, lowing loudly. Its dark eyes were wet and glistening. It tilted its squarish nose upward as if seeking milk from a mother it had never had. The clone-grown calf knew nothing of its own existence.

"Not this one," Maximillian said, squinting at the tattoo in the calf's ear. He moved to a second cage. The other calf let out a bellow, demanding yet shy. "Here."

He unfastened the catch on the wire cage and swung open the door. The calf backed away clumsily, uncertain but with nowhere to go. Maximillian banged the back of the cage with the flat of his hand, rattling the wires. The startled animal stumbled out, lowing again.

Cialben gently put an arm around the calf's neck to keep it from running loose in the warehouse. Grateful, the animal nuzzled his hands with a wet nose. An overturned aluminum water dish sat dry at the bottom of the cage.

"In a water buffalo?" Cialben said. "Is Sondheim running out of ideas? Or is this one of Dieter's sick suggestions?"

"No one asked me how to do it," Maximillian said, then fixed a stony glare on Cialben. "And no one asked you either."

The water buffalo mooed again, and Cialben patted its neck to hush it. The calf nuzzled his hand, running a long, wet tongue along his palm.

Maximillian slipped a long wide-bladed knife from a sheath at his hip, and in a single lightning movement drove the blade hard against the calf's side. A quick thrust between the ribs, then a second full-muscled shove to drive the point all the way into the calf's heart.

The animal bleated in shock, but was dead before it could move. Its eyes rolled up, glassy. Its body shuddered and spilled blood all over the concrete floor as it fell.

Cialben stepped back to keep from being sprayed.

With the carcass still twitching, Maximillian knelt and, tugging on a pair of rubber gloves, withdrew the knife and gutted the calf. He worked without speaking, breathing hard from the strenuous activity.

Cialben watched the slaughter with eager horror, his throat dry, his lips peeled back in a combined grin and wince. Maximillian's arms were slick with red up to his elbows, far higher than the gloves reached. Using both arms Maximillian heaved out the calf's entrails, then sliced open the largest stomach to pull out a plastic-wrapped package.

Dokken's manservant held the bloody packet in his gloved hands and gestured for the sol-pols. The second guard rushed forward from his post at the door. The first man bent over the carcass, choosing the best handhold. The two strong men lifted up the dead water buffalo, and together they lugged it, still dripping blood, out of the warehouse. They disappeared into the night. The fresh veal—a delicacy read about in the archives but never tasted by any living person on the planet—would bring a high price indeed.

Maximillian used his slippery fingers to unwrap the folded plastic of the hidden package. He unrolled the outer wrapping and exposed a treasure.

Cialben gasped. He had never before seen so much in a single shipment. Hundreds and hundreds of sky-blue capsules of the Veritas drug.

More truth than all of Atlas could comprehend.

ii

With a stretching sound and then a snap, Maximillian removed the rubber glove from his left hand, carefully tucking it into the pocket of his gray cotton jalaba, where it left a bloody smear.

Cialben kept his eyes fixed hungrily on the hoard of Veritas, dreaming of the huge number of credits it would bring and also eager to experience the psychic rush again. Because of Dokken's adamant refusal to allow any use of Veritas by his own workers, Cialben had restrained himself, his fear of Dokken's wrath greater than his desire for fleeting entertainment.

With a clean hand Maximillian delicately, reverently, picked up one of the sky-blue capsules with his thick fingers. He held it in the palm of his hand, rolling it around in the creases of his skin, studying it under the uncertain light. Cialben's eyes followed it.

"Do you deserve this?" Maximillian said, surprising Cialben.

"Come on—after all I've done for Dokken?" he answered. "What does he think?"

Maximillian held Cialben's gaze for a long moment. Around them the stillness and darkness of the warehouse seemed to smother all sound. The remaining two water buffalo snorted in their cages, smelling the blood.

The manservant flicked his wrist, tossing the sky-blue capsule toward Cialben. Grinning, he reached out to snatch it from the air.

Maximillian continued in a voice free of emotion. "One and one only," he said. "And you have to do it here."

Cialben held the capsule like a gem, slightly soft and filled with secrets. He looked around him in the empty warehouse. "Here?"

"And now. You know Dokken won't allow it on his own landholding."

Cialben didn't know what the psychic rush would do for him

in such an empty scenario. But the sleeping city lay out there, the identical dwellings, the brick homes, the steel apartment buildings. He considered the thousands of thoughts, the personal mysteries, the muddled dreams the colonists would be broadcasting into the air. The telepathic boost would last only a few seconds, but it would burn very brightly indeed, at peace, surrounded by the city.

And there was Maximillian. Did he really want to read the manservant's thoughts? Yes, he realized, he did. He was astonished that Dokken would allow such a thing, because Maximillian had been the landholder's right-hand man for decades.

Cialben popped the capsule into his mouth, bit down with his back teeth, felt the acrid gush down his throat. He closed his eyes and drew a deep breath, then a second. His scalp began to tingle in anticipation.

He opened his eyes, and opened his mind, and everything came flooding in.

He looked with anticipation at Maximillian. And froze.

At the front of the manservant's mind Cialben read Franz Dokken's final instructions like a sharp-bladed ax coming down. Maximillian must have been thinking the conversation over and over again, keeping his memory fresh, so that the thoughts remained clear in his mind.

He watched as Cialben read them.

"Let him take one capsule and wait until he reads your mind. I want him to know your orders. I want him to know his fate—then kill him."

Cialben caught the rest of the entire appalling setup, the details of what Maximillian would do to his body—planting evidence, distorting clues.

He was already backing away in horror, windmilling his arms. He slipped in the wet blood on the concrete floor from the slain water buffalo.

Maximillian reached out with a fist that moved like a cobra, grabbing Cialben's collar, holding him upright.

Cialben regained his balance and began to struggle. Maximillian drove the long blade hard against his side. A quick thrust between the ribs, then a second full-muscled shove to drive the point all the way into Cialben's heart. He twisted the blade.

Cialben fell, his body losing control, the nerve signals melting into black static. He slumped into darkness, his last thoughts cursing Franz Dokken.

# CHAPTER

## 4

### i

That evening in the damp darkness of Dokken Holding, Guild Master Tharion sat uneasily on a placid gray mare, dutifully following Franz Dokken's chestnut stallion. The ageless landholder rode intently, his body barely visible in dark leather breeches and tunic. His wild blond hair flowed behind him like a comet's tail.

"Thank you for coming with me," Dokken said in his rich, cultivated voice. "This won't take long, but it's important for you to be there. For moral support, you know."

Gusting breezes picked their way around the bluffs like probing fingers. A wide gravel trail wound from the stables down to the foot of the bluffs, and both horses knew their way. Fields of cotton covered the flatlands surrounding the village, extending south to the rolling hills, a mixture of dark and light that gave the landscape a knobbly texture.

Franz Dokken urged his impatient stallion into a trot. Tharion gripped the reins between his fingers, but still felt completely out of control. "Slow down, Franz—please," Tharion said. He would have preferred to take a methane car, but Dokken loved any chance to show off his horses. Luckily, the gray mare maintained a gentle, slow pace—it kept him from looking like a fool in front of the public.

Dokken laughed. "That mare's foal is due in a few weeks— she couldn't manage more than a trot if she tried. Just sit still, pretend you know what you're doing. She'll be careful, for her own sake if not for yours."

Tharion held the reins doubtfully. "If you say so . . ."

Dokken shook his head and flashed a thin smile. "I value your friendship even more than increasing the size of my herd. I'd hate to think of reporting to yet *another* Guild Master just because you fell off and broke your neck. Two in two years' time is enough."

Tharion responded with an uneasy smile. Franz Dokken had worked miracles for Tharion's career, a subtle guardian angel throughout his life at the Truthsayers Guild, a friend as well as one of the most powerful landholders on Atlas. Dokken's outspoken support at the Landholders Council had been one of the reasons Tharion had been chosen for his post.

Two years earlier, the aged previous Guild Master had died in his sleep, leaving Tharion one of the most qualified candidates, but the final vote had favored another Truthsayer, Klaryus. But after a month in his duties, the new Guild Master Klaryus had taken his weekly booster dose of Veritas—only to fall dead from the terrible Mindfire toxin produced by a virulent mutation of the Veritas bacterium. Somehow, his capsule had become contaminated in its processing up on the isolated orbital lab . . . and so Tharion had found himself wearing the royal blue sash of the Guild Master.

The deadly contamination had raised a great many questions, and Tharion himself had submitted to a truthsaying to prove that he had nothing to do with the death of his predecessor. Ultimately, everyone agreed that Klaryus had suffered from a bizarre accident.

Since the elite guard Eli Strone had vanished from the Guild shortly thereafter, Tharion had wondered if Strone might have had something to do with Klaryus's death—but now, after Strone had brutally slaughtered twenty-three people, Tharion knew that subtle poison just wasn't Strone's style.

While many of the other landholders had flocked to assure Tharion of their loyalty, Franz Dokken had been there all along, giving him insightful advice on the new burdens he would have to bear. So, when Dokken asked him to come out to his holding as a special favor on this damp, cool evening, Tharion could not refuse.

At the outskirts of the village the sol-pol sentries stepped forward to verify the identity of the riders. Tharion shook his head in disbelief. Who *else* on the entire planet might be riding up on a horse? The guards pivoted to accompany their landholder to the center of the village.

Incandescent streetlights on wrought-iron poles bathed the town with a harsh glare, burning electricity from Dokken's hydroelectric plant at Trident Falls. Adobe dwellings clustered around the square, where a fountain chuckled over polished stones, misting a flower bed of marigolds.

In the center of the square Franz Dokken pulled his stallion to a halt; the horse snorted, shifting from side to side. The restless animal made Tharion nervous, but the landholder seemed to enjoy the challenge, patting the horse's broad neck.

Dokken sat upright, looking around. "Captain Vanicus, would you ring the bell, please?" he said to one of the sol-pols. "Let's get ourselves an audience, so we can make an effective demonstration." The stallion snorted again, and Dokken patted its muscular neck. The guard jogged over to a tower made of metal crossbars.

"Franz . . ." Tharion said.

"Trust me," Dokken answered. "This benefits you as much as it does me."

As always, Tharion gave him the benefit of the doubt. He could smell the smoke from squat, beehive-shaped kilns, communal electric furnaces used round the clock. Prized terra-cotta pottery from Dokken Holding went for a high price in First Landing.

As the bronze bell rang in clear, high tones, people bustled out to see the excitement. Captain Vanicus tolled ten times before returning to Dokken's side, and another contingent of sol-pols emerged from the garrison in the town square.

The second group of guards folded around five prisoners held within the garrison—a middle-aged, flinty-eyed man, a moon-faced woman whose red eyes were smudged with dirt and puffy from weeping, a young couple who clung to each other despite their bindings, and a sour-faced, matronly woman.

Tharion suddenly paid sharper attention. Did Dokken want him to do a truthsaying? A flicker of annoyance passed through him, though he kept it well hidden. Dokken should have warned him, so he could have at least taken a Veritas boost. Tharion didn't know if his abilities were currently sharp enough to do a thorough mind-reading.

As Guild Master, he had done mercifully few truthsayings in the past two years, spending more time with the Landholders Council, advising the telepathic Mediators, and overseeing the crimes and punishments determined by his Truthsayers. He didn't miss the onerous task of rooting out sins and guilt, though his recent task of sentencing Eli Strone up to OrbLab 2 had not been a pleasant task.

Dokken nudged his stallion closer to the village prisoners. The horse gave a token resistance to the commands, then acquiesced. The five captives looked up at the landholder on his tall mount; they looked at each other; some lowered their eyes to the packed dirt in the square. Tharion could sense the puzzlement and uneasiness in the crowd—these captives were people they recognized, friends or neighbors. Tharion wondered what crimes they were accused of.

"I make no secret of the things I will not tolerate in my holding," Dokken said without further preamble. He didn't raise his cultured voice, but his words carried across the crowd. "My rules are few, but they are firm." He paused just long enough to let them think. "Paramount on my list of crimes is illicit use of Veritas, the Truthsayers' drug. Atlas law forbids anyone but a chosen Guild member to use this substance. Other landholders may be lax in this regard—but there will be no such abuse in Dokken Holding."

He took a deep breath, then let out a long, sad sigh that made him seem intensely paternal. "It seems that not everyone has understood this."

Tharion narrowed his eyes, sitting stock-still on the mare's back. Five users caught in a small village with only a few thousand inhabitants? His stomach knotted with anger and revulsion. His entire life in the Truthsayers Guild had been guided by unforgiving ethical training, knowing what was right and wrong—and this was so *wrong*. Only Truthsayers were supposed to have access to Veritas. Where had these prisoners gotten it? What trivial and mundane thrills did they use it for?

"You!" Dokken said to the moon-faced woman, who cringed and began to sob again. "So desperate to learn whether your husband was cheating on you, you stooped even to this—and for what? Was he guilty, or did your own groundless suspicions damn you?" Her wail was all the answer Tharion needed to hear. "And what will your family do, your children, your husband, now that you have breached their trust?"

Dokken turned to the flinty-eyed man, who flinched and looked away. "You—a craftsman trying to dredge up hidden knowledge about a competitor, stealing trade secrets rather than developing your own skill."

Then the young couple. Dokken's lips flattened into a thin line, and he seemed to be stifling a bemused smile. "And two lovers who wanted to flash into each other's minds during sex, as if Veritas were a toy!"

He shook his head. "You thought working in the cotton fields was difficult? Hear me, because now I'm acting as Magistrate for my Holding. For the next three months, you are all assigned to hard labor at the dry lakebeds, strip-mining salt and processing nitrates. I doubt you'll ever wash the chemical stink out of your skin and hair."

The villagers gasped, but Tharion nodded. Such labor was usually reserved for the worst criminals, and he agreed with the sentence in this case—but sentencing was supposed to be done by a Truthsayer, not at the whim of a landholder.

"These can be punished," Dokken said, then turned to the last prisoner, the matronly woman, whose sour expression intensified. She turned dull eyes up at Dokken, but said nothing. "But the person who *sells* the illegal Veritas cannot be tolerated." He spun his stallion around, turning his back to the drug pusher. "She will be taken a thousand kilometers out into the unreclaimed lands and turned loose. Atlas can do with her what it wishes."

The villagers moaned at the certain death sentence, but Dokken nodded to the sol-pols, directing them to follow his orders. Tharion sat in shock and anger on the gray mare. He could not grant a simple landholder the right to mete out executions; not even Eli Strone had been sentenced to death. "Franz!" Tharion whispered harshly. "Only the Guild—"

With a decisive sweep of his hand, Dokken shushed him. "Wait until we're out of the range of lamplight," he said under his breath. "I know what you're going to say. But there's time. Plenty of time."

One man, muscular and dark-bearded, stepped forward from the crowd, apparently some sort of village leader. "Master Dokken," he said, averting his eyes in respect, "a village representative should be given the opportunity—"

"Not in the internal affairs of my holding!" Dokken said vehemently. "Guild Master Tharion sits here beside me. I need no other authority." He turned his stallion to leave. "Just see to it that I don't need to crack down like this again!"

Tharion's mare trotted beside Dokken as they hurried out of the village. He twisted the reins in his hands, annoyed at himself for being so easily manipulated. As always. His nostrils flared, and the night air was cold.

As they ascended the path into the bluffs, riding together under the stars and the whistling wind, Tharion finally reprimanded his mentor. "Franz, by dispensing justice yourself, you blatantly damaged my power. The Guild can't let this go unchallenged!"

Dokken turned to him, his sea-green eyes shadowed but glittering. He smiled, kept his voice low and gentle. "Ah, but if we say *you* instructed me to do this, Tharion, then nobody is weakened. You were there. Everybody thinks you sanctioned it, probably even ordered me to do the sentencing. You know those people deserved it. Every one of them."

Tharion was unconvinced. "I'd prefer to make up my own mind."

Dokken scolded him now. "Tharion, think! I've been helping you to see the greater consequences, the second and third levels of power and control, not just the obvious cause and effect. These people could have been brought into First Landing, put to a Truthsayer in the middle of the great plaza—but I wanted it done here. In my holding, where it counts most. I want it known that *I*, Franz Dokken, will not tolerate black market Veritas."

"You brought me here so I could pat you on the back, commend your efforts?" Tharion said, his throat tight with frustration.

"No, I wanted you here so we could discuss some new information I have uncovered. It has consequences for your entire Guild as well as my landholding. I've already taken care of it, and you will thank me for it."

"Oh?"

"Let me explain it over dinner," Dokken said, tapping the stallion's sides with his heels. The horse moved at a faster pace. "Come to my villa. Garien is preparing fish tonight."

Unable to think of anything else to say, Tharion rode his mare up the steep hill path to Dokken's home in the cliffs.

ii

Garien, the chef, served a wonderful broiled trout from Dokken's fish farms, seasoning it with herbs from the kitchen garden, served with a sautéed medley of tomatoes, onions, and unfamiliar green pods.

Dokken fell to his meal with gusto; after every three bites he methodically dabbed his mouth with a dyed linen napkin. His eyes were half-lidded as he savored the fish, peeling away crisped skin and flaking the delicate white meat.

Tharion sat at the polished rose-granite table, resting his elbows on the cool, slick surface. He tasted one of the sliced green pods, not a familiar vegetable raised in the greenhouse levels of

Guild Headquarters. He found it tasty, but with an odd texture. "What is this? A new vegetable from the Platform gene library?"

Dokken speared a pod with his fork and held it up from his glazed terra cotta plate. "Okra. It's a relative of cotton, and the kenaf we plant for paper fiber. I decided that since my kenaf was thriving so well, I would try the okra. You should taste Garien's gumbo sometime." He popped the vegetable into his mouth. "It amazes me what still remains untapped up in the Platform's genetic bank."

They finished their dinner with small talk about the season's newly recovered lands, novel crafts and products emerging from the villages, and the annoying activities of the other landholders. Tharion maintained an impassive expression, since landholders always complained about their rivals.

One of the servants came in to clear away the dishes and to refill their wineglasses. Dokken swirled the dark red liquid in his clear glass, then sipped. Tharion drank the sour wine out of politeness, but he didn't like the taste. Dokken seemed torn between criticism and enjoyment of the vintage.

"This is a Chianti," he said, "a dark wine that's traditionally Italian. The bottles are supposed to be wrapped in wicker, but nobody has cultivated the right kind of reeds for old-fashioned basketry. Maybe Sardili will try it down at the delta." Dokken took another sip of the wine. "Let's go sit by the fire."

The landholder's leather clothes creaked as he rose. To Tharion, in his loose white cotton garments and overrobe, Dokken's breeches and tunic looked heavy and uncomfortable.

Tharion followed Dokken across the tiled floor to the sitting room. He took one of the chairs next to a snapping fire that did more to drive off the night's chill than any of the villa's corner thermal units. "Where's Maximillian?"

"Away." Dokken pushed his boots close to the fire and stared at the glowing embers. "I also just returned from another sojourn a few days ago. He'll be back soon."

By now, Tharion had learned not to be bothered by Dokken's evasiveness. He relaxed in a comfortable chair, staring into the flickering flames, uneasy to see such an outrageous waste of wood, which had to be cut and shipped in from the pine forests in Toth Holding.

He sipped his bitter wine again. Dokken began one of his tangential lectures. "Trust me, this isn't how Chianti is supposed to taste. The ground and climate here is dry and rocky, like parts of old

Italy, and it should be perfect for growing grapes and olives. But the fruit tastes awful, even after decades of conditioning the soil. I'm still working on it, though. Either I'm improving, or my sense of taste is irreparably damaged. Maybe I'll try coffee next. I can't remember how long it's been since I've had a good, rich cup of real coffee."

Tharion made a noncommittal sound, though he couldn't imagine where Dokken had ever tasted "real" coffee. He didn't interrupt, though, but tried instead to relax and enjoy the fire.

All through dinner, Dokken had not broached the subject of the allegedly important new information he had learned. He knew better than to push his mentor; Franz Dokken was a master at playing his hints in the right order, drawing inevitable conclusions, manipulating results by virtue of his wise perspective and generous patience.

They sat in silence by the fire, sipping wine. Waiting.

Finally, Dokken raised himself out of his chair and refilled their glasses with the bad wine. "All right, my friend, I know you're getting anxious," he said. "Let's go out onto the balcony."

iii

Dokken set his wineglass on the polished ledge and placed both hands on the stone rail, looking down at the courtyard below. Clay pots filled with explosively colorful geraniums sat in the corners of the balcony.

The main towers of the villa rose up above them, walls of creamy stucco, roof overhangs of red tile, and a satellite dish antenna on the tallest tower, pointed out toward the stars. Below, mulberry bushes adorned the grounds, carefully watered and fertilized.

Dokken turned to his guest. "In civilized Earth society, I would be offering you a fine cigar."

"A cigar?" Tharion asked. He'd never heard of the thing. "What is that?"

Dokken looked up at the veiled stars, as if trying to find the Earth system out in the galactic forest of lights. "Carefully selected tobacco leaves dried and rolled into a cylinder. You light the end, then inhale the smoke. It contained a mild narcotic, which was also a carcinogen. Rather pointless, I suppose, but there was a time when cigars allowed for wonderful social affectations. I hear Hektor Carsus is contemplating cultivating tobacco at his holding, but he doesn't know what he's doing."

"One too many vices from Earth?" Tharion asked, wondering if Dokken would ever get around to the point.

The landholder waved away the thought. "No, the soil and the climate are lousy for tobacco. Not rich enough yet. I looked into it. Give us another few centuries of working the land."

Tharion finished his Chianti and found that he didn't want any more. Dokken would toy with him all night long, avoiding the question unless Tharion pushed. "Franz, about this important information you were going to tell me—"

Dokken smiled, as if he had been wondering how long his protégé would wait—but an interruption from the firelit sitting room disturbed them. Garien was setting out two small glazed saucers of honeyed strawberries, but a dark, slim woman pushed past him.

"No, I don't want a third place setting, thank you," she told the chef with weary patience, heading straight for the balcony.

Dokken frowned, then sighed. "Schandra, could you please excuse us while we finish our conversation?"

The woman, Dokken's longtime lover, placed her hands on her slender hips and widened her coal-black eyes. Her hair was long and silky, like spun obsidian, and her features had a smooth exotic cast that spoke of an African/Asian genetic mixture. She wore a scarlet blouse and a swirling black skirt, both made of the luxurious silk that had made his holding famous. "No, Franz, I won't just excuse you. I've been polite over and over again, and you always forget to make time to talk to me. A few days ago you got back from being gone for two weeks, out of touch with everyone, riding around your holding like some sort of scout, and we still haven't talked. Maximillian won't say a word to me—and I need to discuss our family."

Dokken raised his eyebrows with a long-suffering expression and turned from Tharion as if begging his indulgence. "What family, Schandra? We don't have a family."

"Ah, now you're getting the point, Franz. Everyone else on this planet has children, and we don't. Is it so wrong for me to have a couple of dreams, too?" Obviously, Tharion thought, Schandra had been rehearsing the discussion with her mirror while waiting for Dokken to return from his sojourn in the outer lands.

Tharion thought about Dokken's legendary lack of heirs, the rumors of his sterility. A great landholder such as Franz Dokken should have long ago assured his inheritance, rather than risk losing all the lands he had claimed.

Tharion sympathized with Schandra, though: he, like all Truthsayers, had been rendered sterile by constant use of the Veritas drug.

"Schandra, I don't wish to discuss this now," Dokken said calmly.

"When?"

"Later. Now, if you'd please leave us alone—"

"*When?* Can I make an appointment? You put me off every time I want to talk to you."

"Schandra, this may come as a shock, but I don't keep you around for your conversation skills." Dokken's eyes narrowed, and his voice, though soft, held an unmistakable harshness. "I did not take you under my wing and spoil you with everything a woman could want just so I would have someone to chat with." He glared at her with a fury he rarely showed to anyone. "Now, if you don't leave *immediately*, I will throw you headfirst off of this balcony. Perhaps you'll break your neck in one of the mulberry bushes. Then who will feed your precious silkworms?"

From the landholder's expression, Tharion didn't think Dokken was joking.

After a frozen moment, she forced a laugh. "All right, later then. Let's do lunch sometime." Schandra departed, taking one of the dessert plates with her, as if as an afterthought.

"I apologize for that," Dokken said. "Women become so incensed about little things they have no control over, yet all the while they remain blind to the Big Picture. I never promised her children, yet now she thinks she has a right to demand them."

Tharion toyed with his empty wineglass, set it on the balcony rail, then bent to sniff one of the geraniums. "It's none of my concern, Franz," he said. "My wife Qrista gets incomprehensible sometimes, though with the Veritas we can't keep any secrets from each other."

"A frightening thought," Dokken said.

"Sometimes it is," Tharion admitted. "Now, about this news?"

Dokken smiled, and in that unmasked glance he seemed immeasurably ancient. "I think I might have found some way to stop the black market smuggling of Veritas. You see, by interrogating the woman you saw in the square tonight, the one who was selling the stolen drugs . . . I discovered her source!" He fixed Tharion with his gaze, as if daring the Truthsayer to read his mind. "I know how Veritas is being taken from First Landing and distributed among the other holdings."

Tharion perked up. "How?"

Dokken shook his head sadly. "I regret to say the culprit was one of my own men. Cialben, my associate for twelve years. You've met him. He was behind it all, and I was blinded by my own trust."

Tharion blinked. "Yes, I remember him. How did he—?"

"Don't worry. I've taken care of it. After tonight, much of the black market trafficking will stop. You can rest easy."

Tharion stiffened. "What do you mean you've taken care of it? Did you take matters into your own hands again? I can't allow you to keep—"

"Oh, be quiet, Tharion!" Dokken said curtly. "You're not thinking again. Because this smuggling is chipping away at your Guild's power, the last thing you want is to make a public spectacle of how thoroughly you've failed. Who would believe in a Truthsayer's impartiality when he's digging for knowledge that affects the Guild's own monopoly on Veritas? It is against the law for any person other than a legitimate Guild Truthsayer or Mediator to use the drug. No deliberation is required.

"I have taken care of Cialben, quietly and permanently. It will be an unsolved crime, but the black market smuggling will stop, at least on this end. That's all you need concern yourself with."

Tharion cinched his blue sash tight against the night chill that had suddenly begun to sink into his bones. He pressed his lips together, bristling at how Dokken treated him—like a child. "Where is he? A Truthsayer should interrogate him! We could get a lot more information."

Dokken's cool expression told him that there would be no interrogation. None at all. Tharion shook his head angrily. "When will you ever consult me *before* you do something like this, Franz? I deserve to be part of the decision."

Dokken snorted with impatience and downed the rest of his wine, turning to go back to the fire and his dessert. "I have my own problems, Tharion. Some of the landholders are allying themselves against me. I can feel it, though they're keeping it quiet. We could even have a bloodbath like the civil war sparked by Hong and Ramirez almost a century ago. That's my main concern right now.

"For now, I've stopped the smuggling, Tharion—what more could *you* have accomplished by involving yourself? Get on with your work, and I'll get on with mine. I need you to be strong for my coming battles."

Then Dokken shouted for the chef to bring another plate of strawberries to replace the one Schandra had taken.

# CHAPTER

# 5

## i

Dreaded anticipation made the evening pass with all the speed of a rock eroding. Troy whiled away the hours trying to concentrate on a new painting, his second of the evening. He would have to wait until it was late enough to slip into the slumber-quieted city and fix the stupid mistake he had made.

Before this mess, he had eagerly anticipated a relaxing few hours of experimenting with his new paints—carmine and burnt sienna—but now the thrill was soured. He managed to paint a coppery crimson sunset with a storm rolling in; the orange-gold rays streamed across a lush imaginary landscape sometime centuries in the future, when tall cities spread like monuments across the face of Atlas, where forests grew wild rather than trapped in rigid rectangles of conditioned soil.

But Troy felt distanced from his art, preoccupied with thoughts of dire consequences for his clumsy and unforgivable clerical mistake. He got the perspectives all wrong so that the cities were foreshortened, and the people were far too tall. The rays from the painted sunset streaked out at an astronomically impossible angle.

Terror gnawed at him. What if he got caught keying in the revised manifest schedule when he went back to the warehouse? The sol-pols would haul him off to the brig in Guild Headquarters, and he'd probably be exiled back to the Mining District. Cren would undoubtedly fire him if Troy simply apologized and tried to rectify the glitch in the light of day—though this one was far more easily fixed than his previous mistake of swapping shipments. Cren would also fire him if Troy said nothing and the manifest error wasn't fixed. His choices seemed to funnel to this single option.

On the other hand, it was only marginally likely that someone would discover him out on the streets at this late hour. Logic continued to hammer at his brain, though his emotions were not entirely convinced. Troy shivered.

The viewplate in his living room buzzed with an incoming call. Troy jumped, leaving a trail of reddish ochre across his fresh painting. With a rueful smile he realized he might have to paint that into a meteor flashing down.

Another wash of panic brought pinpricks of cold sweat showering out of his skin as the viewplate buzzed again. Who could be calling him at this hour? Had Cren discovered Troy's error after all, working late? Were the sol-pols giving him sufficient fair warning to pack a few belongings before they marched him off to prison? Was an arrest done that way? Troy didn't know. He had never needed to worry about the sol-pols before.

Pale and frightened, he tapped the Receive button on the viewplate—and was astonished to see the image of his family sitting in the common room in their small communal dwelling. He laughed with relief as he realized this was the day of their weekly communication.

"Look, Rambra," Troy's mother said, "he's actually glad to see us. That's a pleasant change."

"Must be up to something," his father said gruffly in an attempt at humor.

Behind his parents he saw his little sister Rissbeth flaunting a new dress. Rissbeth had devoted her life to demonstrating that Troy was her natural enemy, and had done everything in her power to be his complete opposite. His older sister, Leisa, looked at him fondly. He missed her very much.

"Are you surviving in the big city?" his mother Dama asked. "How is your job? Do you have new friends yet?"

"I'm doing my best, Mother," he answered. Always the same questions. He knew what was next.

"Have you signed up for one of the matching services? You need to be married. You are old enough. Leisa is pregnant. Did we tell you that last week?"

"Yes, you told me that last week, Mother. I'm very proud of her."

Rambra said, "I hope that's not the only set of grandchildren we're going to get." Out of view behind her parents, little Rissbeth tossed her head in challenge, as if to show Troy that *she* was willing to do her duty to have children.

"I haven't signed up for the matching services yet. I haven't had time."

"Time?" his mother said. "What could be more important? People will think there's something wrong with you. Isn't there a stigma attached to single people, those who don't have large families?"

"I'll survive," Troy said. "I just moved here. Starting a family isn't my highest priority. It's only been three weeks."

"You need your own children," Dama insisted. "You simply can't understand until you have your own."

Troy sighed. "Yes, and if I don't have children, the gene pool will immediately begin to deteriorate, thereby leading to the ultimate extinction of the human race."

"Oh, Troy, you're being such a fatalist!" Dama said in alarm.

"If I'm going to be a fatalist, I may as well do it right." Behind his mother, he could hear Leisa laughing.

His mother huffed. "See the way he treats us?" she said. "We've placed our hopes in you, Troy. Your father worked very hard to get you this opportunity. We have faith that you'll pay us back, find a place for us in First Landing. Keep us in your thoughts."

"I will. Thank you for calling, Mother, but it's very late here. We're in a different time zone, and I have lots of work yet to do."

"Oh! We forgot about the time change again," she said. "We should write ourselves a note on the calendar."

"Keep working hard," his father said. "Let us know when you get a promotion—and if there's room for us to move there." Rambra chuckled, but Troy knew that he wasn't entirely joking. "We're counting on you!"

Troy signed off, and the viewplate filled with static, then turned a dull, cooling gray. His heart sank.

Still a few more hours until it was time for him to go.

ii

When Troy peeked out the window in his apartment, he saw rain still sprinkling down, so he chose a dark slicker from the closet. The fabric was too thin to keep him warm, but it had been lacquered with waterproofing resin. His mother had made it for him before he moved to the city. Troy wrapped it around himself, took two deep breaths to buck up his courage, then slipped out into the quiet, lonely night.

He tried to appear casual, not nervous or impatient as he hurried down the puddle-strewn streets. He stopped at a stand, where he purchased a cup of a watery brown liquid the vendor called coffee. The cup steamed in the cool night, and Troy slurped it as he walked in a haphazard path, trying not to look as if he was heading toward the holding warehouse.

*Just going out for a walk,* Troy thought, imagining a confrontation with a night shift sol-pol. *Couldn't sleep. Needed to stretch my legs. Oh, I'm not supposed to be outside this late? Sorry, I'm new here in the city. From the Mining Districts. Ever been there?*

He muttered the excuses over and over to himself, but First Landing seemed to be sleeping comfortably. He wasn't sure if he had ever been awake so late, but dozing was the last thing on his mind. Even the sol-pols must be huddled under awnings or in shelters from the drizzle.

His nose was cold and numb. By the time he finally reached the low warehouse, he was sniffling repeatedly. The building was dark except for a few small lights left burning to comfort the animals.

With a gulp to squelch second thoughts, Troy slid his access card through the reader. The door popped open to admit him. When Cren had given him his own access card, the responsibility made Troy feel tall and important. He had actually called his family to brag about it—and now just days later, he was abusing the privilege, sneaking in to alter records. Once again, it didn't seem like a good idea—but he convinced himself otherwise, wringing his hands as if he could squeeze out more courage.

He had to do this to keep his job, to keep his family's hopes alive, to deny Cren an excuse to fire him (this week at least). It would all be over in a few minutes, just a series of quick keystrokes.

The warehouse was dim, but he picked his way over to his own cubicle, needing nothing more than the peripheral glows from the emergency lights. He flicked on his computer terminal, and the screen's glow helped him see.

One of the water buffalo calves began a repetitive lowing as if it were a machine that needed repairs. The pitiable noise made Troy lose his concentration several times, until he finally succeeded in calling up the receipt file for the day's shipment from the Platform.

Troy withdrew the crumpled piece of paper, the last sheet of the manifest he had found in his pocket. He scanned the erroneous file and erased it completely, then re-input all the items from the manifest so that every entry showed the same clock record. It didn't take long. Troy felt pleased that he was able to eliminate the error; no one would know the difference. The Platform would get the appropriate amount of supplies, and old Sondheim wouldn't complain about being shortchanged. Missing supplies received from the previous day's shipment would not go astray, as had happened before, and Troy would not be reprimanded. He had saved his job.

He keyed in the last entries and sighed. The water buffalo bellowed again, louder this time, startling him. He sat up and sniffed the air, smelling something odd: wetness, a metallic scent . . . like hot copper. The calf lowed another time, as if confused as to why Troy didn't rush over and investigate. He wanted to run back home—but something wasn't right here. The back of his neck prickled.

Reluctantly, he flicked on one of the floor level lights, hoping not to attract attention from any patrolling street guards. He shuffled around the cubicles and headed toward the back of the warehouse where the animals were kept.

One of the water buffalo cages was empty. Had he lost a calf, too? He wondered how he would explain that. It was the first, most ridiculous thought to enter his mind.

Then he saw the dead man lying on the concrete floor, sprawled in an ocean of blood. It reminded him of the crimson sunset he had painted just that evening using his new pigments.

Troy stumbled forward. His legs felt like bars of iron as he plodded forward, gawking down in the low slanted light. He fixated on the blood. He couldn't believe there was so much blood.

A bloody plastic wrapper lay across the dead man's chest along with two sky-blue capsules. Veritas. Troy had seen that substance only a few times in his weeks here. But no shipments of Veritas had come down from the Platform that afternoon. And every capsule of the Truthsayers' drug was supposed to be kept under tight control, heavily guarded until its delivery to Guild Headquarters.

Troy stared down, his eyes wide and dry, but he did not recognize the victim. The man's eyes were glassy, his short hair dark and streaked with gray. The thick blood still oozed, pulled by gravity into a spreading pool around the man's chest. A long stab wound had sliced into the ribs. . . .

Bright lights came on inside the warehouse like flashes from a supernova. Suddenly Troy realized he had been screaming and shouting. His mind was so numb he couldn't understand what was going on. He found himself bending over the body, moaning, his hands trembling.

*Blood—there was so much blood!* Did the human body even have that much blood?

Four armed sol-pols rushed in, dripping rain from outside. Upon seeing Troy, the body, and the blood, they leveled their weapons at him. "Don't move," one said. "You can't get away."

Troy stopped, blinking down at his hands. What were they shouting at him for? He had stopped screaming. His throat was so raw that when he spoke, his voice was hoarse and damaged.

"I didn't. I didn't—not me."

The sol-pols approached him cautiously, rifles ready. When they saw he had no apparent weapon, they grabbed his arms, twisted them behind his back and applied the bonds.

"Uh, wait," Troy said. "I didn't kill him." Terror and shock made him feel sluggish. He couldn't think straight.

One of the sol-pols groaned, "Don't tell me you're going to waste a Truthsayer's time on this?"

"I didn't kill anybody," Troy said. "I'm innocent."

"Aren't we all?" the guard said.

"But I didn't do it," Troy insisted, letting a hint of anger trickle into his voice so that the sol-pols gripped his arms more tightly, with enough force to bruise. "I just found him here."

"We'll get a Truthsayer, and then we'll find out what really happened."

Troy closed his eyes and let them take him away. At least there was some comfort in that. The Truthsayers were never wrong.

# CHAPTER

i

In the stables on a sunny morning after an exhilarating ride, Franz Dokken reveled in the calm he experienced while brushing down his stallion: smooth, soothing strokes, caressing the velvety texture of the chestnut coat that covered the horse's coiled muscles.

The fresh air of Atlas lit the roomy stables with the energy of blue sky and yellow sunlight. Dokken inhaled deeply, smelling the animals, the dusty ground, the rusty sourness from the corrugated steel trough.

The gray mare would deliver soon, and he already had a clean pen ready for the new foal. The other horses made restless sounds—on a day like this they all wanted to be outside, to run and roam, but he had no worthwhile place to graze them.

They ate oats and alfalfa grown on strips of his reclaimed land, and many of his workers quietly resented harvesting food for the animals rather than themselves. The villagers were puzzled by Dokken's obsession, not understanding why he raised magnificent horses instead of "useful" animals—cattle for instance—as other landholders did. But then, it was not their purpose in life to understand his decisions. He was the landholder.

The proud and majestic beasts made Dokken feel noble. He loved the exhilaration of exerting control over an animal physically stronger than himself. It was also a way to show his villagers—not to mention the rival landholders—that Franz Dokken could do as he pleased.

After his two weeks of blessed sojourn, alone and out of touch, he felt ready to tend to all the matters that had slipped during his absence. Maximillian kept the show running smoothly while he was gone; after years and years of practice, Dokken knew how often his presence was truly required, and how many brushfires would burn themselves out without drastic intervention. He thrived on the time alone, when he could get away with it.

He disappeared at least once a month, to the dismay of Schandra. She resented the fact that he kept deep secrets from her, though even in her greatest moments of self-doubt, she didn't dream how little she knew about his real activities. Her failing was that she overestimated her own importance to him, considering herself part of his life rather than a ten-year dalliance. She had no real perspective on time.

Dokken felt refreshed after the morning ride, and after his recent sojourn, but there was so much to catch up on—as always. It would take a few days just to get up to speed, to solve the problems that needed fixing, to tighten a few screws, yank a few leashes. Then he would set other wheels in motion, see that everything was proceeding along its inevitable course . . . and when the laws of human nature grasped his plans firmly, Dokken could afford to disappear again.

The reward was worth all the inconvenience.

After their long conversation the night before, Tharion had left late on a private mag-lev car, bulleting back to First Landing. The Guild Master had walked unsteadily toward the pickup spur, completely unfamiliar with the effects of alcohol and somewhat comically tipsy from the wine. At one point Tharion had accused Dokken of drugging him, which had brought his mentor to side-splitting spasms of laughter, the first true belly laugh Dokken had experienced in recent memory. Tharion hadn't understood the humor.

Through the stable door, Dokken glanced at the sun in the morning sky, estimating the hour. He refused to wear a wrist chronometer, since nothing in his experience required such accuracy. Dokken stroked the stallion three more times with the curry brush before patting the horse's neck and hanging the brush next to the saddle.

"We'll find time to go for another long, vigorous ride, my friend," he whispered. "I promise."

Early that morning Maximillian had arrived back at the villa, prepared to brief him on how the previous evening's work with Cialben had proceeded—but Dokken had not been ready, and the manservant knew better than to pressure his master. Still, it had been two weeks since he had tended to outstanding business, and Dokken needed to know how the world had changed since he had last paid attention to it. He reviewed the primary background like a newscast in his mind.

Returning from his rest, he'd had a few more ideas on how to delay or sabotage the new mag-lev railway between Carsus and Bondalar holdings. It was a bad precedent to set, letting landholders deal directly with each other, rather than keeping them separate and at odds, forced to funnel all their commerce through First Landing. The most dangerous threat to his ultimate goal would be a strong, unified nation of landholdings. Perhaps, if he planted the right seeds, Dokken might even be able to stop the silly proposed marriage between Hektor Carsus and Janine Bondalar. The alliance concept was so . . . medieval!

More disturbing to him were the insinuations that Toth and Koman holdings might also be joining forces as a large cooperative district. They had a wealth of good reasons to do so, but Dokken hated to see the formation of such an alliance. As a first step, he had already set in motion a plan to devastate the fragile pine forests on Toth Holding. Loss of the fast-growing wood would severely damage the economy of the holding, making Toth a less-attractive resource partner.

At Toth, as well as at other holdings, Dokken had made sure the illicit Veritas still trickled out among the populace unabated, creating anarchy and indirectly weakening the Truthsayers Guild as well. Poor Tharion. Exposing secrets caused far more damage than fabricating preposterous rumors.

Meanwhile, young Michel Van Petersden, the son of a landholder Dokken had deposed seventeen years ago, was now reaching his adulthood, still happily living in his adoptive home with Victoria Koman. She seemed to be grooming him as her successor, despite the fact that she had several children of her own, and the boy was completely unaware of the role he might be asked to play. Dokken wondered about the age-old question of nature versus nurture. . .

He had time, but it was no longer all the time in the world. The metaphorical clock was ticking.

Another major colony ship—the *EarthDawn*—was on its way from the home planet, bringing with it an unknown cargo of supplies and people. Citizens constantly speculated on whether the passengers would be hardworking hopeful settlers, more

prison exiles, another group of religious fanatics, or a second
military force with orders to take over. Atlas had weathered all of
these in 231 years—and the *EarthDawn* would arrive in five years.

By that time, Franz Dokken expected to have reduced Atlas
society to a shambles, crushed every one of the rival landholders,
and picked up the pieces in his own hands. He would have the
whole world firmly under his control when he greeted the captain
of the new ship.

ii

Dokken sat on one of the benches in his dressing room and
removed his boots, tugging on the black leather. Sunlight
streamed over the barren bluffs surrounding his villa, shining
through the crisscrossed, wrought-iron window bars and casting
shadows like a spiderweb on the tile floor.

Maximillian stood just inside the door, tall and serene, his
hands clasped behind his back. Schandra had spent the night in
her own bedchamber, and Dokken had gotten a good night's
sleep.

Now energized from his morning ride, Dokken scooped a few
fresh strawberries from a bowl Chef Garien had placed on the
stone end table, then stripped out of his riding leathers. He
sponged himself off with a damp rag, dipping it into a glazed
ceramic basin and wiping his perspiration away with the cool
cloth.

He hummed quietly as he slipped into cool cotton pants and
a white silk shirt, draping his riding leathers on a brass stand to air
out. Unselfconsciously, he dressed in front of his manservant,
paying him no heed. Maximillian had been a fixture at the villa
for so long, Dokken could be comfortable around him.

"All right, Maximillian. I'm listening." He tugged a strawberry stem from his mouth and tossed it next to the fruit bowl.
"How did everything go last night?"

"As planned," the manservant droned. "Cialben is dead—and
very surprised, too, I might add. His body should be found
sometime this morning when the warehouse crew checks in."

"I'll probably get a frantic call from Tharion later today,"
Dokken said.

"Yes, you probably will."

"He knows just enough to put the pieces together the way I

want him to. Tharion is the type of person who doesn't like getting a glimpse of what's really going on around him. It ruins his delusions, and he feels powerless."

"Is that a problem?"

"I won't let it become one. After all his years in the Guild, a few self doubts will be a good experience for him. Anything else?"

Maximillian pursed his lips. "News is that some of the Pilgrim settlements are becoming restive, demanding their own homeland again. They're finally feeling downtrodden. Despite their isolation, they have established channels of communication, so I suspect plenty of sedition must be flying around. Supposedly, no one knows who's starting it."

Dokken raised his eyebrows. "Oh, really? Good. Continue to keep a low profile in your guise as the Pilgrim Adamant. And make sure our own Pilgrim colonies at the lakebeds don't hear any of it."

Maximillian nodded. "As we discussed, I am focusing on the big settlements at Sardili Shores. They have the highest concentration of Pilgrims, and I anticipate an uprising in the near future."

Dokken laughed. "Old Sardili will just wave his hands and hold a meeting and ask everyone to please be friends. It's his style, and he won't be able to comprehend why it doesn't work in a complex system. Else?" He cracked his knuckles.

"Difficult to get firsthand details, but there has been another disturbance in Bondalar Holding, a riot of some kind. A few homes were burned. Apparently, a family feud started when rivals got hold of Veritas and learned how deeply their mutual hatred ran. The brawl lasted a whole afternoon and far into the night. Bondalar's sol-pols put it down severely, and the news has been suppressed, but I made sure it leaked out anyway."

Dokken laughed. "Good, good. You're a master, Maximillian."

"You have taught me much, sir."

### iii

Tharion called much earlier than Dokken had anticipated, even before Garien finished setting out a late-morning luncheon board of fresh bread, kippered salmon, and more strawberries. Dokken walked past the food to reach the viewplate alcove. Maximillian stayed out of range as Tharion's image appeared, his pale skin flushed.

"Good morning, Tharion," Dokken said, immediately trying to soothe the Guild Master.

Tharion groaned. "My head feels like it's got a thunderstorm inside, Franz, and my stomach is upset. I think you poisoned me last night."

"It's called a hangover, Tharion. The unpleasant aftereffects of wine—an ancient Earth malady resulting from overindulgence."

"Is there a cure?"

"Abstinence."

The Guild Master grimaced. "I think I can manage that, especially with the way your wine tastes. But that isn't the only headache I have this morning." He lowered his voice.

Dokken drew himself taller, looking down into the image. "Hmm? What do you mean?"

"The sol-pols discovered your man Cialben murdered, just as you led me to expect. We also found enough evidence to know he was involved in the Veritas smuggling. Just as you said."

Dokken tossed his blond mane and popped his knuckles again. "So what is the problem?"

Tharion leaned forward into the image area, distorting his expression. "I know you did this for me, to help the Guild—but I thought you said the murderer would never be caught! Now this poses plenty of problems."

"He won't be caught, no need to worry. It'll be an unsolved crime. You may need to increase your sol-pol patrols yet again, train more elite guards—but you can weather that. Veritas smuggling will dwindle to nothing in the next several weeks. Your Guild is secure."

Dokken sniffed and turned at a delectable aroma. Garien brought out a tureen of caramelized onion soup, and his mouth watered.

"Franz, they've already caught the murderer, red-handed," Tharion snapped, then paused. "You mean you didn't know?"

Dokken narrowed his sea-green eyes. "What are you talking about?"

The Guild Master's words came out in a rush. "Name is Troy Boren, 23 years old, recently moved in from the Mining District of Koman Holding. Worked inventorying shipments from the Platform —we caught him in the middle of the night. By the body, in the empty warehouse, with blood on his hands. We've also found that he doctored some computer shipment records."

Dokken took a moment to recover, flashed a glance over his shoulder at Maximillian, who shook his smooth head, perplexed. The manservant's brows hooded his dark eyes.

"So what does this prisoner have to say for himself?" Dokken asked.

Tharion gave a dismissive wave of his pale, long-fingered hand. "Claims he's innocent, of course. They all do. But when I bring him into the plaza and set him in front of one of my Truthsayers, will we find evidence linked to you? You really should have let me handle this whole thing, Franz—if there is evidence that ties you to the murder, I'll be forced to prosecute. The law takes precedence over friendship, and you can't keep a secret from the Guild." His expression looked haunted. "I'm worried about what could happen to you, Franz. But there's nothing I can do to help."

Dokken wished the Guild Master could be there in front of him, so he could personally smooth his ruffled feathers. "Tharion, trust me. Listen to what I'm saying. I don't know how this happened, but it's just an accident, a coincidence. This man you've apprehended must have stumbled in at the wrong time, an innocent bystander. Bad luck, that's all."

"I don't believe it. You should have seen him."

Dokken shrugged. "Tharion, you're creating problems where there aren't any. Put the poor sod on trial, let one of your Truthsayers dig into his mind . . . just the way you're supposed to. It's every citizen's right: a speedy and irrefutable trial by telepathy. If the man is innocent, he will be cleared, no doubt about it. And this man is innocent." He jabbed a finger at the viewplate. "The Truthsayer won't find anything in his head—because he knows nothing." He kept his voice low and comforting, repeating himself. "Just a minor inconvenience. Don't worry about it."

Tharion slumped in grudging defeat, still looking uneasy. "This is the last time, Franz. Don't ever put me in this position again. My loyalty is to the Guild—I'm the Guild Master, dammit!" He rubbed his temples. "Oh, my head hurts."

"Tharion, a simple analgesic will help, and drink plenty of water," Dokken said quickly. "It'll pass." The Guild Master snorted as he signed off.

Dokken slipped back out of the alcove. Maximillian stood behind him, saying nothing as Dokken tried to work through his own thoughts. The clumsy innocent bystander complicated the situation, but Dokken couldn't decide if that might be an advantage or a disadvantage.

He took a plate from the luncheon board, piled it with food, and took a steaming mug of onion soup. He told Maximillian to have the chef bring him a cup of watery chicory coffee—the best they could yet manage—then took his food out to a shaded table in the courtyard by the mulberry bushes. He returned to the cold fireplace to retrieve his book from the mantel.

He sat outside, alone and untroubled, as he ate his lunch. Garien brought out a mug of bitter coffee; Dokken sipped it, winced, and tried to soothe his tastebuds by thinking about the coffee he used to drink as a young man, even the bad powdered substitute on the colony ship. Given enough time, it would get better. Everything did.

Picking at the salmon with a long-tined fork, Dokken spread the precious book on his lap. He had self-printed it on flecked kenaf paper and bound the volume in real horsehide, because reading a book like this was an *experience*, not just an information dump.

The treatise was many centuries old, but filled with wisdom that could be transferred from warring Italian city-states to the landholdings of Atlas. A thin, dense book—but Dokken gained more insight every time he studied it.

In the courtyard by the bushes, he began to reread his Machiavelli.

# CHAPTER

i

For days after reading the mind of Eli Strone, Kalliana remained in her chambers in Guild Headquarters, slipping out only at late hours . . . trying to hide from the nightmares she had taken from the killer, nightmares that now resided firmly in her own mind.

The violence, the bloodlust, the *self-righteousness* possessed her, despite her constant efforts to purge it from her thoughts. Not only had she witnessed the crimes in Strone's head, but she had experienced them as well, as if she herself had done them. And in her quiet moments in the darkness of her quarters, a deep suspicion grew that perhaps she herself was capable of the same monstrous acts. . . .

Kalliana sat in silence on her narrow bed, plucking pieces of honeyed fruit from a bowl, but the sweet stickiness contrasted violently with the tacky texture of drying blood in her imagination. A thin skewer of spiced chicken reminded her of pieces of dripping flesh, sliced away with brisk, efficient strokes of a scalpel as a paralyzed victim screamed into the night. . . .

Other citizens might have envied her freedom to indulge in such delicacies, but every time Kalliana visualized the spraying blood and the slaughtered victims, felt the warped justifications flooding from Strone's mind . . . she wondered how many of the common people would still envy her position if they knew.

Outside, in the vastness of the world, she knew other laws were being broken: small offenses out in the holdings that could be dealt with by local, nontelepathic Magistrates . . . or major crimes by people who would be hauled off to First Landing for trial by the Guild.

Kalliana shuddered. It wouldn't be her turn again for some time, though. The Guild had eleven other Truthsayers to share the duties of justice, and nineteen less-powerful Mediators, who negotiated solutions to civil and political disputes. Kalliana was not needed, not now. She would have time to recover, just in case the searing memories assimilated from Strone had damaged her telepathic abilities. She hoped it would be enough time.

Kalliana slept on her pallet in the midmorning, feeling the bright sunlight as it streamed through the outer viewports in the ship wall—and still she woke up sweating, panting hard. She was afraid of the darkness, but nightmares found her even in broad daylight.

The signal at her door startled her, and she had a sudden, wild vision of Eli Strone, escaped from his prison, come back to flay answers out of her with a sharp scalpel. *I'm not guilty. You saw my reasons! You know! How can you call me guilty?*

But the young man outside the door to her quarters was so harmless that she burst out in a shamed laugh, though his good-natured grin was masked by concern. "Ysan, you startled me."

The seventeen-year-old boy glanced away shyly, his white robe and sash looking too large on his skinny build. "You've been hiding, Kalliana," he said. "Nobody's seen you in days. I wanted to make sure you were all right."

The boy was four years her junior, but a gulf of more than age separated them. He was still innocent, a trainee who had not yet been tested for his green Truthsayer's sash.

She began to make an inane reply, but found she didn't have the energy to deceive him. Ysan was a refreshing breeze, a healing kindness that allowed her to see the good side of human nature while recovering from the bad.

Ysan raised his eyebrows. "Let me come in. Tell me how bad it was—that might help you. Besides, I have to get prepared for it myself."

She thought how the razor edge felt as it sliced through skin, an ever-so-faint rasping, a rubbery tug. The blood was thick and wet, smearing like oil, darkening as it mixed with dust. . . . Through Strone's perceptions she had *enjoyed* the sensation—

"I can't talk about it, Ysan," she said in a husky whisper. "There's no way I can describe it. No way I *want* to. I just need . . . time. I'll work through it."

Whenever she tried to focus her thoughts and fortify her

psyche, though, Kalliana felt the battering ram of violence come back at her. The secondhand screams were growing quieter day by day as she tried to erase them—but it was a long, slow process. Recovering from the furnace of Strone's deluded sense of justice was more difficult than anything she had ever endured in her pampered life.

Ysan frowned, leaning on the doorframe. "You've helped me enough times, Kalliana. There must be something I can do." His eyes lit up above his soft cheekbones. His fair skin prickled pink. "Why don't you show me what you saw? I can take some of the burden from you."

"No!" she cried, then looked sternly at him. Also born in the Guild and raised with increasing dosages of Veritas, Ysan had practiced mind-reading abilities from the time he was a child— but the young trainee hadn't yet walked through the shadowed valleys of guilt and remorse. Mental abilities still seemed like fun to him.

"Ysan, this isn't a game. Enjoy your innocence as long as you can," she said, trying to soothe the dejected look that showed on his face. "You'll be tested soon enough."

"I'll be tested in a few weeks. I'll be a full Truthsayer. Can't you—"

"No." She clutched her warm wool wrap closer around her. "I just need a little more rest. I'm going to sleep now—that's all I need. Really." She softened, allowing a smile. "But thanks for your concern."

"Sure," the young man said, fidgeting uncertainly, and then he stepped back into the corridor. "Well, pleasant dreams, then."

ii

Kalliana sat up gasping, hearing the echoes of a shrieking victim in her ears, one of the last batch that Eli Strone had skinned alive, a rugged man with a work-seamed face, whiskered chin, and the misery of barely hidden guilt in his eyes. Filtered through Strone's own memories, the disgust she felt for the victims' imagined sins overpowered her own horror at the crime. They deserved to die. They *deserved* it! The rugged victim screamed again—

But then Kalliana realized the noise was not imaginary. She heard a persistent, whining buzz, a summons from Guild Master

Tharion. Afternoon sunlight streamed through the stained glass windows.

"Yes," she said, taking a deep breath and forcing her voice louder, stronger, as she activated the viewplate.

"Please come and see me on the bridge deck," Guild Master Tharion said, "in my ready room."

Kalliana acknowledged, then dressed herself in a clean white robe. She ran her fingers along the emerald Truthsayer sash; now its bright, honest green seemed tarnished to her. She cinched it tight around her slender waist and walked briskly toward the antiquated turbolift that took her up to the Guild's command center.

The central administrative offices had taken over what had been the bridge of the *SkySword*. The smooth mechanical finery of the decommissioned military equipment gave the Guild Master's seat and the surrounding offices a sterile cleanness and austere technological precision that could not be conveyed by the soft adobe or baked bricks of the other structures in First Landing.

Kalliana stepped down the textured metal stairs onto the bridge deck, and the turbolift doors creaked shut behind her. Other Guild members moved about their duties; many were brown-sashed workers who had none of the rigorous ethical training that a Truthsayer endured or the political education and techniques of rhetoric a Mediator used so well. Thus the Guild workers had no access to the Veritas drug.

Guild Master Tharion sat in the middle of the room in a large chair. Kalliana could imagine a military captain directing space battles from the same point. Tharion scanned a small lapscreen, intent on notes and files, probably from recent Landholders Council meetings. He seemed disgusted and distracted. Kalliana had never paid much attention to the activities of the Council, since that was beyond her expertise; she had heard that at such meetings the appointed representatives from the landholdings spent their allotted time arguing and raising grievances and countergrievances.

The Guild Master blinked at her, preoccupied for a moment, then suddenly seemed to remember who she was. "Ah, Kalliana," he said, "thank you for coming." He set his lapscreen on the side of his command chair, stood, and stepped away. She followed him into his private ready room, dreading his reasons for summoning her. He sealed the door and turned to her with a casual expression.

"How are you recovering from the Strone case? You've been keeping a low profile for several days."

She glanced away to avoid his scrutiny. "Reading the prisoner was a very . . . unsettling experience. The pain is still there, but it's lessening."

"I'm glad to hear that," the Guild Master said. "You are very valuable to us, Kalliana. Every Truthsayer is. But if you feel that your abilities have been worn thin by this ordeal, I'll do my best to see that you're reassigned in some appropriate manner. Toth Holding has requested a new Magistrate, and I don't have anyone qualified to send them."

"No!" she said a little too quickly. "I mean, that won't be necessary." It frightened her to think she might lose her status as a Truthsayer and be weaned from the Veritas drug. That would be the end of everything she knew, everything she had been born to. Her embryo had been grown here in the Guild, and she had been raised for no other purpose, given no other training. That was how it had to be. "No, I'm fine."

"Good," Tharion said. Behind him, the stained glass window filled his ready room with rainbows. "We've taken care of sentencing Strone—he'll spend the rest of his life up on OrbLab 2."

Kalliana could not hide her surprise, considering the over-whelming violence of the murders. "I would have thought he might be executed."

Tharion looked away, then sighed, staring at his twined fingers. "Yes. I gave it thorough consideration—but there are extenuating circumstances. Eli Strone served the Guild well for many years. His record is one of the most exemplary of all the elite guards we've ever had. Until he left us."

Kalliana nodded, unconvinced, but she could not argue with the Guild Master's decision.

He sat down behind his desk. "I wanted to ask you again about my request to check for possible sabotage or a larger plot among the landholders. Did you see any deeper motivation behind the killings?"

"There is nothing," she said, shaking her head vigorously.

"You're sure Strone was acting alone?" Tharion pressed. "You detected no possible connection inside his mind?"

Kalliana shivered. "No. If you don't believe me, feel free to look in his mind yourself. If you can get around the nightmares."

"That won't be necessary," Tharion said. "I've looked in his mind before, when I was younger. Even before he committed his crimes, it was . . . unsettling. So rigid and sharply defined." He looked at her with concern narrowing his eyes. "Are you positive you've fully recovered? You seem . . . shaken."

Kalliana drew herself up, pretending that nothing was wrong. "I'm fine," she said. "I can do my job as a Truthsayer."

He turned in his chair to look wistfully out the stained glass window. "I had always thought I would be a Truthsayer myself for many more years, until Klaryus died." He tugged the blue sash at his waist tighter. "But circumstances don't always cooperate with our convenience. I vowed to do the best job I could."

"I'll do the same," Kalliana insisted, with a conviction she did not feel. She wondered what this pep talk was all about, wanting just to run back to her quarters and be alone again.

Tharion's face was stony as if he had come to a deep decision. "Fine. Then we have a new case for you to read, another accused murderer who claims he's innocent. He may also be involved with . . . other crimes. You will verify that for us."

Kalliana went rigid, as if a spear of ice had shot down her spine. "Another truthsaying?" she said. "So soon? But there are so many other Truthsayers—"

Tharion forced a smile. "I have no control over how frequently crimes are committed, Kalliana. It is your turn again. We've caught this man, practically in the act. The evidence against him is strong, but he claims he's innocent—and I have reason to believe he may be telling the truth. We must grant him a swift trial. I would like you to handle this one in particular. Consider it a test." He paused, apparently seeing her alarm. "Are you saying now that you're not ready?"

Kalliana tried to weigh the shades of terror in her mind. "When will the reading be?"

"In three days," he said.

She opened the ready room door and faced the turbolift on the other side of the command center so the Guild Master wouldn't see her trembling. "I'll be ready." Kalliana left the bridge.

iii

Tharion sat back in the command chair and watched Kalliana leave, masking his expressions until the ready room door had slid

shut. Deeply troubled, he tried to distract himself with other
Guild duties for the rest of the afternoon . . . but he continued to
come back to Kalliana's haunted afterimage.

Tharion sympathized with the ordeal each one of his carefully
trained telepaths went through with every criminal mind-reading—but it concerned him that Kalliana might be unstable. He
pressed his lips together and hoped he was doing the right thing
by assigning her to the case of Troy Boren. It might help her heal
if she could read the mind of a man he knew to be innocent. An
easy verdict that would restore her self-confidence without risking
further exposure to murderous memories.

He prayed that Franz Dokken wasn't wrong.

The distracting thoughts made Tharion less productive, and
it took him an extra hour to review all of the recent disputes
brought before the Guild. The numbers of filed grievances were
increasing as the population on Atlas expanded.

Tharion found himself alone when he finally finished and
walked quietly down the metal corridors to his own suite of rooms,
which had originally been the *SkySword* captain's quarters. The
cabin was dim and empty; the evening lights at floor level suffused
the room with a comfortable yellow-orange glow.

"Qrista?" he called, but heard no answer. Then he remembered that a long and complex meeting of the Landholders
Council was being held in the lower briefing chambers, and his
wife would probably come back frazzled and disgusted at the
uncooperative representatives.

Servants had placed the evening meal on the metal dining
table. Tharion lifted up the thermal cover and sniffed at the meal
of rice and chopped vegetables. He was just debating whether to
sit down and begin without Qrista when she came in, heaving a
weary sigh and closing her ice-blue eyes.

He got up to greet her, ready to offer comfort and support. She
sealed the door to their suite with great pleasure, as if she were
blocking off the problems of the day. She straightened her white
robe then untied the crimson Mediator's sash and came to
embrace him.

"A long one?" Tharion asked.

She nodded, resting her chin on his shoulder as if she wanted
to melt into sleep standing in his arms. "Same old problems," she
said. "Different names, different details.

"Toth claims that Dokken Holding is irrigating their kenaf

fields too much and thereby depleting an underground aquifer that feeds the springs watering his pine forests. Bondalar and Carsus have jointly issued a formal grievance against Koman, alleging that the raw materials the mines are shipping for their mag-lev rail project are defective, resulting in months of lost work. The Koman representative brought out quality inspection sheets to prove that the raw materials had been undamaged when they were shipped from the Mining District, but Bondalar brought out their own analysis to show the flaws in the material as received." She drew a deep breath. "And so on and so on."

Her pale hair was the colorless blond of all Guild members, done up in a long braid that spiraled like a helmet around the top of her head. "I can give you the mental details if you like, but frankly I'd rather spare you the misery."

Tharion laughed. "Let's sit down before our meal gets cold."

She slumped into her chair and closed her eyes. Her sash hung loose, and her white robe fell open. "So how was *your* day?" she remembered to say, keeping her eyes closed.

"Murder," he said.

Now she blinked and stared at him. "What? Another one?"

Tharion nodded soberly. "I'm beginning to suspect the Veritas smuggling goes deeper than I thought. More than just a few stray capsules that somehow managed to trickle into outlying villages."

"And this murder had something to do with it?" Qrista said.

"I believe it's a vigilante killing, removing one of the smugglers. But Franz says our problems are all over now."

"Franz Dokken?" Qrista scowled. "If he's behind it, I'm sure it's not all over."

Tharion took a mouthful of rice and vegetables, chewing slowly to grant himself time to think. "I never said he was *behind* it, Qrista. He's trying to help. Don't be so hard on him."

"Give me the details," she said skeptically. "I want to know what he really said."

Tharion raised his head, and she reached over the small table to stroke his forehead. She closed her eyes and gently ran her fingers through his thoughts, enhancing them with her telepathic abilities.

"Convenient," Qrista said. "And Dokken decides to play his own games with you, getting rid of your only direct connection before a Truthsayer can interrogate him. What about his suppliers?"

"That information is lost. But if it cuts off the Veritas smuggling, I think it's for the best," Tharion said. "Otherwise, we'll raise a lot of questions we don't want answered. How could the Guild lose control so badly? Think of the outcry."

"Think of the outcry if people find out that we're holding a man in the detention chambers who is almost certainly innocent! Dokken supposedly knows the identity of the real killer, but you never bothered to ask him. Are we supposed to ignore the unsolved crime?"

Qrista was visibly upset, turning away from him. "It goes against all our ethical training. We can't just ignore a crime."

"No, we can't," Tharion said. "But if Cialben truly was smuggling Veritas, taking it away from the Guild and giving it to . . . to outsiders who aren't prepared to handle it, and if I declared him guilty—as he assuredly was—it would have been my option to sentence him to death."

"But you wouldn't have."

Tharion sighed. "No, I suppose I wouldn't."

"You're just doing what Dokken wants," Qrista said.

Tharion shrugged. "I do what he wants only if it's the same thing that I want. We can think alike, you know."

"That's a scary thought," she said in a noncommittal tone and fell to eating again.

Tharion felt the need to keep explaining, though his wife already knew every one of his reasons. "Franz has assisted me through my entire career. I'm Guild Master, in part, because of his support. None of the other landholders has been as objective or as helpful. They come here only when they want something. None of the others offered to become my mentor as I was going through difficult times. Now everyone wants my favors, of course—but Franz was there at the very beginning. He's given me no reason not to trust him."

"Have you used Veritas to read him?" Qrista asked, "to see if he's really telling you the truth?"

Tharion was shocked. "Qrista! We took an oath. I would never read a man without just cause and without his consent. Franz has done nothing to warrant such treatment. Why have you always disliked him?"

She met his gaze evenly. "Because you believe everything he says."

Tharion ate in silence, concentrating on the taste of the rice and the spiced vegetables. His hangover headache had faded with the afternoon, but now it threatened to return as a dull throb at the back of his skull. Finally, Qrista finished and nudged her plate off to the side of the serving tray.

"Look, I've had a rough day," she said in an apologetic tone, "and I'm taking it out on you since I couldn't very well slam the Council members' heads together. My mediation didn't work well, even when I could read what each party wanted. I'm upset with all the landholders—and Dokken's one of them."

She stood up and her robe fell completely open to reveal her rounded breasts. "Let's go to bed. Give me a back rub?"

Tharion smiled. "With pleasure."

She smiled back. "That's the point."

On their wide sleeping pallet, with the yellow-orange lights still turned low, Tharion carefully slid the cotton robe off her shoulders and dropped it to the deck. He ran his fingertips along the pale skin of her shoulders, tickling her shoulder blades.

Qrista purred, arching herself up as she rested her head on the pillow, eyes closed. He pressed into her flesh, rubbing the tense muscles. Her skin was so pale it seemed transparent. She'd let down her braid and combed out her long whitish blond hair.

A lifetime of exposure to Veritas had made them sterile in addition to pale. Most Guild members never married, finding it intimidating to be in the presence of a mate who knew every innermost thought—but Tharion and Qrista had no secrets. The two of them had the same expectations, had gone through the same sacrifices.

He gave her a long and luxurious back rub, and then found they were both too tired to make love. They shared quiet soothing thoughts as they pressed together with the lights turned off.

They drifted off to sleep in each other's arms, nestled in each other's dreams.

The Truthsayers Guild had added rugs to the deck plates and tapestries to the walls, replacing sections of the armored hull with reinforced windows and stained glass mosaics—but they had done little to modify the brig.

Troy Boren sat in one of the dim detention cells, fingers threaded through his hair, staring down at his knees. The lower decks of the *SkySword*'s belly lay buried in the dust, blocking all daylight from the smothered viewports.

At least his trial would come within three days, they said. It wasn't soon enough for him, but the Guild was required to send out notice of the public Truthsaying. Despite his protestations, they seemed convinced of his guilt—and why shouldn't they be? Eli Strone had also claimed to be innocent.

Troy had been caught kneeling over a dead body in the middle of the night. Cren had verified that computer manifests from the last elevator shipment had been altered. Records proved that Troy had used his pass card to enter the inventory warehouse long after normal operating hours. Tests showed that the murdered man had recently taken Veritas—illegal Veritas—and two more of the capsules were found on his person.

Troy had tried to explain why he had really gone out late at night. He had done something wrong, to be sure—but certainly not murder. Troy laced his fingers together and swallowed. His throat was very dry, but the sol-pols had given him only warm, alkaline-tasting water.

Though a brown-sashed representative from the Truthsayers Guild had come to make certain that Troy did indeed want to be tried in front of the gathered crowd, it was obvious the worker didn't believe him, thinking that Troy was wasting everyone's time.

But it didn't matter what the nontelepathic administrator thought. Troy was entitled to have his name cleared, and only the Truthsayer's actual verdict counted.

The Atlas system of justice was based on incontrovertible truth, thoughts of guilt or innocence taken directly from the mind of the accused rather than relying on such circumstantial evidence as had piled up against Troy. He felt relieved that a Truthsayer would find out the real story, no matter how unlikely it seemed. *Just wait*, he thought. *Just wait, and everyone will see.*

ii

During the following day, another member of the Truthsayers Guild came, strongly advising Troy to confess and save the Truthsayer the trouble, save himself the public humiliation. The administrator assured him his sentence would be lighter if he admitted his own sins rather than forcing the telepath to tear them out and expose them in public.

Troy continued to shake his head and insist that he wanted the clear Truthsayer verdict. He wanted to be pronounced innocent so that everyone could see.

Finally, toward evening that day—though deep underground in the cell, Troy had no idea what the actual time might be—he received a visit he had dreaded, one he had hoped he wouldn't have to face until after the Truthsayer pronounced him clean.

He heard footsteps, the rustle of stiff uniforms, the clicking weapons of the heavily armored elite guard marching in an oddly echoing lockstep as they escorted several people. Troy hoped it wasn't more Guild representatives come to dissuade him again— instead he saw the swarthy face of his father with his mother and two sisters in tow.

"You didn't have to come," Troy blurted, unable to think of anything else in the moment of his shock.

His older sister Leisa smiled wryly. "Good to see you, too, Troy."

"I mean," Troy said, "I'll be cleared in a couple of days."

"We all had to come," sour-faced little Rissbeth said. "Do you know how much a mag-lev ticket for the whole family cost?"

"Your father got a bonus yesterday," Dama said. "He found a rich molybdenum deposit on his shift, and we had to come and show you our support. You depend on us, don't you?"

Rambra scowled, avoiding the transparent security field by a wide margin. "If you did this thing, Troy," he said, "I can't describe how disgusted I'll be with you." Troy saw, though, a secret glint of confused pride behind his father's eyes. He wondered if Rambra might not be at least partially pleased that his weakling son was capable of fighting a man.

Troy flushed, feeling guilty at what he had put them through, but then annoyance at his little sister rose up. "I didn't ask you to be here," he said.

His mother rolled her eyes. "We've got so much invested in you, Troy—and now look at what's happened. How could you do this to us? And after only three weeks! You should have been so careful, on your best behavior."

Troy's stomach churned. "How can you even think I'm guilty?" he said.

"No matter how this turns out," his mother said, "they'll look down on you forever. I understand you've confessed to manipulating the records in the computers. What were you thinking? Now you'll never get a promotion. You'll never earn any extra credits. It's all for nothing."

Rissbeth made a sound as if she had swallowed a live squirming worm. "Yeah, thanks a lot, Troy."

Leisa shook her head. "I can't believe you're capable of murder, Troy. Or that you would be mixed up in a drug-smuggling ring. In fact, when I think about it I have to laugh."

Troy forced a smile, warmed by the comforting tone of his sister's words. "At least somebody believes I've been falsely accused."

"Falsely accused!" Leisa pantomimed a wail. "A gross flaw in the system. This could lead to the shake-up of our very society."

"To the unraveling of society's moral fiber," Troy picked up the thread. "It could lead to chaos, civil war, and universal Armageddon!"

Dama's alarm escalated with the interchange, as if she had finally realized the magnitude of her son's circumstances. "Oh, you two!" she said stoically. "Stop being so pessimistic. It's not over yet. We'll see this thing through."

Troy slumped onto his bunk, still looking at them through the security field. "Don't worry, Mother. It'll all be over in a couple of days. I didn't do this. Trust me."

"We'll be there watching you when you face the Truthsayer," Leisa said. "Promise."

Troy swallowed the lump in his throat. "I'll try to find you in the crowd but . . . my mind will probably be occupied with other things."

"It better be," Rambra said.

"Afterward," Troy said confidently, "we can all go out and celebrate."

With a clatter of thick red boots on the deck plates, the sol-pol elite guards returned to his holding cell. "Time," one guard said, gesturing with his weapon for the visitors to leave.

As his family filed out, Troy found that he was more shaken now than he had been before their visit.

# CHAPTER

i

After several days of respite, another storm front approached across the continent, bringing a vanguard of ragged clouds over First Landing. Kalliana stood in her quarters, staring out the window up at the sky and fixing her attention away from the gathered crowds that waited again for her in the central plaza. Just like before.

The storm clouds were brooding gray mounds near the horizon, but here the day was merely overcast and cold. A wind sprang up, whipping the fronds of stunted palm trees along the streets, their roots sprawled out in a broad mat to suck nourishment from the heavily fertilized topsoil.

Kalliana stared through the transparent portion of her window, which was surrounded by a sunburst of triangular wedges in green, crimson, and royal blue glass, distorting the view to symbolize the uncertain nature of truth. The central transparent pane was a metaphor for how Truthsayers saw clearly, while others were doomed to see the colors of lies.

Another accused murderer waited for her in the plaza. Kalliana would have to dig into his mind, witness the truth in his own thoughts, and make her judgment.

*Truth Holds No Secrets.*

The Truthsayers' code decreed that the accused was innocent until she read his guilt. But she already knew through grim experience that very few people were truly innocent. She swallowed hard.

Kalliana feared more vivid nightmares that were not her own—but even more she dreaded being transferred from the Guild, being forced to leave her comfortable, familiar existence.

With Veritas she had witnessed secondhand the difficult existence the other colonists endured. She didn't want a pointless life outside the Guild. She wondered if it could truly be as unpleasant as she imagined it . . . out there. She would rather face another murderer.

Only she and the accused could ever know for certain what had actually happened. A Truthsayer had to wear a blindfold to any repercussions of the verdict, decreeing only whether the man was guilty or innocent.

The truth would come out, but Kalliana had to show it the way.

ii

Down in the detention levels, Troy Boren lay motionless on his hard bunk. He kept his eyes closed, willing himself to sleep so that the time might pass more quickly. But his stomach roiled with anxiety, his dry throat burned, and thoughts whirled behind his eyelids, making him squirm with the possibilities of a worst-case scenario. But it wouldn't happen. Truthsayers didn't make mistakes.

He had no idea how many days had passed since his arrest. The guards had taken his personal chronometer; apparently they were afraid he might attempt some sort of bizarre high-tech sabotage with its tiny components. . . .

Though hunger gnawed at his stomach, he felt no real appetite, doubting he could keep anything down if he bothered to eat. The sol-pols had given him only a limited amount of time to pick at his food, then they had taken it away.

When the elite guard switched off the confinement field, Troy was startled to find that he had indeed dozed off, despite his anxiety. He sat up, blinking bleary eyes. His shoulders and back crackled with stiffness from the uncomfortable pallet.

"Got your thoughts in order?" the guard said gruffly, his eyes hidden behind the uniform's tough goggles.

"I'm ready," Troy said, hauling himself off the bunk.

"Do you have a guilty conscience?" the helmeted guard asked with a slight smile in his voice.

Troy couldn't tell if the guard was mocking him or not. "I don't have anything to worry about." He smoothed down his formless prison outfit.

This time the uniformed man did laugh. "If you say so."

Troy followed him numbly out of his cell. The metal deck plates were cold against his bare feet, and he longed to be standing under the warmth of the sun again. At least he could look forward to that part.

iii

"Sit next to me," Tharion said, gesturing for Qrista to take a place on one of the flecked granite benches at the center of the plaza. "I won't be performing for this one. A Guild chanter is announcing the crime."

Most of the audience stood on the open flagstones, waiting for the show. The crowd was smaller than it had been for Strone's trial. This single murder was not as titillating.

Qrista flashed a hurriedly covered frown and fixed him with her ice-blue eyes. Her pale hair was braided again and wound around the top of her head. Angular bones gave her face a finely chiseled beauty that her smile enhanced . . . but now, troubled, Qrista appeared harsh and sharp. Tharion didn't have to ask why.

"This is a sham, and you shouldn't have allowed it," she said quietly, but sat down beside him with a rustle of her white robes, tightening her crimson sash. Because they had shared their thoughts completely, she knew her husband's reasoning, but that didn't mean she came to the same conclusions.

"I know," he answered. "But it's my decision as Guild Master and I have to live with it. We can't announce that we know what the outcome will be, because that would open up a thousand new questions. We must proceed and get this behind us. Let him be declared innocent in open court."

Qrista looked at him uncertainly. "So the damage to our ethics can heal? What if it leaves scars?"

Tharion knew she was right, but he had determined that this path was the best resolution to the complex and uncomfortable situation the Truthsayers Guild had stumbled into.

For a moment he wished that Troy Boren *were* guilty, so they could drain more information about the black market Veritas from him. But since the young man was simply a clumsy bystander, Tharion knew they could get nothing else from him.

He reached out to hold Qrista's cold, pale hand as they sat looking up at the empty podium. "Nothing is ever certain,"

Tharion said. "We'll need to ride this out, and I need your help and support."

She pressed her lips together. "Of course you have my support," she said. "I don't make your decisions for you. I just abide by them."

"This will all turn out all right," he said.

Qrista raised her white eyebrows, allowing him a small smile. "Oh? You can see into the future now as well as reading minds?"

"I wish that were so," he said with a forced smile. "A new kind of drug developed up on the Platform."

He looked up to see the great ship doors opening in the Headquarters building. The Truthsayer Kalliana and the prisoner would be brought forward momentarily.

iv

Quietly anonymous, Franz Dokken stood in the middle of the crowd. He wore sturdy cotton slacks and a warm woolen jacket: expensive clothes but not showy. His ragged hair whipped in long strands in the gusting breeze.

Judging from the cloud bank on the horizon, he guessed it must be raining hard at his holding—good. They needed the water in the dwindling rivers that powered his hydroelectric plant.

Beside him, Maximillian loomed tall and stiff, ready to block anyone who approached his master too closely, though Dokken preferred to remain camouflaged within the crowd. He didn't want Tharion or the others to know he had come to see Troy Boren brought before the Truthsayer.

Dokken wanted to watch the crowd, see how they reacted. He enjoyed observing how all the threads tangled together. He had begun to calculate the earliest possible time when he could disappear for a few weeks on another sojourn. He felt tired already.

"Behind schedule," Maximillian said, glancing at his chronometer.

Dokken pursed his lips. "Don't be such a slave to time."

"Plenty to do back at the villa," Maximillian pointed out. "Another shipment of pine logs coming in this afternoon. And there seems to be some problem with the fish farm. Your presence has been requested to check it out."

"Yes, yes," Dokken said impatiently. "Let's just watch the show and see how much they think they know."

Maximillian's expression was flat and unreadable. "They know nothing about what I did."

"Of course not," Dokken said. "I certainly wouldn't bring you here if they did." He raised his head as the ship doors opened.

The hapless prisoner stumbled out in chains, escorted by the elite guard. Dokken scrutinized this lanky man who moved like a pigeon. Troy Boren was fidgety and nervous, his hair curly brown, his Adam's apple bobbing up and down as he swallowed repeatedly.

"They think *he* killed Cialben?" Dokken breathed a short laugh. "That's funny. He doesn't look like he has enough courage even to harvest vegetables."

Maximillian nodded with no change of expression. "You never can tell," he said. "Sometimes people surprise you."

v

Troy stood alone on the open platform above the crowd. His hands and ankles were wrapped in firm bindings, though he wondered where they expected him to run, how they thought he might attempt to escape. He shivered.

Above, the sky was a bowl of clouds the color of cast lead. Stray breezes hurled the mutters of the crowd toward him like a slap in the face. Troy hunched his shoulders, trying to appear small. He didn't want all these people staring at him. He had never wanted to call attention to himself, just to do his job and make a living, maybe help his family's situation improve.

The noise of the audience rose higher, and he realized what their hopes were. They wanted him to be found guilty. They were eager to see another criminal sentenced. They would be *disappointed* when he was found innocent.

Troy did not dare look out across the crowd. His family was probably out there, watching for him. He knew they would resent having to stay several days in First Landing; they didn't have the money to afford such luxuries. He would try to make it up to them—especially Leisa—once all this was over. A new blanket for the baby, perhaps, or special confections from a sweetshop. Even Rissbeth would enjoy that.

The sol-pol elite guards stood back at the edge of the platform, keeping order through intimidation. Troy remembered the guard asking him if he had a guilty conscience, and he tried to clear his thoughts and think straight—but now the idea of guilt had fixed itself rigidly in his mind.

He knew he was innocent, but that meant the real killer was still on the loose. Troy had stumbled upon the body of the murdered man ... there had been so much blood. If he had arrived an hour earlier—even fifteen minutes—the killer might have caught him as well. Troy shuddered. If only he hadn't botched those manifest sheets in the first place. If only he hadn't gone back to fix his mistake, creating an even bigger error in the process. He had changed what would have been a private (though still disastrous) reprimand into a murder trial.

The image danced across his mind: the dead body, eyes wide, two capsules of the Veritas drug, the wound where the blade had stabbed between the ribs and up into the heart.

And the blood. The dark blood spreading across the concrete floor.

So much blood!

Troy squeezed his eyes shut. He just wanted this entire ordeal to end. He gulped, hunched down even further, and waited for the Truthsayer to come out and free him.

vi

The promenade doors to Guild Headquarters split open, leaving Kalliana to stand in their center. A thin fingernail of cold breeze scraped along her white cotton robe. She straightened her green sash around her narrow waist. Her translucent skin flushed in the chill air as she stepped barefoot toward the plaza. The gold ceremonial collar felt heavy on her shoulders.

She saw the crowd, saw the accused, and was reminded again of Eli Strone—but this skinny young man looked so different, so quiet and lost, like a terrified waif. He insisted he was not guilty. However, Strone had also been certain of his own innocence, convinced that he had done nothing wrong. A Truthsayer could not judge on the basis of outward appearances. Because Troy Boren looked *so* unlikely, he seemed paradoxically more suspect.

Kalliana came forward and waited as one of the Guild chanters listed the case and the details, describing the crime of which Troy had been accused. As the chanter summarized, the crowd booed and jeered. Kalliana frowned. They needed to be reminded that the accused was innocent until *she* pronounced him guilty.

*If* she pronounced him guilty.

She came forward, an angel in white, holding the power of this man's life in her hands. She received one of the sky-blue capsules of Veritas from its ornate brass-and-copper box, the small pill that protected Atlas from the deceptions of criminals. She popped it into her mouth, cracked it, and swallowed, taking a deep breath.

"If you're innocent," she said to Troy Boren, "you need not fear the truth."

He drew a quick breath and answered in a quiet voice that no one else could hear. "I'm not afraid," he said. "I am innocent."

Kalliana tried not to show that fear engulfed her as well. She hoped that her exposure to Strone hadn't set up echoes in her mind that might dampen her telepathic abilities. She felt the power of the Veritas surging through her, but she had difficulty focusing her thoughts.

Kalliana reached out and placed both of her hands flat against Troy's temples. She closed her eyes as he blinked up at her like a wounded and confused animal.

She worked to sharpen her truthsaying ability into a usable tool, then went inside Troy's thoughts, tentative and skittish. She brushed the surface of his memories, unwilling to go deep—and there she found it sitting like a black stain on the top of his mind: a guilt, a fear.

She probed deeper, feeling herself stiffen and grow even more wary, afraid to see—but it was her duty. She was a Truthsayer. She had to see.

She looked into Troy's memories for just a glance, a snatch, a vision—

—and saw the sprawled body, saw the blood, heard the scream echoing in his mind. *My God, there was so much blood.*

The body lying there in the dim orange light.

The blood.

The overpowering guilt.

Kalliana froze, trembling until her shuddering became so violent she could not go deeper. She didn't have the strength to probe for clearer details of the actual murder, but the answer was obvious to her. Too obvious.

She pulled back, jerking her hands away and cried out in a hoarse gasp. "Guilty," she said. "Guilty!"

Troy's face drained completely of blood. "No," he whispered. "You're wrong."

But Kalliana staggered away, hiding from him. She did not wish to see any more. "Guilty," she said again, then fled into Guild Headquarters, to safety.

## vii

Guild Master Tharion leaped to his feet as the crowd yelled.

"That can't be right," he mouthed, but caught himself before saying it out loud, knowing the terrible consequences if he, the Guild Master, accused a Truthsayer of making a faulty judgment, of distorting the truth . . . of finding an innocent man guilty! That simply could not occur. On Atlas it would never happen. The Guild would fall apart if the faith of the public faltered.

Qrista grasped his wrist and squeezed so tightly that her fingernails bit into his skin. Tharion looked down at her, his face devastated. How would he be able to remedy this? He couldn't announce that he knew Kalliana's judgment was in error. He couldn't admit *how* he knew.

"You can't let this happen," Qrista said, her words stabbing like knives.

"I can't do anything about it," Tharion said. "Not at the moment."

He looked up to see a pair of familiar figures in the crowd: bald Maximillian, then Franz Dokken with his blond hair and ageless face. Both Dokken and his manservant looked bewildered by the outcome, and Tharion wondered what could have gone wrong. Had Kalliana intentionally given a false verdict? Was she involved in the black market sales somehow? He realized that someone in the Guild might be a link—but *Kalliana*? The possibilities swam in his mind, making him dizzy.

He wanted to rush over to the landholder, to grab him by the collar and demand to know what had gone wrong, but Dokken and Maximillian looked as confused as Tharion.

Troy should not have been found guilty—but now that the judgment had been pronounced in public with full ceremony, Tharion knew of no way he could rescind it. This was all so impossible!

The uproar continued, and he looked up to see the elite guard grabbing a limp Troy Boren by the bindings on his wrists and hauling him toward the armored walls of the Guild Headquarters. A convicted murderer.

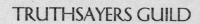

TRUTHSAYERS GUILD

# CHAPTER
# 10

i

The *SkySword*'s library contained a repository of knowledge from old Earth. Many of the old ship files were locked with long-forgotten military passwords and thus unavailable to members of the Guild. However, once the Truthsayers had learned to use the computer databases and gain access to files, they had begun keeping track of their own work, maintaining files of the cases they had determined.

Kalliana sat alone inside the metal-walled library room. The consoles were discolored and scuffed, the swivel chairs worn by time. She gazed at the phosphor-filled screens as if they were deep wells into a universe of information. The reflection of her pinched face stared back at her, distracting her. She blinked to restore her concentration and tapped again on the keyboard, summoning the next list.

The names were just a blur, one after another, accompanied by capsule summaries of their trials, the crimes of which they had been accused: thievery, vandalism, rape, murder, conspiracy, arson. The far column listed the most important data of all.

Innocent.

Innocent.

Guilty.

Innocent.

Guilty.

Guilty.

Over two centuries, the colonists had come to Atlas in waves, ships full of wide-eyed colonists, exiled criminals, military forces, religious fanatics. . . .

According to transmissions, a new ship called the *EarthDawn* was on its way. Atlas had heard nothing from Earth in decades, not since the Pilgrim exiles had come forty-two years earlier, spouting tales of social upheaval and Armageddon. However, the Pilgrims were Millennial religious fanatics and saw the end of the world in everything—so the veracity of their news was in question. But without a doubt, something terrible had happened on distant Earth.

Kalliana viewed another screen of data, working her way down through the years. She wasn't searching for anything in particular, just a confirmation of the work the Guild had done, a salve for her doubts and the pain that so many guilty readings had brought her.

After his trial Troy Boren had been sentenced to permanent exile up on OrbLab 2, the separate orbital processing facility where he would work in the dangerous Veritas-processing chambers. There had been an increasing number of disastrous accidents in the past few years, so the free-floating lab always needed new workers. Troy Boren would be shipped up on the space elevator and transported from the Platform to the orbital laboratory as soon as the proper contingent of guards could be arranged.

More names flashed across the screen, but the words were blurred through her dry burning stare.

Guilty.

Guilty.

Innocent.

Guilty.

So many names . . . for every bad one the Guild removed from society, Atlas seemed to breed another, and another. . . .

ii

Kalliana went to one of the military briefing rooms that had been converted into a classroom, where Ysan was teaching (and playing with) seven young children. All were dressed in little white gowns and had the pale hair and complexions of those exposed to Veritas since they were embryos.

Though visits to help train the children were part of Kalliana's regular duties, she also wanted to divert herself, watching the innocence and exuberance of the young ones.

"Ah, Kalliana!" Ysan said, climbing to his feet as the white-robed children scattered, giggling and laughing. He surrendered his maroon chair at the head of the meeting table. "Look who's come to play with us, kids. Sit down, Kalliana. We were just doing the mind practice game."

"I don't want to disturb you," she said.

"No, you'll help us," Ysan answered with a grin.

"All right." She flashed a small smile of her own, then sank into the padded fabric chair, running her hands over the polished black armrests.

The children gathered around her. Ysan knelt next to them, much taller than the six- to eight-year-olds. He lowered his voice to a stage whisper. "She's a real Truthsayer, you know, so we'll have to work hard now. No more playing."

The children snickered.

"You know how the game is played," Kalliana said to them. "I think of something, then you try to read it from me. The first person to get it right wins, then we'll try another."

The children sat around, watching her obediently with their bright eyes. Observing them, Kalliana felt a healing force, the goodness of children raised within the protective arms of the Guild.

"All right," she said, "I'm picturing something." She closed her eyes, summoning an image in her mind. "Try to read it from me."

The children concentrated, looking comical with their focused expressions, their furrowed foreheads. Ysan picked up the image immediately and nodded at Kalliana, but she continued to project, not letting herself get distracted. That might throw the children off.

"It's a white ball," one little boy said.

"No, it's glowing," a girl interrupted. "It's a glowbulb!"

"No, the sun," a third child said. "The sun—the sun up in the sky!"

"Yes," Kalliana said and smiled. "It's the sun."

Next, she thought of one of the tall palm trees that grew out in the plaza.

"It's a stick!" one of the girls said.

"No, a broom," another girl challenged, "thin and dry."

The boy grew suddenly incensed and pointed at the little girl beside him. "She's thinking bad things about me!"

"I am not!" the girl answered. "You were doing it first. You thought I look like one of the rock lizards."

"I didn't think that."

"Yes, you did."

"Well, I couldn't help it. That's what you look like."

Losing her temper, Kalliana stood from the maroon chair. "Enough! You shouldn't be reading each other's minds unless you have explicit permission to do so. That is *not* something a Truthsayer would ever do.

"Thoughts are private, unless we have cause to go inside another person's mind. I've given you permission to read me while we play this game, but you must never, *ever* read another person just for fun."

Kalliana sat down again, alarmed at her own temper. The children stared at her uncertainly, and she wondered if they had caught a backwash of her inner turmoil. "All right," she said, getting down to business. "Let's do the game again and try to focus once more on the picture in my mind."

Trying to calm herself, she realized that with the mental wounds still stinging, she had once again been considering her onerous obligations to the Guild, whether it was worth everything her life had granted her. After the unpleasant lives she had witnessed in the minds of criminals, she was afraid to lose it all, no matter how difficult her Truthsayer duties were.

But she couldn't stop thinking of the recent violent trials . . . the bright images of bloody corpses lying in shadows, the wide-eyed stares of victims, the brooding anger and disregard for life, *how good it had felt to kill.*

Suddenly three of the children screamed and began to cry. Several of them backed away from her, horrified and sickened. Kalliana slammed down on her thoughts, knowing what images she must inadvertently have broadcast to them.

Ysan shooed the startled children out of the room. "That's it. No more game for today. Go and play in the upper corridors."

"I'm sorry," Kalliana said quietly to Ysan as the children scattered.

He glanced at her strangely, with a glimmer of uncertain fear behind his eyes. Yes, he had read it too—and unlike the little children, he understood what he was seeing. "I'm worried about you."

Masking her thoughts and her expressions, Kalliana straightened her white robe. "I'll be all right." She left the teaching room.

# CHAPTER

## III

i

Exactly on schedule, six sol-pol elite guards appeared at the sealed receiving hatch of Guild Headquarters, bearing a new shipment of Veritas capsules sent down on the space elevator. Guild Master Tharion himself stood at the doorway to meet them, using his own access code. He waited on the threshold where hot air scented with baked dust from the streets met the cool mustiness of rarely used levels in the grounded spaceship.

"Standard shipment from OrbLab 2," the lead guard said.

"And someone has accompanied it every step of the way?" Tharion asked. "Never been out of your sight?"

"Fully accountable, Guild Master. It has never left my own hand," the guard said. His face was a stony mask partially covered by his dark helmet. "I personally received it from OrbLab 2 and counted the capsules. I rode down the space elevator with the case on my lap, and carried it here."

Tharion nodded. "I don't suppose there's much chance of any having been stolen, then."

The guard stood at attention. "I can't see any way it would have been possible, sir."

Tharion let the armed escort pass into Headquarters. It took only one man to carry the locked case containing a gross of the sky-blue capsules—a week's production from OrbLab 2—but five other sol-pols guarded him. Though Franz Dokken had suggested that the black market activities would stop with the death of Cialben, Tharion had increased the size of the Veritas escort. Even so, neither the additional guards nor Dokken's assurances had stopped the smuggling, according to continued rumors of the drug out in the populace in the past week. Tharion did not know what else to do.

He marched with the escort down the echoing metal corridors of the converted military ship, observing their backs, their dark armor, their scarlet gauntlets, boots, and kneepads. The Guild's elite guard wore *genuine* old uniforms from the long-defeated *SkySword* soldiers, rather than imitations, as did the regular sol-pols.

Back before he became Guild Master, Tharion had spent much more time and attention getting to know the elite guards. The soldiers had been an important part of his upbringing, ever-present, impressive. Their loyalty fascinated him.

Eli Strone had been one of them, obsessed with duty, rigid in his awe and admiration for the Truthsayers, trustworthy to the point of being an automaton. Yet somehow he had cracked, and left the Guild, wandering aimlessly for two years until finally driven to murder.

Tharion tried to look at the ranks of elite guards objectively for a moment: armed with deadly weapons, padded with body armor, a powerful force entrusted with protecting the Truthsayers and the Veritas stockpile. He wondered how close any of these others might be to falling into a maelstrom of unpredictability. Like Strone. Though all the sol-pols ostensibly reported to the Guild, they could be dangerous assets.

Deep in the isolated central deck, Tharion used his access code again to enter the shielded chambers that had once been the military ship's armory. Now, the armory held something more precious and threatening than any high-tech weaponry.

In tiny sealed bins along one wall, the Guild's stockpile of Veritas capsules had been separated and stored, divided according to potency: the strongest dosages which were given to Truthsayers immediately before pronouncing a verdict; maintenance doses for himself and standby Truthsayers every three days; weekly capsules for the Mediators; and bodyweight-dependent doses of Veritas for children as well as the embryos growing in the infirmary sector of Headquarters.

Lengthy research by the Guild's biochemists had shown that the drug did not deteriorate over time, and so the stockpile would last them through even a lengthy disaster. He had rarely considered it, but now it made him dizzy to think of how many vital capsules rested in airtight chambers behind their numerous security interlocks. Tharion drew a deep breath.

*Truth Holds No Secrets.*

He keyed in his access code again, used the *SkySword*'s

thumbprint reader, and finally opened an empty bin to receive the current shipment. The elite guard carrier unlocked his case while the five sol-pols stood outside the armory door. Tharion recorded the control number of the shipment, a precaution he had instituted since the accidental poisoning of Klaryus.

Inside the case lay twelve dozen sky-blue capsules of fresh Veritas cultured over the past week in the isolated, orbital lab, wrapped in translucent packing material. Tharion stood by, counting out each pill to double-check the shipment. The total came out right, as it always did. He checked the documentation and appended his initials.

The entire process seemed so meticulous—yet mistakes continued to be made. Veritas was leaking into society somehow, even though every single capsule could be accounted for, from the beginning of the production line up on OrbLab 2 until it was sealed here in the Guild armory.

Was it someone from *inside* the Guild? Truthsayers giving up their own dosages, for sale to some high-paying users in the public? But why? Truthsayers had a golden life, given every luxury and amenity they could imagine. What could they be selling the drug *for*?

The Truthsayer Kalliana had made an error in her verdict of Troy Boren. Had she actively lied? And if she had lied, could the reason be because she herself was somehow involved in the black market smuggling? Had she convicted Troy to cover up any further search for the perpetrators, to conveniently answer all questions, sacrificing an innocent man in the process?

The only other alternative he could imagine was that some foolhardy ring had established a Veritas-culturing and -processing station somewhere here on the surface of Atlas, though the horrifying probability of a Mindfire mutation and the dangers of contamination and plague made that unlikely. The simplest mistake could result in a plague that might wipe out thousands. Errors had been made before, and the current technology available to the colonists was far inferior to that originally brought from Earth.

Upon assuming the royal blue sash, Tharion's first act as Guild Master had been to order a crackdown on the production facilities of OrbLab 2, tightened constraints, quality checks, and an overhaul of the process line, much to the consternation of station exec Dieter Pan and the OrbLab crew. They hated being called to task for a job they considered beyond Tharion's authority—but the contamination of the Veritas capsule that had killed Guild Master

Klaryus was simply inexcusable. The Guild Members—and the entire population of First Landing—had simply been lucky that the poison present in that pill had been merely the distilled toxin, not the wildly spreading plague organism itself.

But though all work on OrbLab 2 had been tightly watched for the past two years—the smuggling had been steadily increasing.

The lead guard sealed the bin containing all twelve dozen capsules. "Finished, sir," he said. Tharion added his thumbprint lock to secure the bins, then followed the elite guard out into the corridor, where he sealed the armory hatch. Air hissed, draining the atmosphere from the armory vault. Frost crackled around the edges as the temperature dropped.

The Veritas was safe.

Supposedly.

Leaving, Tharion decided to place an extra guard at the door to the stockpile. Probably an empty gesture, but he ordered it anyway.

ii

Tharion searched out the most calming influence he could imagine. Qrista. He sat back in one of the audience seats, alone but certainly not unnoticed, as he watched the Landholders Council session in progress.

Qrista, wearing her Mediator's sash, sat at the center of the gathered representatives. She looked icily beautiful and stern in her position. Qrista glanced up at him and smiled. Tharion smiled back, waiting for the warming influence of her presence to burn through the glacier surrounding his heart. His Guild was threatened, and he didn't know how to fight it.

The next speaker on the agenda entered through the broad rear doors, and immediately all the representatives shifted uneasily. A tall muscular man with gray hair in long dreadlocks came forward, wrapped in a dirty brown robe with a ragged hem and patches on the elbows. The Pilgrims wore their uncomfortable robes all day, every day, during their hours of difficult labor, and when they relaxed. It was no wonder the fabric became stained and dirty before long.

"Speak," Qrista said as the gray-haired man shrugged back his hood and stood silently in front of the Landholders Council, his head bowed. The skin on his cheeks was a weathered, ruddy brown from a lifetime spent outside in the harsh winds and desert sun.

"My name is Kindness," he said. "Of the Holy Order of Pilgrims from Earth."

"We know who you are," Qrista said, glancing at her agenda. "Please be brief. We have no time for sermons or lectures on our sins."

"Very well," said Kindness. "I come again to request an allotment of land on Atlas, a barren area unworked by other landholders. Some fifteen thousand of our Pilgrims from Earth are a part of your Atlas society, scattered among the landholdings. We have worked diligently since our arrival here decades ago. We fled the evils of Earth and came to seek a land of our own—but instead you have taken us, separated us, made us your slaves."

"Now wait a minute—that's not true," said the representative from Bondalar Holding.

"A matter of semantics," Kindness said. "I have no wish to argue words, only to make my point."

"I think we know what your point is," said the hard-faced woman representing Koman Holding.

The Pilgrim continued as if he hadn't heard, or didn't care. "We Pilgrims have labored without complaint, but we deserve to reap the rewards of our own efforts, or suffer the burdens of our own failures."

"In short, you want a homeland," Qrista said, hoping to curtail any further embellishment on the issue.

"Yes," Kindness answered. "That is exactly what we wish."

"I sympathize with the Pilgrims, but that will cause immeasurable damage to our fragile society at this point," said a fresh-faced young Sardili representative. "As you know, Sardili Shores accepted a much larger proportion of the Pilgrim refugees than did any other holding. We are glad to have your labor, and we give you all the freedoms you ask for. I can't believe you find the conditions too harsh."

The Pilgrim nodded slightly, but did not comment.

"Much of the economy of our holding depends on the labor of our Pilgrim settlers. If suddenly five thousand of our hardest workers were to pick up and leave, Sardili Holding would collapse."

"Your economy is not our concern," said Kindness. "We have waited long enough for a homeland. You are stalling, and we have limits to our patience."

"Very well," Qrista said firmly, frowning at her chronometer.

"We'll set up a meeting to discuss the matter thoroughly. At that meeting we will consider a timetable for a gradual displacement of the next generation of Pilgrims. For now, that is all. On to the next matter."

"But nothing has been decided," Kindness said, raising himself up and tossing his graying dreadlocks away from his high forehead.

"*Nevertheless*," Qrista said, her voice turning brisk, "that is all for today. As it was, we were hard-pressed to accommodate your request for an audience on such short notice."

Two elite guards marched forward to escort him out. The Pilgrim stood like a statue for a full three seconds. From where he watched, Tharion worried that there might be violence—but then Kindness turned and allowed himself to be led from the meeting chamber. Tharion closed his eyes, heaved a thin sigh.

Qrista looked around at the other landholders' representatives and sat up rigidly as she spoke. "Next, I must introduce a problem that concerns me greatly. As you all know—but many of you are loath to admit—the Veritas drug is being sold secretly to the holdings. The common populace uses it in ways that are morally offensive to us—for thrills, personal gain, spying. . . ."

She looked up and down the long table at the representatives, as if challenging them to deny what she had said. "It has crossed my mind that even some landholders may be using black-market Veritas for their personal advancement." She shook her head as if she couldn't believe it.

"I will begin this discussion by suggesting that we look yet again into the process of packaging and delivering Veritas on OrbLab 2. With the establishment of the Guild a century ago, the landholders all agreed to a delegation of authority, a dispersal of responsibilities. Truthsayers, and Truthsayers *alone*, are permitted to use the telepathic enhancement. It is dangerous—physically, economically, and politically—for untrained people to dabble with its powers. We are justifiably concerned."

Qrista raised her colorless eyebrows, and Tharion sat forward, wondering what his wife was about to do.

"I propose that we begin a new outside investigation, using representatives from several landholdings to study the chain of Veritas production and delivery, starting with a team sent to OrbLab 2. The Veritas begins there, so we will begin there."

"I object, most strenuously!" said the representative from the

Platform. The old balding man sputtered, but could not seem to put his thoughts into words. "Even this hint of suspicion—what evidence do you have? Look to the law of the Guild—not even a Truthsayer can probe into private matters without just cause."

"The very existence of black market Veritas is certainly sufficient cause to suspect that something, some*where*, is not going right," Qrista pointed out. "We have been dealing with rumors of lost Veritas for the past decade. Guild Master Tharion conducted such an investigation two years ago after the unfortunate Mindfire contamination killed his predecessor Klaryus. Many changes were implemented at that time as a result of the investigation—but the drug continues to slip through our fingers. We must find out where and how."

Tharion sat back, nodding proudly at his wife, but she gave no sign that she saw him. He knew that he had already garnered a great deal of resentment from the workers and the station exec on OrbLab 2 because of his first probe two years earlier. Qrista knew the Guild had nothing to lose by calling for another investigation.

The representative from Toth Holding cleared his throat and spoke up. "It might be sufficient as a first step that Kareem Sondheim appoints an *internal* investigation to see if he can verify the existence of these alleged problems."

Seated next to the Toth representative, the representative from Koman Holding agreed. "That might be best," she said. "Let Sondheim poke around. If you're not satisfied, or if anything concrete is found, then we can discuss more drastic solutions."

Several other Council members nodded, and Tharion watched from the visitors' gallery, studying the representatives and trying to sense the invisible threads of secret alliances between them.

Historically, the landholders had been notorious for their lack of cooperation, but here they showed some common ground. It encouraged him to see that they agreed on *something*, even if it might be at the Guild's expense.

# CHAPTER
# 12

i

As he rode his chestnut stallion over the rocky rise, Franz Dokken paused to look across the flatlands, down toward the chain of shallow artificial ponds that made up his prized fish farm.

The ponds were fed by fresh water pouring out of the mountains, down a thin arroyo. Greenery and bushes planted by Dokken's workers made the streambanks a lush ribbon of life.

The fishponds themselves had been stocked with trout and salmon from embryos old Sondheim had delivered from the Platform. Several prefab shacks stood at one end of each lake to hold fishing equipment, food-prep and -storage units, and small dwellings for the fish harvesters.

Even from this distance Dokken could see figures going about their daily chores. His fish production had increased steadily over the years. Of all Dokken's attempts to conquer the waiting land, his fish farms had been among the simplest and most successful—until now.

Dokken looked up into the periwinkle sky. High cirrus clouds looked like daubs of white paint. The chill air was sharp and thin in his nostrils.

Atlas's atmosphere was perfectly breathable, containing the right mixture of oxygen, nitrogen, carbon dioxide, and inert gases. But the air always tasted powdery to Dokken, without the organic nuances and complexities he remembered from Earth . . . but it had been so long he wondered if perhaps his imagination was adding details that had never actually been there.

Atlas was a virgin world, with all the right chemical ingredients to make it an eventual paradise . . . much like Earth must have been billions of years in the past, with a burgeoning ecosystem in the seas but a barren landscape. A few hardy lichens, algae, and primitive grasses had made the transition from the ocean onto dry land, but the species had not diversified sufficiently to give rise to dense forests and large insect or animal populations.

Life had spread like wildfire since the arrival of the first colony ship, as hardworking settlers performed surgery on the rugged lands, laying down heavy fertilizers, first-wave plants, mosses, and grasses to establish an organic matrix. More and more acreage was claimed every year as landholders exploited resources, recycled their compost, coaxed agricultural lands to life.

Franz Dokken had had a huge stake in taming Atlas, and now he frowned in defensive concern as he thought of how someone might strike out at him. His fish farms were such an easy target. . . .

"Let's go see," he said to the stallion. He used his bootheels to nudge the horse into a gallop.

The fish harvesters saw him coming. Some rowed in small two-person boats out on the circular ponds, others stood outside the prefab shacks. One man, obviously the foreman, waved his arms to signal Dokken.

He dismounted beside the group of people clustered near the foreman. He handed the reins to a young woman, who cast her gaze down at the pebbly ground. "Hold these," Dokken said, "and stay with him. He might want to get a drink at the stream. Let him." Then Dokken ignored the girl, turning to the foreman. "My manservant tells me you've reported a problem. Show me."

"Yes, sir," the foreman said. He had a long, narrow face, as if someone had tugged down on his chin to stretch his features. His gray-brown hair looked as if it hadn't been washed in some time, or combed for that matter, but right now Dokken was concerned only with the threat to his fish.

"It happened quite suddenly, sir," the foreman said as he led Dokken toward a metal-grating pier by the swirling influx of the stream.

The water was murky with churning silt mixed with greenish algae added to the ponds. Several varieties of lakeweed had thrived on the chemical fertilizers Dokken had added to bring the lake into organic equilibrium for the fish.

Each pond was monitored to be hospitable to different species—trout, bass, and perch in one, salmon in another. Thousands of dragonfly larvae had been introduced into the water. The fish ate many of them, but some matured and hatched into emerald-green dragonflies that buzzed over the water surface, eating the other waterbugs Dokken had added to the system.

Standing on the metal grate, Dokken's attention focused on the dozens of fish floating belly up, like tiny overturned boats in the center of the pond, trapped by the swirling currents from influx and outflow.

"They started dying three days ago," the foreman said. "Just a few at first, then more and more each day."

"What's causing it?" Dokken asked. "Have you tested the dead fish?" His mind suggested several possibilities: that the water wasn't being oxygenated, that an underground volcanic bubble had released sulfur compounds into the water, that something had caused the temperature to fluctuate. . . .

"We tested them using a portable analyzer," the foreman said. "It's some kind of toxin. The meat is poisoned."

"What kind of toxin?" Dokken demanded.

"We don't know, sir," the foreman said. "It appears to be similar to that produced by native Atlas bacteria—like the Mindfire plague organism, for instance, or the paralysis drug *stenn*—but we aren't sure." Dokken nodded grimly, keeping his gaze focused on the fish that bobbed gently as ripples from the current caressed them.

Occasionally something strange appeared from Atlas biochemisty, as the fledgling biosystems produced mutations right and left, trying new species, new adaptations. Perhaps something similar had happened here, a deadly bloom of natural microorganisms that poisoned Dokken's precious fish, spreading from pond to pond.

"There's one other thing, sir," the foreman said, looking very uncertain.

Dokken faced him, bringing to bear his full intimidating persona. "Yes?"

"We don't have heavy security here, only a few patrols, but the two sol-pols spotted someone hanging around the ponds on the night just before the fish started dying. They pursued, but the intruder escaped. We would have thought little of it—except for this." He gestured at the pond.

Anger flamed within Dokken. He could picture one of the rival landholders salting the fishponds with an Atlas-derived toxin, something that would look like a natural bloom. Possibly Emilio Toth, in retaliation for Dokken's tainting of the aquifer that had destroyed part of Toth's pampered pine forests. If he were weakened sufficiently, Dokken Holding might become an easy target for a takeover. He knew all too well how landholders were ready to grab fertile lands. He had done it himself.

Fertile lands on Atlas were more precious than gold; with additional resources the landholders were allowed to produce more, and thus develop even more land. It was an upward spiral, and any landholder not able to hold his claim risked forfeiting his lands by direct or covert military action.

Nearly a century ago a civil war between Hong and Ramirez holdings had left their lands torn apart and leaderless; the newly formed Landholders Council had divided up the acreage among the remaining landholders.

For decades the holdings had been self-absorbed with increasing their resources and gradually building up an infrastructure. One landholder, Abraham Van Petersden, had been an incompetent leader, more wrapped up in his wife and newborn son than in exploiting the land to the fullest extent.

Dokken had seen no reason not to grab the opportunity, especially since he had developed his own secret weapon and wanted to try it out at an exorbitant price. He had wheedled a few illicit capsules of the Veritas drug from his long-time friend Kareem Sondheim. Dokken had then turned loose his ambitious, overeager aide Cialben on Van Petersden's Holding, sending him to infiltrate as an out-of-luck worker.

Cialben had used Veritas to peep into the minds of those in charge of Van Petersden's security systems, his schedule, his plans. The spy was gone for only two weeks, but he returned with knowledge of the vulnerabilities of Dokken's rival. Planning the invasion and coup had been a simple matter.

Dokken had killed Van Petersden and his lovely young wife . . . but, to display his compassion, he had presented a squalling infant boy to the Landholders Council. "Though this is a critical mistake according to mythical fiction, I'll allow Van Petersden's newborn son to live—if one of you will take care of him."

The boy, Michel Van Petersden, was adopted by Victoria Koman and raised on her lands. The Council roared in outrage, and the Truthsayers Guild sternly reprimanded Dokken for the bloody takeover and unprovoked violence. Neither the Council nor the Guild quite knew what else to do with him—and he had expected nothing else. Dokken had formally declared war, defeated his enemy, then ceased hostilities. Of course, he contritely apologized, even allowed the Guild to assign additional solpol troops to his holding (which he quickly subsumed under his own command). As if to demonstrate how powerless the Council was, the furor died away before long . . . and Dokken was left with the new lands.

That had also been the beginning of Veritas smuggling. Dokken had applied political thumbscrews to an initially reluctant Sondheim, pressuring him with their long friendship, until the Platform landholder had relented and leaked a few shipments. Ten years ago, Dieter Pan on OrbLab 2 had also joined the game with great enthusiasm.

The Veritas trickling into other landholdings exerted an enormous destabilizing influence. After people used the telepathy drug, they refused to trust each other—and no government could function without that basic trust. Consequently, Dokken had been an ogre about keeping his own holding clean, because if any Veritas user came close to him, all of Dokken's own plans could be pried from his mind. He could never allow that.

Until recently, Cialben had been the funnel for distributing the drug from First Landing, but he had grown too difficult, too demanding. The ambitious assistant was no longer a problem, though.

Now Dokken stared as if hypnotized at the sunlight glittering on the fishponds. The fishery foreman cleared his throat. "What shall we do about it, sir?"

Dokken spun and walked back off the metal pier. His boots made loud clanging sounds that reverberated through the water. "Have you seen any effect in the salmon ponds yet?"

"None, sir. Perhaps they weren't poisoned."

"Very well," Dokken said. "Block the inflow of water from the other ponds. Maybe we can salvage these two." He breathed rapidly, feeling helpless rage in the pit of his stomach. "We'll have to drain the other ponds, let the arroyo water flush any leftover toxin. Then we'll start again from scratch."

He crossed his arms over his leather jerkin. "We have lost some time, but there's a lot of time in the world. We can replace everything. We received a new shipment of fish fry from the Platform on a recent elevator run. We'll restock the ponds once they're purged. You'll just have to eat something other than fish for the next few months."

Dokken went back and took the reins of his stallion from the frightened girl. He thanked her cursorily, then turned back to the foreman. "Keep this quiet," Dokken said. "If it was truly a natural seep of an Atlas toxin, then there's no need for anyone else to know about it. If the fish were poisoned by a saboteur, I won't give them the satisfaction of our outrage."

Dokken swung into the saddle, and the horse snorted, ready to be off again. He did not look back at his wounded fish farm as he rode out into the open land.

ii

A soft whisper of moth wings greeted him as he entered the solarium annex of his villa. Sunlight streamed through the transparent panes; mist generators kept the air balmy and humid, perfect for the pampered silkworms.

Dokken was covered with dust and tingling perspiration that had rapidly dried during the ride. He was tired and still simmering with frustration. He had convinced himself of the best way to release his tension so he could think clearly again.

"Schandra!" he called, looking around. The room was filled with wire cages that held fat silkworms, gray-green caterpillars that were voracious eating machines. The caterpillars consumed fifty times their weight in fresh mulberry leaves within the first few weeks after hatching. Schandra and shifts of workers from the town fed the silkworms fresh clipped leaves every two or three hours around the clock.

A few of the fat-bodied, furry-winged moths fluttered about in breeding cages while caterpillars by the thousands spun glossy cocoons. Very few of the cocoons were allowed to hatch, because as the white moth emerged it rendered the silk strands useless. Most of the cocoons were baked under low heat, just enough to kill the metamorphosing moths and leave the tightly wound husks ready for unreeling into glossy fiber.

The few mature moths mated in a blazing flash that ended their life cycle. The exhausted and fulfilled female laid hundreds of eggs, which Schandra kept in cold storage until the cages were ready to receive more hatchlings.

Dokken pondered the unpleasant implications of a creature that mated only once in its life and then died. He was glad humans didn't suffer the same fate.

He strode through the solarium, while the workers kept out of his way. He ignored them.

A door opened at the far end of the glass-walled solarium, and Schandra entered, wearing a trim work outfit that accentuated her curves, even without the glamour or dazzle of the dyed silk negligees she used to entice him. Her eyes beneath her long, dark hair were depthless pools that did not allow him to see her real thoughts. She carried a basket of fresh leaves plucked from the mulberry bushes out in the courtyard.

Schandra saw him standing there and froze, taken by surprise. She handed her basket of leaves to one of the other workers, who took it silently and began to open the wire cages, dropping in handfuls of the glossy dark leaves. The silkworms fell to their meal voraciously.

"Franz, what a pleasant surprise," Schandra said sarcastically, raising her voice so the other workers could hear. "Have you come to visit, sparing me a moment from your busy schedule so we can talk—or do you just want something?"

Dokken bristled. He had been growing less and less enchanted with her aloof and derogatory demeanor. "I want you to come with me," he said. Seeing her beauty made him ache. "We need to make love. It's been too long."

Her eyes blazed, and she gestured around herself. "Franz, can't you see I'm busy? It's the middle of the afternoon."

He locked his eyes on hers. "So? I'm being spontaneous."

"I don't know what to tell you. What's the point of making love," she said, "if you don't ever intend to have children? Are you taking sterility pills, or are all the rumors true?"

He glared at her. "Don't concern yourself with rumors. Rumors are started by people who have nothing more important to do." He gestured. "Come with me back to our quarters."

"You are assuming that I want to, Franz."

He grabbed her wrist and squeezed. She winced. "It doesn't concern me whether you want to or not," he said, his voice low. The other workers were clearly listening, though they studiously continued their duties.

"Perhaps you're forgetting just who you are and where you came from. I can always find another farmer's daughter. I've raised you for your role in my holding since you were a pretty little girl. If you're unwilling to pay the price for the lap of luxury you live in, I'll be happy to find a replacement."

"Maybe that's why I'm beginning to resent you so much: you continue to flaunt the fact that I don't mean anything to you," she said. "You would be just as happy to find a replacement. You've never invested anything in me but some money and a few years." She stared sharply at him. "Years . . . just how old are you, Franz Dokken? You haven't changed in all the years I can remember you."

He smiled at her, trying to soften the moment. "I'm old enough to know what I want—and when I want it."

He held her hand in a locked grip, and Schandra rigidly followed him out of the solarium, leaving the silkworms behind. They went to the upper turrets of the villa, where she performed admirably for the next hour.

# CHAPTER

# 13

i

Kalliana sat in the uncomfortable metal chair, smoothing her white cotton robes across her lap. She looked away nervously, wondering why Guild Master Tharion had summoned her again to his private ready room.

Tharion went to the stained glass window where he could stare out at the city. Glimmering silver threads of mag-lev rails spread out like the spokes of a wheel toward the outer holdings. The Guild Master was uneasy but trying to hide it, as if he suspected her of something but was unwilling to speak his suspicions out loud. She wondered what she had done.

After a stifling moment of silence, he said without turning toward her, "Kalliana, I believe you have been greatly affected by your exposure to the violence you've read recently. Eli Strone. Troy Boren."

She sat up quickly, clenching her hands in her lap. "I can still perform my duty, Guild Master." Her voice was weak as water.

Tharion studied her, as if considering whether to touch her mind directly. "That is not at issue," he said. "I'm talking about *you*, Kalliana, your mental state. I have an assignment you may find relaxing, perhaps even healing."

Kalliana frowned. "If that's what you wish, Guild Master." She couldn't think of anything that she really wanted, other than to be left alone.

Tharion rubbed his hands together and stood tall. "At one time it was common for Truthsayers to go out among the people, but in recent years we've allowed ourselves to grow too isolated within these walls. Guild Master Klaryus had intended to continue this practice with greater enthusiasm, but he never got the chance. Myself, I've gone to meet all the landholders at their private estates, but I think it's time other Truthsayers do the same. You'll be going out on a brief diplomatic visit . . . you might even think of it as a vacation."

Kalliana felt the ice of sudden fear crystallize around her. "Go out . . . out there? But I've never been away—"

"Yes." Tharion waved his hand to dismiss her concerns. "Joachim Sardili submitted a request a while ago, but I haven't been able to visit him. I'd like you to go there, see the people, meet his Magistrates, show them that the Guild really does exist and cares about them. Most of those people in the outer lands have never been to First Landing."

"But . . . but I don't want to leave," she said. "I'd rather stay—"

Tharion drew a quick breath, and Kalliana caught herself. The ready room's curved lifeless walls sealed her away from the bustle and conversation of the workers on the bridge deck.

"I need to send you away from the Guild Headquarters for a while, Kalliana. Don't ask me why." Tharion spoke in a sharp voice. "It is important for a Truthsayer to know the people. It's time for you to stretch yourself, see how the world works.

"This will not be a difficult assignment. Usually the holdings have local Magistrates to take care of family squabbles, petty thievery, minor crimes—they aren't any challenge for a real Truthsayer to read. You'll be there as a symbol of our esteem for the landholder, conveying more power and prestige than if I had sent a regiment of sol-pols. And, frankly, Sardili is probably the nicest of all the landholders.

"I want you to leave by mag-lev tomorrow afternoon."

ii

She had the small VIP car to herself as it shot through the twilight, heading westward toward the edge of the continent where the main mag-lev spur ended at Sardili's burgeoning central city.

Acceleration pushed her backward into the padded seat. Kalliana looked at the worn fabric and thought of all the other travelers who had ridden the train to various parts of Atlas, inbound to the central hub of First Landing or outbound to new lands.

Mining shipments, raw lumber, packaged food, fresh meats and fish, bins of grain, everything came to First Landing for distribution. Kalliana thought of the bustling trade and how it would be threatened by the interconnecting rail line between Carsus and Bondalar holdings. Toth and Koman were talking of doing the same thing, and soon First Landing might be bypassed entirely. But the Truthsayers Guild still had its firm grip on society, and First Landing remained the only anchor point for the space elevator.

She felt the acceleration pressure ease up as the mag-lev car gained proper velocity and continued its rocket-whisper forward, away from First Landing. Kalliana fought down her panic again. The great unknown seemed ready to swallow her up.

She reached into her satchel and withdrew a tin of assorted sweets, selecting a couple of her favorites: honey squares and taffy flavored with mint oil. She munched to soothe herself, but the candy only made her thirsty, not calm. . . .

Hours later, deceleration coils kicked in, and the mag-lev car slowed and finally docked against its buffer collar in Sardili Station. The station building was a big airy structure like an aircraft hangar with wire-reinforced glass and titanium struts riveted with polished copper studs. The mag-lev car door hissed open on pneumatic pistons, and Kalliana stood up, preparing herself to face a strange new world.

Outside waited a thin smiling man with rusty brown hair and a neat goatee laced with strands of silver. Surrounded by laugh wrinkles, his eyes were a clear golden brown. He stepped forward to greet her, extending his hand. "You must be Kalliana, our visting Truthsayer? Welcome."

She took his hand with her own, afraid he might squeeze too hard. His grip was firm but gentle.

"I'm Joachim Sardili. Pleased to meet you. Thank you for coming all the way out here. It's good to have a visitor from the Guild." He indicated two taller and younger men behind him. "Franklin and Russell, my two sons. Russell's the shorter one. We wanted to meet you ourselves."

Kalliana was taken aback, surprised that a landholder had greeted her without a retinue of sol-pols. Most of the other landholders she had seen were grim and fearful, showing off their personal power by the number of retainers they could demand for personal protection.

"I . . . I'm happy to be here," Kalliana lied. "I've never been away from First Landing before."

Sardili took the satchel from her hand and gave it to his son

Russell. "You'll like it here. We certainly do." The two young men nodded in perfect unison, as if they were clones.

They led her through busy crowds that made her uncomfortable, but Kalliana was surprised to note how different these masses were from the chanting spectators who appeared in the plaza before a scheduled truthsaying. Here, the people were intent on their own concerns. She felt an unexpected backwash of joy from many of those around her at the station, elation at meeting friends and relatives come to visit or returning home. Despite their hard lives, these people seemed happy and satisfied with their lot. It puzzled her.

With her escorts, Kalliana walked across the concrete floor, listening to the voices and the sounds echo in the big enclosed structure. Maintenance vehicles hummed outward along the tracks, checking the braking coils and testing the collision avoidance systems for the high-speed trains.

Kalliana saw many Pilgrims in the crowd. Most of them were walking, but others pedaled bicycles with tires made from rubberized seafoam polymer. Small cargo haulers puttered about, bringing baggage and supplies from the cars.

Kalliana looked around, already drowning in the new sights and sounds. The smells here were different, vendors selling exotic spiced fish and vegetables. The clothes and customs seemed unique to her, emphasizing the dyes and fabrics most easily created from the resources of Sardili Holding.

Joachim Sardili saw the amazement in Kalliana's eyes and chuckled. "Don't worry," he said, "we'll take you someplace more peaceful. Out to the ocean." Russell and Franklin both nodded.

"Trust me," Sardili said, squeezing her shoulder. "The first time you look out across the sea, you'll be amazed. It's like nothing else you've ever seen in your life."

iii

Still bleary-eyed from tossing and turning on an unfamiliar bed and surrounded by strangeness, Kalliana shivered in the misty morning stillness on the ocean shore. Joachim Sardili had awakened her before dawn, grinning like a child with a surprise. They were going to spend a few days out on his yacht.

Now, Kalliana warily eyed the leaden water rippling against the pebbly beach where Sardili's boat was anchored. Russell and

Franklin were already aboard, tying up the ropes and preparing for departure.

Morning fog swallowed the horizon, but still the water extended as far as she could see, and a muffled back-roar extended beyond the edge of the world: the growling of waves, the distant crashing of surf. Kalliana felt a hollowness in the pit of her stomach as the immensity overloaded her senses.

"We'll have to wade out," Sardili said, kicking off his sandals and plucking them up as he strode into the gently swirling water. "Just a little ways. Come on." He gestured toward Kalliana, but she looked in dismay at the uncertain surface of the sea. "It should only be up to about your knee, probably less. I'll give you a hand up onto the boat."

Uneasy, Kalliana hiked up her white cotton robe and stepped into the shockingly cold water that lapped around the pale skin of her calves. Goose bumps prickled her body, and she hurriedly sloshed toward the boat across the disconcertingly rough floor of the lagoon. She thought she felt ridged shells, crawling aquatic creatures. Sardili had already hauled himself up on deck. He reached down with a strong hand to yank her over the deck railing. She stood gasping and dripping.

The yacht was modest, but it would carry the four of them comfortably. The hull was made of enameled fiberglass with extra metal sheeting at the waterline to protect it from rocks near the shore. The brass rails and fittings gleamed in the dim morning light.

Sitting in a seat on the foredeck, Kalliana accepted a rough towel from Russell and dried the chill water from her lower legs. She slipped on thick woolen socks from a supply satchel inside the cabin. That, along with the inner wrap she wore under her robe, warmed her in a few moments.

"Where exactly are we going?" she asked, trying not to sound nervous.

Working in precise unison, the two sons hauled up anchor. Sardili powered up his methane engines and began to move away from the shore into deeper water. A breeze picked up, numbing her cheeks and mussing her pale hair. The smell on the wind was sharp and salty with a tang of iodine.

The landholder sat comfortably at the captain's wheel and stared straight ahead, scratching his goatee, though what he could see in the thinning mists was a mystery to her. "Oh, we'll just spend a day or so puttering up and down the coast. There's a marvelous reef farther north if we have time to reach it."

"What is there to see?" Kalliana said. "Why do you go there?"

He looked at her with a childish smile. "I go there because I like being on my boat," he said with a laugh. "But if you want a more-practical answer, then I'm checking out the terraforming progress on my lands." He gestured into the unseen vastness lost in the morning fog.

"My sea ranch stretches all up and down the coast. I've put in an awful lot of effort, spreading rich plankton, Earth algae, and kelp in the protected bays and lagoons where they've got a better chance of getting a good foothold. I've added krill—little shrimp— and some fishes. I can't do it all myself, of course, but Nature'll take over before long. The sea is an untapped resource. I guess it's too uncontrolled for the other landholders—they prefer to plant their crops and know that the grain will stay where they put it. The ocean isn't like that."

The mist broke up as the morning went on, and suddenly, with a surprising shift, the boat passed out of the fog. Kalliana gasped, standing on the swaying deck as she looked across the infinite ocean. The vista made her dizzy, with no grounding point. She wrapped her hands around the cold brass rail, holding tight to keep from fainting.

"There, now," Sardili said, resting a firm hand on her shoulder. "See what I mean? Impressive."

Kalliana blinked at him in alarm. "But where's the shore? How do we find our way back? Are we lost?"

He laughed. "No, we're still in sight of the shore, once the last of this fog burns away. We'll keep moving for a time yet. This boat isn't made to go out to the deep ocean. That's for future explorers. On my holding we're still worrying about making enough food to eat."

As they continued up the coast, the surf grew choppier; the mist-fuzzed shoreline became rugged, black cliffs of lava rock that had been chewed away by tides. Her trip on the mag-lev had gone by so fast that Kalliana couldn't comprehend the distance to Sardili Holding, and the scale she had seen on maps meant nothing. For the first time, now, she glimpsed the vastness of the planet and was awestruck.

Colorful algae brightened the sheltered coves. Sardili pointed them out. "A few of the strains are native to Atlas, the blues and the vermilions," he said. "But lots of the more successful ecosystems come from Earth stock brought down from the Platform."

Waves crashed into white froth against the rocks, and Sardili ordered Franklin to take the boat to calmer waters. The engines thrummed, turning propellers that drove the boat onward. Eventually, they drifted into a shallow bay of blond sand beneath water that was far deeper than it appeared. The clarity had a lensing effect that allowed her to see the magnificent creatures moving about below.

Sardili had installed thick glass on the bottom hull, and he took Kalliana belowdecks, so that she could kneel, spreading her palms out on the cool hull and gaze down at the underwater societies of mollusklike shells and strange crab creatures with purple and black tiger stripes scuttling about on ten segmented legs foraging for prey. Rounded pink seaweed waved about like feathery mushrooms, a squirming fungus that arose from the seabed.

"These are the critters Atlas has experimented with," Sardili said. "Life is forming in its mother ocean just like the life Earth must have developed billions of years ago. Those things there are worms or crustaceans. Those"—he pointed to a colony of disclike multilegged creatures ducking for cover from the boat's looming shadow—"remind me of trilobytes in ancient Earth fossils."

Sardili stood up and led Kalliana back onto the deck under the warm sun. "Those Atlas organisms are just beginning a war against the Earth species we introduced. Their biochemistries are incompatible, so they're not really competitors for the same resources—but I doubt they'll find an ecological truce." He smiled and looked up into the empty blue-white sky. "I wonder who'll win?"

Suddenly off to their left—the port side, Sardili called it—a monstrous creature like a great serpent breached the surface of the water. Russell and Franklin shouted, running out on deck as Sardili gaped in surprise. The serpent rose out of the sea, splashing spray and hissing.

The monster was a metallic blue-gray, with armored scales, each as large as Kalliana's outspread hand. A comblike fan ran the length of its sinewy neck. It looked like an eel with a mouth impossibly full of serrated fangs and an array of glittering eyes: two large faceted spheres set on either side of its head and an equilateral triangle of smaller black eyes in the center of its forehead.

Kalliana froze, then backed quickly away from the brass rail. The creature bellowed again, circled the boat with a rapid churning ripple, then dove below the water, leaving a straight line of turbulence as the long creature shot out of the lagoon toward deeper water.

Franklin and Russell both stood on deck, shouting to each other. Sardili shook his head in amazement. "Never seen anything like it," he said. "I knew Atlas had plenty of those dinky creatures down there, but—well, well!" He guided Kalliana back to the deckhouse with trembling hands. "I guess every once in a while we need a reminder that we humans know very little about this planet we've made our home."

Toward sunset they reached the silty delta of a river that flowed from the rocky highlands into the ocean. Kalliana could see sprawling green rice fields planted in the marshlands. People waded in the water, some planting shoots, some harvesting the grain. Despite the heat of the fading day, the workers all wore thick robes, like burdens they had to carry. Kalliana recognized them as a colony of Pilgrim workers; upslope from the swampy river's edge she noted a small village, a cluster of dwellings.

"Those Pilgrims are very productive," Sardili said, gazing at the village. "They're hard workers, but they like their privacy. I try to respect that. This settlement here is pretty far out, but we installed a new rail spur so we could take the rice they produce in exchange for supplies they need."

"So you let them have their freedom?" she asked.

Sardili shrugged. "As much as I can." He turned to her with a perplexed expression. "As long as they do their jobs, I don't really care what else they do. That's none of my concern. I try to give them every concession I can manage. The other landholders complained about being forced to take refugees from a ship full of religious fanatics, but my father accepted as many as would come here. They've proven to be a valuable asset to our economy.

"Oh, a lot of the Pilgrims still aren't satisfied." He dismissed that with a wave. "I don't know what else I can do for them. They want to go off into the unclaimed lands and set up a paradise for themselves, but they'd be in for a rude shock. Atlas isn't so cooperative. We colonists have been working with our full resources for over two centuries, and we're still barely holding on by our fingernails. "

He continued to watch the workers who had stopped in the rice fields to stare at the distant boat. "I don't understand their problems, but I'm sure we can all work something out, if we're reasonable."

The boat continued its slow pace along the shore as the sunset poured molten gold into the sea.

"Are we going to stop there for the night?" Kalliana asked.

Sardili looked out at the Pilgrim village and a frown creased his brow. "No, we'll anchor farther out to sea. You haven't really slept until you've slept on a boat. The rocking motion is just like being in your mother's arms."

Kalliana looked away. "I didn't have a mother," she said. "I'm from the Truthsayers Guild."

iv

The gentle rocking of the deck made Kalliana queasy when she concentrated on it, and relaxed her when she did not. They had anchored the boat in a quiet harbor. Waves roared against a stunted black reef that made a natural levee, keeping the bay placid as Sardili and his sons bedded down in bunks for the night.

They had eaten a quick meal prepared in the self-contained microwave in the boat's galley. As full darkness folded around them, Kalliana looked far out to sea, observing a lime-green glow that rippled like witches' fire beneath the water—natural phosphorescence from plankton in the Atlas sea.

Sardili and his two sons lay back on their narrow beds inside the covered deck house. They gave Kalliana a wool blanket, but she had a hard time drifting to sleep on her bunk. She stared out the thick portholes, saw pastel colors rippling across the sky as the aurora continued its magnetic dance. She listened to the three men fall quickly into slumber. They snored contentedly, as if cramped quarters didn't bother them in the least.

Kalliana let her guard down and dozed off at last. Her anxiety had robbed her of deep sleep for days . . . and now she fell through the trapdoor into unguarded dreams.

*Blood.*

*Pain.*

*A slash of the scalpel.*

*Eradicating sin and evil from the world. So many who deserved the ultimate justice!*

As the dream crept into her, insidiously working its way down her spine, through her nerves, into her mind, Kalliana felt Eli

Strone's anger, felt the justification, felt the crime—and the elation—of murder.

Gasping, she fought her way to wakefulness and finally burst through the deep red bubble surrounding her imagination. She sat bolt upright on her bunk drenched with cold sweat, trembling from the deep-buried experience that had spewed up from her subconscious. The night was dark and deep.

With a sick dread, Kalliana realized that even here, far beyond land's edge, memories that were not hers had given her nightmares that did not belong to her, making her relive crimes she had not committed—and still it all lived in her mind.

Her heart pounded, forcing adrenaline-suffused blood through her veins. Trying to control her rushing breaths, she sucked cool sea air through clenched teeth and closed her eyes, waiting, calming.

Near her in their bunks, Joachim Sardili and his two sons slept untroubled, filling the cabin with their faint wheezing.

Far off in the distance, in deep water beyond the black reef, she heard mournful songs sung by unseen aquatic creatures. The mysterious wails rose and fell in an unsettling music, as if the ocean dwellers had shared Kalliana's dreams.

# CHAPTER

# 14

i

Though the young Truthsayer trainees had numerous teachers, Tharion occasionally lectured them in morality and the law. It was important to instill an abiding faith in the Truthsayers and also to show them that even the Guild Master spent time with those who had not yet received their colored sashes.

On a walk through the ship, Tharion led the nine oldest students, those able to comprehend the esoteric nuances of ethics. He stood taller than any of the pallid-skinned students, and the teens clustered together, some fascinated, others risking brief roughhousing when they thought he wasn't looking.

As Tharion looked at them, he realized that some might not pass their final testing. Then each would have to choose either to remain in the Guild as an administrative worker, accept a job as a Magistrate out in one of the villages, or find work like any of the other colonists.

The group entered the cavernous rear engine compartment of the Guild Headquarters. The *SkySword*'s rear bulkheads had been torn out and replaced with reinforced glass so that light streamed in, transforming the entire bay into an arboretum with carefully tended trees growing in planters. A pair of sol-pol elite guards marched on their regular rounds, attentively ensuring that Guild members were not disturbed in their duties.

The tubes once designed for launching orbital missiles had been modified to make fountains that spilled water into irrigation troughs running through rows of vegetables and bright flowers. Gardeners worked on a line of dwarf pear trees. Tiny angled mirrors reflected dazzling sunlight to all corners, making the engine bay sparkle. Mist hung in the air, and butterflies flitted about, colorful species sent down from the Platform as a gift from Kareem Sondheim to the Guild.

Tharion found a private spot near one of the fountains gurgling from a missile tube. He hauled himself up to a casual sitting position next to the running water. A few droplets splashed onto his robe, but he didn't mind.

He tried to be at ease among these teenagers who had undergone so much rigid training. The constant instruction was necessary, because they alone held the fate of the accused in their hands. A Truthsayer must be absolutely trustworthy, of rigid moral character, open to no suspicion whatsoever.

"Our work might seem simple," Tharion began his lecture. He directed a stern glance at two young boys who hung back so they could keep surreptitiously jabbing each other in the ribs. Seeing his silent reprimand, the boys flushed, their white skin flecked with red pinpricks.

"The citizens think all we need to do is glance at their minds to reveal whether someone is guilty or innocent. But you know from your exercises that the answer to a question of personal behavior is rarely black and white. Humans do not behave logically, and we often don't know the reasons for our own actions. You'll be surprised to find that people outside the Guild are even more complex. They have complicated reasons for everything they do, whether it's legal or illegal."

Tharion let the pouring water trickle over his fingers, as if he could wash away all doubt. "A Truthsayer must sift through a jumble of memories and rationales to apply a verdict *against the framework of the law*. No excuses, no extenuating circumstances. You must determine whether the accused was right or wrong, innocent or guilty. It's a difficult, difficult question."

Only young Ysan—the oldest trainee—seemed interested in the lecture. The others were distracted. They had heard it all before, but sometimes they didn't comprehend the full meaning until they had wrestled with the ethical arguments for themselves, repeatedly studied their shape and texture.

Ysan raised his hand, his lips upturned in a half smile. Tharion wondered how much of his personality would change once the young man was given a Truthsayer's heavy responsibility. Tharion was glad his duties as Guild Master had freed him from the onerous task of truthsaying. "Yes, Ysan?" he said.

The youth looked away, pursing his lips as if to reconsider his question. "If the laws are so clear, how can there be any question in the mind of the accused? They must *know* they are doing something wrong."

"Ignorance of the law is no excuse," Tharion said.

Ysan shook his head. "That's not what I mean." He looked at his long fingers. The other trainees grew restless, but Tharion stilled them with his gaze. "Every citizen is required to know the law, right?" Ysan continued. "Therefore, when they commit a criminal action, they must realize it goes against that law. And if they *know* it goes against that law, then they are clearly guilty. If it does not go against the law—the law they all know—then they're innocent."

Tharion grasped the question. "Not every colonist is as familiar with the law as you all are. To them, the law is an invisible net that provides safety for most and traps the few. In the Guild we view the law as rigid and unalterable, but many citizens see it as a flexible set of . . . of suggestions."

Some of the trainees tittered at that, while others looked appalled.

"They rationalize ways to fit their actions within the framework of law as they understand it. They might think they're innocent, when they are in fact guilty." Tharion pulled his hand out of the fountain and looked at the droplets of water on his fingers. "Let me give you a recent example. Recall the murderer Eli Strone? His actions were so blatantly against the law that there can be no question as to his guilt. Correct?"

Ysan nodded vigorously.

"And yet, Strone was utterly convinced of the 'morality' of what he did—so much so that he believed he operated outside the law. Let me tell you something about Strone. He used to work here in the Guild, as one of the elite sol-pols. I knew him rather well in my younger days, as I suppose some of you have gotten to know the regular guards."

Tharion lowered his voice. "Even then he had strong convictions. A man like Strone has a clearly defined moral path burned deeply into the core of his mind. It was possible to guess exactly how he was going to react, how he would interpret someone else's actions—but unfortunately, Eli Strone's moral path diverged from ours. He left his service here imagining that he was a dispenser of justice, actually helping the Guild do its work. So how could the Truthsayers possibly object?"

"But he killed people," Ysan said.

"In his mind he was probably punishing them for their crimes. Filled with self-righteousness, he was obviously not afraid to be caught and called to account for his actions. Strone granted himself the right of Truthsayer and sentencer, but that's . . ."

"Wrong," Ysan said.

"Exactly," Tharion answered with a thin smile. He gestured to the glass arboretum walls that looked out on the city of First Landing. "The people out there don't always understand how clear-cut the law is."

"That's why we're superior to them," said one of the rowdy boys in the rear. "We get to live in the Guild Headquarters away from the dirty homes and the dirty people out there."

"They must be very jealous of us," said a girl, looking smug.

Tharion scowled at the trainees. "First," he said, "you must understand something very important and very unpleasant: they are not *jealous* of us—they don't *like* us. They are relieved that we live in isolation, because regular citizens are uncomfortable around us."

The trainees looked shocked, as if they had never considered such a possibility. Ysan spoke up. "But why are they so afraid?"

Tharion crossed his arms over his chest and nodded grimly. "Because they know what we can do."

## ii

Tharion took the group up to the bridge deck during luncheon hours when the command center was deserted, an empty stage on which he could perform his dramatization of the story of the Truthsayers Guild. The trainees already knew the basic facts, but he had never before performed it for them.

"Our heritage," he said in a low, whispery voice that forced the trainees to lean forward. They were rarely allowed on the command deck, and they had certainly never been here alone before with the Guild Master himself.

"There wasn't always the Guild, of course. Veritas itself was discovered only 160 years ago, but never used to determine guilt or innocence until many years later, when the *Botany Bay* arrived carrying its exiled criminals from Earth. The colonists were terrified of so many felons joining our society, so in anticipation of a rash of crimes, many citizens began to use the brief and intense rush of Veritas to test their own truthsaying abilities.

"But much to the colonists' surprise, the exiled criminals proved to be devoted settlers, hardworking people glad of a second chance, happy to be away from Earth. Many of them were political prisoners cast out by a government that was growing more and more repressive—as we saw for ourselves when the *SkySword* arrived unannounced.

"Oh, the *SkySword* crew pretended to be just another wave of settlers, smiling and bowing politely. Since the established colonists couldn't see details of the warship from such a distance, it was difficult to guess their primary purpose."

Tharion stood on the command platform of the bridge. He drew himself taller, playing the role. "Captain Gul had traveled fifty years across space, in deepsleep two-thirds of that time, training his soldiers to take over the colony of Atlas for the degenerate Earth government.

"The ship arrived, contacted our Platform, and sent down a scout shuttle carrying Captain Gul himself and numerous tactical officers under the guise of diplomatic emissaries. They came with sweet words, bringing greetings from Earth"—Tharion leaned forward, deepening his voice—"but their true mission was to scout out our colony, to determine our weaknesses and develop a plan to dominate us quickly and efficiently. They wanted a bloodless takeover, if possible, but they meant to take over in any case."

Tharion smiled. "What Captain Gul and his military advisors saw did not impress them, but they kept up their charade, thinking it would be a simple exercise to establish their fortresses and clamp down on any resistance.

"We were mere colonists. We spent our effort encouraging crops to grow on our new land. We had no defenses, no military forces, nothing comparable to the *SkySword*'s high-tech weaponry."

From behind, Tharion placed both hands on the old command chair and swiveled it right and left. "But the captain and his emissaries didn't know that one of the members of our own welcoming committee was a shrewd and daring man named Archimand, who had spent years experimenting with the Veritas drug. One of the landholders—the records don't say which one— had the forethought to have Archimand accompany the reception team. As soon as the new 'ambassadors' departed in their shuttle, Archimand divulged Gul's true plans—that the *SkySword* meant to take over Atlas."

Tharion released the command chair and walked through the

group of trainees to the viewing window that looked toward the anchor point of the space elevator. "The landholders met in an emergency session, but they had more of an advantage than they first realized. They knew what the military forces anticipated, and they knew Captain Gul had concluded that we were incapable of mounting much resistance. Archimand worked with the landholders to set up a trap.

"Spouting words of goodwill, old Kareem Sondheim—yes, he was old even then—proposed an exchange of visitors. Captain Gul and some of his staff would come over to the Platform, while Archimand and several of the landholders, our most important leaders, would visit the *SkySword*."

Now Tharion turned from the viewing window and rubbed his hands together. "Captain Gul thought this was a fine idea. It allowed him to take important hostages aboard his own ship, while he could send a military crew aboard the Platform—an unparalleled opportunity to strike against First Landing, a perfect setup.

"An escort shuttle brought Archimand and the landholders to the *SkySword*, while at the same time Captain Gul secretly dispatched two military assault vehicles on a mission to secure First Landing. Gul himself shuttled over to the Platform. He left his ship in the docking bay, like a Trojan horse filled with armed occupational forces. While his hidden strike force waited for the right moment, Gul congenially toured the Platform with Sondheim and then asked to ride down on the space elevator to be received in First Landing. He left his soldier-filled ship behind, ready to strike as soon as he transmitted the signal."

Tharion paced the control deck. He had read the story many times, told it to dozens and dozens of trainees, yet it always inspired him. His heart raced as he thought of the glorious victory.

"As soon as Captain Gul and his tactical officers began their descent on the space elevator, Kareem Sondheim filled the docking bay with diluted *stenn* vapor. It paralyzed every one of the attacking soldiers, allowing Sondheim and his crew to take them prisoner.

"Meanwhile, once Archimand and the hostage landholders arrived on board the *SkySword*, they knew for certain that it was a battleship with a military mission. The hostages were taken to the control deck to watch and wait." Tharion walked about, running his hands against the control panels, the lifeless computers. "Here," he said.

"Archimand and the others were forced to look out this

viewing window," Tharion pointed, "down at their supposedly helpless planet, which the gloating soldiers claimed would soon be under military rule.

"But Archimand had already seen into the mind of Captain Gul and knew all of the military ship's secrets. He knew the commander's passwords, codes that not even the other officers knew. As the soldiers waited, feeling smugly superior to what they considered hick colonists, Archimand positioned himself near an auxiliary console. While one of the landholders created a diversion, he quickly punched in Captain Gul's private self-destruct sequence for the *SkySword*. The orbital missile tubes inside the armory bays were locked down, preventing launch, while the missiles themselves were armed and powered up, propulsion fluids pressurized, timers set. The *SkySword* would become a nova in mere minutes."

Tharion's eyes sparkled with distant amusement. Some of the students were enraptured, some giggled, others seemed terrified. They had all heard the story before, of course—but never like this. "Meanwhile," Tharion continued, "Sondheim froze the space elevator, stranding Captain Gul and his officers at the edge of the atmosphere.

"The countdown on the *SkySword* continued ticking as the military officers ran about frantically, threatening Archimand and the hostage landholders with immediate execution. But Archimand knew they could do nothing, because only Captain Gul—and he himself—knew the release code to halt this particular self-destruct sequence. The captain was so paranoid that he had shared his password with none of the other officers. And Captain Gul was trapped in orbit. He couldn't possibly come to their aid.

"At the same time, the blustering attack shuttle arrived just outside of First Landing—exactly where the citizens knew the soldiers would set down expecting no resistance . . . and there the colonists sprang their ambush. They struck the instant the shuttles landed, before the soldiers could lock down and prepare their orderly, intimidating assault.

"The people launched crude liquid-filled grenades, splattering the doors with an overwhelming barrage of instant-hardening epoxy that grew stiffer second by second. The soldiers inside the assault shuttle hesitated, taken aback by the ambush—and every moment they waited sealed their doors shut even tighter." Tharion dropped his voice to a whisper. "And they waited too long!

"Up in orbit, with the timers ticking down, the *SkySword* crew had no choice but to surrender to Archimand." Tharion sighed wistfully, walking around the dead computer terminals.

"As you can see, the ship was grounded, landed here in the city and stripped of its valuable components. The would-be invaders were sent out as penal workers or married off in the outer holdings. It took only a generation to integrate them into our society.

"Because he had been so instrumental in preventing the takeover of this world, Archimand used this opportunity to bring a group of people together under a central authority, the Guild, whose objective members were charged with uncovering truth and keeping the peace, like benevolent overseers. Because of its symbolic value, we established our headquarters inside the empty wreck of the *SkySword*.

"The landholders created a force of soldier-police to help defend our society against attacks and other turmoil, both external and internal, and they agreed to put all the sol-pols under Archimand's command."

"And the sol-pols wear military uniforms from the crew?" Ysan asked.

"Yes," Tharion answered. "The elite guards wear the actual uniforms, while the other sol-pols wear something similar." He sat down heavily in the captain's chair, swiveling to look at the trainees.

"With the Guild in charge, life on Atlas has been relatively smooth ever since, because we are impartial. Soon you"—he pointed to Ysan and then at the other students—"will be given that same responsibility. We have a long tradition of honor to uphold."

# CHAPTER

## 15

i

After two days on the boat Joachim Sardili guided them into the mouth of a wide river. Several times a day their radio crackled with messages, administrators and managers from his main holding offices requesting clarifications or important decisions. Sardili took all the interruptions with good humor, dealing with the necessary matters to keep his holding running so that he and his two sons could stay out longer.

The riverbanks were twin walls closing in on the boat, embracing arms that confined the quiet water. They breakfasted on smoked fish and toast. Franklin poached one egg each for them, preparing them over a little alcohol burner in the galley.

Kalliana ate quietly, savoring the salt-smoky taste of the fish. She dipped her toast into the grayish yolk of her egg, altered from its natural yellow color by the additives and rough feed Sardili used on his chicken ranches.

"A nice breakfast, Franklin," she said. "Thank you." The tall boy grinned as if she had blessed him, then hurriedly found something to do on the deck. Though Sardili was a relaxed and interesting conversationalist, his two sons remained in awe of her.

Kalliana went onto the deck and looked up at the low, gray clouds peeling back, revealing shreds of pale sky that promised a clear day. Russell turned the winch that hauled up the anchor, and Franklin started up the methane engines. She had trouble telling the brothers apart, though she didn't think they were twins.

Sardili came out to stand beside Kalliana, and they watched the bow slice through brownish river water churning with silt and mud. As they proceeded upstream, bluffs rose high on either side. Kalliana eventually made out a dark smear extending into the sky from one bank: smoke rising from factories or furnaces.

"That's one of my towns. These people make my holding's best bricks, which are sold far and wide," Sardili said, stretching out his arm. "We'll stop there and do a little old-fashioned king's justice."

Kalliana reacted with alarm. "Justice? What do you mean?"

"The villagers are a little restless." He smiled apologetically, stroking his silver-streaked goatee. "They don't always submit their reports or respond when I make a request."

"So you're going to punish them?" Kalliana asked.

"No, no!" Sardili shuffled his feet. "Just make myself visible, remind them of their landholder's presence."

"And do I have to do anything?" Kalliana said. "A truthsaying?"

He shrugged. "Think of your old Earth history tapes, the medieval ages when a king would hold court among the people. Anyone who had a dispute could present the case to the king, and he would make his decision. That's what we'll do here, you and me. The villagers have the usual range of petty differences—land disputes, charges of thievery, brawls and assaults. Their Mediator usually takes care of everything. I'll sit there and try to look like an imposing leader, and you use your truthsaying abilities to provide the right answers. With a landholder and a Truthsayer we'll make quite an impressive team."

Kalliana stammered and looked away, focusing on the ripples in the river. "Guild Master Tharion did say that I would be asked to use my ... my abilities." She drew a deep, resigned breath and gripped the cold brass rail. "I apologize. I haven't been sleeping well."

"Oh, I'm sorry to hear that," Sardili said with genuine concern. "Need another blanket for your bunk?"

ii

Most buildings in the village were constructed from the local bricks. Tall smokestacks traced dark fingers in the air above the kilns. People in muddy overalls worked at the riverbanks with pallets, shoveling wet clay into barrows, which were hustled off to the molds and ovens.

The bluffs above had been excavated into terraces, each with a concrete lip, to keep the fertilized soil from washing down into the river. The barrenness of Atlas's land eliminated the need for herbicides and extensive weeding, since nothing grew except what was planted and nurtured, but the vegetables and grains had to be watered and nourished carefully. The terraces sported green crops, like agricultural islands.

Sardili's boat was such an unusual sight chugging up the river that all work stopped as they passed. Russell and Franklin heaved the boat close to the bank in a tiny semicircular inlet. Because the landholder visited so rarely, the village had not built its own pier, and Sardili and his sons had to jump over the railings into the muddy water. As Kalliana looked overboard, smelling the rich, silty water, Sardili came back to carry her to the shore, keeping her dry, as Russell and Franklin glanced down in embarrassment.

Villagers came forward to greet them, led by the town administrator, a dark-skinned woman with a harried expression.

"A rare and unexpected pleasure, Master Sardili," she said, grasping Sardili's forearm in a strange handshake, then did the same to Russell and Franklin. She seemed uncertain as to what to do with a Truthsayer. Kalliana nodded a greeting, and the town administrator accepted that as enough.

The town administrator gave them a brief tour of the village. The town's small group of Pilgrim inhabitants kept to themselves in brightly colored old prefab shelters made of durable plastic from Earth and shored up with tan bricks. Pilgrim representatives came out dressed in their heavy robes, heads bowed under their hoods.

The rest of the villagers stood watching. Kalliana was uncomfortable to see how filthy they were, their overalls smeared with clay from the brick-making work, boots thick with mud, smelling of chemical fertilizers or natural manure from the agricultural terraces. *What an unpleasant life these people lead*, she thought, longing to be back in the clean comfort of Guild Headquarters.

While they waited for workers to set up a platform and move aside the debris and piled pallets of bricks waiting for shipment on the next mag-lev train, Kalliana and Sardili were treated to a small but delicious meal of barley soup and a fresh salad of ripe tomatoes and cucumbers.

Though Sardili joked and continued his easy conversation with the town administrator, Kalliana kept glancing out at the sunlit streets, dreading an afternoon of looking into the minds of these people. True, no one had been accused of more than a minor offense—but she feared she might uncover something far worse . . . and then what would she do? She had not had any cause to take a dose of Veritas in the several days since she'd arrived at Sardili Shores, so her telepathic powers were already somewhat diminished. It was time for her booster dose.

Joachim Sardili set aside his glazed ceramic bowl, wiped a

forearm across his mouth, then straightened his mustache and goatee. He lifted his eyebrows at Kalliana. "So, are we ready?"

She tried to muster enthusiasm, but found she could only nod and stand up, tightening her green sash as if it might give her strength. Digging into the folds of her white robe, she withdrew one of the sky-blue Veritas capsules and slipped it into her mouth.

"Russell, Franklin," Sardili said, gesturing, "I want you to stand on either side of our chairs." He turned to the town administrator. "How many sol-pols are assigned to this town?"

"Only three," the woman answered.

"That'll be enough." Sardili raised his eyebrows. "Kalliana?"

She felt the bitter drug working its way through her system like tiny fingers running along her neurons and into her brain. The telepathic waves swelled and crested, but lower than she expected. Her thoughts seemed blurred, less focused, and she wondered if she was *too* disturbed at the prospect of truthsaying. Hiding her uneasiness, she followed Sardili out the door.

Kalliana concentrated on her Truthsayer powers, on intensifying her ability. She was led to a low platform made from stacked cargo crates topped with metal plates for a floor. She had to climb a step stool to reach the stage, then seated herself on a padded chair just like the ones they had used inside the administrator's hut. The town's assigned Magistrate, a rotund man with a large bald patch, sat back at the rear next to the sol-pols, looking unsure of what to do.

Sardili greeted the audience. "Welcome! Thank you for coming. I know you must hate being taken from your labors for the afternoon—but I don't visit too frequently." Some of the villagers chuckled.

Kalliana stared at her white hands, the translucent fingernails. Her heart pounded as she breathed deeply, trying to calm herself. She hated doing this, hated even more the fact that her own once-beloved duties had become so abhorrent to her.

She heard little of Sardili's speech as he told the villagers how, because his landholding was large, he couldn't see them in person as often as he wished, but that he still cared for their needs. He had brought them the formidable Truthsayer Kalliana to help them smooth their disputes and to keep them from wasting time on legal issues when there was so much work to be done.

She stood, and the first accused person was brought before her, led up the ladder by two of the sol-pols. A brutish youth, eighteen years old with a heavy brow, broad shoulders, and hairy arms, the accused clenched his teeth as if he wanted to bite down hard on something. He glared at Kalliana, at Sardili, at the rotund Magistrate, at the Pilgrims in the audience.

The Magistrate read the crimes, looking nervously at Kalliana, as if unhappy about being upstaged. "Accused of vandalizing several Pilgrim prefab structures on the outskirts of town and finally burning one of their homes. A Pilgrim family barely escaped with their lives."

Behind the youth's blustery, angry exterior, though, Kalliana could see that he was frightened. He had never imagined he would be brought before a Truthsayer, but rather had expected the town Magistrate to dispense a more lenient sentence.

Kalliana touched the young man's temples. He flinched. The uniformed sol-pols tensed. She reached out with her thoughts, but found that her telepathic power penetrated little, stumbling over the thick surface of this man's mind.

She shuddered and tried again, afraid to push deeper. She found a wall of hatred, of disgust, directed toward the quiet religious fanatics—but as she probed to find whether he was guilty of the crime of which he was accused, her telepathic powers splintered into a jumble. She couldn't control her thoughts, couldn't find the strength. Panic over the possibility of losing her powers disrupted her focus even more.

Kalliana forced herself not to let her expression change, despite her alarm. The accused man stiffened, ready to unleash violence upon anyone nearby. The Magistrate looked on with nervous concern, rubbing his hand across the top of his head in an unconscious attempt to cover his bald patch—and suddenly Kalliana grasped the situation: the Magistrate also hated the Pilgrims. The sentence had been prearranged. This young man, if brought to trial, was supposed to have been found innocent for lack of evidence . . . but he seemed so guilty, so afraid of the verdict, so full of violence and hatred. She didn't need her Truthsayer powers, not in this case.

"Guilty," she said and stepped back, heaving a great sigh.

The Pilgrims and the others in the audience murmured, some with satisfaction, others with annoyance—but no citizen could argue with the verdict of a Truthsayer. Truthsayers never made mistakes.

Kalliana's power waned further as the next cases were brought before her. A woman accused of stealing a bolt of fabric. A man accused of attempting to poison his wife. Three men who had hurt each other in a brawl after consuming too much grain beer and were now arguing over who had started the argument and who was, therefore, to pay for the damages.

Kalliana's thoughts were so scattered she found herself unable to use her Truthsayer abilities to determine any of the bald facts . . . but these people were so readable, so obviously guilty or terrified or outraged at being falsely accused that she found she could judge them anyway, just by their expressions, their actions. They were intimidated by Kalliana's presence, fearing her infallibility, knowing they were caught, or relieved to be set free. She could tell what the people had done just by witnessing them.

Finally the last case was brought before her—an old Pilgrim woman whose leathery skin was softened by wrinkles. Her eyes were knives, dark and flinty, flicking over the audience. Her name, incomprehensibly, was *Serenity*.

The Magistrate spoke up. "Accused of spreading sedition among the Pilgrims. Holding secret meetings. Trying to organize the religious fanatics to violence. Advocating a bloody takeover of Sardili Shores so that the Pilgrims can have their homeland."

Serenity looked angry, but Kalliana couldn't tell if she was angry at the people who had accused her, or if she felt such anger toward the other villagers that she might indeed suggest such a revolt.

Kalliana looked into the old woman's eyes, slid the hood down over her head, and touched her wiry gray hair, pressing in. Serenity kept her eyes open, her gaze boring back into the Truthsayer. Defiant.

Kalliana let her eyelids fall closed, attempted to use her telepathic powers—and found nothing but a blank wall. According to the Magistrate's description, there was no actual evidence against Serenity. No one had seen these alleged seditious meetings. No one had actually heard her speak against Joachim Sardili or the other villagers. Her accusers cited only secondhand reports, hearsay evidence.

Normally, such a case would never even have been brought to trial—but Serenity was a member of the disliked and aloof religious community. The other villagers wanted her found guilty so that the Pilgrims could be kept under tighter control.

Blindly naive, Sardili saw none of the nuances. He just wanted everyone to be friends . . . but everyone didn't want to be friends.

Kalliana stared into the careworn face and could not find the old woman guilty. Not on such a basis. "Innocent," she said, and released her hold.

Serenity snapped away like a released spring from a crushing burden. She stood up, blinking and surprised, but she quickly pulled her hood back into place, shrouding her face. Kalliana thought she had seen a ripple of amazement cross her expression— but was it amazement that Kalliana had been impartial after all . . . or amazement that a Truthsayer had made a mistake?

iii

On the mag-lev ride back to First Landing and her blessed home at the Guild Headquarters, Kalliana sat alone in her padded car, eyes squeezed shut, trying to sort through her confusion. She was filled with revulsion at what she had done. Deciding verdicts without telepathic evidence! Toying with lives! Unthinkable!

She had been raised in the Truthsayers Guild, given constant and implacable ethical instruction on what was right and what was wrong, on the responsibility she had to justice. *Truth Holds No Secrets.*

A Truthsayer was not a normal human being. Kalliana was not *allowed* to guess someone's guilt or innocence. She had to *know.* She had to see it absolutely, with no question. If she couldn't do that, she was no longer a Truthsayer. Something was wrong, terribly wrong—and she feared it was deep inside herself.

Kalliana shuddered. She had been programmed to be honorable and true, to despise lies—and now she found herself living a lie.

She had to rectify the situation, somehow. Maybe Guild Master Tharion would allow her to take a sabbatical until her thoughts stabilized, until her turmoil faded so she could perform her duties again. But it would have to be kept quiet. She couldn't understand what was wrong with her.

The escort of elite guard met her at the First Landing mag-lev station and took her quickly through the cobblestone streets to the tall metal ship of Guild Headquarters. The guards were grimly attentive to duty and wasted no time with lighthearted conversation, which she appreciated.

Once behind the stoic and unchanging facade of Headquarters, though, Kalliana noted a dramatic shift in the mood of the Guild. Though she saw no altered decor, something had definitely changed here. The eleven other Truthsayers, the red-sashed Mediators, and numerous brown-sashed Guild workers seemed to be discouraged. She saw none of the children trainees anywhere as she made her way to her cabin.

Finally she stopped a gardener on his way to the greenhouse alcove in the engine bay. "Something's happened," she said. "Tell me."

The gardener blinked at her in surprise, as if wondering why she didn't know, how she couldn't just read it from his mind. "It's Ysan," he said. "Quite a shock." He shook his head.

"What happened?" Kalliana demanded.

"He's in his quarters," the gardener said, and Kalliana backed away, rushing to the nearest turbolift. She took it down to the trainee levels and made her way to the young man's small cabin, thinking all the while of the boy's humor, his constant smile, his . . . unshakable innocence.

What could he have done that was so terrible? She signaled twice at his door, and after a long moment he unsealed the electronic lock. She was stunned to see him.

Ysan looked broken, his eyes bruised and puffy from hours of private weeping. He wore a warm woolen outer wrap, yet shivered as if from some inner cold. His white cotton robe lay discarded in a wad in the corner.

"Kalliana," he said. "I thought you might come . . . as soon as you got back."

She pushed him into his quarters so that he could close the door, understanding his need for privacy, whatever had happened. "Tell me about it."

He shrugged and looked away. His movements were jerky, as if his muscles had been cross-wired. "What can I say? I failed. Guild Master Tharion tested me. I was supposed to be promoted to Truthsayer yesterday. I've passed all my training. But when I was told to read one of the test cases . . . I couldn't. I've done it before with others here in the Guild—with you even—but this was someone from the outside. A citizen.

"The thoughts were all jumbled. Nothing was clear-cut. I must have been frightened. For some reason I just couldn't summon the strength, couldn't go deep enough. It was as if the Veritas didn't work for me." The words poured out of him and he looked up at her, pleading for understanding. "What if it had been a real trial?" he said. "Guild Master Tharion is right. I can't be trusted with the responsibility of a Truthsayer."

Kalliana blinked her dusty blue eyes at him in shock, recalling with dread her own recent inability to use her powers. But no one would question *her*, because she had already been blessed with Truthsayer status. Ysan, though, had blanked during his most important test.

"All my life was leading up to that moment, and now it's gone." Ysan slumped on his bunk and knotted his fingers in the drab woolen wrap. "All my life," he said again. "Now I have to start over."

"What are you going to do?" Kalliana said, trying to smother her own fear—for Ysan's sake, if not her own. The Guild Master could not test the young man again, since the public had to believe a Truthsayer was one hundred percent reliable. One chance only. Even if Ysan passed the second test, he had already proven that he *could* fail. One failure could be enough to let an innocent man face punishment.

Ysan shifted the anger toward himself again. "I can't stay here with my shame obvious to everyone. What would be the point? I don't have the training to be a Mediator, and I won't stay here for seven more years. Guild Master Tharion offered me the chance to become a worker, maybe a scientist . . . but I just want to be far from here, away from Guild Headquarters."

Kalliana shuddered, unable to comprehend this terrifying decision. He should never have failed. Never! Ysan had been so talented! Something was wrong. "But where will you go?"

Ysan looked toward his small table, and she saw that he had collected images of mountains, pine forests, a distant rugged land. "Toth Holding," he said. "I'm being assigned there as regional Magistrate. Even without Truthsayer powers, I have all of the legal training. It'll be difficult—" The young man swallowed. "But not as difficult as staying here."

Kalliana hugged him. He hugged her back for a moment, then stiffened. "I'd like to be alone for a little while longer," he said.

She nodded and left, feeling his turmoil acutely within herself. She was even worse than Ysan because she had *pronounced sentence* while uncertain. A hypocrite! She had to decide what to do. She sensed a great shadow hovering over the Guild, darkening.

A Truthsayer had lied, and now the consequences were rolling toward her like an avalanche.

# CHAPTER

# 16

i

The gray mare had borne a fine foal several days earlier, a dappled colt that stood on spindly legs and looked about the world in absolute wonder. But since the mother was in no condition for a long ride, Franz Dokken chose a different mount for Schandra as he took her out on a wilderness trip, despite her repeated complaints.

The two of them rode with Maximillian away from the villa, leading a packhorse behind their own mounts. They traveled to the colorful badlands, a raw painted desert of sedimentary soils, bright bands of reddish iron oxide and green-black copper ore.

The thin air was brisk and so clean it scrubbed Dokken's nostrils as he took deep breaths. Schandra wrapped herself in a woolen poncho and wore the resigned, long-suffering expression that most annoyed him. Maximillian, as usual, wore his gray jalaba, riding in silence behind Dokken and Schandra.

Schandra's dark hair flowed behind her like strands of ebony silk. She tossed her head, squinting into the bright sky, managing to look defeated, yet still annoyed. "How far are you dragging us out this time, Franz?" she asked. "I want to prepare myself mentally."

Dokken sat up on his chestnut stallion, gazing toward the horizon, the serpentine hills, the canyons that sliced through the badlands. He marveled at the magnificent landscape, glad to be free of management headaches. He felt his mental batteries recharging just looking at the rugged beauty of Atlas.

"Enjoy it, Schandra," he said. "Relax."

"What about my silkworms?" she said.

"They'll be fine," Dokken answered. "The workers will take

care of them, so there's no hurry. Be patient."

Her hands clenched the reins, but her face remained placid. "Just because you enjoy this doesn't mean we all find it relaxing to live like barbarians. I'd rather be reclining by a fire."

"We'll have a fire," Dokken said with forced cheerfulness, "just for you."

Schandra rounded on him. "What's the point of these expeditions, Franz? What am I supposed to get out of them? You never ask if I want—"

"Think of it as a family vacation." He tossed his head to include Maximillian in their group.

"Don't talk to me about families," she snapped.

Dokken decided to leave the conversation there and rode on ahead, shutting out Schandra's further complaints. She was in one of her resistant moods again, and he didn't want to bother with it. Once, she had been starstruck and charming, but lately she'd become so difficult, unappreciative.

They camped at the edge of a dying sea, a primordial ocean whose aquifer had long since been shunted elsewhere. The evaporating water had left a dazzling white pan of mineral deposits, salts, and chemicals that crunched like a brittle crust under the horses' hooves.

In these waters lived the native Atlas bacteria progenitors of the species that, once mutated, provided the Veritas drug. The chemical flats were a gold mine of resources, and Dokken Holding was the greatest supplier of the first-stage bacteria to the Platform and OrbLab 2.

Small puddles remained in the drying lake, alkaline mirrors that swarmed with transplanted brine shrimp. Hardy algae created rafts of slimy foam in the shallow pools. The air swarmed with buzzing sand flies, bred on the Platform and now surviving in the inhospitable ecosystem, filling the air with a faint hum and the shore with their blackened carcasses and egg cases.

The late-afternoon sun spilled orange-yellow light across the landscape like a heat lamp, making it ripple with long shadows. Monolithic spires of dried tufa looked weirdly surrealistic, tortured pinnacles of calcium carbonate deposits that had bubbled up from beneath the seabed and been left high and dry as the ocean receded.

Dokken chose a spot near the edge of the water, and Maximillian pounded cast-iron stakes deep into the ground so they could tether the horses. The manservant set out their bedrolls and folding chairs.

Schandra held a fistful of the crumbling whitish powder that formed the lakebed. She let it run through her fingers, then looked skeptically at the smear left on her dark skin. She rubbed her palms on her poncho. "Delightful," she said in a dull voice.

Dokken, losing patience, glared at her. "Make the best of it."

ii

Maximillian had loaded a bushel of aromatic pine with a few slivers of cedar onto the packhorse so they could have a genuine campfire. The smoke curled its sharp spicy scent around them. Dokken rubbed his hands above the flickering flames, feeling warmth rise into the night.

"Too bad we don't have any crickets," he said with a sigh.

Maximillian prepared a meal of self-heating ration packs, then warmed distilled water over the fire for tea. They sat back in their folding chairs and ate. The manservant was a lousy conversationalist, and Schandra was too wrapped up in her selfishness to say anything, so Dokken was able to capture a moment of peace.

He slid his fingers into one of the stiff pockets of his leather jerkin, feeling the smooth round capsule of Veritas. His fingertips tingled with the thrill of the forbidden. This capsule was one of the dozen he had confiscated from Cialben years ago, and he knew its potency remained undiminished.

Upon catching Cialben with the forbidden capsules in his villa, Dokken had confiscated them. He had locked the powerful drugs away, though he always knew they were there waiting to be used . . . inviting him . . . seducing him.

After several months, the temptation had been too great even for him. Dokken had taken the first dose alone, standing on the balcony of his villa and looking out at the workers in the courtyard, the gardeners, the dim forms in the greenhouse solarium where the silkworms were tended.

He felt the sudden rush of telepathic intensity like an orgasm in his mind, its climax a bright flash of insight, overloaded with the thoughts of all the people he could see. It was a cacophony in his head, but he rapidly learned how to narrow his focus to the mundane concerns of two men snipping leaves from the mulberry bushes: a stomach cramp, a full bladder, a worry about his young daughter being pregnant.

But since Dokken's body had not built up a tolerance to the

Veritas, his own resistance systems rapidly purged it from his mind. He had seen enough, though, to be aware of the drug's possibilities. . . .

Over the years Dokken had sampled the capsules sparingly. He never tried to obtain more, because he didn't want to admit to himself that he intended to use further dosages. Through Veritas, he had once ferreted out a traitor among the servants in his villa—someone spying for Victoria Koman. The traitor had suffered an unfortunate accident, not even aware she had been caught.

Using another capsule, Dokken had tested the loyalty of Maximillian, sifting through the manservant's innermost thoughts, searching for evidence of betrayal—but Maximillian exhibited absolute loyalty. His thoughts were well-ordered and clear-cut; the world existed in black and white for him. The gaunt man's devotion was a bit frightening . . . but such loyalty was a comfort, because Maximillian knew everything about the ongoing plans.

As the campfire burned down, the manservant went off to set up his own lean-to tent near the horses, out of sight around a tufa outcropping to give Dokken and Schandra privacy for the night.

iii

Making love under the stars held a special magic for Dokken, and he hoped it might even penetrate Schandra's distaste. She'd probably rather just be *talking*. The night was crisp around them, the pale green aurora rippling like a snapped tablecloth overhead. Everything was absolutely silent. The water in the dying sea was still.

Schandra lay back naked, reclining on a warm blanket that covered the salty ground. She breathed quickly, seeming to enjoy his caresses . . . but Dokken couldn't tell if it was just an act. Her body was beautiful and exotic, silky to his touch. Her dusky skin flowed in gentle curves over her hips, her breasts, her buttocks, softened by a lifetime of luxury. He rubbed one of her nut-brown nipples between his thumb and forefinger until it hardened, then he kissed her other breast. She sighed, a sound of quiet contentment.

Dokken had chosen her as a lovely little girl from one of the rugged kenaf plantations. He had seen the potential beauty behind the grime and the weariness of tending irrigated fields all day long. Planning ahead, he had taken Schandra as his ward, grooming her to be his mate and consort for as long as she proved worthwhile. He had patience. He had time, and she had been sparkling with exuberance, demure, intelligent.

Now she took it all for granted, as if she had already paid enough, as if she were more than just another servant.

For years Schandra had been a fine student, a true courtesan. She learned much from him about cause and effect, about complex consequences arising from seemingly simple actions. He had shown her how to set an avalanche in motion by moving the right pebble at the right time . . . but Schandra had grown increasingly irrational and volatile, obsessed with bearing children, like some common villager.

Now he stroked her inner thigh, raising goose bumps, feeling the warmth of her skin beneath his flat palm. He spread her legs apart, then climbed on top of her and slid inside, nestled between her legs. Working through the fuzzy texture of the blanket, he placed another hand at the base of her back and pushed her closer against him as he ground into her.

Schandra looked over Dokken's shoulder, staring up at the stars. She seemed resigned, making the required sounds . . . but gradually she grew more involved, genuinely excited. Her eyes drifted closed. Her expression showed contentment, then pleasure; finally, she began to groan in ecstasy.

Now was the time. Dokken shifted the capsule he had held in the back of his mouth. He had hoped for this, waited for this—and now he could experience his own lovemaking through Schandra's senses, read it from her mind and share her sensations.

As he continued thrusting with his hips, he cracked down on the Veritas capsule, felt the rush of the bitter drug. In less than a moment his thoughts increased to a pounding intensity. He felt his own sensations . . . and then a flood of hers, nerve endings firing in places Dokken had never before felt, *inside*, a delicious intrusive pressure, throbbing. . . .

Schandra groaned again deep in her throat, a guttural animal sound. His own telepathic boost continued to build as she prepared to come—then the Veritas penetrated deeper into her mind. Her thoughts swept over him, her fantasies, the scenes her mind painted as she rode Franz Dokken toward climax—

And Dokken saw the image she had conjured behind her closed eyes: a vivid picture of rutting with Garien, the chef.

He read deeper through his anger, looking for some sign of collusion from Garien, but saw that this was sheer fantasy on

Schandra's part. She pictured the other man, imagined how he felt, envisioned how he might do things to her body—and that alone brought her to the peak of orgasm. She breathed sharply, arching her hips and grabbing Dokken's back, clutching him.

In outrage, Franz Dokken reacted like a triggered land mine. "Bitch!"

Schandra's eyes flickered open, confused for a second, uncomprehending.

Still on top of her, he slammed down with a balled fist, crushing her larynx with the force of a sledgehammer. She gasped and choked, writhing, unable to breathe. Her mouth opened wide. Spittle dribbled down her cheek. She thrashed about, clawing at him with manicured nails as he encircled her neck with his large hands and squeezed.

Dokken kept his voice low and calm. His eyes burned bright. "How dare you!" he said through clenched teeth, breathing the words. "I gave you everything. *Everything!* And all I asked for was your loyalty." His anger was so great that adrenaline doubled the strength of his muscles. He grunted as he squeezed again. "I gave you everything," he said again. "Now I take it all away."

He heard her neck snap.

Dokken left Schandra there on the shore of the forgotten sea as he stood, wiped himself with a corner of the blanket, then casually dressed. He called for Maximillian's assistance, and the gaunt manservant climbed out of the lean-to and came over to the campsite. He gave a long appraising look at Schandra's naked body, lying like a squashed bug, arms and legs akimbo.

"I'll need you to help me," Dokken said.

Maximillian hesitated for the briefest instant, then nodded, saying nothing.

They dumped Schandra's body in an isolated ravine. Dokken wasn't the least bit concerned that some lonely explorer might find her out in this wilderness. It wouldn't matter anyway.

Dokken looked toward the lightening sky, where the blackness became a pale purple, and sighed. "Maximillian, I think it's time for another sojourn," he said. "I need to disappear for a while. By myself this time—you've got better things to do. You'll take care of everything?"

Maximillian nodded. "Yes, sir."

Dokken climbed into the saddle on his chestnut stallion and patted the fine horse's muscular neck. He turned to Maximillian.

"This will be a short one. There are still plenty of issues that need my attention," he said. "I'll be back in about a week—feeling much better."

Maximillian gave a thin, pale smile. "You always do, sir." The manservant finished packing up the camp, loading Schandra's riderless horse with the remainder of their belongings.

Maximillian and Dokken rode off in different directions, into the Atlas dawn.

ORBLAB 2

# CHAPTER

## 17

i

The delay was interminable.

Troy Boren didn't know how he could stand waiting in the brig any longer. He wished it would just be over, but that wasn't an option. He wondered how the sol-pols could possibly need so many preparations—stationing extra guards, preparing a secure path to the space elevator, loading and double-checking weapons—all for him. *Him.* He was impressed . . . flattered . . . frightened. They thought he was a vicious murderer and intended to take no chances.

Troy huddled on his bunk inside the detention cell until the elite guards finally brought him out of the gloomy underground decks after some unknown number of days. "Hold your hands out," one of the guards said. He extended both arms, and the sol-pols wrapped his wrists tightly with resin-soaked ropes. "Don't let it touch your clothes until the cement stiffens."

"You're going to have to use a saw to get these off!" Troy said, striving for a light tone in his voice.

The guard captain turned his goggled helmet toward Troy. "Yes we will. But not until you reach the Platform."

The sol-pols marched Troy briskly through the buried decks of the old military ship. Troy had feared there would be a bloodthirsty mob of screaming citizens waiting for him, but the guards had been discreet, taking him out a side access door without fanfare.

He breathed the outside air after the musty closeness of the brig. The sky was dressed in funereal gray draped with a layer of icy clouds that promised no rain and no sunshine, only gloom. Once he reached OrbLab 2, Troy would be looking down upon the clouds from above for the rest of his life.

He stopped to blink, but the sol-pols continued marching, and he tripped. The guards tensed, as if afraid he might be making an escape attempt. One of them grabbed Troy's arm so that he kept his balance. It was difficult to steady himself with his arms lashed rigidly together.

The armed escort walked him through back streets, between low adobe buildings and corrugated metal warehouses. He heard the vendors, the accountants, the merchants exchanging commodities that funneled through First Landing. The citizens studiously ignored the sol-pol troops, though Troy was convinced everyone was staring at him. Everyone knew who he was—and everyone was glad to see him go.

When they finally reached the anchor point and the facilities that had sprung up around it, Troy felt a leaden lump form in his stomach. Within the fenced enclosure, people bustled about in comfortable overalls as they prepared the elevator car for its ascent. Troy looked with a great pang at his former coworkers.

He missed unloading the elevator with them, keeping track of the items that came down from the Platform. If only he had paid more attention. If only he hadn't been distracted by the escaped chicks, he would never have made his inventory mistake, would never have felt compelled to fix it . . . would never have stumbled upon a dead body late at night. And a Truthsayer would never have convicted him of a crime he hadn't committed.

Troy's surly former boss Cren moved like a hawk around his work crew, clapping his hands and urging them to greater speed. He seemed more harried than ever, and enjoying every moment of it.

As the procession approached, the work crew turned to stare openly at Troy. Cren placed his hands on his hips and glared, in uncharacteristic silence. The others wore open expressions of disgust or outrage at Troy's supposed betrayal. But what could he say?

No one would believe him that a Truthsayer had lied or made a mistake, that he was actually innocent. Both possibilities were equally ridiculous. When he had insisted on his innocence to the guards, they had made the security field around his cell opaque to sound, so that his words echoed back at him like mocking whispers. After a while, he gave it up. Now Troy merely bit his lower lip. What else could he do?

He focused his attention instead on the large elevator car, at the packaged cargo strewn about, canisters of purified oxygen, tanks of water, shipments of grain and fresh vegetables. Some of the dry goods had been set aside for the next elevator run because of the added space and breathing air required by the prisoner and his guards. Two more sol-pols stood outside the space elevator car, prepared for him.

Troy chose not to look pleadingly at his former coworkers, for that would only increase his shame. But even as his gaze locked on the vessel that would take him on a one-way trip from Atlas, from his home, he could feel the looming emotions of the work crew, of those who might have become his friends given a little more time. He sensed their hatred and fear. He knew what they were thinking.

*My God! I worked with him.*
*What if he had killed me instead?*
*Who would have guessed?*

Troy heard a rattle of the chain-link fence surrounding the secure compound that guarded the anchor point. He turned stiffly, and the sol-pol guards let him move just enough to see his family gathered there. Just like when he had gone off to First Landing, they had come to see him off.

ii

"Wait," Troy tried to say, but only a brittle breath came from his throat. He spoke louder. "Wait!" He struggled, and the armored guards folded around him like a clenching fist, placing their hands on their weapons. Troy calmed his pounding heart, took a deep breath, and said, "It's my family."

One of the younger guards seemed about to make a sneering retort, but the sol-pol captain, a middle-aged man with dark stubble on a sunburned face, seemed to be giving Troy a hard stare behind his goggles. "We've got a long trip together, all of us," the captain said. "I'll take you over there for just a minute, if you promise to cooperate and not cause us any trouble."

"I don't intend to cause any trouble," Troy said, as if it were the most obvious thing in the world. "I'll be quiet. I'll cooperate in anything you want me to do." Which he would have done anyway. "Just let me talk to them."

The captain nodded grimly. "We had a very unpleasant experience with our last prisoner," he said. "I'd prefer a little relaxation this time."

Troy nodded. "Yes, sir."

The guards marched him over to the chain-link fence. Troy had a difficult time walking, feeling top-heavy with his arms lashed in the resin-hardened ropes. He kept his eyes on his mother and father, his two sisters.

As Troy approached, his mother and younger sister flinched. His father stood motionless, shoulders hunched, anger and confusion showing on his face. Leisa stood closest, her fingers wrapped around the links of the fence as she gazed at him, defeated.

Troy felt a deep longing for the past, to be with his family in their crowded dwelling in the Mining District, living a dead-end life. Once, he had found it so intolerable . . . but now it seemed the happiest alternative in the world.

He leaned toward the fence—though the guards wouldn't let him get any closer than two meters—and searched for words, but tears came out instead. Leisa, standing by the fence, also began to weep. Her eyes were red-rimmed and puffy.

Rambra clenched and unclenched his hands, as if trying to sort and re-sort his own fingers. "Leisa wanted us to come," the big man said grudgingly.

Troy wondered how many days it had been. He looked long and hard at his older sister, memorizing her face, his eyes pleading as he searched for something to say. Leisa had to believe he was innocent—but she couldn't speak. Lips trembling, she yanked her fingers from the fence and whirled, running off into the streets.

"Leisa!" Troy finally called after her. He had so much he wanted to tell her, so much he wanted to ask, to explain.

His mother came forward. Dama looked as if she had been pummeled by circumstances, her body imploding, her confidence collapsing into herself. She looked at him with eyes like fading embers. "Troy," she said, "how could . . . how could you? You lied to us, betrayed all our hopes!" She shook her head. "Thinking of yourself again. That's all you ever did. Before you committed this . . . this horrible act, couldn't you have paused to consider what it would do to us? Your family? Now how are we ever going to find a place in First Landing? Good thing you never wanted children of your own."

His little sister pushed her way to stand beside her mother, clutching Dama's arm. "Yes, Troy," Rissbeth whined, her face hard and pinched like a crone in training. "I had already listed on the marriage market and now with this . . . this blot on my family name, who will ever consider me? I'll never find a respectable husband, thanks to you."

Troy flushed with a deep annoyance at her attitude. "Of course, Rissbeth—it could never have anything to do with your *own* failings, could it? For a person with your personal charm and deep inner beauty, there must be some . . . *creature* on this world willing to marry you."

Looking at him in disgust, Rissbeth ran fingers through her mouse-brown hair. "With you as my brother, I'll probably have to wait until that new colony ship comes in. It'll probably carry another batch of worthless exiled criminals, and *that's* what I'll be stuck with." She looked as if she wanted to spit.

Rambra, alone and silent, suddenly bristled, barely restraining himself from backhanding her with his meaty hand. "Enough, Rissbeth!" he said. "How do you know even an exiled criminal would want a shrew like you?"

She gaped at her father in shock, and Troy could hardly contain a pleased smile. Rissbeth should have known better than to let loose such a comment, since Rambra was himself descended from families exiled to Atlas on the *Botany Bay* generations earlier.

Now, though, they had another criminal in the family.

Rambra swept his wife and younger daughter away from the fence. "Go find Leisa," he snapped. As the big man turned, he looked back over his shoulder at Troy standing there with his hands bound. The rugged miner's face was a kaleidoscope of emotions, more complex than anything Rambra knew what to do with. Troy felt sorry for him.

iii

He didn't notice the bindings anymore. By now his entire body felt dead and detached.

The sol-pol captain had arranged for him to sit beside one of the space elevator's narrow rectangular windows, with one guard stationed on either side of him. The chamber was cramped, not built for comfort. People traveled regularly from the surface to the Platform and back again, but it had never been intended as a luxury cruise.

It had been a long time since his last meal, but Troy didn't feel hungry. Though they had fed him in the brig, the elevator would take ten hours crawling up its cable, and he wouldn't have a chance to eat again until they freed his hands. He doubted the sol-pols would want to spoon-feed him.

He sighed and closed his eyes. Every moment took him farther and farther from the world. The space elevator continued to climb the wound-diamond fiber, ascending higher and higher into the darkening sky. Troy opened his eyes and stared through the pitted glass panel, watching as Atlas dropped away forever.

# CHAPTER

# 18

i

After ten hours the space elevator finally approached the sprawling Platform that hung over the equator of Atlas.

Troy had spent the first few hours of the long journey up the cable bemoaning his circumstances, then paying attention to all the unusual details around him. Then the trip had degenerated into straightforward tedium—and finally that changed to alarm and discomfort as gravity began to cut loose. The space elevator climbed above the tenuous outer atmosphere, and Troy found himself displaced and disoriented. His fascination at the way his internal organs seemed to drift about inside his body cavity ended when he became desperately queasy. Two of the armed guards accompanying him appeared equally distressed, grayish and sweaty, adjusting their gauntlets and helmets, squirming in their uncomfortable body armor.

The sol-pol captain watched his prisoner closely. Finally, when Troy could no longer contain his nausea, the captain sprang across the chamber like a fish leaping out of water and stuffed a bag over Troy's head.

Surprised, Troy spewed the contents of his nearly empty stomach. The bag blinded him, but also prevented the spray from flying in all directions. Troy struggled, certain he was going to choke from the bile because his arms were still bound in front of him. The captain removed the saturated sack, careful to contain most of the vomit in the zero gravity.

Troy retched again, but nothing came out. His mouth tasted sour and awful. His face, his hair, his eyelids were all caked from the flying droplets.

"You won't have to get used to it, since you won't be traveling up and down anymore," the captain said. "Your body will accustom itself to low gravity on the station."

One of the other guards found a tattered rag and soaked it with a pungent-smelling disinfectant used to swab out the animal cages the elevator often delivered. The potent odor burned Troy's nostrils, but at least it scalded away the reek of his own nausea. The captain used another scrap of cloth to dry Troy's tingling face and damp hair. Troy blinked and briefly nodded his thanks, though his eyes stung from the fumes. He shuddered, working to regain his composure, and trying to endure for the rest of the trip. . . .

The guards seemed wrapped up in their own thoughts. Two quietly played a card game. Others sat and stared at the prisoner, though Troy couldn't imagine what could possibly be so interesting about him.

A prerecorded voice announced, "Docking at the orbital Platform will commence in fifteen minutes." Troy could not see the looming space complex directly above them, the only remnant of the original colony ship. Long ago the precious space elevator cable had been unreeled like a fishing line from the Platform, establishing a ready surface-to-orbit transportation system that required no expendable rockets, and fuel, or an astronautical infrastructure that Atlas did not have.

Even after getting his job at the anchor point, Troy had never dreamed he would be taken up the elevator himself. Such travel was reserved only for special personnel, a change of crew up on the Platform . . . or for convicted criminals like himself, doomed to be shipped off to the free-floating OrbLab 2.

With a jarring thump, the elevator's roof locked into place; the sudden change in inertia knocked Troy hard against his seat and made two of the sol-pols slide to their knees. One of the small cargo boxes sprang free of its lashings, hit the far wall, and ricocheted, slowly spinning until it hung dead in the middle of the cabin.

Troy blinked, still smelling the thick disinfectant. He looked up at the blank metal ceiling. Rather than exiting from the elevator's side egress doors as Troy had when unloading cargo on the ground, the sol-pols undogged a circular roof hatch and swung the lid up.

One guard pushed against the floor with his feet, propelling himself upward like a fish into a tunnel. He vanished into a small storage crawl space overhead, then unsealed a second hatch in the main roof of the elevator. Two of the guards followed him, then the captain picked up Troy like a piece of luggage, holding him by the resin-hardened bindings at his wrists, and nudged him through the opening.

Troy drifted out of control, floating upward into a new world.

## ii

Thick, soft clamps folded around special rings on the side of the elevator car, forming an airtight seal like a pair of steel-strong lips. The first three uniformed guards bobbed in the air at either side of the egress hatch, reaching down to catch Troy as he drifted upward.

He found himself in a spacious docking chamber that had once been used to house shuttlecraft, large hoppers of supplies, crates of prefabricated dwellings, and machinery for the original colonists. Someone had long ago painted the domed ceiling a beautiful sky blue, with a bright warm sunrise at deck level. Cottony clouds floated across the curved plates, and confident words were stenciled in an arc over the painted sunrise. "Atlas— a new dawn." Because of his own dabbling with paints, Troy found the scene breathtaking. He wondered if the painter of this idealistic scene had ever visited Atlas, or if this dream had lived in the artist's imagination alone.

Rotating green lights flashed outside sealed doors marking deck levels along the hemispherical ceiling. Because gravity imposed no restraints here, corridors spread into the main body of the Platform in all directions and at all angles, bypassing design limits for gravity-constrained systems.

Platform workers came forward to unload the meager cargo that had been crammed into the attic crawl space of the elevator car. The sol-pols clustered around Troy, who still couldn't move his hands.

Near the apex of the domed sky-ceiling one of the hatches slid open, and an odd creature emerged, accompanied by two uniformed guards who flew headfirst, arms stiff at their sides, like remoras following a shark.

The withered man behind them reminded Troy of a troglodyte, twisted and deformed—an ancient, *ancient* man who looked to have grown up in a very confined, dark cave. His skin was pale as paper, dry and crinkled. His snowy hair frizzed around his shriveled face like a tattered corona from a dying sun. The hair had begun falling out in patches, leaving him with weird pattern-baldness.

The man's thin arms had big bony elbows and sticklike fingers with swollen knuckles. His biceps were overdeveloped from constant exercise, while his legs were curled beneath a tightly wrapped loincloth. The feet were lumps, the legs contorted at the knees.

Troy's guard captain looked up in surprise, intimidated. "Master Sondheim," he said, "thank you for coming to greet us. We didn't expect such an honor simply for the delivery of a new prison laborer."

Kareem Sondheim, the "landholder without land," carried a small jetpack on a belt at his waist, a canister no larger than his hand. He expelled bursts of pressurized gas to move him toward them, sliding the belt around his waist like directional settings on a dial.

Sondheim's black eyes were set in a labyrinth of wrinkles surrounding an aquiline nose. When he smiled, his teeth were tablets of white porcelain—obviously artificial. "It'll be good to return to normal production after the tragic loss of those other two workers," Sondheim said, his voice nasal and unpleasant as he scrutinized Troy. He bent closer, sniffing. "Disinfectant, eh? Space sickness is really a bitch."

At first, Troy averted his eyes, but the misshapen man fascinated him, and he found his gaze wandering back to the ancient landholder. If he remembered his history right, Kareem Sondheim had been one of the children born on the colony ship en route from Earth. He had been horribly deformed from birth, possibly because his mother had spent too much of her pregnancy in a deepsleep chamber.

When all the colonists had disembarked on their exodus to the surface of Atlas, Sondheim had been old enough and intelligent enough to stay behind and run the Platform. In zero gravity he could scuttle about and maneuver as well as any other human, but down on Atlas the gravity would truly handicap him.

Sondheim had access to a few Earth geriatric treatments, but the secret to his immense age was supposedly that the weightlessness vastly reduced the strain on his fragile body. He had been here more than two centuries. Troy wondered if he had come to inspect the new prisoner simply because he was bored.

Sondheim looked at him with a wild expression in his ebony eyes, as if he knew more about Troy than Troy himself did. It made him uncomfortable, and in a moment of dangling silence he blurted out, "Sir, what happened to those other two workers I'm replacing?"

The guards glared in annoyance, but the fragile old landholder pulled his cracked lips together like a purse string drawn tight. "A tragic industrial accident. Because of the risks of processing the Veritas drug and distilling out the Mindfire mutation, we have stringent decontamination systems on OrbLab 2, placed there at the request of Guild Master Tharion, though the systems themselves have proven to be quite difficult. Two unfortunate workers accidentally triggered an emergency alarm. The automatic safeguards flushed the entire contents of the bacterial sorting chamber out into space."

Floating free in midair, Sondheim shook his head, and the nimbus of white hair rippled around his skull. "A great pity, too, because upon further investigation we feel that the alarm may have been triggered in error. The two workers were jettisoned along with a full month's production of Veritas. Tragic in both senses." He smiled, flashing his enameled teeth again. "You won't be so careless, will you, Mr. Boren?"

"I hope not," Troy answered, his voice hoarse through a lump in his throat.

"Good," Sondheim said. "Enjoy your new life up here. In orbit there's absolutely nothing weighing you down!"

The ancient man cackled with childish laughter, spun a backward somersault in the air, and then swam off, boosted by air jets and accompanied by his two silent guards.

iii

The sol-pol captain finally had to slice through Troy's bonds in order to get the prisoner into a pressurized spacesuit for transport to OrbLab 2. Gasping with relief, Troy flapped his hands and rubbed them briskly. He felt the sting of returning circulation and flexed his fingers, but the buzzing electric sensation continued to increase until the annoying pinpricks became a burning agony in his wrists and arms. He hissed in pain.

He wanted to go home—but he was almost home now. His new home. Troy fought to hold back a groan.

The captain and three others crammed with Troy into a suiting room adjacent to the external launching tubes. With numb, clumsy hands Troy worked his way into the bulky suit, an ancient Earth design to keep him pressurized and protected during the brief orbital sled ride over to the space laboratory. He checked the interlocking connections as best he could. The sol-pols tried to help him but were apparently as unfamiliar with the donning procedures as Troy was.

When they all had their helmets in place with the faceplates up, the sol-pol captain pushed Troy's hands against his sides and activated a switch that magnetically locked steel wrist bracelets to holding clamps on the suit, effectively immobilizing him again. Troy tried to squirm, then finally gave up in resignation.

Emerging from the suiting room, they entered the launching tube for the ballistic sleds that traveled between the Platform and OrbLab 2. The snub-nosed, bullet-shaped craft were little more than empty canisters five meters long with viewing windows at the front, thick plating in the rear, and nozzles placed at strategic points for the attitude-control system.

A large coiled spring would launch them along a rail into space. A battery-powered generator wound the spring tight, drawing the orbital sled into position along its rails until the mechanism quivered, ready to be released. The contraption looked deceptively simple to Troy. He had expected to see a shuttle system comparable to the flashy chromes, the slick plastics, the dazzling computer systems on the high-tech Platform. The transport sled was little more than a ballistic slingshot.

Moving slowly, the group of suited figures climbed into the open cabin of the stripped-down sled. There were handholds for keeping balance, and only one seat—for the pilot. The vehicle seemed sturdy enough, solid, airtight. Troy asked, "Why do we need to wear these suits if the vessel is pressurized?"

The sol-pol captain looked at him. "These craft have been repaired many times over the centuries. Their integrity . . . no longer instills confidence."

"Oh," Troy said. One of the other guards snapped Troy's faceplate shut before he could ask another question.

Using a ring on the back of his suit, they clipped him to the wall like a hanging satchel. The captain sat in the pilot seat and punched the large-buttoned controls with his gloved fingers. "Casting off," he said. "Hang on."

The sled lurched forward, shot from the released spring. It barreled along the rails, fired into space like a cannonball. Troy, thrown to one side by the sudden acceleration, closed his eyes, but that only made things worse. His brain broadcast messages of shattered equilibrium in the weightlessness.

OrbLab 2 hung within line-of-sight distance. Once launched, the sled's momentum carried them forward. The speed of their flight would vary depending on the efficiency of each particular spring release and the coefficient of friction on the floor rails. If the pilot steered correctly, they would arrive at the isolated laboratory.

The captain gently touched buttons, and hissing air bled from the nozzles on the side of the ship, slightly adjusting their course toward the facility in space. Flying by dead reckoning wasn't necessarily the most accurate, but it was certainly good enough.

Troy heard nothing but silence in his sealed suit, since the sol-pols had shut off his radio and continued their conversation on a private channel. The silence roared around him, and he finally squeezed his eyes shut again, ignoring the disorientation.

The trip across the gulf of space took half an hour. Troy could see OrbLab 2 was a collection of spinning, self-contained pods or armored canisters linked together: discarded external fuel tanks and cargo holds cobbled together into a separate facility, with life-support systems and structural reinforcement added as an afterthought.

The lab station rotated slowly, and Troy wondered how much artificial gravity the centrifugal force provided, how much applied force the biochemical procedures needed to function properly.

The slight spin made the docking procedure more difficult for the pilot. As an open port rotated slowly into view, the captain jetted forward by releasing pressurized air in the stern; with its increased velocity the sled neatly slipped into the open bay like a pill popped into a waiting mouth. The docking doors slid shut behind them. The rotating wall finally came up and nudged them gently, imparting angular momentum and creating a sudden sense of gravity, faint but undeniable.

When the chamber had finished repressurizing, the bay lights switched on. The captain opened the sled hatch, flipped up his faceplate, and went to an intercom on the wall next to an inner airlock door. "Reporting from the Platform," he said. "We are here to discharge possession of prisoner Boren. Acknowledge receipt."

A rich voice came over the speaker. "Acknowledged, boys. Send him through the main airlock. We have your exchange shipment there in the cargo bins, waiting for transport back to the Platform."

"Thanks, Dieter," the captain said and switched off.

One of the other guards unfastened Troy from the sled's inner hull and disengaged the magnetic clamps holding his arms immobile. The sol-pol captain gestured over to the wall. "Take off your suit and stow it in one of those lockers."

Troy struggled out of the bulky fabric that refused to cooperate at every step. His helmet drifted out of reach in a halting descent toward the floor plates. One of the sol-pols grabbed it and helped Troy squirm out of the suit. The smell of lingering disinfectant had made the air in his helmet nearly unbearable. He gasped the stale recycled atmosphere as if it were the most refreshing breath he had ever taken.

They hung his suit next to several others in the metal lockers. The rest of the sol-pols busied themselves, stacking packages for delivery to the Platform into the empty sled. More Veritas, no doubt, and perhaps other dangerous pharmaceuticals better suited for processing aboard the isolated facility.

Troy stood shivering in his thin prison jumpsuit, and the captain gestured him into the open airlock. "In you go," he said. "You'll have to strip down and be completely disinfected. No foreign microorganisms allowed on OrbLab 2." Then the captain's hard expression softened. "Good luck inside," he said. "I hope you make the best of it."

Troy blinked away the sudden moisture that sprang to his eyes, overwhelmed with emotion for this one man who had shown him a glimpse of kindness. "Thank you. I'll try." He entered the airlock, which sealed behind him.

Harsh white light shone from above in the small chamber. The intercom told Troy to shuck his jumpsuit. A warm rain of disinfectant splashed around him. He coughed and sputtered, squeezing his eyes shut, then a blast of cold water showered down to rinse him off.

The inner door opened, and he was forced to step cold and wet into the secure facility of OrbLab 2, dripping all over the floor plates, given no opportunity to dry. He felt completely miserable and helpless—which was no doubt the intent. He blinked the chemical residue out of his eyes and shook his head to release water droplets from his hair.

In front of him stood a wiry, well-muscled man, whose lithe muscles and fluid movements resembled those of a dancer or gymnast. He had rich brown hair, large eyes, Mephistophelean eyebrows, and a pointed chin. He wore a clinging dark green jumpsuit and smiled humorlessly at Troy's bedraggled form. The man floated in the air, gradually drifting to the floor in the low gravity, until—with a slight, unconscious hop—he propelled himself upward again.

"Ah, another lost boy to join us! Welcome to OrbLab 2." He came forward as if out of long habit to pump Troy's hand in a vigorous greeting. "I'm Dieter—Dieter Pan, the station exec. So good of you to come."

The burly guards beside Dieter wore magnetic boots that kept them anchored sturdily to the floor.

"We'll have a lot of fun and a lot of time for training, son," Dieter said with a grin. "But after that last accident, I can't risk the loss of any more of my skilled workers—so I'm going to assign you to work with our other newbie. That way if either of you klutzes happens to trigger an alarm, it won't be any great loss." He chuckled, raising his curled eyebrows and observing Troy's wretched expression. "Just kidding! But I do like to have our new boys work together."

He hopped again to keep himself aloft and spread his arms as if he meant to reach out and fly at any moment. "Boys, let's get our friend here a nice warm outfit." He gestured to the two guards. "Then take him to meet his new partner—Eli Strone."

# CHAPTER

## 19

### i

Still trying to get warm after the cold, antiseptic-smelling decon shower, Troy dressed himself in the shared quarters to which he had been assigned. With damp fingers he fastened the adhesive strips of a papery outfit that felt more like loose pajamas than real clothes. He tugged on thin slippers.

Finished, he realized with a dawning horror that eventually he would have to think of this place as *Home*.

He looked warily at the empty bunk on the other side of the cell, feeling himself shrink inside. His roommate had meticulously placed his own possessions, every item of clothing, in one half of the minimal room, dividing it with an imaginary wall. Troy stood there, blinking. He wondered if the man had cleared part of the cell in anticipation of the new arrival, or if he had automatically marked his own territory, ignoring the rest of the precious space.

The door popped open, and Dieter Pan hovered outside. "Time's up, my boy! What's the matter—having trouble deciding what to wear?"

Not wanting to be difficult, Troy muttered an apology. He lurched out of the cell in the low gravity, walking like an inebriated ballet dancer, wobbling and overbalanced. Making his way down the metal corridors, Troy was accompanied by guards clomping along in magnetic boots. Their heavy rifles made him nervous, not just from the threat of the weapons but from a concern that their bullets might puncture the space station's walls. Then he remembered that they used molded ceramic cartridges up here, just hard enough to cause a lethal injury to prisoners, though they shattered to dust upon impact with a metal wall.

Dieter Pan flitted ahead, hopping and drifting, as if he had been sprinkled with fairy dust. Dieter and Troy slipped up a metal rung ladder to the second level, then waited outside an access hatch as the two guards ascended in their heavy boots.

The station exec chattered a memorized speech that served as both a pep talk and a lecture on the rules. Dieter went over the basic information about regulated rest periods, and how prisoners were expected to be in their cells during off shifts.

Troy tried to pay attention, but the words swarmed around him like gnats, overwhelming him with details. He blinked in an attempt to clear his head. Not long ago, when he had left the constant noisy company of his family in the Mining District, he had adjusted to a new job and lifestyle in First Landing. Now everything had changed again. But he would have plenty of time to adjust. Too much time . . . the rest of his life.

"Come along now, my boy," Dieter said, gesturing with an overlarge circle of his arm as he bounced ahead. "We've got work to do. Hi-ho!"

ii

Seen from outside, the hodgepodge complex was clearly composed of disparate components. Inside, as they passed from section to section, Troy noted dramatic changes in the floor color, wall plates, and texture; one compartment would be slick and clean, the next battered and corroded. The suspended ceilings hovered low, making him claustrophobic. He would never again see the wide-open sky, only gray-plate panels.

Oh well, he sunburned easily anyway, Troy thought. The black humor kept him from collapsing into shuddery sobs.

Once they entered the actual processing complex, Troy noted observation cameras sprouting like eyestalks in every upper corner, tracking their movement. Troy, Dieter, and the two guards continued through a double airlock that served as the first compartmentalized barrier to the hazardous work areas. The smells inside were pungent, penetrating even the residual burning in his nostrils from the disinfectant wash. He could just imagine how much fun it was going to be working here.

The station exec rapped his knuckles on the thick glass of a wall-window that looked into an enamel and chrome clean-room. Troy leaned forward, while Dieter Pan beamed like a proud father.

Inside the clean-room white-suited figures concentrated on their work, staring into enhanced microscopes, their hands covered with filmy gloves and the lower half of their faces masked with woven breathing filters. One worker glanced up at Dieter Pan outside the window, then ignored the spectators.

"What are they doing?" Troy asked. "Will I be working in there?"

"Not yet, boy. That's a real plum of an assignment. You've got to work your way up." He rubbed his fingers on the thick glass, raising his curled eyebrows. "These are the culturing sections, where we grow the Veritas precursor bacterium. The people in there are our microlivestock breeders." He laughed at his own joke.

"The Veritas precursor is a hardy little bug that thrives in the drying alkaline lakebeds downstairs." He gestured at the floor plates to imply the planet far below. "This critter is one of the few bits of native Atlas biochemistry our human bodies don't ignore—in fact, our systems celebrate it!"

Dieter tried to swallow his last words, as if realizing he shouldn't have been emphasizing the pleasurable aspects of the mind-reading drug. Clomping guards followed on either side, saying nothing.

"Ah," Dieter said, approaching another sealed laboratory. "There and there, we have the distilling chambers, and the encapsulators that place the cultured Veritas toxin inside a coating of hardened starch-gelatin. What comes out the other end is a pretty little blue pill that I'm sure you've seen before —" He slapped his forehead comically. "Of *course* you've seen them before, if you've been smuggling! Hah. Forgot why you were sentenced here in the first place."

Troy held his tongue and resisted the urge to make a pointless denial of his guilt. He certainly didn't expect the station exec to believe him.

"But you, my lucky boy, will be working in the bacterial sorter lab, down at the end of the line. You'll have thrills and chills isolating the superior strains from the unaffected bugs and the deadly stuff. What fun! It's the riskiest assignment on the station—but hey"—he shrugged—"you're the new kid on the block, and you get last pick."

Dieter stopped at an equipment wardrobe outside the door to the final lab complex along the curved corridor. The lights down here were brighter, shadows banished by the enameled walls and the scoured floor plates. "On the other hand," he said, "your partner Strone seems to enjoy the work. To each his own, I guess."

From the storage wardrobe Dieter removed a full-facemask respirator and settled it snugly on his head, clipping the air hose into a small air canister, buckling the straps around his head. He didn't offer similar protective gear to Troy.

Dieter opened the airlock door, pulling Troy with him into the small booth as if he were as light as a soap bubble. The sol-pols remained behind, but the station exec didn't seem worried. After a long, silent pause, the second door detached from its seals with a hiss, and they entered the lab space with Eli Strone.

Troy's stomach lurched and his skin turned clammy as he prepared himself to meet the mass murderer, expecting to see some inhuman monster with dripping fangs, blazing eyes, and scaly skin. Instead, Eli Strone was deeply preoccupied at a pulsed-laser bacterial sorter, a processing sieve that separated out desirable species from the unwanted ones. Adjusting focusing knobs with his large-knuckled hands, the big man hunched over a magnification viewer. His chocolate-brown hair was disheveled, and he hummed to himself, a long, uninterrupted note, like the drone of a machine.

"Strone, my boy!" Dieter Pan said, his voice muffled through the respirator. "This is Troy Boren, your new playmate."

Troy realized that as a convicted cold-blooded murderer, he himself was supposed to be as evil as this man! The thought nauseated him. Once again Troy shivered from the pervasive coldness that penetrated every deck plate, every breath of recycled air.

Strone, still intent on his work, repeatedly blinked his round, fixated eyes. "I work alone. You didn't ask me if I wanted a partner."

Dieter's face darkened. "I don't have to ask you anything, my boy." He turned to smile at Troy. "Mr. Strone here doesn't seem to understand the concept of authority here on OrbLab 2. I've tried to teach him over and over again, but I believe he's mentally deficient."

"Don't interrupt me," Strone said without flinching. "Dangerous stuff."

Dieter held Troy back near the airlock door, but the murderer didn't look the least bit interested in stopping his work. Dieter scowled, as if trying to think of some punishment for Strone.

"Why is this part of the process so dangerous?" Troy whispered.

Dieter rubbed his hands together, as if trying to start a fire with friction. The motion sent him bobbling against the metal wall. "Dangerous?" he said. "Ever hear of Mindfire, boy?"

Troy nodded. The unpleasant smells in the air suddenly took on a more ominous edge. Was he breathing the deadly plague organism right now?

"New employee orientation," the station exec said. "I'll only go into the gory microbiological details once, since prisoners don't usually care. But you're a bright kid, right?"

Troy shrugged uncomfortably. "Uh, I try to be."

Dieter gestured toward the wall to indicate the other lab complexes they had seen. "After being exposed to a certain mutagen, the precursor bacterium is likely to form two separate mutant strains after reproducing. One strain—thirteen percent of the offspring—makes Veritas. Do they still teach chemistry downstairs, boy?"

Troy tried not to look stupid. "I've audited class packs on the network."

"Good, then this should be easy for you. When the Veritas bacteria enter the human nervous system, they increase the efficiency of the dendrites to transport chemical messages across the synapses in the brain. The Veritas toxin acts as a chemical catalyst for the transport of ATP and ADP across nerve endings." He laughed. "Supercharged gray matter! You with me so far?"

Troy nodded.

"This results in an explosive increase in the sensitivity of nerve receptors, which allows a Truthsayer to—in effect—receive messages another person's brain is sending to itself."

Over at the pulsed-laser sorter, Strone suddenly grunted in alarm and lunged backward. A red light flashed on the side of the apparatus, and Strone moved like a manic whirlwind, sealing the system and exhausting it to space.

Dieter Pan clamped his hand against his respirator mask and made ready to leap for the airlock booth. Troy froze, unable to cry out. But Strone finished his emergency procedures, purged the system with cold nitrogen, blinked at them and spoke in an absolutely calm voice. "No problem," he said. "No problem."

Dieter relaxed, then immediately resumed his lecture. Troy found it difficult to concentrate, unable to switch gears from utter panic to quiet normalcy. "That's what happens with the good thirteen percent of the offspring," the station exec continued. "However, twenty-eight percent of the mutated bugs will be a horrific organism that causes a deadly encephalitic plague, like an incredibly severe form of meningitis. That's the Mindfire. It leaves its victims complete vegetables, their brains so dead that in most cases the heart and lungs cease to function as well. Nasty stuff. You don't want to catch it, boy."

"No, sir," Troy said.

"Want to know how it works?" Dieter asked eagerly, hopping into the air again so that he floated above Troy's eye level.

"Uh . . . sure," he said. Over at his station, Strone went back to work, apparently oblivious to his visitors.

Dieter's breath hissed through the hollow shell of his respirator mask. "The Mindfire mutation also produces a neurological toxin, but this one *inhibits* the transfer of nerve signals across the synapses. Shuts them right down. Naturally, as the disease spreads, the entire brain switches off, unable to send even the signals to keep the heart beating and the lungs filling. Dead as a door hinge. The poison that killed Guild Master Klaryus."

Troy pressed his lips together, breathing shallowly.

"So, if you added the numbers in your head—as I'm sure you did—you know that those two mutations account for forty-one percent of the first generation from the precursor bacteria. The remaining fifty-nine percent are unaffected, used as seed stock for the next generation, and we start the process all over again before they kill us."

Troy looked at the equipment, Strone's workstation, the emergency blowout hatches to the vacuum of space. "So, uh, the challenge comes in exposing the precursor to the mutagen, separating out the offspring we want, and dumping the deadly bugs into space."

"Bingo!" Dieter said. "That's what you'll be doing."

"Wow, what luck," Troy muttered.

Strone finally turned and spoke to them slowly, as if passing down a pronouncement from on high. "Accidents happen only to those who deserve them. Remember that, Dieter Pan. We'll be careful. Very careful."

"You'd better be," Dieter said to them sternly. "We have no intention of making an OrbLab 3."

Strone nodded, his eyes sparkling, as if the subject fascinated him. "You know, no one has ever gone back to dispose of the corpses on OrbLab 1. Still drifting there, alone. I wonder what the bodies look like by now."

Dieter Pan looked at Troy and Strone from behind his transparent facemask. "I can see that you two are going to work just fine together. Mr. Strone is falling behind, so you can help him catch up."

"I'm not falling behind," Strone said.

Dieter acted as if he hadn't heard. "He'll show you what to do."

Eli Strone gave Troy a deep, appraising look, as if judging his new companion. The station exec slipped into the airlock booth again and sealed it behind himself. Troy found himself alone with the mass murderer.

Strone nodded at him. "Partners."

# CHAPTER
## 20

Over the next several days Troy focused on his work with wild concentration, if only to keep his sanity. He spent his evenings locked in the cell, tense in the company of Eli Strone; they were silent companions, each in his own impenetrable world. Strone didn't seem to see Troy at all, and Troy was too nervous to attempt small talk.

Dieter Pan pretended to be a generous and benevolent administrator, though it was clear that he hated Strone. Troy observed that the station exec had a chaotic streak, reacting to certain situations and suggestions with overblown enthusiasm and a gleeful raising of his demonic eyebrows.

In a halting voice Troy had asked if he might be allowed to have pencils or paints to attempt a few sketches. Dieter Pan had clapped his hands with such gusto that the inertia sent him spinning adrift. "An artist!" he cried with feigned delight. "Be my guest. Mr. Strone will probably be annoyed with you, but he can be such a bastard sometimes."

Hours later Troy received a pack of bright grease pencils, safe and soft, which Troy could use as crayons. Paper was far too valuable a commodity, so he decided to use the grease sticks on the enameled wall of his cabin.

Troy selected one of the soft grease pencils from his cupped left hand. After polishing the smooth wall with his thin sleeve, Troy began to draw. He gazed out the cell's single windowport at the isolation of space. Below, the bubbly surface of Atlas swirled with the blue of oceans and the brown of continents. If he looked closely, Troy could discern small patches where the landholders had brought acreage to life.

He saw the half-eclipsed hemisphere of the Platform just emerging from the planet's shadow. Off in the distance, like a bright star, he could make out the other orbital lab, the canister that had been OrbLab 1—now dark and abandoned, reflecting sunlight but showing no outward signs of life, a grim reminder of the utmost need for caution in processing Veritas.

On his own side of the cell, Strone lay back on his bunk, legs stretched perfectly straight. He cradled a stringed musical instrument across his chest: a resonating box, a fretted neck, and a single long string that the killer twanged, sounding a lone hollow note. Strone plucked the string, listened to the vibrating overtones until they gradually faded, then plucked again, playing his single note over and over. It seemed to calm him, though each note was like an ancient form of water torture to Troy. He bit his lips, refraining from any complaint.

Strone caught Troy's sidelong glance. "Do you like my music?"

Troy jerked in alarm. What answer did Strone want to hear? Was he plucking his string just to see if he could agitate his cellmate? Would he grow furious if Troy gave the wrong answer? "It's . . . deceptively simple," Troy said.

Strone eyed the vibrating string as the note died into silence. "Yes—simple, but elegant." He strummed his instrument again.

Despite himself, Troy found the monotonous, hypnotic rhythm gradually relaxing. He studied the view out the windowport and dove into his new grease painting, intent on drawing the image in his mind. He thought of the Mindfire plague and the Veritas drug; its development interested him more acutely now that he was trapped inside the facility where it was produced. Information he had learned long ago, now seemed very important.

About 160 years ago a microbiologist named Foeria had been developing pharmaceuticals from Atlas microorganisms. In one of the few primitive bacteria able to lock into human systems, Foeria had accidentally discovered the telepathic boost obtainable through a simple mutation—and had used it to uncover the identity of a thief at their isolated laboratory. That had been the beginning of Veritas.

Foeria had unfortunately also stumbled upon the Mindfire mutation, and it had killed her. She had been its first casualty, and Troy fervently hoped that the drifting graveyard of OrbLab 1 would be the last. . . .

Troy sketched quickly, switching colors, using the side of his hand to blend the greasy pigments, smudging sharp lines into softer, broader strokes. Again he chose to draw an imaginary scene from an imaginary future. The land masses of Atlas were stippled with a lush and life-filled green. The sky swam with gauzy clouds that shone with reflected sunlight. OrbLab 1 sparkled brightly, lit with bustling activity. Sleek new shuttle-sleds traveled back and forth, carrying supplies in a burgeoning economy. The first orbital lab prospered, no longer just a great coffin in space. . . .

As Troy finished, he scribbled the black background of space, leaving random pinpoints of the white wall shining through as stars, more stars than were ever visible from the surface because of the colorful aurora.

He realized with a start that Eli Strone had stopped playing his single-note melody. Troy turned around to see the tall man looming over him, inspecting the new painting with a detached gaze.

"So . . ." Troy mumbled, at a loss for words, "do you like it?"

Strone stared for a long moment, his square jaw clenched as creases of concentration furrowed his brow and cheeks. He reached forward with one blunt finger and smeared downward at the very edge, wiping a few stray colored lines that had crossed the imaginary dividing line down the middle of their quarters onto Strone's side of the wall.

Troy flinched, waiting for an outburst of anger—but once Strone had rubbed away the trespassing lines, he nodded in satisfaction. "It's fine." He turned away and climbed back onto his bunk.

Troy shuddered. His heart pounded, imagined terrors whipping dizzily through his head. He felt as if he were living and working beside a ticking bomb.

Strone lay back on his pallet and embraced the stringed instrument again, plucking out its long, low note over and over into the night.

# CHAPTER

# 21

## i

Trident Falls thundered over the cliff, plunging in a headlong drop of three hundred meters into a rocky basin below and spraying up a rainbow mist.

Franz Dokken stood at the headwaters on a flat rock that extended into the milky turmoil of rapids above the falls. He looked out at the tumbling river that produced a wealth of energy for his hydroelectric plant to harness.

Above the cliff twin granite crests thrust out of the river, splitting it into the three ribbons of water that gave Trident Falls its name. Black overland wires stretched across the landscape, extending to substations where the electricity was sold to other landholdings.

After disposing of Schandra's body, Dokken had disappeared to his usual spot for a week-long rest while Maximillian returned to manage business activities—particularly to find a new foreman for the silk-production facilities.

Dokken had returned fresh and full of energy, ready to get back into tinkering with dozens of plans. No one questioned Schandra's disappearance. Maximillian leaked a story that she and Dokken had had a falling out, and most people assumed Schandra had been sent off to one of the outer villages.

Dokken had begun working on other transitions as well, since the loss of Cialben and his direct link with Veritas smuggling operations. Dieter Pan had not liked to slow down any of the shipments, but Dokken had insisted. Dieter was not to be trusted, far too enthusiastic, a loose cannon. But he did his part.

For a moment Dokken wondered how the poor patsy who had stumbled upon Cialben's body had fared. Troy Boren. He had probably been sentenced up to OrbLab 2 as well. What an irony! The unexpected scapegoat had smoothed over some of the rough edges in his own plan, because now the sol-pols were no longer investigating a murder. Guild Master Tharion must be tying himself into ethical knots with the quandary of knowing his Truthsayer had made a mistake.

Now, though, Dokken had other problems to solve.

One of his hydroelectric generators had begun faltering, and the Trident Falls engineers had finally taken it off line. Dokken used that as an excuse to go out to inspect the problem. After only nine days at the villa he was already growing restless. He enjoyed it better when he could "fast-forward" through the slow progression of his plans, to see the large-scale effects before he became interested in something else.

The gray mare was recovering nicely from the birth of her foal two weeks earlier, and Dokken had considered taking her out for the exercise—but he knew he would be gone for longer than a day, and she was still nursing. So Dokken rode his chestnut stallion on the long exhilarating trip out to Trident Falls. He had tied the stallion upriver. Now, as he squatted on the flat rock overlooking the falls, he could let his eyes drink in the vast distances and let his mind roam. . . .

He would go down into the warrens cut into the cliffs where the engineers tended the turbines, the hydroelectric generators. A waterwheel converted power from each of the three streams flowing down the cliff. Dokken had salvaged the generator systems from the original colony ship's stores. They had been pieces of vital equipment for establishing a thriving colony, and Dokken was the first landholder to put them to use.

Along the misty cliff faces, fast-propagating kudzu had spread up and down the river in only a few years' time. Downstream, still pools were now clogged with lush water hyacinths that also grew at a remarkable pace. These were originally considered garbage plants, unwanted weeds on Earth—but they grew well enough here to provide a usable biomass, vegetation that could be converted into methane gas or processed into animal feed.

Dokken had also introduced a community of fishes that fed on the hyacinths, insects that pollinated the flowers, and cliff swallows that ate the insects. It was remarkable, he thought, how such tiny footholds allowed living creatures to dig in their claws and hold on.

He stared out beyond the falls, through the mist rainbows, and out across the flat landscape painted by the raw morning sunlight. Dokken Holding was vast and untamed . . . yet it wasn't enough. He refused to be content when there was so much more on the entire world.

ii

When the original colony ship had arrived, the three captains studied the high-resolution images and divided up the main land mass by committee. They used their best satellite-scanned resource maps, allotting twenty landholder districts in the fairest possible manner.

They were so naive then, Dokken thought. He found it embarrassing to think back on those days.

Atlas offered plenty of room, but the land required a great deal of work before it could be made habitable. The twenty highest-ranking crew members became the first landholders, granted administrative power over vast sectors filled with a variety of natural resources. They bore names still familiar to most people on Atlas, though many records had been destroyed over the years—some of them by Dokken himself—and few of the struggling colonists spent much time reliving history.

Because every holding was different, specific lands were assigned by lottery, and all twenty landholders were supposedly content with what they received. The colonists, the supplies, the equipment were equally divided to put everyone on an equal footing.

The colony had to be set up with great planning—during their flight here, they had had five decades to plan, to model infrastructures, to decide on the best way to transplant an entire society. But on board the ship, with every aspect of life predictable and planned, they had forgotten how random nature could be. Their solutions were simplistic and wrong-headed, and the harsh realities of Atlas proved quite a shock.

Machinery broke down faster than specifications had predicted, and spare parts were at a premium before industrial facilities could be established to manufacture new equipment. As the machinery proved troublesome, actual manual labor became more valuable. Workers were constantly in demand.

The first-wave colonists remained in contact with Earth, in a one-way conversation with a twenty-year lightspeed transmission lag. Their intermittent reports were rosily skewed, showing doctored images of a beautiful planet with untapped potential. The ploy worked, and within sixty-nine years of their arrival, a second, fully equipped colony ship came filled with wide-eyed settlers: additions to the worker pool, who also had no hope of returning to Earth. Oddly, even though Atlas was a more difficult place than they had been led to believe, the second-wave colonists seemed happy to be away from the tightening repression at home.

Since that time, three other groups had arrived in their ships—the exiled criminals in the *Botany Bay* 147 years ago, the military mission in the *SkySword*, whose abortive attempt at a coup had been foiled by Dokken's friend Archimand 103 years ago, and finally the ill-advised Pilgrim refugees with their barely functional craft only 42 years ago.

The new ship on its way, expected to arrive in five years, claimed to be filled with new equipment and hardworking settlers—exactly what Dokken wanted to hear. The *EarthDawn* would knock Atlas society out of equilibrium, and Dokken had to be ready for it. None of the other landholders had made plans *big* enough, and so they would be taken by surprise.

But Dokken had proved he could be stronger; he could be patient. Given enough time, he would hold all of Atlas in his hand.

iii

Dokken descended the metal stairs bolted to the side of the cliff. The steel had been enameled to protect it from corroding in the constant spray. His leather riding gear was drenched by the time he finally reached the entry hatch to the cave chambers behind the waterfalls.

He undogged the lock and swung the heavy metal door open, slipping inside and yanking it shut behind him. Though the tunnels shone with bright glowpanels, the contrast between the brilliant sunshine and the harsh artificial light made him wait for the colors to stop dancing in front of his vision. He ran his fingers through his long hair to slick down the strands, and made his way to the intersection of the three tunnels, where the access grottos spread out into generator rooms.

One of the engineers, a young square-faced woman, came to meet him. "Ah, Master Dokken," she said and rubbed a hand across her cheek, leaving a smudge of dark graphite lubricant. "I'm glad you could come and help us inspect the third turbine. We found the problem, but it will take us a few days to fix it."

Dokken was annoyed at the delay but didn't let it show. Sweating despite the damp coolness inside the rocks, he unfastened his leather jacket, letting his loose cotton tunic air out. The walls were slick with a fine sheen of dew that reflected the harsh light. A subsonic hum surrounded him, vibrational echoes from the plunge of the water. "Was it something you could have planned for?"

The woman engineer grinned uncertainly. "I don't think anybody could have expected this, sir," she said. "Have a look. We've never seen anything like it."

The engineer led him into the large chamber where the waterfall spun huge turbines. The thundering waterfall was a white wall of static, directing electricity through transformers and distributed throughout the settled areas on Atlas. Pools of water lay like mirrors on the floor. Movable lights hung from the low rock ceiling, shining yellow-white illumination throughout the room.

Four technicians and engineers worked on the large piece of dark machinery. They had taken the main flywheel off-line, and the many-toothed gears stood like hungry grinding jaws. The engineers scrambled through the machinery and emerged covered with sludge, blackened silt that had been carried down the waterfall and shunted into the machinery.

One of the technicians, a rail-thin boy who couldn't have been more than sixteen, popped up from two interlocked gears holding handfuls of a dripping organic substance that resembled shorn hair washed in toxic sewage. "It's all over in here," he said. "Um, hello, Mr. Dokken." The boy held out his hands to show his disgusting prize. "You've never seen anything like this."

Dokken came forward, frowning and perplexed. The woman engineer said, "It's gotten all through the machinery somehow, tangling up the mechanisms."

Dokken poked at the mass in the boy's hands and plucked out a few strands. It was long and rubbery, but tough as piano wire, strands of gray-green and lavender that exuded a gummy mucus. "What is this?" he asked.

"Apparently native to Atlas," the engineer said. "A new strain of algae. It's in the rivers and now it's settling into the machinery."

Dokken wondered if this were some sort of destructive organism that another landholder had turned loose against him—but that was foolish, because everyone benefited from his hydroelectric plant. The primeval world of Atlas constantly proved far more unpredictable and hostile than even the most vindictive of landholders.

He scowled, then flung away the alien algae. "Scour it all out," he said, "then purge the whole generator with harsh caustics. You'd better take the other two generators off-line, one at a time, and do the same. But be careful with the runoff water—the caustics could kill the water hyacinths and the kudzu. Capture all your waste disinfectants, then find a cave or a dry canyon somewhere to store them."

The engineers nodded. The young boy climbed back inside the labyrinth of the generator turbine.

Everything on Atlas was so delicately interconnected. Dokken couldn't afford to make even a single mistake. He had woven his tapestry so carefully, he wouldn't be able to bear watching it unravel in his hands.

No, *that* he would never allow.

# CHAPTER

## 22

i

As their daily routine continued, Eli Strone refused to let Troy do any of the meticulous, dangerous work. Troy didn't mind, though being sealed in the quarantine-rigged compartment placed him in no less danger. He preferred working on computers anyway.

Self-absorbed, Strone reveled in dancing on the razor's edge of risk and survival. He monitored the sorting apparatus as mutated strains of bacteria sifted through the intersection of pulsed laser beams that separated the three types of offspring.

As the first week in prison bled into the second, he grew accustomed to the aching terror that was always present, reminding him that he had been falsely sentenced to OrbLab 2 and partnered with the most notorious mass killer in the history of Atlas. Troy longed for something more, and there was little to be had.

He did his share of the work with the inventory of bacterial specimens. He found that the percentages of Veritas offspring, Mindfire mutations, and unaltered precursors varied from the tallies Dieter Pan had specified, though on average the totals remained about right. Day by day, Dieter avoided the two of them, leaving them sealed in their isolated lab compartment; from the flick of his eyes and the forced sarcasm in his voice, Troy suspected the station exec was afraid of Strone.

They had a break for a few days when Dieter left the orbital lab to go down to the surface "for an important powwow." Troy wondered what the station exec could possibly be talking about; Strone didn't seem to care in the least.

Inventorying the bacterial specimens was similar to his work at the anchor point in First Landing. With his mind unoccupied, Troy used the integrated computer systems to double-check productivity along the drug-manufacturing line. The tracking didn't need to be done, and the station exec certainly had not requested it, but Troy wanted to be useful. No doubt the exact inventory specifications were calibrated and monitored, but Troy thought he might be able to make suggestions to increase the efficiency.

At his station Eli Strone hummed to himself, wrapped up in his work.

From studying production records, Troy learned that the two recent accident victims had been engaged in activities similar to what he and Strone did every day. The lost prisoners had been slammed outward by explosive decompression. They probably hadn't even had a chance to hear the alarms as the air blasted them into empty space.

Troy checked the station log, found no apparent reason for the triggered emergency system. A mistake, old Kareem Sondheim had suggested.

Glancing over at Strone, who was concentrating like a hungry predator on his work, as if daring a mistake even to suggest itself, Troy recalled something else: Sondheim had bemoaned the loss of an entire shipment of Veritas in the accident. But if the disaster had occurred in *this* compartment ... why would finished capsules have been stored here? As the accident had proved, this was the spot most likely to suffer a catastrophic dump of its atmosphere. Why risk placing such valuable supplies in this chamber? Finished capsules didn't belong here.

Troy researched the incident further and discovered to his surprise that an entire month's production had indeed been transferred here on the very morning of the accident. According to the computer records, the loose shipment had been sucked out into space when the airlocks automatically blew.

Troy sifted through additional files, captivated by the mystery, and did not notice when Strone ceased his humming. He looked up with a start to find the tall man standing over him and studying the screen with his impenetrable eyes. Troy forced himself not to squirm away.

Strone continued to study fixedly. "Those are old records," he said. "What have you found?"

For a moment Troy considered pretending that he had found nothing at all—then he decided it would be very dangerous to lie to Eli Strone. "A ... a discrepancy, I think," he said. "Probably nothing, but it caught my eye."

"Explain it to me," Strone said with intent interest. Troy took a deep breath, then summarized what he had learned about the lost shipment of Veritas.

Strone jabbed at a new line at the bottom of the screen log, using his blunt finger to indicate an access record. "Here, just before the accident," he said. "Two guards entered the lab area to inventory 'various materials.' They could have taken the shipment with them and not recorded it. Some of the guards on this station have a shadow of guilt about them—I've sensed it."

Troy blinked in astonishment. "But that would imply they knew the airlock was going to blow. And they left those workers inside, to certain death!" He paused as the train of thought kept rolling. "In that case, the records would indicate that all the Veritas capsules were lost—even though somebody still had them."

"Interesting," Strone said, but his jaw was clenched and unforgiving. "This is a prison station," he said. "Crime should not be happening here." Strone's big knuckled hands squeezed into fists that looked as powerful as meteors.

Troy grinned uncertainly. "If a staged accident like that could happen, all sorts of things could go wrong. Why, OrbLab 2 could smash into the Platform, knocking it down into the atmosphere in flames, striking the planet with enough force to alter the orbit of Atlas and maybe even send the whole world crashing into the sun itself!"

"Ah," Strone said with a solemn nod, "we think alike."

ii

"So . . . why did you do it?" Troy said to the wall in their quarters. He held the grease pencils in his hands. He had decided to use his free time creating a mural that would cover every speck of free wall space on his half of the cell.

Strone lay back on his bunk as always, plucking the single string on his instrument, staring up at the ceiling. Troy held his breath, not looking at the other man and praying that his question didn't trigger a violent rage.

He was surprised, actually, that it had taken him so long to ask Strone, though he doubted his partner would ever inquire the same thing of him. Troy had thought that such questions were inevitable and had dreaded the prospect of making excuses, trying to explain that he was actually innocent, that he had killed no one, that a Truthsayer had lied. But he didn't expect Strone would care.

"Why did I do what?" Strone asked as the tone from his plucked string faded. At last he seemed to be accepting Troy as part of his daily existence.

"Kill all those people," Troy mumbled, then busied himself scrawling colorful streaks across the wall to draw the low hills of the Mining District where he had grown up—but of course he would landscape it much better than he remembered. He would plant forests and beautiful flower gardens, with livestock on grassy hills rather than smelter smokestacks and mounds of discarded tailings from the mine shafts.

Strone remained silent for a long moment, not even strumming his instrument. "I had my reasons," he answered.

"Good reasons, I hope?" Troy said, suddenly doubting the wisdom of this line of conversation.

"Somebody had to kill them," Strone said. "I couldn't trust the Truthsayers. No one should trust the Truthsayers. They are as tainted as everyone else."

A cold shiver rippled through Troy. "What . . . what do you know?"

Strone speared him with a sharp glance. "Why do you care?"

"Because . . . because the Truthsayer lied about me, too. I thought I was the only one."

Eli Strone shook his head, then lay back on his bunk again, strumming the single string. "No. They are corrupt, too. I worked for them. They were my ideal of justice—perfect, impartial, *clean*. But I know they poisoned Guild Master Klaryus. I saw him die twitching from the Mindfire poison. I saw that the tainted capsule was no accident, though I can't be certain who did it. It wasn't Tharion, though—he is a good man. I trust Tharion."

Troy tried to reconcile what he remembered of the events from the past several years, but he had been isolated out in the Koman Mining Districts, and the internal conflicts of the distant Truthsayers Guild had never been a high priority in the miners' gossip. "So what did you do?"

Strone took a long time to answer. "I could not reconcile what I had learned about secret treachery within the Guild with what I believed justice should be. I could no longer work for the Guild, and so I left. I wandered the landscape, working, searching—until I realized that *I* must be the dispenser of justice. I could not rely on anyone else. The people I met needed justice. So I punished those people, all twenty-three of them. For starters."

The big man sat up on his bunk, and Troy tried not to tremble as he continued to sketch with the grease pencils.

"Guilty people should be punished," Strone said. "Everyone on OrbLab 2 is already being punished"—he frowned as if deeply disturbed by something—"but everyone continues to think evil thoughts. It sours them, corrupts them. I can see it all." He raised his eyebrows. "I can read their thoughts, you know. I have my reasons for what I do."

Troy gave an uneasy chuckle, trying to impose a more light-hearted tone on the grim conversation. "Well," he said, "I hope *I* never give you a reason." Then he clamped his mouth shut, mentally kicking himself.

"You haven't . . . yet," Strone said.

THE BURDEN OF PROOF

# CHAPTER

## 23

### i

The storm struck First Landing with a wild, forceful last gasp to end the rainy season. The weather scopes on the Platform above had issued strident warnings, but nothing had prepared the colonists for such severity.

The Truthsayers battened themselves into the protection of Guild Headquarters and listened to the howling gale that thrummed against the thick hull. Sheets of rain sloshed against the stained glass windows.

Guild Master Tharion brooded out at the darkness, seeing bright lights from the industrial complex near the mag-lev station. Every sensible person had gone home for the night, and even the sol-pols on patrol spent their shifts huddled under doorway overhangs or behind rain-protection fields.

In their shared quarters Qrista finished scrubbing her face at the water basin and patted it dry with a plush towel. She wound the braid around her head, then tied a crimson sash around her slender waist.

"Ready to join me for the meeting?" Qrista said.

Tharion nodded. "I'm curious about what she's going to report," he said, though he already guessed what the head of Sondheim's internal investigation team would say. "They've resented me as Guild Master anyway, ever since I called them to task after the death of Klaryus."

"And well you should have," Qrista said.

"That doesn't mean they've forgiven me for it. They'll issue their findings, but I don't expect to believe them."

Clad in his formal white robes, Tharion held out his arm, and Qrista took it. The two of them walked together in proud silence to a turbolift that took them down to the large gathering chamber.

All representatives from the Landholders Council had taken refuge inside Headquarters just as the storm struck. The atmospheric turbulence was great enough that the descending space elevator had been halted and sent back up to the Platform—the first time that had happened in thirty-four years—along with most of the investigators.

Only the OrbLab 2 station exec himself, ostensibly the head of Sondheim's internal investigation team, was available for the meeting, since he had come down to First Landing a day early on "other business." With all the other Council members already gathered, Tharion refused to postpone the presentation. Dieter Pan knew the findings well enough.

The other members of the Landholders Council sat in their seats chatting with each other, their expressions guarded, secrets veiled behind placid faces. Some drank warm beverages, feeling an irrational chill because of the muffled howling of the wind, though the temperature diffusers had increased the room temperature two degrees above its normal level.

Dieter Pan, wearing a dark green jumpsuit and wrapped in a warm cape, as if he were cold, sat isolated in the guest speaker's chair, looking cranky and nonplussed. His body was wiry and lithe, but he moved slowly in the planetary gravity, as if it required an effort just to lift his gaze from one person to another. He did not look pleased to be giving this report unsupported by the rest of his team, the ones who would cite all the numbers and back him up with jargon from the process line. He did not look pleased at all.

When Tharion and Qrista walked in, all heads turned in their direction. Qrista's two supporting Mediators had already arrived, sitting together and watching the other attendees with bemused interest.

"All right," Tharion said, "let's get this over with so we can all get back to our nice warm quarters and ride out the storm." Some members of the audience chuckled. Others nodded in agreement.

While Qrista took her place at the Speaker's pedestal, Tharion fetched them each a terra-cotta mug of herb tea, then sat beside his wife. All eyes turned in anticipation toward Dieter Pan.

After Qrista had dispensed with the usual announcements, Dieter raised his curled eyebrows and waited impatiently for permission to speak. "I can't give you all the details without full documentation from my team members. I wouldn't want to step on anybody's toes—especially not in this gravity! But, so sad to say, they are now stranded up on the Platform." He cracked his knuckles with a loud sound like snapping bamboo. "There you have it. But, all is not lost! I can share the summary data on my computer pad." He held up a small granite-colored plaque.

"I can copy the files to each of you, but the final result is indisputable. We've checked every step of Veritas processing, manufacturing, and shipping from its creation at OrbLab 2 to its being shuttled over to the Platform, and finally its shipment down the space elevator, at which point it falls into the hands of the Guild's elite guard." Dieter snorted, as if that explained everything. "Look, we found no evidence whatsoever that there has been tampering on *our* end of the production line. All samples we tested checked out. So, you'll have to find some other way to harass us, Guild Master. Fabricate some other trumped-up charge.

"The team members interviewed good old Kareem himself, and all the OrbLab 2 workers. Frankly"—he turned a false jovial smile at the Guild representatives as he spouted his poison—"I think we're chasing ghosts here. Our friend Mediator Qrista should look elsewhere for her wild conspiracies from now on."

Qrista stiffened, and Tharion placed his fingertips at the center of her back, as if he could bleed off the pressure building within her.

"Hey, I've got an idea," Dieter Pan said, holding up one finger. "Maybe you should look into members of your own Guild. They've got the greatest opportunity to sneak around here on the surface."

Qrista lunged to her feet, her pale face flushed, though she managed to keep her voice calm and professional. "Mister Pan, you are out of line. Our Truthsayers are above reproach, and all Guild workers submit to regular scans of their minds. Your conjecture is ill considered."

Dieter Pan crossed his arms indignantly over his chest. "Whatever you say. Just offering a suggestion. Didn't realize you wanted to find a scapegoat rather than track down the truth. I would have said that my own OrbLab workers are 'above reproach,' but that didn't stop you from insisting on yet another investigation."

Qrista sat down quickly without replying. She whispered to Tharion, "Can you believe that?"

He made a noncommittal sound; his own thoughts had tied themselves in knots. He knew that Dieter Pan had made a

perfectly legitimate suggestion, especially when coupled with
Tharion's own suspicions about Kalliana's involvement, her cover-
up. Even upon returning from her assignment at Sardili Shores,
she had been just as withdrawn and confused. That, added to the
recent failure of the talented young candidate Ysan, made him very
uneasy indeed. Something was definitely wrong. Perhaps the
heart of the smuggling was to be found here inside Guild Headquarters after all.

As the Council members buzzed among themselves with
gossip—oh how they loved to see the Guild put down!—Tharion
stood up and struck the brass bell that demanded silence of the
audience.

"I suggest we take our time to study Mr. Pan's data. You are
all welcome to stay here and finish your tea. I, on the other hand,
am going to retire for the evening."

He and Qrista left, and as the wind and rain hammered down
on Guild Headquarters, Tharion wondered if an even greater
storm might be brewing within the metal walls.

ii

Because of his position, Guild Master Tharion was politically
required to see any landholder who came to the Headquarters and
requested an audience.

Two days after the furious storm, Victoria Koman made the
trek into First Landing and pounded on the sloping metal doors
of the SkySword. She brought her seventeen-year-old adoptive son
Michel Van Petersden.

The elite guard outside Headquarters gave the two of them a
pro forma search for hidden weapons, then led them through the
cargo doors and into the smooth corridors. Brown-sashed Guild
workers manning their computer stations at the bridge center
looked up curiously as the guards showed the visitors in.

Tharion stood by the door to his private ready room. Smiling,
he motioned them inside. "Welcome, Landholder Koman," he
said, squeezing the leathery hand that gripped his. She was an
iron-hard old woman with a hatchet face and eyes so bright and
darting they seemed made of quicksilver. Koman's entire body
was sinewy, toughened from a life of excruciatingly hard work in
her Mining District, which provided the bulk of metals and alloys
for Atlas.

Michel Van Petersden's straw-colored hair was neatly cut. With his high cheekbones and firm jaw, the youth looked very little like his father, Abraham Van Petersden, whom Franz Dokken had slain in his violent takeover of the holding. Victoria Koman—who had family troubles of her own—had adopted the infant Michel, raising him in her own holding.

Tharion wondered if his two guests resented how much time he spent with their enemy Dokken, his own mentor. Franz Dokken was no chivalrous knight, Tharion knew. Dokken was a man who took advantage of every opportunity and twisted it to his own ends. So long as Tharion's actions did not contradict Dokken's desires, the two would remain friends and close allies—but he suspected that situation would quickly change the moment the Guild Master became a hindrance to Dokken.

"I am pleased to see you, young Michel," he said, gesturing for his guests to be seated. "You've grown quite a lot in the year or so since I last made a visit to your adoptive mother's holding." The young boy seemed incredibly alert and attentive. His eyes drank in every detail.

"True," Victoria Koman said; her voice was harsh but strong. "You should get out more, Guild Master. The world is not entirely contained within these walls."

Rather than taking offense, Tharion laughed. "You're exactly right, Lady Koman. I wish I could. Now, what can I do for you?"

Koman leaned forward in her seat, like an animated piece of human leather. "I want you to truth-read him, Guild Master," she said.

"But . . . why?" he asked. "What has the boy done?" Tharion looked probingly at young Michel, who stared through the stained glass window.

Outside in the streets work crews were still cleaning up after the storm, replacing shattered greenhouse panels in the agricultural complexes. Others, shirtless and in tattered slacks rolled up to their knees, used brooms and shovels to clean the cobblestone streets, brushing silt and mud back into gutters where it would eventually be washed away. Bedraggled, once-colorful banners had been soaked and torn to shreds over merchants' kiosks.

"Michel has done nothing," Koman said, looking at her foster son. "Nothing that I know of. I want you to reassure me as to what I already believe is true. Is he a good man? Let me know the color of his heart."

Tharion folded his hands, stared at the faint lines on his

knuckles as he tried to collect his thoughts, and finally looked back at Koman. "This is a very unusual request. Even though I assume he is willing to submit to a reading, I need to know why you are doing this. My abilities to look into another person's mind are not to be used for sport."

Victoria Koman shook her head. "No, Guild Master, not for sport, but to determine the fate of a holding. As you know, my oldest son was killed in an accident in the mining tunnels some twelve years ago. My oldest daughter had no interest in management and ran off to live with a potter out in one of my villages, where she refuses to use her family name. My next daughter is retarded, and though I love her in my own way, she is unable even to read and write. I have two other sons who are boisterous and unreliable—and though they are my own descendants, they are not fit for the responsibility of running an entire holding.

"Michel is my adopted son," she said. Tharion could see she was trying to smother an outpouring of maternal pride. "He is exactly what I wished for in a child—intelligent, dedicated, loyal, not afraid to speak his own mind, and not too proud to do what he's told." She lowered her voice.

"There are events afoot, Guild Master, great changes ahead. I'm a tired old woman, and though death will take me kicking and screaming, I have no doubt that I'll be gone before too many more decades are out. I want to make sure that I have trained someone to be a worthy successor. Michel seems to have an instinctive understanding of power. Look into his mind and tell me if he is the person I believe him to be . . . or if I must resign myself to leaving my holding in weaker hands."

Tharion considered this. "I agree." He stood up, smoothed his robes, straightened his royal blue sash as if to emphasize his rank, then leaned forward to brush his fingertips against the straw-colored hair at Michel's temples. "This won't hurt," he said. "You won't even notice it."

"I know," the boy whispered.

Tharion closed his eyes and opened his thoughts, letting himself fall into the young man's mind . . . cruising over Michel's thoughts, his feelings, his conscience. It had been a while since he had done such a thing, and the images were oddly blurred. Tharion had difficulty penetrating, though he had taken his weekly booster of Veritas only two days earlier. It was easy enough to see into this innocent mind, though. . . .

He withdrew from the probe with a sigh, blinking his granite-gray eyes and smiling at Victoria Koman. "You should be proud of your son," he said, intentionally using the term. "He is everything you believe him to be."

Michel Van Petersden beamed, and in a surprising and unexpected show of warmth, the brittle old woman leaned over to embrace the boy. "I'm so relieved," she said. "Now my planning can continue."

The two were led out of the ready room, but Tharion remained in his office, pondering the growing troubles that Victoria Koman seemed to anticipate.

# CHAPTER

## 24

### i

The fire in the hearth crackled, shedding orange light across the tiles and warding off the evening chill. Franz Dokken lounged in his chair with a glass of Chianti in his right hand, cupping his palm around the smooth crystal. He sipped the wine, for once not noticing its sour taste as he studied the wall map of Atlas.

Dokken ran a fingertip along his lips and stared at the topography from the ocean's edge and river deltas of Sardili Shores, to the metal-rich hills of Koman, the tall mountains of Toth, the rolling pasturelands of Bondalar, the lake district of Carsus, and others, including his own rocky desert.

Red dots marked the locations of the scattered Pilgrim settlements. Many landholders had wisely kept the settlements small and widely dispersed, but Joachim Sardili, the kindhearted buffoon, had allowed the hooded atavisms to settle wherever they wished. Sardili claimed it kept the fanatics happy. But to what purpose? They were a disruptive influence, a random factor, people who didn't operate under the same rules and mores that Dokken understood.

But Sardili liked being tolerant, for some reason, letting the Pilgrims pursue their own lifestyle . . . live and let live so long as they followed certain simple rules of human behavior. Sardili was incapable of seeing how good intentions could easily be twisted.

Joachim Sardili had assembled the components of a bomb— and Dokken himself was busily priming it.

Maximillian, who frequently slipped into villages disguised as the Pilgrim "Adamant," whispered treason, spread sedition, and occasionally even performed nighttime vandalism that could be blamed on others. It was laughably easy, and Sardili remained completely baffled by it.

Maximillian had spread the word that the Pilgrims were to make a show of solidarity: three weeks hence they would all gather at the main village of Sardili Shores, and as a unified force, demand a homeland. The Pilgrims were so dedicated and unmindful of adversity, they would walk overland for days just to reach the appointed gathering place. Sardili would be forced either to carve up his holding or butcher the Pilgrims . . . and Dokken knew Sardili would never hurt his own workers.

Maximillian/Adamant had also dropped hints that he feared for his own safety, that the evil Sardili and his sol-pols were on his trail, outraged . . . that he, Adamant, was soon to be imprisoned for his work to win the Pilgrims their freedom. This fostered an angry atmosphere of mistrust and suspicion.

Dokken couldn't imagine how the setup might work any better. Finishing off the rest of his Chianti, he ran a tongue along his lips, then began to study the boundaries of the other holdings.

Maximillian stood at the archway with an insistent expression on his craggy face. "Master Dokken," he said. "A message, sir. The incoming colony ship has sent another broadcast. We are recording the transmission, but I thought you'd want to watch it real-time."

Dokken flung himself out of the chair. The *EarthDawn*'s captain usually repeated the broadcast—but just in case . . . They ran up the spiral stairs in the northernmost turret of the villa. On the roof a wire mesh dish antenna spread out, pointed toward the stars.

The approaching colony ship was still years out on its half-century voyage, and though the *EarthDawn*'s distance diminished with every moment, the transmission lag was still seven months . . . which made direct conversation impossible. However, the occasional update transmissions allowed Dokken to plan.

The new colony ship had begun transmitting to Atlas thirty years earlier, and Dokken had begun his long-term mission. The *EarthDawn* had broadcast an announcement that the great crisis on Earth was past, and decades of that new dark age had finally come to an end.

The captain, a bearlike black man named Omar Psalme, had transmitted his news and images on the open colonial frequency. His thousands of hardworking colonists, families wealthy with supplies and much-needed technology, were anxious to set up their lives and become part of the new world.

The news had created quite a stir on Atlas. Long ago, Dokken had taken communications gear from the original colony ship, and periodically he tried other frequencies, attempting to contact the *EarthDawn* privately so he could transmit his own version of events to contradict the official messages from the Truthsayers Guild. For several years now, he had been engaged in a private dialog with Psalme . . . not overly fruitful, but a good foundation nevertheless.

On the Platform, Kareem Sondheim had also established contact with the ship; he and Dokken would have the incoming *EarthDawn* passengers completely brainwashed by the time they arrived here. . . .

As he and Maximillian reached the tower room, Dokken saw the image of Captain Psalme finishing his transmission, adding his concluding remarks, and ending the message.

"We've recorded it, but the loop should repeat anyway, sir," Maximillian said.

Dokken hunched close to the viewplate. The captain's image reappeared after a flicker of static. He had a wide puffy face, and his jaw ballooned out in a frizzy, coal-black beard. Psalme had aged during the last few years of the journey, though the high velocity of his ship made him experience time in a slightly compressed fashion from an outside frame of reference.

"Once again we send our greetings to you, all people of Atlas," Captain Psalme said, obviously reading from a prepared text on an unseen screen in front of him. His voice was a deep growl. "Our anticipation grows with each passing day. We know Atlas may seem a bleak and difficult place to you—but to us, after leaving a bruised and wounded Earth, and after voyaging through cold space for decades, your world will be like paradise.

"There will be many differences between my voyagers on the *EarthDawn* and your people. Our societies have diverged greatly in the centuries we have been apart, but we look forward to working with you, to integrating ourselves into a new life. Though we are saddened by our need to leave the homeworld, we bring with us many lessons learned from years of hard experiences on Earth, repression, and dictatorships. We hope we can apply what we have learned to make Atlas a better place."

Dokken snorted at that and looked at Maximillian, who nodded in agreement.

"We have little to report here. Several more births. Two accidental deaths. Life goes on, and we look forward to making our lives on a new world. End of transmission," the captain said and switched off. Because his message was so brief this time, the *EarthDawn* repeated it a third time, but Dokken wasn't listening.

As he watched the captain's face and studied the details of the cabin behind him, Dokken found himself drifting into a reverie, recalling what it had been like on the original ship: the long years . . . the endless waiting . . . the boredom . . . the scheming. . . .

ii

Subjective time on the fifty-year journey had been shortened through several effects. The ship itself, traveling at a significant fraction of the speed of light, experienced a noticeable time dilation, which shaved off a few years. Because of the immensely long trip—not to mention the simple need to conserve supplies for so many people—the crew and passengers spent much time in deepsleep chambers, where they did not age as time passed. The original refugees from Earth had no wish to arrive at their new home as withered old cripples.

The colonists knew all the hazards before they left Earth. They had read the warnings, the disclaimers. But en route the difficulties and the tedium became personal. Dokken remembered it well.

Irreparable neurological damage occurred if the human body was placed in deepsleep for more than fifty percent of the trip, or for more than two weeks at a time. The deepsleep allotments were carefully monitored; no matter how bored or depressed the passengers might become, they could not sleep away into eternity.

That forced a constant transition aboard the ship: some colonists waking, others going down to sleep. Dokken never knew whom he might encounter, when he might see someone again. The setup required there to be three alternating captains on board, so that one could be on duty, while a second was off shift, and a third frozen in deepsleep.

Franz Dokken had been one of the three original captains. He was the only survivor of the original complement of crew and passengers that had landed 231 years before. Kareem Sondheim, a deformed baby born on the journey, had spent his entire overlong life in zero gravity, too handicapped to survive on the surface where his birdlike bones would snap from his own bodyweight.

The other two captains, long since dead, had founded the

powerful landholdings of Toth and Koman many generations earlier. Their descendants knew nothing of Franz Dokken's real background. He had subtly altered records enough times in the preceding two centuries, resetting his recorded birth date every few decades so that no one knew how old he truly was. By being patient, he remained ready for whatever opportunities presented themselves. And they always did. He had lived much longer than anyone else could remember.

The time aboard the ship had passed as a monotonous blur . . . but the centuries since the landing had been engrossing. Dokken found it fascinating to watch the developing colony on Atlas, the emerging and pliable society. It was a great sociological experiment, and he found he had the time and patience to watch large-scale events, causes and effects. He understood human nature, perhaps better than anyone else who had ever lived.

His lips formed a calm, self-satisfied smile.

Beside him Maximillian stood, curious as to why Dokken wanted to watch the *EarthDawn* message again. "Did I miss something significant in his words, Master Dokken?"

Dokken shook his head. "No," he said. "In fact, it was a particularly uninteresting transmission." He cracked his knuckles. "Are you scheduled to become Adamant and go to Sardili Holding soon?"

Maximillian nodded his bald head. "Soon."

"Good," he said. "Everything is going exactly as planned."

"Naturally, sir," Maximillian said, as if the point was obvious.

*Naturally*, Dokken thought.

# CHAPTER
## 25

### i

The nightmares were relentless, and Kalliana woke up screaming again.

Though she found herself in the safety of her comfortable quarters in the Truthsayers Guild, she gasped for breath. Her heart raced along at the speed of a mag-lev train, but she focused on the familiar smooth walls, the cool whiteness of enameled deck plates, the out-of-place wool rugs on the floor. No bloodstains, no echoing screams. Just her room.

She could not live like this.

Becoming a Truthsayer was not a choice she had made herself. She had been taken as an embryo from the genetic library up on the Platform and raised in the Guild with no family other than her fellow Truthsayers. This was her existence. She had been shaped for this. Her life had been blessed and easy because of her status—but now it was killing her.

Cold sweat encased her, like a sheath of ice on her pale skin, raising goose bumps. She clasped her arms over her small breasts, shuddering, and turned up the heaters in her quarters, knowing it wouldn't help. She could smell the spicy aromas of her uneaten dinner still sitting on her low table. Kalliana had had no real appetite for some time.

Her nightmares were the same, always the same. Eli Strone's bloody, brutal justice. His rationale, insidiously working on her own conscience, insisting that she *understand* what he had done. But the dreams were mixed with the guilt and horror she'd found in Troy Boren's mind as well: his startling visions of the murdered victim lying in a darkening pool on the concrete floor. His guilt felt so different, though—different. . . .

*Why?* she thought. Why was there so much evil on such a small, isolated world—and why did she have to confront it?

The turmoil she'd seen in Troy's mind struck a discordant note opposite, if that were possible, to Strone's cold viciousness. Something wasn't making sense here. It was as if her subconscious, programmed by years of training in ethics, was sending her a signal. *Something wasn't right. Not right.*

In darkness she felt her way over to the window that looked out across the sleeping city of First Landing. Kalliana placed her fingertips against the cool barrier of stained glass and watched fixedly through the colored wedges at the distorted streetlights that twinkled like counterfeit stars across the landscape. As she breathed against the glass, a fog of steam clustered there. The weather must have grown cold outside. The city slumbered . . . so quiet, so secretive.

*Truth Holds No Secrets.*

The motto of the Truthsayers Guild burned through her mind like a brushfire, and she shuddered again. She recalled the tragedy of Ysan, with all his hopes dashed because of one failure . . . now condemned to a life of exile in Toth Holding, away from the Guild, away from all the safe and stable things he had known. She thought of her own inexplicable mental blanking during the truthsaying at Sardili's village—and the unfathomable surprise she had seen on the face of the old Pilgrim woman Serenity.

Something was wrong. And not just with her. Ysan should never have failed his straightforward test—Kalliana had exercised with him, knew the depth of his truthsaying talent. He had the skills, and the willingness, but somehow he had not been able to render a correct verdict. What had he missed?

As it continued to haunt her, Kalliana felt again that the sensation of guilt she read in Troy's mind had been *different*. She had been too frightened, too mentally crippled to dig deep enough to find the real answers. The true answers. She had made assumptions. She had relied on her instincts—but *Truth Holds No Secrets*. Had she been unwilling to dig to the core of Troy's truth—or *unable?*

What if she had been wrong? Could she have made a mistake? A mistake! Truthsayers were not allowed to make mistakes. Never. The nightmares and her conscience wouldn't leave her alone.

She squeezed her eyes shut and concentrated, trying to throw her thoughts out like a net across the sleeping city, to touch the

citizens, capture a glimpse of their drab lives, their uneasy dreams—
but she heard only a roaring silence from the populace. She had
been struck mind deaf.

Kalliana's heart knew what she was afraid to admit to herself.
She had to face what she had done, and she had to make it right.

ii

"I need to speak with you, Guild Master," she said, trying to
find strength for her voice. She had located him down on the
arboretum decks. "There's something I must tell you."

Tharion stopped inspecting one of the dwarf pear trees and
gave her a stern look. She hadn't realized until this moment just
how much taller he stood, how small she now felt.

"I'm glad you finally came of your own free will, Kalliana," he
said. "I was planning to begin a rigorous investigation, and you
would have been its first subject—as I'm sure you could guess.
How could you do such a thing? The shake-up from this will
damage the Guild for years!"

He kept his voice low so the brown-sashed workers in the
engine levels could not hear them over the background noise of
water pouring through pipes, ventilation fans whirring at the
ceiling. He motioned for her to follow him into one of the narrow
greenhouses, where sunlamps compensated for the gray dreariness
of the skies outside. They walked between rows of pepper and
tomato plants under mist-irrigation systems.

"But why?" Kalliana asked in astonishment, remembering
now how he had looked at her with suspicion the last several times
they had spoken. "How could you know?"

Two agricultural workers entered the far end of the greenhouse and stopped abruptly as they noticed the Guild Master and
a Truthsayer apparently looking for privacy. Tharion gestured
dismissively, and the two workers scurried out, still carrying their
empty baskets.

Tharion turned back to look at her. "I know Veritas has been
leaking from our stores out to the citizens. You're the only link I
know. I just don't understand how you succeeded in smuggling
the capsules out of the armory vault."

Kalliana's baffled expression must have surprised him. "Smuggling Veritas? I don't know what you're talking about."

This time Tharion was taken aback. He must have known no

Truthsayer would tell another a bald-faced lie, since Tharion could easily read the truth from her if he chose. "Then why did you want to see me? It's something about your verdict of Troy Boren, isn't it?"

Kalliana took a long, deep breath to summon up all her courage. She looked away from him, focusing on a bell pepper ready to be picked. "Yes. My abilities . . . the Veritas—I think I made a mistake," she said, "and found an innocent man guilty."

The Guild Master appeared suddenly surprised, with an odd undertone of . . . relief? she wondered. He frowned, deeply perplexed. "What made you change your mind? Have you found new evidence in the case?"

"No," Kalliana said. She filled her lungs again with the lush greenhouse scent, then let her breath out slowly. Her mind whirled, and finally the explanation bubbled out in a rush: the nightmares, her abortive truthsaying at Sardili's village, the unfocused dismay in Troy's mind that she had misinterpreted as guilt.

"And Ysan—I can't believe he failed his test, either, Guild Master. He was young, yes, but stronger than I was." Kalliana looked away. "I'm worried. The Veritas no longer seems to be working for me, maybe not for Ysan, either. What if we've lost our tolerance?"

Tharion stared at her, his expression both appalled and disappointed. "The Guild can no longer trust you to perform your duties, Kalliana."

The words struck panic within her. "I know," she said miserably. "I know. I may have to resign."

Tharion shook his head, a saddened, lost look on his face. "My investigation will still proceed. There is much more going on here than you suspect. Please let me read you so that I can know the extent of your mistake."

Kalliana was startled, but agreed. She hadn't been probed by another Truthsayer since her original confirmation in the Guild— but Tharion was right, and she stepped closer to him, tilting her narrow elfin face up to him. He cupped both of his hands at the sides of her head, resting his fingertips in her hair, touching her temples. He closed his eyes, then she closed hers.

Kalliana waited, enduring stoically. She felt nothing . . . but then, she didn't expect to. The tendrils of Truthsayer thought were invisible and subtle. To make it easier for Tharion, she recalled everything she knew, what she had seen in Troy's mind and also, reluctantly, the images she had taken from Strone.

Tharion held her head for a long time; his grip tightened, squeezing until it hurt, as if he were trying to crush the thoughts out of her head. Kalliana flinched. He released her. She opened her eyes to see the Guild Master flustered and surprised, unsure of himself.

"Do you agree?" Kalliana said. "Do you think I might be right?"

"Yes, yes," Tharion answered distractedly. "I must think about this further." His brow furrowed, and he turned away from her. "I need to think about this," he said again, then faced her one last time. The hissing sprinkler systems in the greenhouse came on, filling the air with a faint mist. "Are you willing to do what must be done to rectify this mistake? Will you do what I ask—if I can find a solution?"

Kalliana's stomach twisted itself into a painful knot, but she had gone too far to back away now. "I have no other choice."

# 26

i

In the darkness of his private stateroom Tharion sat shaking in Qrista's arms. His wife had turned all the lights down, and she hugged him tightly. As he squeezed his eyes shut, he could smell the cotton of her robe, the fresh scent of her skin, her hair.

"I couldn't read her," he said again. "Nothing! That's never happened before. It terrified me."

Qrista pressed his shoulder with her hard fingers, emphasizing that she was there to support him. Tharion let the words and the shock continue to pour out of him. "It was a loss of balance. My thoughts slipped away like water through my hands. I don't think Kalliana noticed anything—*but I couldn't read her.*"

Qrista's breathing grew more rapid, and he could feel her tension. Without trying, his mind caught a flicker of her emotions, enough to show that perhaps he might still have a spark of Truthsayer abilities after all. She was rigid with rage.

"Your suspicions were misplaced. Something must be happening to the drug itself," she said. "And Kalliana raises the same questions I did. You know Ysan's abilities—he should *never* have failed his test. He was destined to be a Truthsayer, far more powerful than even a Mediator like me. You already knew Kalliana had made a mistake with Troy Boren's verdict.

"So the problem is more widespread than we thought." She sighed heavily, turning her face away so that her words projected into the darkness. "It's affecting all of us. Tharion, it's your responsibility to do something about it! Find some answers— you're the Guild Master."

Qrista had found exactly the right thing to give him back his sense of direction and distract him from his turmoil. He had to get to the root of the Veritas problem, to capture and sentence those people who were undermining the power of his beloved Guild. His need bordered on obsession . . . which wasn't necessarily a bad thing. He had waited far too long, ignoring clues and innuendos, reluctant to put the pieces together.

Qrista's lips were so close to his ear that he felt the hot steam of her breath. "Test the Veritas. We need to know if it was tampered with."

Tharion lowered his lips, kissing her shoulder. "You're right."

Qrista increased the room lights to a rosy glow. Her ice-blue eyes bored into his from above high cheekbones; her expression brooked no compromise. "And if you *do* find something wrong with the Veritas, you must bring Ysan back—and you must set Troy Boren free. He's innocent."

Tharion closed his eyes. "Ysan must never find out. That would cause too much damage—he's been sent off to Toth, and I'm sure he'll be quite happy as a Magistrate. As for Troy Boren, I know he shouldn't be in prison. . . but it will damage the Guild's credibility to set him free."

"That's a poor excuse," she said sharply. "Just say there is new evidence. Retract the verdict."

Tharion pulled away from her. "We can't do that. Think of the Guild!"

She scowled at him. "What am I missing? An innocent man has been sentenced to OrbLab 2, and you know it! What am I missing?"

Tharion held his hands out to her, beseeching. "If we change this verdict, then we'll be admitting that truth is not as absolute as we've always insisted. Truthsayers are not allowed to make mistakes. We can't just shrug and change our minds. If we cite some mysterious new evidence and let Troy Boren free, we'll be buried under an avalanche of appeals on other cases."

"And what if there *have* been other mistakes?" Qrista asked coldly.

Tharion avoided the possibility. "The Guild would have to spend all its time for months endlessly reconfirming the guilt of everyone we've already sentenced. That's what our whole system on Atlas was set up to prevent!

"You've read how it was on old Earth, with legal systems as full of pits and traps as quicksand. Once you stepped into the legal labyrinth, victims and criminals alike spent the rest of their lives lost in appeals and counterappeals, with never a firm decision being made. Here, Truthsayers make that final decision: we read the truth and we announce our verdict. Period."

Qrista faced him squarely, not backing down. "I'm not a child, Tharion. I was raised in the Guild just as you were."

He lowered his voice, looking down at his fingers to avoid her accusatory expression. "Our system will not function unless we are perceived as infallible, utterly beyond reproach. If the citizens stop believing in the Truthsayers, then we lose everything."

She crossed her arms over her chest, annoyed and disappointed in him. "Think of your own ethics, then. Is it better to sacrifice an innocent man? Or two? Or ten?"

Tharion paced the room, chewing his lower lip. He had been noticing a brooding tension in Guild Headquarters even before young Ysan's failure. He wondered if other Truthsayers had experienced mental lapses, as he had just done while trying to read Kalliana. What if the dozen Truthsayers were themselves hiding secrets from their Guild Master?

Qrista came up behind him, massaging his shoulders. Her voice was quiet and conciliatory. "If we are losing our abilities, then we will make more and more mistakes."

"I know," he answered. He had to find out what was going on, before it was too late. "I've got to test the Veritas."

She cradled him in her arms, and he leaned back into her embrace. He turned around to slide his own arms around her waist, pulling her close.

Taking one sky-blue capsule each, they dimmed the lights and slipped together into the familiar paths of each other's thoughts . . . but Tharion found little solace there.

ii

With some trepidation, Tharion answered the summons of his chief chemical analyst, Khirkos, to his lab in the topmost levels of Guild Headquarters.

Years ago, under Khirkos's guidance, workers had replaced the bulkhead plating in one of the laboratory rooms with thick panes of clear glass that let warm sunlight spill in, eliminating the need for artificial illumination. Khirkos dabbled in astronomy, and on cloud-free nights he sat in a lounge chair with one of the *SkySword*'s military spy telescopes, staring out at the blackness, hopping from star cluster to star cluster.

Tharion stepped off the turbolift and came into the laboratory rooms, blinking from the bright light overhead. Acrid whiffs of escaping vapors, alcohols, and other organic fluids bombarded his nose. His eyes burned for a moment, then adjusted as Khirkos came forward.

A short man with massive thighs and a belly going to paunch, Khirkos had a round face, close-set eyes, and long yellow hair tied back in a ponytail. His white cotton robe—stained and burned from many experiments, and enhanced with numerous hand-sewn pockets for holding instruments and writing implements—was tied across his girth with a plain brown sash.

Khirkos had been raised in the Guild, originally groomed to be a Truthsayer. Though he had shown promising abilities during his childhood, the biochemical changes of puberty had caused his tolerance to go haywire, making his body reject the Veritas drug as rapidly as an unmodified human would. Though unfit to be a Truthsayer, Khirkos had continued to serve the Guild. He had discovered his calling in analytical chemistry and worked with the strains of native Atlas bacteria to be shipped up for processing into Veritas on OrbLab 2.

Khirkos turned from his testing and spoke without preamble. "So, I've finished the analysis for you, Guild Master, and I've got some startling results." He fumbled in one of his pockets and pulled out a swatch of kenaf paper on which he had scribbled numbers, displaying them in a table for easy comparison.

"Were my suspicions correct?" Tharion asked.

Khirkos fixed him with his sharp gaze. "Even worse—or at least it's getting worse. Good thing you found out when you did." He handed the small square of paper to the Guild Master. "Look at those numbers."

Tharion squinted at the rows and columns of shrinking values. "This means nothing to me," he said. "Explain it."

Khirkos took the paper back and thrust it into the pale fire of a methane burner. The paper burst into flame and crumbled into brown-gray ash. He rummaged around the detritus on his worktable and picked up a flat glass dish on which lay a capsule of Veritas. With a scalpel he had sliced it in half, and the syrupy liquid spread out in a fingernail-sized puddle.

"The drug is diluted," Khirkos said. "Substantially. Since we maintain a set of control doses in the armory vault, I've also analyzed five separate samples from different batches. Same story."

Tharion's throat felt brittle, as if a cough had petrified inside it.

"The drug has been cut," Khirkos said. "Inert substances added to the Veritas. Each capsule contains a much smaller dose than our Truthsayers require."

"And the rest is being skimmed off, sold on the black market?"

Khirkos shrugged. "I can't determine that in the laboratory. You're the one with the telepathic powers, Guild Master."

Tharion didn't comment that his own abilities seemed to be diminishing as well. He poked his fingertip into the sticky blue drug suspension on the plate and touched it to the tip of his tongue, as if he could notice a difference in its sharp sour taste.

If each Veritas dose were gradually weakened over months or years, would the Truthsayers notice their mind-reading abilities slowly growing dimmer? What if they could no longer determine with razor clarity the distinction between guilt and innocence, truth and lies?

Khirkos looked at the curled ashes from the burned kenaf paper and frowned, then recited the information from memory. "It's been most greatly weakened in the doses ordered for the embryos in our cloning facility. The babies . . . the ones least likely to notice the difference."

Tharion stared at him. "The babies are weakened too? This is . . . appalling."

Khirkos nodded. "That's a good word for it—appalling. I'll have to remember that. So, the embryos are getting about half the dose that's necessary to build up a full base level. A few years from now, when they grow up and are being trained as Truthsayers, who knows how their ability may be diminished."

Khirkos held out a pudgy finger, spotted something under his nail, and picked at it. He took the glass dish from Tharion's hands and said eagerly, "I can run some more tests if you'd like . . ."

"That won't be necessary," Tharion said. The chemical analyst looked disappointed. The Guild Master spun on his bare feet and walked away from the sunlight toward the turbolift, wrapped in his dark, disturbing thoughts.

iii

Machinery hummed; amniotic fluid bubbled; deep subsonic vibrations trickled through the air . . . all of which combined to make the embryo-cloning chambers an island of silence swaddled in white noise within Guild Headquarters. Gratings on the floor and light panels on the wall of the infirmary were visible around the stacked chambers where baby Truthsayers were grown from anonymous embryos.

Tharion walked down the rows with his hands clasped behind his back while the workers watched him, uneasy at the presence of the Guild Master. He could tell their emotional state from the unshielded vibrations of their thoughts. The extra dose of Veritas must be working.

Tharion studied the small chambers, thinking how similar they must be to the embryonic-restoration vats up on the Platform, where the library of Earth genomes rested, awaiting requests from landholders.

Here at the Guild, though, Truthsayers tapped into the stockpile of original colonists' embryos, keeping the genetic makeup confidential. It was imperative for the sake of justice and objectivity that their parentage remain unknown. Tharion himself had been grown here, without a family, with no connection other than the Guild itself.

While still in their amniotic vats, the embryos hung in mechanical wombs, exposed to increasing doses of Veritas so that their immune systems became accustomed to the drug and did not purge it completely from their bodies.

Tharion watched the bubbling oxygenation fluids, breathed in the warm salty smell—a tang that reminded him of blood. This generation of Truthsayers would be weakened because of the tainted dosages. All might fail their tests, as Ysan had.

While Ysan's expulsion was unfair, if Tharion overturned it he would have to admit a blatant mistake, the consequences of which were worse than any injustice. Yet Tharion knew that the Truthsayer Kalliana had already erred in at least one verdict. What if she had misjudged Strone as well?

His beloved Guild was already mired in an ethical swamp, and there was no lifeline in sight.

In a way, he was relieved to learn that the drug wasn't just being stolen from the vault and sold on the distant holdings. The leak wasn't with one of his own Guild members, as he had dreaded. If the Veritas *inside* the capsules was diluted and the rest presumably sold on the black market, then the original crime must be committed in the processing centers on OrbLab 2. The scam did not begin and end here in First Landing—and the murder victim

Cialben was not the only link, as Franz Dokken had thought. It was much larger than that.

As he stood, and pondered, and dreaded what he might learn if he continued to pursue the question, Tharion was suddenly struck with another thought. His predecessor, Guild Master Klaryus, had died from a poisoned dose of Veritas, a capsule that had somehow been contaminated by a toxin distilled from the virulent Mindfire strain. OrbLab 2 had insisted it was an accident—but now Tharion questioned that.

What if they had killed Klaryus, intentionally giving him the Mindfire-infected capsule? But why? Certainly not to place Tharion in the position of Guild Master! What would OrbLab have to gain by that? As he had proved from the outset of his administration, Tharion was no friend to the orbital lab, tightening restrictions and quality control.

The answer lay up there somewhere, though. He had to find out what it was, and he had an idea how he might get the information he needed and right another wrong in the same stroke.

There were more wheels within wheels, and Tharion suspected—and *feared*—that if he kept poking around, he would uncover an entire clockwork of conspiracy against his Guild.

iv

After he had summoned Kalliana to his private ready room, Tharion waited, uneasy about the confrontation, but knowing he must go through with it. His expression was grim as the Truthsayer entered his ready room and sealed the door, blocking the curious gazes of the administrators at their bridge stations.

He said nothing, and Kalliana finally spoke up. "Have you decided what to do with me, Guild Master?" Her voice was very small.

Tharion stood as tall as he could manage. He had put on a new sash of royal blue, and his white cotton robes were bleached clean and dazzling. He drew a deep breath, flaring his nostrils, and delivered his pronouncement.

"Kalliana, I hereby strip you of your rank as a Truthsayer." He held out his hand, palm up, waiting.

She flinched as if he had physically struck her, and grasped the edge of the metal desk to keep herself from falling. Finally,

Kalliana fumbled with the emerald-green sash, drawing it free. She held it, a dangling verdant ribbon draped across her trembling fingers, and Tharion pulled it away. Without the sash she seemed naked and colorless—her robes white, her skin pale, her hair the lightest blond, her skin pink with shame. She began to weep.

"It is necessary," Tharion said.

Kalliana nodded jerkily. She squeezed her dusty blue eyes shut, and tears flowed from between her lashes, streaming down her cheeks. Unable to speak, she nodded again and again.

Tharion came around the side of the desk and touched her, raising her face up so that she was forced to look at him through the blur of her tears. His words were gentler. "It is necessary, Kalliana . . . because now it frees you to fix everything."

She drew a short breath. "How?"

"We both know that Troy Boren does not belong up on OrbLab 2—but we can't just march in and free him," he said, seating himself back at the desk, playing his role as Guild Master again. "It would be disastrous to admit our error and hope that the citizens would forgive and forget. They won't let us survive such a mistake, and they won't forget so easily. We must keep it a complete secret."

"Then how will we rectify this injustice?" she asked. "If we can't free the prisoner, how is he going to get off of OrbLab 2?"

Tharion took another breath. His heart was pounding. "You will have to help him escape."

Kalliana drew back in astonishment. "Escape?"

He held her hand in a firm grip. "Yes. I am arranging everything. You will know the details as soon as I've established them."

"But if Troy Boren escapes, he—he can't just have his old life back," Kalliana stammered. "He will continue to be a fugitive no matter where he goes."

Tharion raised his eyebrows. "Only if we choose to pursue him. It can be forgotten. Troy Boren can make a new life."

Kalliana started to say something again, as if to argue with him, but the Guild Master cut her off. "It's the best we can do. Live with it."

She looked down at the desk. The tracks of her tears still glittered on her cheeks, but she had stopped crying now. "What about me?"

Now Tharion smiled. "There's something else you must accomplish."

He briefly explained to her how a certain amount of the Veritas was being siphoned from the sky-blue capsules. Kalliana's eyes went wide with disgust and disbelief.

"It's all true," Tharion said. He raised a finger. "Since the Veritas capsules themselves have been altered, we must assume that at least the first part of the crime is being committed in OrbLab 2. Recently an internal investigation from the Platform found no evidence of tampering. I don't believe we can trust this result, however. Sondheim's team might not have had the proper . . . incentive to find the truth, and so I—as Guild Master—am gathering an impartial group of representatives from the Landholders Council, scientists and inspectors from the various villages."

He waited for her to comprehend. "These inspectors will be unfamiliar faces. You, Kalliana, will accompany them in disguise. No one will know you have been trained as a Truthsayer."

Kalliana was confused, unable to sift through possible answers to her questions. "But why must I be disguised? Why hide the fact? They would be more intimidated if you brought a Truthsayer."

"Not necessarily," Tharion said. "Kalliana—I want you to use Veritas to learn what you can. Secretly. OrbLab 2 and the Platform will no doubt cover up the evidence. Even my investigators are not likely to find anything incriminating . . . except in someone's thoughts."

Kalliana gasped at the suggestion. "But . . . but I can't read a person's mind without his permission, Guild Master. I took an oath as a Truthsayer!"

Tharion folded his hands together and leaned forward, resting his elbows on the desk so that she understood with perfect clarity. He wound the green sash he had stripped from her around his wrist and clenched its ragged ends in his fist.

"Kalliana—*you* are no longer a Truthsayer."

# CHAPTER
## 27

### i

With the decision made, Tharion felt as if a great weight had been lifted from him. In high spirits for the first time in weeks, he met Franz Dokken for lunch in Guild Headquarters.

Dokken came alone and was shown inside by an elite guard who recognized him and did not question his business. The other landholders visited the Guild Master rarely—and then only when they wanted something—but Dokken came to see Tharion at least once a month, usually for a meal and conversation, nothing more.

When Tharion had once cautioned his mentor that the Guild could show no favoritism because of their friendship, Dokken scowled at him, offended at the suggestion. "Tharion, I've known you since you were a boy," he said. "I've been very pleased with the progress you've made within the Guild—but I would still come and visit you even if you wore the brown sash of a lab technician. I had no way of knowing you would eventually be asked to take the place of Klaryus as Guild Master." Dokken sniffed. "You don't see me befriending every young child in hopes that I'll pick a future leader, do you?" Tharion had shaken his head, then forced a laugh at his own paranoia.

Today, because the erratic rain showers had finally cleared for the season, Tharion instructed the Guild servants to set out lunch in the bright conservatory, where he and Dokken could have a bit of privacy.

The conservatory was housed in a glassed-in blister that had once held the *SkySword*'s targeting lasers and computer-guided plasma cannons. Several similar blisters studded the long hull at strategic positions, and Guild members could spend some time over a pleasant meal or afternoon cup of herb tea, surrounded by the sky or a view of First Landing.

Tharion shifted until he found a comfortable position on his cushioned metal chair. He looked out across the rooftops that radiated from the space elevator's anchor point. Mag-lev rails rayed outward like silver bolts to the far-flung holdings. Strips of green made a patchwork quilt on the barren lands surrounding the city, and tall palm trees waved in a slight breeze.

Dokken scraped his metal chair across the deck plates, drawing closer to Tharion so he could share the view. "You look very pleased with yourself," the landholder said and raised an eyebrow in puzzlement. "Is it because of this new investigation team you're sending up to the Platform? Tell me about it."

Tharion gazed off into the distance. "Well, Sondheim's private inspectors found no evidence of Veritas tampering—and of course I don't believe a word of it." He turned toward Dokken. "And neither do you, nor would any reasonable person. Sondheim is involved somehow. So is Dieter Pan. After Pan provoked us when he delivered his report, it can't come as a surprise that I'm calling for yet another investigation. I've always been a thorn in their side anyway."

Dokken leaned forward. "But Sondheim knows they're coming," he said. "If he has anything to hide, surely he would have removed it by now. You don't really expect your team to find anything, do you?"

Tharion shrugged. "They can look, can't they?"

"Yes," Dokken said with growing exasperation, "but what's this about you alone picking the team members from names suggested by us landholders?"

"Only way I know to keep it impartial, Franz," he said with a secretive smile. Though he trusted Dokken, he could not risk revealing his plans to anyone, especially not a landholder.

Dokken pressed him. "What? What is it? You're keeping something from me, Tharion."

Two servers came in bearing covered dishes. Tharion lifted one metal lid and drew in a deep lungful of the sweet spicy aroma from a sauce drizzled over rice, cut carrots, snow peas, and small chunks of turkey meat.

Dokken inspected the small dish beside his plate: sliced maroon circles swimming in crimson juice. He tilted the bowl so that the bright red liquid sloshed to one side.

"Sliced beets pickled in rice vinegar. I think you'll like it," Tharion said with a mischievous upturn of his lips. "In fact, it reminds me of that Chianti you make."

Dokken scowled. "I've always hated beets." He pushed the bowl aside and set to work on his rice and vegetables.

The moment the servants had departed, Dokken leaned forward again. "So what is this secret you're keeping? You know how I like secrets."

"Yes," Tharion said, "especially when they're not your own. You've told me before." Dokken gestured insistently for Tharion to continue. "Really, Franz, I thought you were a much more patient person than this."

Dokken sat up, taken aback. "I am, of course—when I'm the one controlling the conversation. What are you up to? Tell me."

"My Truthsayer finally realized she made a mistake in sentencing Troy Boren. You know and I know the man was never guilty—but I couldn't find an acceptable way to rectify the error. Until now."

Tharion leaned forward, lowering his voice to reveal only the part of the plan that Dokken needed to know. He required the landholder's cooperation to make everything work perfectly. "We're using this new investigation team as a diversion—to arrange for Troy Boren's escape! We're going to smuggle him back down to the surface, and I would like you, Franz, to arrange a job for him at your holding. Nothing extravagant—just a new shot at life."

Dokken's expression filled with skepticism. "You're breaking a man free from OrbLab 2? Impossible! Really, my friend, how do you expect to accomplish such a thing?"

"Kareem Sondheim has already agreed to help me. I think he's a good man at heart."

Dokken's face was awash with disbelief. He spluttered, then took a sip of his tea.

Tharion leaned forward with an intense stare. "It'll work, Franz."

Dokken chewed in silence for a few moments, looked sidelong at the plate of beets (while Tharion ate his own with great relish). Reluctantly, he speared one of the red circles with his fork and nibbled it, making a sour face.

At last, Dokken nodded slowly, after more contemplation. "I'm proud of you, Tharion. Are you giving up the rest of the Veritas investigation, then?"

Tharion poured them each a second cup of tea. Off in the distance they watched the space elevator begin to rise on its long slow climb to orbit.

"Don't worry about it, Franz. I think I can handle this."

"Very mysterious," Dokken said around a mouthful of rice. "I think all my years of advice and training are beginning to sink in."

Tharion raised his eyebrows. "Could be."

ii

In her quarters Kalliana went through the motions like an automaton. She shed her white robe and picked through the clothing options Guild Master Tharion had provided her. Though each piece was the right size, everything seemed incredibly drab and uncomfortable. The colors were gray or brown accented with a narrow band of red embroidery. The weaving was coarse, the wool prickly, rather than combed soft. Even the lightweight tunic felt scratchy, as if made from rougher linen instead of fine cotton.

She dyed her pale hair a rich auburn, then used face paints to color her eyebrows. She added makeup with inexpert strokes, daubing a flush on her cheeks. A stranger looked back at her from a mirror: not the petite angel in Truthsayer robes, but a small waif with red-brown hair and a narrow face, eyes large with surprise, her clothes common.

Each step in the process of disguise was like closing another door on her life. She kept thinking of her young friend Ysan and the despair on his face when he had been cast out from the Guild, how he had clung to a desperate hope of a tolerable future as a Magistrate in the outlying lands.

Kalliana didn't have such an anchor. She had no idea what her future might hold. Her only goal was a short-term one—to see that an innocent man was freed from unjust imprisonment. She also hoped she could uncover the people responsible for stealing Veritas from its rightful users. Perhaps then the Guild Master would reconsider her future.

Kalliana had done her best to remain hidden in her room for the past three days. Her missing green sash would have been a blatant indication to the other Truthsayers that something terrible had happened to her; neither she nor Tharion had offered any explanation.

In the hour after noon, elite guards inside the Headquarters helped everyone go to a large assembly Tharion had called—for the express purpose of emptying the corridors so that the disguised Kalliana might depart unseen. She stopped at the entry to her quarters, looking back at them one last time, amazed at how little she was actually leaving behind. Then she sealed the door behind her forever.

That day the Truthsayer Kalliana vanished from the world, and a quiet chemical analyst—coached for jargon by the Guild's lab specialist Khirkos—emerged to take her place on the new investigation team sent up to the Platform.

# CHAPTER

# 28

## i

Kalliana sat cold and alone among the other inspectors. She was an island of silence, not listening to their conversations or joining in. The seven team members met and introduced themselves. They had been instructed to keep their holdings confidential, though in many cases their accents and clothing gave them away. Everyone was excited to be going up to the Platform.

Tharion's confidence in her, and her own desperation to return to the ways she loved so well, combined with her own guilt at sentencing an innocent man, gave her the inner strength to keep going—though at times she felt swept along by circumstances out of her control. Kalliana tried to find some measure of stability by grasping her single hope: She was going to rectify an injustice—could a Truthsayer have any higher goal?

All eight people sat together with a minimal sol-pol escort inside the space elevator. Because of the unusually large number of passengers, this entire run would carry no major cargo (although the anchor point supervisor, Cren, had managed to cram the small overhead compartment with canisters of air and water).

At the midpoint of the ten-hour journey, a few of them shared packages of dried rations; others were too queasy to eat. The inspectors occasionally glanced at Kalliana, either curious or dismissive, but she avoided conversation, afraid she might let slip the wrong information, that she might contradict herself if she didn't remain tight-lipped. The other four women and three men discussed analytical possibilities or inventory methods, forming strategies for their investigation.

Kalliana had never been off Atlas before. Very few Truthsayers had. For a moment she thought of old Archimand, the hero who had saved Atlas and founded the Guild. He had done something similar . . . but Kalliana could not consider herself a legendary figure.

She sat in her itchy clothes, still shivering. The cold would never go away. She closed her eyes and leaned back. So many new things. One mistake had opened up a wealth—or a hell—of novel experiences for her.

As the elevator hummed upward on its impellers, Kalliana felt as if she were cutting loose from her life, her entire past.

ii

In the high tower room of his villa, Franz Dokken sat at a computer station, accessing the satellite uplink. Maximillian had departed two days earlier to continue his subversive work in the Pilgrim settlements, and, without Schandra, his home seemed quiet and empty. It left him free to concentrate on all the delicate details to which he needed to attend.

Such as warning his friend Sondheim.

The direct link chimed, and an image from Sondheim's personal quarters blinked. The old man accepted the call, pressing his simian face close to the viewplate until he recognized Dokken. Then he withdrew slightly, blinking his rheumy eyes.

Dokken began without preamble. "Tell me about this deal you made with Guild Master Tharion. I think he's got more up his sleeve than you suspect."

Sondheim drifted backward, allowing Dokken to see his cluttered private room, a shrine to the surface of Atlas. Dokken himself had provided the crippled landholder with high-resolution images of desert vistas for a mural across the wall of his Platform quarters, masking the sterile metal plates.

Sondheim's furnishings were made of polished wood from the surface, glazed terra-cotta tiles and pots, stained glass, all expensive items from Dokken Holding. The "landholder without land" repeatedly denied it, but Dokken knew he longed to come to the surface, if only once. Kareem Sondheim had spent nearly two and a half centuries trapped in the station, never once having touched solid ground.

"What did the Guild Master tell you?" Sondheim asked in his phlegmy voice.

"I know about this crazy escape plan. I think it's going to be very difficult," Dokken said. "Difficult to cover up. How are you going to explain it?"

Sondheim shrugged and looked away. "I'm leaving the details to Dieter. He's good at that sort of thing. Once the two escapees manage to get to the Platform, I'll smuggle them down on the elevator during a cargo run."

"Dieter?" Dokken snorted. "Kareem, you have too much confidence in that flighty man. He's caused most of these problems with his eagerness to dump more and more Veritas onto the public. When I first pressured *you* to let loose a few stray capsules for my own purposes, I thought it would end there. Nobody would notice. But these last ten years since you put him in charge of OrbLab, Dieter has been going overboard. A shipment inside a *water buffalo*? My god, what were you thinking, Kareem?"

Sondheim lashed out, indignant. "Dieter has also greatly increased the production efficiency on OrbLab 2. We're making more of the drug than ever before. He's fixed a lot of the problems. Tharion should appreciate that rather than snooping around all the time." The old man seemed ready to pout. "You're not the only one who can take on a protégé, Franz Dokken!"

Dokken stared upward at the ceiling, as if seeking divine help. "Yes, but I picked someone talented and malleable. Tharion isn't damaged merchandise, like Dieter Pan. Your protégé may be sharp, but he's missing a few character points."

"Wise words from a man who knows exactly what it's like to have warped sensibilities," Sondheim said acidly.

Dokken laughed. "Oh, don't talk to me like that, Kareem. I remember when you were just a toddler." Despite Sondheim's obvious advanced age, Dokken knew the crippled old man looked up to him almost as a father figure.

For a moment, Sondheim drifted out of view, and when he returned, the shriveled old man was obviously doing his best to control his temper. "You and I have had a longer friendship than anyone else on the entire planet, Franz. You've stated your piece, but there's nothing I can do about the escape attempt. It's been agreed to. Now leave me alone."

"No!" Dokken insisted. "I haven't stated my piece. There is more afoot here than a simple plan to free one prisoner. What, exactly, did Tharion promise you?"

Sondheim sighed, seemingly contrite. "That he wouldn't

reveal any results of the investigation team if I arranged the escape of Troy Boren. They probably won't even look very hard. It seemed a reasonable deal."

Dokken leaned back in his chair, pondering. The wood and leather creaked. "He's keeping the identities of his team members a secret. To me, that means somebody isn't who he or she appears to be. My best guess is that Tharion has infiltrated one of his own Truthsayers into the group of investigators, probably the one who falsely convicted Boren in the first place. Imagine what would happen if a Truthsayer began snooping around up there, Kareem. It won't matter how much cleaning up you've done if she comes in contact with any of your people who *know*." Dokken scowled, allowing Tharion a moment of grudging respect for the plan.

Sondheim listened, and the web of deep wrinkles around his eyes spread wider and wider until they were grayish chasms in his papery skin. "A Truthsayer up here? Do you really believe he'd do something like that? I thought you had better control over him!" Sondheim's nostrils flared. His hunched shoulders slumped as if gravity had just increased on the Platform. "Maybe *your* protégé isn't as wrapped around your finger as you expect."

"Don't worry about Tharion. I'll keep him in line. Now I'm going to tell you what to do about this mess." He let out a long slow breath, wishing again for a good cup of coffee or a decent glass of wine. "Troy Boren and the Truthsayer are both dangerous loose ends. I wouldn't be surprised if an unfortunate accident happened to them during this wild escape attempt."

Sondheim scowled. "I'm not going to kill anybody. Not for you, and not for me."

"Then do it for Dieter." Dokken's expression hardened. "Don't make me use a threat neither of us wants to hear. If these two escape and manage to deliver their information, I don't need to explain to you how many of our plans will come tumbling down. All of Dieter's dealings will be exposed, and your precious little adopted son will be ruined, not to mention the damage it'll cause you and me."

The withered old man drifted across the image area of the viewplate, like a spider on a web, his entire body trembling with sudden fear. Dokken continued, "You thought you had it all taken care of, but you stepped right into Tharion's net. There's only one way to get out. It's dangerous up in orbit, after all. Accidents happen."

Seeing Sondheim's continued reluctance, Dokken grew impatient. "The team is on its way, Kareem! They are ascending in the elevator at this moment. We don't have the luxury of long contemplation."

"All right!" the old man shouted. "I'll do it for Dieter. But I despise you for this, Franz." Sondheim picked up one of the decorative glazed pots as if he wanted to hurl it at the viewplate.

"Me?" Dokken said with hurt innocence. "All I did was warn you."

Sondheim annoyed Dokken by terminating the connection without a response. The twisted old man was still a child in many ways.

iii

When they docked at the orbiting Platform, the anxiety among the team members increased tangibly. Kalliana had to force herself not to read the turmoil of their thoughts. She had taken a double dose of Veritas immediately before departing, though her powers didn't feel particularly enhanced. She would return to the surface long before she was due for another booster.

One of the sol-pol guards led the way, and Kalliana floated up into a hemispherical chamber that depicted an idealized sky. When she read the words "Atlas—a new dawn," painted near the imaginary rising sun, Kalliana felt her heart turn to lead.

As workers hustled off with the supply cylinders, Kalliana waited with the others, a small chick in a flock of birds, hanging weightless and disoriented in the air. A shrunken old man who looked like an animated mummy drifted down, accompanied by two guards who floated in the air beside him.

Kalliana recognized the man by his gross deformities, his underdeveloped legs and sticklike bones; Kareem Sondheim had been in charge of the Platform since the beginning of Atlas history. He had figured prominently in her Guild history lessons, but now she looked toward him with hope. He had promised to assist her in setting Troy Boren free, though his position on the Platform also made it likely he was involved in the illegal Veritas activities.

"So, welcome to the Platform," Sondheim said to the team. "I am saddened that the Truthsayers Guild considers your presence necessary, but I promise my full cooperation in your investigation." His wrinkled face stretched as he grinned. "I'm sure you'll find everything *exactly* as it should be—I hope you don't prove me wrong."

A painted thundercloud split down the middle as an access hatch opened halfway up the wall, and Kalliana almost expected a cloudburst to pour down. Sondheim and the guards directed them upward into the open corridors, nudging them when they needed assistance in the zero gravity. Kalliana constantly had to readjust her perception of the directions Down and Up and Forward.

"Today we'll give you a tour of the Platform facilities, and tomorrow you'll all be shuttled over to OrbLab 2, where our actual Veritas work takes place," Sondheim said. "If there's anything else you wish to see, we'll look into it. The space elevator is scheduled to depart midway through tomorrow, so you'll have to wait for the next run anyway. I hope that will give you sufficient time to complete your investigations."

Over the next few hours Kalliana and other inspectors endured tours of machinery and facilities: chip imprinters where lasers drew incredibly small patterns through focal lenses onto ultrapure substrates, pharmaceutical culturing labs where tiny petrie dishes were surrounded by cold air and ultraviolet light. Materials synthesis labs used extreme cold, extreme heat, and extreme vacuum to create exotic new alloys, sponge metals, and ceramic films. Tanks in the cloning lab and the genetic library bubbled and hissed, growing new species that would have their chance on the new planet. The details of everything overwhelmed her, and Kalliana ceased to absorb anything new after the first hour.

The Platform's fixtures, the walls, the windows, were a dazzling array of plastics, enameled metal, and chrome—everything perfect, everything exact—manufactured on long-lost Earth to tolerances that were inconceivable on modern Atlas.

The walls and false windows were decorated with Earth images brought by the original colonists long ago, reminders of their former home. Kalliana had never seen anything like the enhanced photographs of spectacular natural formations and amazing cities. The faded propaganda posters depicting Eden-like dreams of Atlas seemed just as strange.

Their inspection team moved along, streaming into the flow of traffic in the main corridors. In the weightlessness people worked or swam around, jetting with compressed-air packs, some expertly, some flying out of control. Others clanked along in magnetic boots.

Kalliana noticed that nearly everyone had well-developed arm muscles from pulling themselves around the Platform. She used the clumsiness fostered by zero gravity as an excuse to bump into people, making superficial mental scans of some of the sol-pols, a few of the lab technicians—but nobody knew anything about what she sought. Kalliana could barely even find the word *Veritas* in their thoughts, so concerned were they about their own tasks.

As he scuttled ahead, Kareem Sondheim glanced directly at her several times, fixing her with his hooded gaze. She expected him to make some sort of contact, but he ignored her. She had hoped for an opportunity to touch him, to snatch a few of *his* thoughts so she could study them. Guild Master Tharion would have considered that very important. But Sondheim did not allow her to get close enough as he bobbled along pointing out Platform activities.

Fuzzy with confusion, Kalliana followed along with the group to the next stop on their inspection.

iv

At the end of the day Kalliana paced the floor of her sterile, unfamiliar guest quarters, seeking some answers to her own questions.

Once crammed with impatient colonists, the station high above Atlas was now nearly empty, an enormous structure left alone in orbit, connected by a frail tether to the ground. Most people wanted to live on the surface, despite the hardships involved in making a home there.

Kalliana's mind and stomach were twisted into knots. So far she had gleaned no insights at all about the Veritas smuggling. Troy Boren was still a prisoner aboard OrbLab 2. She was supposed to free him, but she had no idea how. No plan. Guild Master Tharion had said he would *arrange* everything—but how much would be left up to her? She didn't know.

The buzzing door signal startled Kalliana. She unsealed the hatch to find the hunched landholder Sondheim floating just out of reach.

"Hello there," he said and handed her a self-playing disk. "This is for you." She took it instinctively, and he backed away, waving. "It's all you need to know."

"Wait!" she called, but he was already moving down the

corridor. Sondheim avoided her, as if superstitiously afraid to let
her touch him. But he wasn't supposed to know that she was a
former Truthsayer, only that she meant to free Troy Boren. . . .
What had gone wrong? Where had he gotten his doubts?

"Play the disk," Sondheim called. He jetted away with his
compressed-air pack, somersaulting through the air.

Kalliana looked at the square disk in her hand and sealed the
door. *This was all she needed to know.*

Sitting on the bunk she played the disk, focusing carefully on
the words, because it was marked as a one-time-only file filled with
self-erasing text.

Intent on her goal, she drank in the step-by-step instructions
for a prison break.

# CHAPTER

i

The investigation team suited up and climbed aboard the ballistically launched sleds that propelled them across space to the orbiting laboratory.

Kalliana's stomach filled with acid, and her muscles ached from tension. She played and replayed the steps of Sondheim's plan in her head, hoping she didn't make a mistake. She had to be brave. She had to follow through. This one act would stop the chain reaction of wrongs she had inadvertently started in motion.

Reaching OrbLab 2, the team members moved through the airlock booths and the decontamination shower, one by one, then entered the prison labor complex, shivering in their damp new clothes.

Inside, Kalliana let her gaze flick from side to side, absorbing the locations of the entrance booths and outer guard quarters, the schematics of the station—all items she would need later. Sondheim's escape scheme seemed preposterous, and would have been unthinkable without all the information he had provided. Kalliana had no choice but to follow each step, precisely as the old man had laid it down. She just had to hope it would work. . . .

The station exec Dieter Pan drifted forward down the long corridor that housed crew quarters, a ring of cabins separated from the locked-down central complex that held the prisoners' cells and the isolated processing labs. Dieter bounced along, focusing on Kalliana. He raised his mercurial eyebrows and grinned as he approached. "Welcome, welcome to OrbLab 2." Reaching the first team member, Dieter reached forward to shake the woman's hand vigorously. "We've been expecting you, boys and girls."

As sol-pols thudded forward, moving slowly in their mag-boots, Dieter went down the line, grasping every team member's hand in an enthusiastic welcome. Kalliana braced herself, and when Dieter Pan reached out to take her grip, she squeezed back hard, seizing the chance. Marshaling the Veritas strength in her mind, she dove in—

—to a swirl of images, details Kareem Sondheim had not wanted her to find, all the machinations that the previous investigation teams had not discovered . . . or to which they had turned a blind eye:

Sondheim, who had taken Dieter under his wing, raising him like a foster son, grooming him for this position on OrbLab 2, where he reigned as king—Sondheim on the Platform, Dieter Pan on OrbLab 2, the masters of space. . . .

Withered, sentimental Sondheim, who could never refuse the young man anything. . . .

Dieter staging accidents, rescuing supposedly lost and written-off shipments of Veritas that he could sell to those greedy people "downstairs."

The thoughts came to Kalliana in an unsorted jumble, made more difficult because she didn't know exactly what she wanted to find, no simple yes or no answer, guilty or innocent. But now she knew incontrovertibly that OrbLab 2 was behind the smuggling.

Disconnected details continued to flood into her with the speed of thought:

How Dieter Pan loathed Eli Strone—and even the background thoughts about the serial killer had the power to make Kalliana shudder. Strone's stoic perseverance and refusal to be intimidated made Dieter want to lash out at the man.

The escape plan, overturning Troy Boren's false conviction . . . Dieter planned on helping them. She caught glimpses of his plans, saw how he intended to stage a spectacular emergency to cover the escape—but she couldn't read any details . . . only that he looked forward to it with great glee.

The flicker of Dieter's emotion did not inspire her with confidence, though, because in a rush she saw more—many more—indications of darker thoughts. . . .

Then Kalliana was set adrift as Dieter snatched his brief grip away, suspecting nothing as he moved on to the next person in the team with another bobbing handshake.

Kalliana let out a long, soft sigh. It had been easy after all, so easy that it had taken her by surprise. Everything had changed with a half second's worth of memory dump from the station exec.

Now she held some of the information Guild Master Tharion wanted. His suspicions were confirmed, and he would now have to take drastic action. Her revelations would cause a great upheaval as soon as she returned safely to First Landing. But that turmoil would be necessary to shore up the crumbling foundation of the Guild before it was undermined any further.

Perhaps it would even be enough to get her reinstated as a Truthsayer.

"Well then, boys and girls," Dieter Pan said, rubbing his hands briskly together as he flitted forward, "we'll split into separate groups so you can nose into everything. Shall we get on with it?"

ii

Troy Boren toiled away in the sealed high-risk laboratory. He had no chronometer, no way of telling how many hours he put in each day. He simply worked when they told him to and quit when they told him to. It didn't matter. Each day had already become a drab gray limbo.

It would be this way for the rest of his life.

He already felt as if he had been trapped on the orbital laboratory for years, though he knew it couldn't have been much more than a month. He wondered if his sister Leisa had had her baby yet—of course not, her pregnancy probably wasn't even showing. He wondered how many men had fled from his shrewish sister Rissbeth.

Time dragged so slowly. Once, he even wished Eli Strone would go berserk—just to give him something to remember and think about, something out of the ordinary.

Troy had long since stopped smelling the mélange of chemical odors wafting through the recycled air. He had ceased feeling the station's bone-penetrating chill. He did his daily duties.

Beside him, Strone remained as engrossed as ever in his job, never wavering, never complaining.

The airlock booth hissed. Troy and Strone both looked up to see Dieter Pan cycling through from the outer corridor. The airlock popped open, and the wiry man drifted in, wearing his ubiqitous forest-green bodysuit. He gave a push with his right hand to drive his body up into the air, then hung about a meter off the ground.

Dieter carried a bubble-wrapped package, which he set on the table beside Troy's terminal. "Change of routine for this morning, boys," he said. "We've had overflow from the capsule-processing labs, and we aren't going to make this shipment down, since the space elevator departs the Platform in another hour or so. We'll have to hold this until the next run."

"But why bring it in here?" Troy asked warily.

"This is the most sterile of the labs," the station exec answered, "and I don't want it cluttering up the capsule facility. Log this in, Boren, then accompany me. You and I have more to do this morning."

"What do you mean?" Troy asked. "Me?"

Dieter's eyes widened beneath his curled eyebrows; the pupils contracted to pinpricks of black. "What is this, an interrogation? Just pay attention, boy. There's a VIP inspection team here snooping around to make sure we aren't hiding Veritas in our armpits or something like that. One of the inspectors is too dim to use our computers and needs someone to help her through all the basics. You're stuck with the task. Remember, the new boy always gets last pick of jobs."

Troy blinked in confusion, but Dieter clapped his hands, making his floating body move. "Come on, boy! The inspectors are waiting."

"Uh, sure," Troy said, then picked up the bubble-wrapped package. "It'll take me a while to divide up all the lots in here and double-check—"

"We don't have time for that," Dieter said. "Just log in the package as a whole. You can do your cross-checking later, after the team leaves."

Reluctantly, Troy left the package beside his terminal and pecked in the numbers with his fingertips, then followed Dieter Pan to the airlock booth.

"Strone, don't talk so much," Dieter said with a glare. "You'd better keep up production even without your partner here."

"I always have," Strone said.

As the booth door sealed behind them, Troy looked out through the transparent wall back into the confined lab. Eli Strone glanced at the package with a mixture of uneasiness and annoyance. Troy realized that the killer, too, had a bad feeling about this turn of events.

### iii

Assigned to a small inspection cubicle, Kalliana drifted over to an unoccupied computer terminal. The muffled room was tiny as a coffin and empty; bright phosphors from the screen listed numbers she could not comprehend. "What am I supposed to do with this?" Kalliana asked the guard, who stood like a medieval knight anchored to the floor by mag-boots.

He shouldered his rifle. "Wait. We're bringing someone to walk you through the inventory procedure."

She suddenly realized this was the connection, and so she wasn't surprised to see the scarecrowish young man, Troy Boren, brought into the chamber with her. She took a deep, chilled breath. His face had become more gaunt, his eyes hollow, his lips thinner—and he had been here no more than a month!

"This is Chemical Technician Kalliana," the guard said to Boren. "Help her out. Tell her what she wants to know." Paralyzed with dread, Kalliana looked at Troy—but he didn't recognize her. With her disguise of face paints and different clothes, Troy would have no reason to suspect her identity as the pale Truthsayer who had convicted him.

His hands fluttered like wings, and he swallowed before bending over the computer terminal. "I'm here to help you," he mumbled.

Kalliana spoke in a low voice, though the sol-pol at the door didn't seem to care. "And I'm here to help *you*, Troy Boren," she said.

### iv

The package of capsules sat by itself on the table beside Troy's terminal, unsettling Eli Strone. It was an item out of order, a loose end. He hated pieces that didn't fit into place.

Why had the station exec brought the package here? Why had he removed Troy? Why had he insisted that the capsules not be inventoried? None of this was part of the routine.

Since coming to OrbLab 2, after the Truthsayer mysteriously rejected Strone's careful efforts to mete out justice to Atlas, he had found that his own truth-reading abilities had begun to wane.... He squeezed his eyes shut and forcibly drove the thought from his mind. He still had much work to do.

He *could* read minds. He *could* smell out sin and guilt, and he would deal with it as necessary. He had been unable to read the mind of Dieter Pan, yet still he had sensed something wrong, something out of the ordinary. The station exec had moved with a discreet furtiveness, had spoken with the silky ease of a practiced liar. What had Dieter really meant? Why? He didn't trust the maddening station exec.

Strone finished a run with the pulsed-laser bacterial sorter, then moved over to his partner's computer station. He would double-check and log in the shipment of Veritas, since Dieter Pan had not allowed Troy the time. Once Strone took care of this outstanding task, perhaps the pieces would fit together again, and he could get back to his own job. Then he'd be able to concentrate better.

He unrolled the bubble pack, spilling out small packets that contained separately numbered lots of the precious drug—but he saw immediately that a mistake had been made. The capsules were empty: grayish translucent shells made of hardened gelatin in the right size and shape, but containing only air or some inert substance, not the sky blue of Veritas.

As his anger built at the thought of being tricked, Strone squeezed one of the capsules between his blunt fingers like a vise. A clear liquid—water?—spurted out of the empty shell.

He then remembered what Troy had uncovered by digging through the station records the previous time an entire shipment had been lost to space. Something strange had happened there as well: a loose end, a disaster. Would Strone be blamed for the mix-up this time?

He felt the anger building and snatched up one of the packages, deciding to confront Dieter Pan with this gross mistake. If everyone would only do their jobs as they were supposed to, nothing bad would ever happen.

His palm filled with the false capsules, Strone went immediately to the airlock booth, stepped in, and sealed the door behind him—

—just as the screeching contamination alarms sounded. The red emergency portal blew outward in an unexpected explosive decompression, dumping the lab room . . . though the bacterial sorter had been sealed and empty, offering no hazard whatsoever.

Strone spun about in the confined airlock booth, placing his palms flat against the transparent wall, and watched the death chamber. The air screamed away into space, all loose items flying out as the hard vacuum ripped everything free. The empty package of fake Veritas capsules spiraled out into the star-strewn blackness.

A moment sooner, and the emergency systems would have flung Strone out as well, tearing the air from his lungs faster than he could scream.

The airlock booth locked itself, imprisoning him. Eli Strone had no choice but to stand there, his eyes round at his narrow escape.

The magenta alarm lights cycled, and he could feel the pounding sirens vibrating through the walls. Louder than everything else he heard his heart thumping as he realized that the pieces did indeed fit together, that he had answers to his many questions—but not the answers he had hoped to find.

i

Even though she had expected the alarm systems to begin shrieking through OrbLab 2 at any time, Kalliana still had to bite back a startled scream. The guard standing outside the small inspection chamber looked about wildly, his feet anchored to the floor as he held his weapon out, ready to fire at some oncoming enemy.

Speakers in the enclosed corridors rang out with a harsh synthesized voice. "Major decompression event in bacterial sorter lab. Warning! Major decompression event—"

Troy Boren looked around in panic. "That's my lab. What happened?"

"All guards report to bacterial sorter laboratory. Repeat, major decompression event—"

The sol-pol whirled, jabbing the end of his rifle toward Troy. "Stay here," he said, then trudged off like an armored knight.

Kalliana waited a moment, then snapped to Troy, "This is our chance!" she said. "I'm getting you out of here."

Troy's eyes seemed to bug from his face in a "major decompression event" of their own. "What did you say?" he asked.

"I'm from the Truthsayers Guild," she answered quickly. "We know you were sentenced falsely, and we have to get you out of here."

"But," Troy said, unable to find words. "I can't. They won't let—"

"Yes, they will! It's all been arranged, but we have to *move now*. We won't get a second chance."

Troy suddenly narrowed his eyes, suspicious in a way he would never have been before his time in the orbital prison. "How do I know you're not trying to get me killed in a prison escape attempt to cover the Guild's mistake?"

Kalliana sighed in exasperation. "You don't. But I'm your only hope for getting back to Atlas." She fixed him with an intense, impatient gaze. "Unless you'd rather stay here for the rest of your life? Do you want to go, or don't you?"

Troy's lips trembled, but he shook his head vigorously. "No, I want to go home."

Kalliana didn't have the heart or the time to explain that he could never go home. At least he'd get back to the surface, though. She grabbed his wrist and pulled him with her, bounding out into the corridor in the featherlight gravity.

Lights flashed. Doors sealed shut automatically, trapping people inside. Kalliana was aghast to see that the door to their inspection cubicle hissed to an airtight seal only moments after they had slipped out. If she hadn't moved immediately . . .

Sol-pols rushed down the corridor, their loud bootsteps thundering. "Get to shelter," one shouted at Kalliana, then hurried on his way. Several workers without mag-boots scuttled along, like fish swimming away from predators to a safe refuge.

Kalliana tried to recall the OrbLab 2 blueprint, but the noise, the lights, and her own panic, only served to transform the diagram lines into a tangled nest in her mind. "Help me find the outer portal," she said. "To get to the suits and the sleds!"

"Oh!" he said, as if it had suddenly become real to him that they were actually going to leave the prison. "But we're sealed in," he said. "We can't just leave—they'll know."

"We'll worry about that when we get there," Kalliana said in an effort to purge her own self-doubts.

They reached the main entry station where two sol-pols supposedly sat armed and waiting to prevent any such escape attempt—but even these two had left their posts in the emergency. Kalliana doubted that was standard procedure; Sondheim had assured her they would be given explicit orders.

The big metal door sat shut, as if welded against the outer docking chamber where the slingshot sleds waited. She raced to the keypad and punched in the code phrase Sondheim had told her to memorize—but her trembling fingers stuttered, and she hit the wrong buttons. A warning flashed up, telling her she had one more chance before the entire station would be locked down.

Breathing fast and hard, concentrating to keep the numbers and letters from swimming in front of her eyes, she picked out the input one key at a time, her lips pressed together.

"Are you sure this is going to work?" Troy said.

"I am," she answered and finally completed the last keystroke. The airlock door swung open. "Inside, hurry," she said. "We'll have to cycle through."

It took forever for the pressure equalization to allow them access to the docking chamber. "We're going to slip off of OrbLab 2 during the confusion," Kalliana continued. "I was planted on the inspection team. Nobody knew who I was. The team members will be evacuated separately, in small groups. No one will know I'm not with some other party. And you," she pointed at Troy, "the records will show that you got ejected from the airlock in the decontamination dump, though the lab was really empty. Clean, efficient, and simple—and you'll be a free man."

"I . . ." Troy's Adam's apple bobbed again. "Whatever you say. But that lab wasn't empty—"

"Just get moving," Kalliana said.

The second door finally unsealed. They bounded into the docking chamber where the two sleds still waited for their return journey—but the large craft were not yet cranked into the heavy-gauge spring-launchers in preparation for launch. Kalliana went to the big equipment closet mounted to the wall and opened it, sorting through the suits dangling there like empty silver skins.

"But how are we going to get back down to Atlas?" Troy said.

"One step at a time. First we have to get to the Platform."

Exasperated, Troy said, "But how do we get to the Platform? You can't fly one of those sleds can you? They're too big for just the two of us to launch."

"True," Kalliana said, knowing how preposterous it would sound. But Sondheim's message had insisted this was the only way. She pulled out one of the spare suits and thrust it at Troy.

"We're going to jump."

ii

With his head sealed inside the spacesuit helmet Troy's breath roared around him as he panted with fear and disbelief. He could hear his heart pummeling his chest and the blood rushing through his ears.

They toggled through the communication systems on their suit, finally connecting each other with a low-power line-of-sight radio link.

"Now what do we do?" he asked.

Kalliana seemed just as frightened as he was. She went over to the hull door controls and punched in a sequence that began the decompression cycle.

The waiting was tense and interminable as the docking bay drained of air, seemingly one lungful at a time. Troy felt his suit ballooning as it strained to protect the pressure of his body from the empty maw of space. At any moment he expected the Orb-Lab 2 guards to stop them.

He fought against a violent shiver and a distant roaring in his ears that made him suspect he was going into shock. He had no idea what he was doing here. He had hated his hazardous yet monotonous life in prison. He knew he wasn't guilty of his crime—but this escape attempt was insane. What if the sol-pols caught him? They would shoot to kill. And this emergency, the sudden depressurization in the bacterial sorting lab—had Eli Strone been a victim of the planned escape?

Troy felt like a tiny piece of flotsam in the midst of a hurricane as he looked out the opening door that led to the bottomless pit of space. "And you want us to just . . . swim?"

"Swim," Kalliana's voice crackled over the speaker, bouncing around in his ears. "There's a way we can bleed air from our tanks, use it to propel ourselves across the gulf and get to the Platform."

"But if we jet with our air, we won't have enough to breathe," Troy said. This "solution" seemed to get worse every moment. Standing by the equipment cabinet, he snatched two of the small compressed-gas packs, and tossed one to her. It tumbled slowly, end over end in the soup of nothingness, and she caught it, nearly overbalancing herself. "Here. Maybe these'll help us. I saw Kareem Sondheim using gas canisters to move himself about."

"It isn't really all that far. Sondheim assured me we could do it," she insisted, working her way to the edge. Troy gulped as he looked across the black canyon of space. The gold and blue planet hung immeasurably far below, and a sense of unreality overtook him.

Before Troy could remember his terror again, the two of them pushed off, drifting through the open doors and out into the abyss.

OrbLab 2's decompression cycle timed out and began to

reverse itself. Behind them, the thick doors ground shut in silence, sealing Troy and his rescuer from the hodgepodge of canisters and sterile laboratories.

The yawning distance below and around him seemed incomprehensibly vast. Troy found himself dizzy and nauseated again, as he had on the space elevator ride, but he clamped his teeth together. The thought of vomiting inside the space helmet made him doubly queasy.

Across space Troy could see the Platform, and the space elevator with its razor-thin thread of diamond fiber just disengaging to begin its descent.

They experimented with their compressed-air canisters, sending themselves into spins and lurching with increased inertia. Troy felt a great uneasiness at being so disconnected, so disoriented, out in space.

"We're supposed to go to a particular external airlock on the Platform," Kalliana said over the line-of-sight link. "There's a holding chamber inside. Sondheim will see that we get hidden in the space elevator on the next cargo-only run."

Troy recalled the cramped elevator, thought of what his surly boss Cren would say if the anchor point crew opened the hatch to find two fugitives hiding inside. It might be worth it, just to see the bug-eyed expression of surprise on Cren's face.

The winking hemispherical Platform hung in orbit, precariously connected to the planet below. They drifted closer, faster—and Troy realized with alarm how much they had jetted with their canisters. They had better start decelerating now.

He sprayed the nozzle in front of him, and white vapor puffed out. It slowed him down like a fist slammed into his chest, but gradually counteracted his forward motion. Kalliana did the same.

"There!" she said, pointing toward the convoluted topography of the outer dome. Troy squinted through the polarized glare of starlight and saw a circular outer hatch marked *X15*. Using tiny jets from her canister, Kalliana maneuvered herself closer and closer to the designated opening.

"If Sondheim was correct," she said, "I should be able to open this from out here. Then we'll be inside and home free."

Troy heard the words with a sluggish sense of joy. *Home. Free.* Two concepts he had never thought he could apply to himself again.

Kalliana struck the hatch like an insect, landing with spread hands and booted feet. Troy gave a final blast from his gas canister, which slowed him down just enough so that he wasn't thrown off-balance by the impact.

Kalliana fumbled with the access controls. Troy wondered when this entryway had last been opened. These emergency entrance chambers had been placed by the original workers when they had disconnected the Platform from the main bulky framework of the colony ship.

The door swung silently open with a puff of crystal steam, remnants of air that hadn't quite been drained away in the cycling procedure. Inside, the chamber was full of shadows. A good place to hide.

Kalliana drifted in, groping for Troy's gloved hand to pull him after her. She had turned and looked behind herself to get a good grip and tugged Troy along, so that they both saw the threat at the same time.

Sondheim's guards were waiting for them.

Within the cramped chamber three suited figures stood around a massive cannonlike weapon that gleamed with solenoids and magnetic rings along its barrel: some sort of bizarre and powerful plasma-discharge launcher, Troy guessed, far different from the simple projectile rifles carried by sol-pols. It was obviously aimed at them.

The suited guards reacted frantically, moving about in vacuum silence—their communications link must have been tuned to a different channel—as they wrestled the plasma-discharge cannon into position.

In a snapshot of terror, Troy noticed a curiously familiar insignia emblazoned on the cannon's barrel. He had seen the same design on the outer wall of the Truthsayers Guild, partially worn away by time. This weapon had come from the *SkySword*, part of the military ship's stockpile of high-tech armaments that had supposedly been destroyed when the invaders' vessel was grounded.

"We're betrayed!" Kalliana shouted over the radio link. She still clutched his wrist; Troy planted his foot on the hatch frame and shoved with all his might.

They tumbled backward just as the three figures managed to trigger the plasma discharge. A bolt of crackling, fizzing incandescence sprayed outward through the center of the opening, a screaming path of disintegration. The weapon blasted a second time.

Troy and Kalliana reeled out of control, tumbling endlessly into space.

# CHAPTER

## 31

i

Though Maximillian was generally dour and serious, Dokken caught him smiling as the two of them galloped their horses out for another rigorous ride deep into the badlands.

Dokken was in no particular hurry, but he enjoyed the feeling of his stallion extending his muscles, snorting with effort, hooves pounding on baked clay as they thundered across the desert. Dokken's long hair swept wildly behind him. Though the rainstorm had washed away all previous trails, the stallion seemed to know where he was going.

When both horses were exhausted, Dokken slowed his mount to an easy walk. Maximillian squinted, as if his cheekbones were squeezing upward toward his craggy forehead. They carried plenty of water and supplies. Though it was dangerous to ride off into the rugged wasteland alone, Franz Dokken and his manservant had done this so many times it had become old habit to them.

Back at the villa Dokken had once again grown weary of constantly shepherding his myriad plans, each designed toward guiding the great tapestry, a plan that would leave him, Franz Dokken, fully in control of Atlas by the time the *EarthDawn* arrived. His work was not merely a petty power-grabbing scheme, of which the other inexperienced landholders were so fond—he was sculpting history.

Now, though, he also felt eager for the restful oblivion, to recharge his batteries in the way that had allowed him to maintain himself for nearly two and a half centuries. It also helped "dodge the bullet" of his own more extreme actions, such as the sabotaged escape attempt of the Truthsayer and that scapegoat Boren from OrbLab 2. Some things just needed time to sort themselves out.

Tharion would be utterly outraged when he heard of it, but the Guild Master simply had to believe it was an accident, a tragic mistake. In time Tharion might even be made to see the ultimate advantages of removing the scapegoat and the Truthsayer. Dokken simply hoped he had trained Tharion well enough that he would come to such a realization on his own. He had the potential for greatness, though he must never suspect any deeper scheme. The powerful Guild Master's greatest value lay in the fact that he *thought* he knew what was going on . . . but in reality he knew very little, and therefore remained malleable.

Riding across the desert, lost in thought, Dokken was taken by surprise when they encountered a deep, fresh ravine across their path. When he pulled his stallion to a halt at the edge, Maximillian rode up beside him, and they looked down the long shadowy ribbon of sliced earth.

They rode along the edge for some time until they finally found a spot narrow enough for the two horses to leap across. Some of the crumbly clay broke away and slid in a small avalanche down to the thin damp line of mud on the gully bottom.

Dokken looked back to see the white ivory of exposed bones in the fresh-cut strata, ancient fossils of large misshapen animals. He did a double take, surprised to see evidence of extinct life here on this supposedly dead world. Atlas, too, had secrets that it kept carefully hidden.

Finally, as the sun reached noon, Maximillian asked the question he always asked. "Please tell me the specific items you wish me to oversee while you are . . . away, Master Dokken. How long will you be this time?"

Dokken had already been assessing the same issues, but hadn't yet come to a clear answer. "I have so many things going on," he said, "but I'm torn between resting for our big events in the near future and needing to stay on top of things *now*, making sure that all the plans are nudged when necessary. Two weeks, I think."

"Two weeks?" Maximillian sat up in the saddle, his eyes flashing sudden surprise—but he covered it well. "Yes, sir."

"The big Pilgrim rally won't happen before then, will it?"

Maximillian shook his head. "No. I went from village to village and riled them up. They are going to meet in three and a half weeks. I don't believe Sardili suspects a thing."

Dokken snorted. "He never does. You're sure no one will recognize you as the Pilgrim Adamant?"

Maximillian shrugged, as if it wasn't a concern. "How could they? We met in the dark. I wore one of their hooded robes, and the Pilgrims themselves are not . . . cosmopolitan enough to keep tabs on the assistants of distant landholders."

"You're right, Maximillian," he said, "again. What would I do without you?"

The tall manservant sidestepped the rhetorical question. "One thing you *will* miss though, sir," he said, "is the final dismantling of the Carsus-Bondalar marriage alliance. Next week is the culmination of our efforts, after which their alliance will no longer be a problem."

Dokken made a sour face. "I'm sorry I won't be present to enjoy the fun."

They rode on in silence as the land around them grew more rugged. Black rock like rotted teeth thrust up from the clays, and tall cliffs of shale tilted above the surface as if some powerful force deep below the crust had elbowed them up.

Back in the flatlands, a dust devil stretched to the sky, gray-brown as it thrashed from side to side, plowing up clouds of debris as it moved. It was a short-lived phenomenon, though, and dissipated, leaving only settling dust.

"One concern does seem to be growing, sir," Maximillian said. "I believe Emilio Toth and Victoria Koman have indeed joined forces to oppose you. From all indications they have a vendetta against you."

Dokken raised his eyebrows. "Well, they have ample cause— I just didn't know they realized it. Too bad we don't have Cialben to slip inside and bring back a report."

"They're keeping their plans secret, but most likely they have set their own plots in motion to back you into a corner."

Dokken made a rude noise. "Amateurs! They're out of their league." He shook his head then snorted in derision. "If only Koman knew how she's been set up, she'd crawl down one of her own mine shafts to hide."

They rode into a narrow canyon in the gray and red cliffs. Sheltered by a broad flat overhang, the cave lay before them. Dokken grew more and more excited as they approached the hideaway.

It had been so much more difficult to disappear when Schandra kept nagging him about his whereabouts, insistent upon knowing his every movement. Maximillian, on the other hand, knew all of his plans, and Dokken didn't need to keep up the tiresome charade. They dismounted, tied the horses outside the cave, and went inside, powering up the lights from the antique generator.

Dokken felt bone-weary, and he stretched his arms, looking around with a heavy sigh. Inside the cave, hooked up to its well-maintained diagnostics systems and its recirculating routines, lay one of the stainless-steel-and-Plexiglas deepsleep chambers he had long ago taken from the original colony ship.

"I feel as if I could sleep for about two weeks," Dokken said with a grin.

ii

He had been impatient once, despite the fifty-year journey from Earth and the expected slow progress of the terraforming efforts on Atlas. Franz Dokken wanted to *see* the results of his many labors. Cause and effect, global changes.

As one of the three captains aboard the colony ship, he had seen the first seeds planted on their new home. He had been given special geriatric treatments that extended human life by decades—by virtue of which the infant Kareem Sondheim, now a withered old man, had also kept himself alive since the ship's arrival.

But ever since their first landing, Dokken had also used the deepsleep technology to pad his life span. He could spend up to half of his time frozen in stasis, letting others continue their work while he stopped aging, and then reemerge to see the results.

Over the years, as he had implemented his grand plan for placing the world in the palm of his hand, he had used the deepsleep chamber like time-lapse photography to watch his schemes develop. Skating across the history of Atlas, shape it, plan it, make modifications, and observe the results in what—to him—was real time.

Whenever it suited him, he had altered records, installed false entries of previous Dokken landholders from many decades past to make everyone think there had been a regular succession of landholders. . . .

The cave was cool, but not at all unpleasant after the ride across the hot and dusty wastelands. Dokken stripped out of his riding leathers and sponged down with water, then an alcohol-based disinfectant. Maximillian gave him the slowdown injection so expertly that Dokken barely felt the sting of the needle as he set the timer on the control panels.

The chamber, centuries old now, still shone as if new. He had maintained this apparatus with more care than he expended on the equipment in his villa. Inside the chamber, the fabric was warm and slick, some synthetic polymer that reminded him of Schandra's precious silk. This was far more durable, however, and heated with recirculation systems to make him comfortable . . . until the coma carried him down.

Dokken climbed into the deepsleep chamber and lay back, sliding his naked skin against the padding. Each time, it reminded him of a coffin.

Outside the cave the horses snorted, finding nothing to eat in the ravine. Maximillian leaned over him, made sure the diagnostic leads were attached properly, then stood erect. "Will there be anything else, sir?"

"No," Dokken mumbled. Already his body felt sluggish as his metabolism started cycling down. His internal temperature began to drop. The deepsleep chamber grew colder, but he couldn't think clearly about it. He lay still, ready to be engulfed.

"Very well," Maximillian said. "I will see you in two weeks." He sealed the glass top of the chamber, and Dokken, allowing his eyelids to fall closed, breathed deeper. The sound of the rushing air was hypnotic, a flowing river. A rhythm that ran slower and slower . . . and slower.

Like a one-way time traveler into the future, Dokken would slumber through the days, let weeks pass, allow the wheels to grind along . . . until Guild Master Tharion cooled down from his anger.

Maximillian rode off with the two horses, leaving the secret cave behind.

Franz Dokken slid into timelessness, and the world of Atlas sped up, passing him by. . . .

# CHAPTER

# 32

i

The bottomless universe tumbled around Troy. He flailed his stiff arms within the spacesuit, pinwheeling out of control.

The glittering metal Platform and the cracked sphere of Atlas spun about him like a tornado; in all directions the infinite gulf of space seemed to suck him down. The white sun blazed incredibly hot and bright.

Troy couldn't steady himself, but he wrestled through his panic enough to use the compressed-gas canister, instinctively spraying in the direction opposite his spin. It took him several tries, repeatedly overcompensating, but finally he managed to get himself reasonably stable again.

Another searing plasma blast roared out of the Platform's emergency access hatch, streaming bright and tenuous fire, but in the wrong direction. Sondheim's murderous sol-pols could not easily aim their bulky weapon. Troy didn't think they saw anything, though. To them it must appear that both he and Kalliana had been disintegrated in the first explosion.

*Kalliana!* he thought, and struggled in his suit, craning his head inside the rigid helmet to find his rescuer, hoping he wouldn't see a lump of molten debris that had once been a petite young woman inside an environment suit. Instead, he saw her silhouette, a dark, unreflective blot as she passed between him and the metallic hemisphere of the Platform. She was still tumbling, arms waving frantically for some kind of handhold.

Troy had had time to get accustomed to the negligible gravity on OrbLab 2, but Kalliana seemed completely unfamiliar with the changed rules of motion. He was about to call out on their line-of-sight radio transmission, but stopped himself just in time.

Something had gone desperately wrong here, and he didn't want any eavesdroppers on the Platform to realize that both he and Kalliana had survived. No radios. They couldn't risk it.

She faced away from him, heavy air tanks strapped to a framework on her back. Troy jetted toward her and collided from behind, moving faster than he had anticipated. He grappled with her shoulders. Kalliana struggled wildly, as if he were attacking her, until he managed to spin her around so she could see his face. Her eyes were wide and white with terror.

He pressed his faceplate against hers, hoping his voice would carry. "Are you all right?"

Kalliana's voice came ragged and high-pitched, humming through the faceplates. "We've been betrayed!" she said. "Guild Master Tharion must have betrayed us. He was the only one who knew. He and Sondheim set this up—they wanted to kill us."

"I knew this was a mistake," Troy said.

Kalliana was paralyzed with confusion. As they spun together, sharing momentum, she said, "We have to get into the Platform, announce this scheme to the Truthsayers Guild. They'll take care of everything."

"I don't know which part you missed, Kalliana," Troy shouted, "but somebody at the Platform is trying to *kill* us. They don't want us to get away."

Kalliana moaned, but said nothing.

"You helped me escape," Troy continued. "After we're dead, they can make up any explanation they want."

"Where can we go?" Kalliana said. "We'll die out here before long."

Troy knew only one possibility, and—weird as it seemed—he thought of Eli Strone's ability to keep absolutely cool in an emergency. "Down there," he said. As outrageous as it seemed, it couldn't be any more dangerous or unlikely than the other phases of this escape plan. "And we have to move now."

He pointed with a gloved finger toward the space elevator descending on the gossamer thread. Its impellers moved it along, accelerating down from the Platform. Every second took it farther and farther from them.

Troy cartwheeled in the air, still holding Kalliana. When they were facing the descending bulk of the elevator, Troy clicked his helmet against hers again. She was still shouting "—never make it! It's going too fast. Too far away. We'd better just—"

"No," Troy said. "We'll use our compressed-gas canisters. We won't be able to decelerate, but I think that the elevator will be going fast enough that our speed differential won't make the impact too bad . . . I hope."

Looking forlorn but determined, Kalliana ceased her complaining. "I guess there's not much choice, is there?" she said.

Linked together they both shot their canisters, pointing the nozzles behind them. Troy felt a gentle hand pushing them, harder and harder, straight toward the huge planet below. If they didn't catch the descending elevator in time, both of them would continue their headlong plunge all the way to the surface.

In a way it was like the sol-pol captain piloting the shuttle-sled over to OrbLab 2, a dead reckoning that adjusted course by feel, making mistakes and then correcting them, wasting their precious propulsion gas. Troy was glad they had brought the extra canisters along, because by now they would have emptied their oxygen tanks.

They followed the cable down. In sunlight the wrapped-diamond fiber looked like a wet spiderweb, seemingly far too delicate to hold up the elevator. Troy thought of all the times he had stood down at the anchor point, gazing upward in wonder as the big shape came down from orbit. Never had he imagined he would be riding it down in such a crazy stunt.

He and Kalliana accelerated toward the complex mass of the incomprehensible machinery on the elevator roof—impeller housings, sensors, boxy battery packs—but the elevator itself continued to pick up speed, so that they closed the distance only gradually.

Kalliana's gas canister sputtered, then ceased its flow. Troy had carried both of them with what little remained in his own, though their acceleration decreased considerably, and the elevator seemed to lurch ahead. Still holding Kalliana, Troy felt a sinking in his stomach.

Suddenly a great fist punched him from behind—and they soared toward the elevator at dizzying speed. Kalliana had cracked the emergency valve on one of her air tanks, propelling them forward in the way she had originally intended to fly over to the Platform.

The elevator slammed up at them fast—too fast! Troy gripped her arm. "Enough!" he shouted into her helmet.

Kalliana squeezed off the valve, and both of them braced for impact. It was like dropping to the ground from a three-story rooftop, but their suits were tough and padded. Kalliana reached

out for the superstructure on top and snagged a brace pipe. Troy
struck and rebounded, starting to spin off into space again, but he
managed to grapple one of the top towers, swinging around until
he finally damped his inertia. Panting, he moved hand over hand,
his legs dangling behind him in space.

Troy hauled himself down to the roof of the elevator car,
where he found Kalliana clinging to one of the support bars, as if
afraid she might fly off. Far above, the receding Platform appeared
as little more than a flat silvery coin, lit on one side by the sun.
OrbLab 2 was just a bright star. He wedged himself in the
sheltered area beside her.

Kalliana looked at Troy, then clutched his arm. He could feel
her fingers pressing even through the thick suit. She refused to
release her grip on the support strut, but she needed to be reassured
by his presence. They crouched face-to-face, pressing helmets
together.

"Well, we made it this far," Troy said, trying to be optimistic.
"I mean, what else could go wrong? I suppose our impact *could*
have caused the cable to disengage from the Platform. Then the
elevator would fall through the atmosphere and slam into First
Landing, obliterating all the people there and us along with it,
thereby stranding everyone up on the Platform, where they would
slowly die from starvation . . . not to mention the fact that it would
destroy the economy of Atlas and the fragile society in which all
the landholders depend on each other."

"Or maybe it'll turn out right after all." Kalliana looked uncertainly at him, and he said. "We can relax now. It's a ten-hour trip."

Then Troy gulped as a very real possibility struck him. "In fact
we'd better conserve energy," he said, "I don't know if we have
enough air to last us all the way down. Hold your breath."

ii

Kalliana clutched her precarious anchor as the elevator continued its rapid descent to the fringes of the atmosphere. Over the
past hour she had worked her way into a state of calm, but was not
yet ready to plan for what would happen when they reached the
anchor point below.

Troy spent the time talking with her through the helmets.
Some of his words were fuzzed, but she understood most of them.
The conversation soothed her, and him as well.

Kalliana was afraid to tell him much about herself. After all, he still had no idea who she was and what she had done to him, but she listened as Troy told her stories about living in what sounded to be utterly miserable crowded conditions in a tiny dwelling in the Koman Mining District . . . how his father worked all day long and came home filthy and exhausted. Troy sounded bright and cheerful as he spoke of his sister Leisa, of her recent marriage and pregnancy—which would add yet another mouth to feed in the family's already-crowded dwelling.

How could people live like that? Kalliana wondered. She thought of her own gentle and spacious upbringing in the Guild, her every need taken care of, her only requirement to study and to become a Truthsayer.

So she could face the minds of twisted men like Eli Strone.

"And then there's my little sister, a complete opposite," Troy continued, "who's focused like the point of a stiletto on getting what she wants—"

"Troy," she finally had to interrupt him, "you will never be able to go back to your family. That was a condition of your escape. I know you're innocent, but we're trapped in our circumstances. The Guild was only willing to free you on the condition that their . . . that *my* mistake remain a secret." She paused, then continued, waiting for him to realize what she had admitted. "You will have to be a different person, live a different life, if we survive this at all."

Tróy looked at Kalliana, his eyes narrowing in the shadows of his rounded helmet. "What do you mean *your* mistake?"

"Look at me," she insisted. "Take a good look. Don't you recognize me?"

Troy searched her face, but did not seem to know what he was supposed to find. "Imagine my hair white," she said. "My skin paler . . . wearing white robes." She could feel him tense inside his padded suit.

"You," he said. "You're the Truthsayer."

She nodded helplessly behind her faceplate.

"You lied!" he shouted, his voice muffled and distorted through their touched faceplates. He broke contact so that she lost some of his words, but then picked them up again as he slammed his helmet against hers.

"—sent me up there. *Up there.* Everyone thinks I'm guilty. I didn't kill anybody. You lied!"

"I made a mistake," Kalliana said.

"But Truthsayers can't *make* mistakes."

"I did," she said, "and I'm sorry for it. When I found out I'd made an error, when I discovered that my abilities were no longer reliable, I wanted to make it right. I went directly to the Guild Master . . . but now it seems Tharion didn't want everything right after all. He didn't want anyone to know."

"But," Troy said, sounding flabbergasted, "but what did *I* do? Why me?"

"Nothing," Kalliana said. "You were just in the wrong place at the wrong time. When I truth-read you, all you could think of was the blood, the horror. Your mind was so filled with guilt about something, I jumped to the wrong conclusion."

"Guilt," Troy said, then he laughed. "I was feeling guilty about the mistake I'd made in the manifest sheets. I was attempting to fix it when I discovered the body."

"I know—now," Kalliana said. "That's why I helped you escape."

Troy looked around himself, and Kalliana wondered if he was thinking of his father, his family, how they had looked when the sol-pols had marched him in bindings off to the elevator.

"Thanks for all your help," he said, his voice steeped in bitterness.

iii

Hours after entering the scarce outer atmosphere, Troy finally began to feel wind against his suit. The empty black of space faded into a wispy lightness without color. Above, the stars continued to shine, and he could still see the bright dot of the distant Platform. But now they were much closer to the surface of Atlas.

Kalliana had remained withdrawn since delivering her shocking news. Troy felt a burning, helpless anger toward her, but he tried to ignore it. Venting it at Kalliana now would only waste more air. Though her mistake had ruined his future, she had also risked her life to undo what she had done. Brooding resentment wouldn't do him any good. She was as cut off from her former life as he was, and right now they had to support each other if they were going to get out of this. Somehow. But he found it difficult to tell her that.

Troy braced himself and leaned over the edge, where he could look down the elevator cable. Though he could still see the curvature of the planet, Atlas filled the view beneath them with the deep blue of ocean and the coppery brown of untamed continents. Immediately below, he saw a brooding knot of clouds, a thickening storm system. It was supposedly too late in the season for the heaviest storms, but Atlas weather was notoriously unpredictable.

"Anchor yourself well," he told Kalliana. "Bumpy ride ahead. Looks like we're heading into some clouds." He dug into the utility pack of his suit and used bits of paraphernalia to lash himself to a strut, clipping a line onto it so that even if he got jostled, he wouldn't be thrown off to plummet to the surface. Kalliana dutifully did the same.

When the elevator jostled, Troy reached over to grip her. Kalliana responded without words, hanging on to him tightly.

Wisps of cloud tore past, as if the elevator had plunged through a boll of raw cotton. Even at the upper cloud level the atmosphere was thick enough that Troy could hear the wind singing, scratching around the superstructure. The diamond cable emitted a high-pitched whine as the wind sliced past it.

The elevator continued downward, and suddenly they were plunged into a gray, wet limbo. Tiny droplets drenched every surface, cracking into a patina of frost on the chilled metal. The wind slapped at Troy and Kalliana like invisible paddles.

He had no idea how thick the cloud layer might be. The grayness seemed to go on forever, the clouds fogging his faceplate, glittering on his suit. Distant lightning sizzled through the clouds, illuminating the mist with diffuse explosions.

By the time the clouds slipped above them, letting them continue their descent through a dreary, fog-laden day, the tension in his body had grown worse. Despite the cold, he felt warm and sleepy. Breaths echoed in his ears as if some invisible rider were panting down his neck. The blood thrummed in his head, and he felt tightness like a vise around his skull. Each lungful became a labor now, and he looked at his chest pack to see that the gauge on his air tanks read EMPTY. Kalliana fared no better.

Troy could see the ground below. They were still high above the ground, and he had no idea how thin the atmosphere was—but they had no choice. Taking the first risk himself, he drew a last lungful of the heavily reused air in his suit . . . and then unsealed the helmet at his neck.

With a gush of outrushing air and a blast of icy wind, the

helmet was torn from his hand, a round, shiny cannonball sailing into the infinite sky. His ears popped. A bright pain stabbed through his skull. He drew long gasps of the sharp air, breathing, then breathing again. His ears rang. His head pounded—but already he seemed to be stealing a bit more oxygen than what had remained in the tanks. The thin air smelled damp and saturated with ozone, but even though the cold made his lungs raw, the fresh atmosphere seemed blessed indeed.

Kalliana did not move. She watched him, apparently unable to comprehend what had changed. He reached over to fumble with her helmet. As if in slow motion, she batted him weakly with her gloved fists, trying to keep him away, not understanding—but at last he popped her helmet off, and she gasped, her chest heaving. Her lips, normally pale, had turned blue. She fought to breathe, coughing and sucking in huge lungfuls.

"Thank you," Kalliana said, her eyes finally clearing. "I think I passed out."

Troy nodded. "My old boss would have had a hard time explaining two dead people in spacesuits hooked to the top of the elevator."

Kalliana hung her head. "How will they explain two *live* people on the elevator?"

"They won't need to—not unless they find us," he said. Troy's mind spun again. He'd been trying to think of a solution, and he knew only one way that might work. "You told me this elevator car had no passengers, just supplies that were preempted by the investigative team. So there's no one to suspect if we pop the upper hatch and climb inside."

Kalliana frowned at him. "But they'll find us as soon as we dock at the anchor point. When they open up the elevator to unload, they'll see us."

Troy shook his head. "Not necessarily," he said, raising his voice above the cold wind. "We'll climb into the upper crawl space—it isn't usually used on the downward trips. Nobody will bother to look—I know, because I've helped unload the elevator enough times. They'll have no reason to check up there." *At least I hope they don't,* he thought.

It was a relief to be speaking with their own voices rather than faceplate to faceplate. Kalliana's expression grew stormy. "Why couldn't we have gone there from the start, then?" she said. "Instead of hanging on up here for the entire ride?"

"The elevator is pressurized," Troy explained. "If we opened the hatch, it would have blown everything out, certainly all of the air—and the people at the anchor point would know as soon as they unloaded the elevator. This way, we're deep enough in the atmosphere that we shouldn't lose so much air when we climb in. We can wait there, and we can breathe."

Troy unclipped his restraints and carefully worked his way around the superstructure until he found the upper hatch. He was relieved to see that it required no special security code. When the disk swung upward on its hinge, a strong gust of musty air puffed out.

He dropped down into the small crawl space, then decided it would be best to remove his bulky spacesuit and throw it overboard. The crawl space was cramped enough, and if they did manage to sneak out onto the ground, their escape would be hindered by the Platform environment suits.

Still with his shoulders above the roof level, he shucked the slippery metallic fabric. The bulbous empty oxygen tanks slowed him down, but Troy finally dropped the whole suit over the side, letting the wind rip it away. They were still kilometers above the surface, and breezes would carry the suit far from any chance of discovery.

Kalliana did the same, tossing her outfit overboard. It flew like a severed silhouette, vanishing into the distance under the gray-lit clouds. Troy sealed the hatch again, and together, they huddled in the crawl space. They lay across from each other, shivering in the sudden cold and looking warily into each other's eyes . . . dreading the next step.

iv

Troy felt the abrupt, vibrating thump as the elevator settled onto the annular docking ring at its anchor point in First Landing. He feared the Platform might have sent down a warning, that sol-pol guards were even now surrounding the elevator and making ready to charge in to capture the stowaways. The cargo door below slid open with a loud *thwoop* of equalizing pressure.

Above the ceiling Troy and Kalliana lay absolutely still. He caught the Truthsayer's frightened gaze, noting that her dusty blue eyes were bloodshot. She said nothing, not even a whisper. He heard the boisterous conversation as workers moved in to take out the heavy packages. Troy remembered the clumsy oafs who had tipped over the water buffalo cage, and accidentally released the frantic chicks. He tried to recognize voices, longing to hear even the harsh reprimands of his former boss. Someone down there must have taken his own place, Troy realized—someone else hired by Cren to do the inventory checklists, to enter the data on the manifests. *Someone else.* That part of his life was gone forever, regardless of his guilt or innocence.

Troy chanted a silent litany over and over in his mind. *Please don't come up here. Please don't come up here.* Kalliana's lips moved, as if she were saying quiet prayers of her own.

After many minutes of bustle and clatter and congenial conversation, the elevator became quiet again, and Troy waited, hoping the workers had finished unloading. He counted to a hundred again and again, stalling for time, waiting, hoping someone hadn't set a trap for them.

When he guessed a half hour had passed, he whispered, "They won't reload the elevator until tomorrow," he said. "They always take a twelve-hour turnaround." His voice, though hushed, seemed explosively loud in the dead silent chamber.

Kalliana sighed with relief. "Is it safe to go out yet?"

He shook his head. "It's still daylight. We'll wait for full darkness, and even then there'll be lights and guards. We just have to hope they're not watching too closely—and that we can disappear into the streets."

"Where will we go?" she asked.

Troy shrugged in the cramped crawl space. "Away from here," he said. "But it's going to be a while yet. We're both tired and hungry. There should be a pack of emergency rations here, and then let's try to get some sleep. I think we could both use it."

For the next several hours, they lay restless, dealing with their own anxieties. Troy dared to open the top just once, raising it the barest crack to see dirty gray daylight still spilling in, then resealed the heavy hatch. And they waited some more.

Finally, in the deep blackness of night, Troy peered out again. The veil of clouds obliterated even the greenish glow of the aurora. This was as dark as night ever became on Atlas. Despite the security lights burning all around the fenced-in anchor point, Troy knew this would be their best shot.

With stiff shoulders, he lifted the elevator's hatch carefully, with Kalliana close beside him. Both were ready for anything.

They might have to run and dodge weapons fire . . . or they might slip out undetected. Stranger things had happened. The concrete apron surrounding the elevator looked like a desert plain in daylight under the bombarding streetlights.

"I sure hate to cross that space," Troy said. "But there's no avoiding it." Kalliana nodded wordlessly, her pale lips pressed together.

Two sol-pols stood outside a guard kiosk, patrolling the area. They seemed inattentive, and Troy hoped he and Kalliana could slip across the wide-open space. The chain-link gates were locked with a keypad code—but Troy still knew the access number unless Cren had changed it. He doubted that: with Troy sentenced to OrbLab 2, why should the boss worry about a convicted murderer knowing the codes?

"Shall we go one at a time?" Kalliana asked.

Troy shook his head again. "That wouldn't gain us anything. As it is, we'll have a slim enough chance that they won't notice us dashing across the concrete. Let's not risk it twice." Troy looked sheepishly at her. "Might as well get it over with."

Some of the massive shipments stockpiled for the next trip up had already been brought to the concrete apron. Stacked cylinders of compressed air and containers of filtered water lay on pallets, providing islands of cover for Troy and Kalliana.

Troy hauled himself out onto the elevator's roof, but this time the superstructures looked more sinister, nested with shadows and sharp edges. He ducked low, hoping no one would see them moving. He made sure Kalliana closed the hatch and sealed it.

"What difference does that make?" she asked.

"The longer we can keep them from suspecting anything," he said, "the longer we'll have to get away. We don't want them thinking something unusual happened here."

They crawled to the section of the elevator most deeply in shadow and opposite from the patrolling sol-pols. Gripping her hands, Troy helped lower Kalliana down, but she still had to drop the last meter to the concrete. She seemed so slight, as if a powerful gust of wind could carry her back up into the air.

He dropped beside her, then caught his breath. They looked at each other for a long moment, finally clasped hands. "Ready to go?" Troy asked.

She nodded. They bent low, peeked around the side of the elevator, and agreed on the first stopping point: behind several tall crates of packaged food. They waited until the sol-pols had marched out of sight and then sprinted until they reached the shadows of the containers and crouched down. The sol-pols reappeared and continued their patrol around the corner once more.

From that point Troy and Kalliana ran to the next scant shelter, and the next, until they had worked their way over to a gate on the perimeter fence, a side gate that led to the clustered district of warehouses that served as holding points for material that had arrived on the mag-lev trains. Even at this late hour, high-speed cargo containers zipped off with a humming whine as they accelerated along the frictionless rails and shot away into the night.

Troy gazed longingly at the departing trains, remembering when his family had come to Koman Station to see him off from the Mining District, dressed in their finest outfits. Even Rissbeth had looked downcast to see him go, but hopeful that he would get his big break in the city. They had all waved farewell as Troy boarded the packed passenger pod to First Landing, looking back over his shoulder. . . .

Now, seeing no sol-pols, Troy made a final dash to the fence. He reached through the chain-link, twisting his wrist to reach the keypads outside of the gate. Clumsily, he punched in the four-digit code and activated the lock, yanking his hand back just as the rattling fence trundled aside. The racket was thunderous, and he dashed through the opening as soon as it was wide enough, gesturing frantically for Kalliana to hurry, as she scurried across the last distance and leaped through the still-opening gate. Troy headed toward the shadowed warehouse district.

Barely a moment after they disappeared into the shadows, sol-pol guards came running onto the scene and sounded the alarm.

"Run!" Troy whispered into Kalliana's ear, and they sprinted down narrow alleys, between buildings, behind waste disposal units and piles of discarded parts to be refurbished or rerouted. Troy glanced back toward the blazingly lit anchor point, spotting half a dozen guards already crowded inside the fenced area, weapons drawn as they searched for intruders.

Troy could not restrain his jubilant smile. "They think someone broke *in*!" he said. "Keep going."

Though Kalliana gasped and panted, she did not complain. Troy decided their best bet would be to get to one of the cargo transports, find a way inside, and ride it far from First Landing. . . .

At the mag-lev station in the industrial section, several containers were just now being loaded by automated cargo systems that transferred shipments from one landholding onto a spur bound for other villages.

Kalliana doggedly followed Troy as he slipped from one loading container to another, dancing across the silvery rails into other murky areas. Finally he found a battered auxiliary car hooked up to a long chain of cargo containers just preparing for departure.

The two fugitives let themselves fall into a darkened, empty enclosure that smelled of pine wood and fresh sawdust, and slumped to the floor, safe at last. In the distance they heard weapons fire, the tinny muffled shouting of sol-pols. Troy's heart thudded with renewed fear that the guards had guessed where he and Kalliana were hiding, that they would stop and search every outbound vessel.

But with a thump, their cargo pod lurched as the entire transport train powered up and lifted on its magnetic cushion. Its accelerators heaved the transport into motion.

Troy and Kalliana huddled alone in silence, both of them too numb to wonder yet about their new destination as the mag-lev train carried them off to nowhere.

# CHAPTER

## 33

### i

As his image sharpened in the viewplate, Dieter Pan's face wore a foolish grin. "Hi, Kareem! What a pleasure."

Sondheim could never tell when Dieter was serious or when his words were meant to mock him. He had watched the boy, born and raised on the Platform, reach to the peak of his ambitions and still grow more enthusiastic about his work as the years went by.

"Don't be so cheerful, Dieter," Sondheim scolded. "Two people are dead."

"I know—and Strone isn't." Dieter shrugged, then gave a little hop into the air. "But mistakes happen, and people die. What we *do* with our lives is all that's important."

"And is smuggling Veritas all that important?"

Dieter grinned. "Makes our mark on the world."

Around him in his private quarters, Sondheim looked at the breathtaking scenery of the yawning desert landscapes, the immense vistas that seemed too large for the tiny planet below: the sunlight on rock, the shadows spilling into canyons, life finding its desperate footholds. Atlas must be incredibly beautiful, he thought. If only his frail body could withstand the crush of gravity.

Over the centuries, he had grown to hate the Platform, and his forced exile from any other experiences.

"I'm not sure that's the kind of mark I want to make on the world," Sondheim said.

In raising Dieter Pan, teaching him all he knew, Kareem Sondheim had done the next best thing, sending his protégé down to the surface for a stint to see how a less insular society worked. Dieter had stayed with Franz Dokken for nearly a year, learning from the other landholder, until that . . . incident with the horses. Young

Dieter had been sent back to orbit, at which point Sondheim had finally considered him capable of managing OrbLab 2.

But Dieter had perhaps learned too well from Franz Dokken, often taking the idea of power plays to extremes, with no end in sight. Sondheim had to rein him in, somehow. At least Dieter always listened to him.

He toyed with an enameled tile Dokken had sent up to him as a gift, then let it float loose in the air, turning back and searching for words that might have a great enough impact on the young station exec. "My hands are now bloody because of you, Dieter! It should have been a simple escape attempt. Those two people didn't deserve to die, but I had to protect you. Now I've made far worse errors in trying to fix things."

"Oh, blood washes off, Kareem. You worry too much." Dieter flapped his hands in an exaggerated dismissive gesture.

"You don't worry enough—and it's time you started," Sondheim scolded, taking on a lecturing tone. "You have only lasted this long in your position because *I* have been protecting you. And I don't like being painted into a corner."

Dieter looked at his wrist chronometer, though Sondheim couldn't imagine what might be more important than this conversation. "The only loose end is Eli Strone," Dieter said.

Sondheim shook his head. "What do you mean? I thought it was a miracle that he didn't die in the airlock explosion. You said you were going to evacuate him before the alarm."

A storm crossed Dieter's face. "Just an oversight, Kareem. But if he had popped out of that airlock, he would have been out of my hair once and for all—but that man has devilish luck. I can't stand him, but there's no place else to send him." He grinned furtively. "Guess what? I slipped a harsh laxative into Strone's food yesterday—it was rather amusing. But don't worry, Kareem. I'll take care of him."

Sondheim wrung his clawed hands in dismay mixed with anger. "What, another accident? That's murder, plain and simple, Dieter—and murder is wrong!"

Dieter smiled. "All those other deaths really were accidents, Kareem. Honest. I had no way of knowing people were going to be in those rooms. Trust me. I hate the bloodshed."

Sondheim backed off, wondering just how much his paternal feelings for the young man had blinded him to Dieter's true personality. What had Dokken called him—"damaged merchandise"?

"I'm going to take a trip down to the surface, so I'd like you to arrange for me to get a spot in the elevator, maybe with some of the last team members," Dieter said. "I want to stretch my legs, watch the sunset, take care of some business. You know what I mean. I need to get away from OrbLab for a few days, especially after all this mess."

Sondheim didn't know if Dieter was intentionally rubbing his mentor's face in his handicap, but the barb stung nevertheless. "I'll get you a spot, but I will no longer cover up for you, Dieter," Sondheim said with a weary sigh. "Please control yourself. The matter is now at an end. I will forgive you if you really decide to change."

"I'll change." Too quickly, it seemed, Dieter raised his hand, palm forward in a solemn gesture. "I promise."


ii


Eli Strone lay on his pallet, alone in his now empty room. All traces of his cellmate Troy Boren had been removed, scrubbed away, disposed of. He was alone again. He trusted being alone.

Dieter Pan had tried to kill him in the separation laboratory. The "emergency" had been no accident—Strone knew that without a doubt. The station exec had always been a foul, twisted one, a corruption of the balance of justice, where an evil man lorded it over the righteous—such as Strone himself—in a mockery of punishment.

Rich new apparitions of guilt had appeared in the windows beneath Dieter Pan's mercurial eyebrows. Strone could see it in him.

He plucked the single string on his musical instrument, letting the tone soothe him. A long, low note, fading into silence. Silence, then music again.

He could think best that way.

# CHAPTER
## 34

### i

His thoughts scrambled with a turmoil of despair and undirected anger, Tharion left Guild Headquarters and strode out into the streets of First Landing. He moved purposefully, but with no clear direction in mind.

He had tried to call Franz Dokken, and one of the servants in the villa told him that the landholder was "not here at the moment." But Tharion needed to burn off his unsettled energy now.

The elite guard assigned to the Guild Master hurried to follow, but the brooding expression on his face kept them at a distance. They marched along, weapons shouldered, scarlet boots and gloves polished, dark blue uniforms sucking up the sunlight.

Other people on the streets stayed out of their way. . . .

Days before, during the ill-fated escape attempt of his Truthsayer and the falsely convicted young man, Tharion had sealed himself inside his ready room, instructing the other administrators that he was to be left alone. He hadn't wanted to be disturbed until he received word from Kareem Sondheim that the escape had successfully taken place.

He had waited, checking his chronometer as he paced the small room and looked out at the unchanging landscape. He stared at his knuckles, at the walls, out the window, hoping everything would work out as planned. Every second plodded along.

Earlier, Tharion had insisted that Sondheim transmit to him an exact copy of the instructions given to Kalliana, and the crippled old landholder grudgingly did so. Tharion had studied the data file, choreographing the events in his mind.

The escape scenario seemed too risky; everything depended on timing, on the predictable reactions of the sol-pol guards and

OrbLab 2 station personnel. It seemed so unlikely—and yet it just might work. He had to pray it *would* work. Sondheim thought it was the only way.

Finally, half an hour past the time when Sondheim had promised to report, his private videoplate buzzed with a burst of static in an encoded transmission. The image of the Platform landholder appeared, drifting from one side of the frame to the other. His snow-white hair bristled around his head. The color values in his image were shifted and distorted, made garish by the data compression and security coding.

Tharion rushed into the transmission area. "Ah, Sondheim," he said. "I've been waiting for your message. Do you have word of Kalliana?"

"I —" Sondheim said with great agitation, then hesitated. "I'm sorry to say there has been a terrible accident. So terrible." The old man shook his head. "A great tragedy."

Tharion felt as if he had been dropped into ice water. "What happened? What went wrong?" He reached behind himself to find his chair, groping blindly in the air until his trembling fingers snagged on the armrest. He collapsed into the seat, keeping his gaze glued to the videoplate.

"They got close," Sondheim said. As if that mattered in the least. "Very close. All the steps happened exactly as they were supposed to. The original alarm was triggered—rather a blundered event I must say. We almost lost another worker, who miraculously made it to an airlock booth before he could be tossed out into space. Your operative and the prisoner did get free of OrbLab 2 and traversed the distance to the Platform."

Sondheim looked away, blinking his obsidian eyes. "But I'm afraid they were unfamiliar with routine operations in space. They didn't know the full safety procedures and depressurization routines. When they attempted to gain access to the emergency entrance chamber, they encountered a sudden decompression explosion. The hatch blew open, and the blast knocked them away from the Platform. They must have been killed instantly. I'm afraid their bodies are irretrievable."

The image made Tharion squeeze his eyes shut. He pictured the two spacesuited bodies spinning silently away into space, or spiraling down until they screamed through the upper atmosphere, trailing fire like embers tossed against the curtain of the aurora.

"I'm truly sorry, Guild Master," Sondheim said. "We did the

best we could, but it was a complicated and dangerous undertaking. If there is any way I can . . . anything else I can do, don't hesitate to ask. I'll be busy mopping up the aftermath here."

Tharion whispered, his voice only a husk of its former commanding tone. "Thank you."

He switched off the videoplate and sat looking at the dull gray screen, but he found no answers written there. His vision blurred, and his heart hammered in his ears. He grieved for the loss of the two innocents, feeling as if *he* had betrayed Troy Boren and Kalliana. The young man had not asked for this rescue, and Kalliana had only obeyed her Guild Master's instructions.

It was *Tharion*'s fault. He had put them up to this.

But the mishap itself still seemed odd. Too convenient. Too unlikely. He frowned at the viewplate, wondering belatedly if Sondheim had had an agenda of his own.

He had to think about this.

ii

Now, the day was clear but breezy as Guild Master Tharion left Headquarters and wandered the city streets, either to settle his thoughts, or elude them. The tall palm trees scratched dry fronds together, and their long trunks swayed. Dust devils scudded across the open spaces, rippling colorful awnings in the merchants' district. Tharion headed there.

Before leaving Headquarters, he had swallowed a fresh capsule of Veritas, and now he felt the conflicting thoughts of the populace surging around him. Ever since his inability to truth-read Kalliana, Tharion had insisted on taking regular booster doses, overcompensating for his one-time lapse of telepathic abilities. He also issued an order that the eleven other Truthsayers take increased doses, though he refused to explain why. This, in turn, created a greater demand for the capsules, and OrbLab 2 complained about providing the additional supplies.

As Tharion moved through the city streets, he felt the psychic babble around him like a comforting white noise. He filtered out all the lush and seductive details, screening his mind without difficulty, yet took comfort in the fact that everyone's thoughts were ready for the taking, a thousand perceptions, a million experiences.

Mist from an ornamental titanium fountain sprayed toward

him as a gust of air funneled through a narrow alley. Tharion brushed some of the damp spray from the front of his robe, then continued into the bazaar.

The merchants' district in First Landing was much larger than similar places in the landholdings. This was where craftsmen and hobbyists could display unusual wares from distant lands. Many of the metal framework stands exhibited fabric and clothing of cotton, silk, or wool from the outer holdings. Some were outrageously decorated with flecks of crystal or sequins or ornamental embroidery. Other garments looked plain, but comfortable.

Tharion stopped to run his fingers through the soft richness of some speckled brown trim. "It's rabbit fur, Guild Master," said the merchant, his eyes widening as he recognized the identity of his customer. "Very fine."

"Rabbit fur, eh?" Tharion said. "Who's raising rabbits these days?"

"Carsus Holding, sir," the merchant said. "Those creatures breed faster than we can feed them." Tharion nodded, but he was in no mood to buy.

Other merchants displayed enameled tiles and prized terra-cotta pottery from Dokken Holding, or wind chimes made from crystal shards and polygonal scraps of beaten brass. Tharion flitted from stall to stall, distracted by the baubles and unique items, but still he felt at a loss. He kept picturing Troy Boren and Kalliana as human meteors streaking across the sky.

He swore he would find out the real answer behind the sabotaged Veritas capsules and the black market ring. Obviously, Sondheim wanted Tharion to ignore the problem. Even Franz Dokken had hoped that the smuggling would stop now that the guilty party—Cialben—had been "taken care of." But Tharion's sense of justice was not satisfied. A buried crime remained a crime; it did not become forgivable once everyone forgot about it.

And the smuggling had continued.

A spicy, sweet scent tickled Tharion's nostrils as he passed a vendor selling incense and potpourri, burning flower petals and herbs in a strong but pleasant smoke. Another merchant offered Tharion a free sample of a new-season mead.

"Mead?" Tharion asked. "What is that?"

"Blackcurrant wine made with fresh Toth honey," the woman said proudly. Tharion quickly declined, wanting nothing more to do with wine after his bad experience with Dokken's Chianti.

Other people moved about the bazaar, designated buyers for villages or landholders. The most jaded were the citizens of First Landing, to whom such variety was available every day.

The accompanying elite guard drew closer to Tharion as a small methane-powered scooter hummed directly toward them. Other pedestrians moved out of the way. When Tharion turned to look at the approaching driver, he recognized the station exec of OrbLab 2, Dieter Pan—whose blind or incompetent team had found nothing out of the ordinary in the Veritas processing, and who had supposedly helped set up the disastrous escape attempt for Kalliana and Troy Boren.

"Dieter Pan," he said, preempting the conversation. "I'm surprised to see you here on the surface again. I thought you would be anxious to stay away."

He was surprised to see the comically false sadness on the station exec's face. "Hey, it was tough to get space on the elevator to come down, my man," he said. "Everything's such a mess since that crazy scheme you set in motion. I don't think you have any idea how much damage you caused up there, the lost work time, the endangered crew members. Tsk, tsk.

"Not to mention, my man, that because of your new team coming back home, and the cargo we bumped to make room for them, the elevator is still playing catch-up."

He heaved himself out of the scooter's seat to stand and confront him more squarely. He seemed continually surprised at how much he weighed. "I needed to come down here on some errands of my own—none of your business, tut tut. There wouldn't have been passenger space available to me," he said, "if I hadn't pulled a few strings with old Kareem just to get a place to sit." He chuckled thinly. "Sometimes it pays to have powerful connections, doesn't it?"

Tharion looked at him with narrowed eyes. "What is it you want, Dieter?"

The mercurial eyebrows shot up. "What is it I *want*? Would you like a list, my man? No, I don't think so. But at least I trust you're through sticking your nose in our business up in orbit?"

Tharion stiffened as he wondered again about the botched escape attempt, whether Sondheim had indeed betrayed him. "I can't speak to what the team has found until I study their results in detail," he said. "But if you'd done your task more thoroughly in the first place, Dieter, you would have had nothing to worry about."

As if he had pushed a button to unleash the wiry man's anger, Dieter bunched his fists at his sides, and held his shoulders high even though it seemed to require a great effort in the Atlas gravity. "Me, worry?" he squawked. "I delivered that first report in good faith. We work to the best of our ability—and all for you, my boy, I might add! Do you think *I* get anything out of all that Veritas we make for the Guild?"

The elite guard stood alert, weapons ready. Tharion began to answer him, but Dieter interrupted. "Kind of interesting, wouldn't you say, how you Truthsayers manage to self-righteously demand a complete monopoly on our production of Veritas? We work harder at it than anyone on Atlas, don't we? And it's dangerous! But I'm sure the Guild considers the risks to be acceptable. Lives are lost regularly every year to create this *exclusive* blue goop you hold so precious—but others could use it as well. Yes, indeed! Use your imagination—for teaching, for sharing experiences, for communicating, for, uh, recreation . . . and yet you Truthsayers keep it locked up in your vaults and deny it to everyone else. Now I ask you, does this *really* sound fair?"

Tharion kept his voice low and threatening as he thrust his answer into a gap in Dieter's speech. "The Guild's Truthsayers deserve Veritas because only we have the moral strength to use it. We are incorruptible—you are not."

Ferociously indignant, Dieter Pan pushed himself up straight, using the rail of his methane scooter—but Tharion had momentum. His anger forced the words out in a rolling stream. "If you didn't want to raise further questions, if you didn't want a second investigation team sent," he jabbed at the station exec with a fingertip, "then you should not have lied to me in your initial report. I want to find out what's really going on."

His retort brought flooding back the confusion that recent events at OrbLab 2 had begun in him. He thought of Kalliana, of Troy Boren, of the Veritas mystery, of the unlikely "accident" at the Platform.

*Everyone lies.*

He could trust no one until he had read them himself. Only a Truthsayer could know the irrevocable truth. *Truth Holds No Secrets.* What people said and what they did were often carefully constructed masks to hide their true thoughts . . . and the only way to get to those thoughts was through Veritas.

Tharion felt himself perched on the edge of a slippery,

uncertain slope. But hadn't he already taken the first step over the brink? He had sent Kalliana in disguise on a covert mission to find some answers, had asked her to probe the minds of other suspects, without their prior approval . . . was there any real difference between that, and doing it himself?

While Dieter Pan was speechless, one eyebrow cocked, still trying to formulate a response, Tharion reached forward to grip the man's shoulders and physically turned Dieter around to face the methane scooter again. In the heavy gravity the station exec's muscles were weak, and Dieter could not resist, despite his outrage.

Tharion used the brief touch during this contact to throw a swift, sharp probe into Dieter Pan's mind. After all, Tharion reasoned, Dieter *had* to know more than he was telling. The station exec of OrbLab 2 must understand the truth behind the drug smuggling.

Tharion probed with all the power from his fresh dose of Veritas—and, in the flash of his reading, was overwhelmed by the shocking information he uncovered. It had all been a setup, more so than even he had dared consider. OrbLab 2, the Platform, and Kareem Sondheim were all involved, though their connections were well covered, as Tharion had expected.

Tharion read about the smuggling, the joy Dieter took in bypassing the system, reveling in the power he felt because he could do something that was forbidden. . . .

Dieter actually enjoyed the challenge of staging accidents, killing workers just to hide a missing shipment of Veritas . . . implanting packages of capsules in large animals due to be shipped down on the elevator . . . wheedling old Kareem Sondheim into arranging for the opportunities. . . .

Tharion squeezed, dug deeper—

He saw Dieter's years of training when Sondheim sent him to live on Atlas with Franz Dokken to observe how real society worked apart from the artificial menagerie up in orbit. How Dokken had actually trained him much more than Sondheim suspected . . . how Dieter Pan had to leave quickly under difficult circumstances, when Dokken had caught the young man maliciously whipping his precious horses. . . .

The Guild Master had been blind. In spite of himself, he marveled at the magnitude of these deceptions—and then Tharion felt the wind knocked out of him, as he saw that Sondheim was not the ringleader after all.

Although Sondheim had long thought that Dieter Pan and Franz Dokken still resented each other, the two had entered into their own alliance, manipulating events, working a master plan to see the Guild destroyed and the landholders laid low. . . .

*Dokken himself* was at the center. Dieter Pan was the focus on OrbLab 2—but Dokken ran the black market. Dokken pulled all the strings, made all the plans. Cialben had been a red herring, a diversion, a ripple on the surface of a sea of plans within plans.

Tharion squeezed, trying to read more deeply—but Dieter jerked away, indignant at the Guild Master's accusation, though he had no idea that he had been truth-read. Dieter climbed onto his scooter and, without looking back, pressed the accelerator and careened down the street, forcing pedestrians to scatter out of his way.

"Are you all right, sir?" one of the elite guard said, steadying him.

For a moment, disoriented, Tharion nearly sent a thought probe into the guard as well, suspecting conspiracies at every corner, traitors everywhere.

But he caught himself. Tharion, still dizzy with the truth he had been avoiding, hurt and sad and angry, realized that the clues had always been there—as if Dokken had been *expecting* Tharion to solve the problem. The arrows of all his suspicions pointed to the same target. He could not deny it.

Franz Dokken.

His own mentor.

# CHAPTER

## 35

### i

As Tharion watched through his ready room window, the sun came up slowly, like acid fire across the forge of desolation beyond First Landing. He hadn't stirred for hours, watching, thinking.

He had been such a fool, all his life. Dokken had been manipulating him.

Since returning from his walk the day before, Tharion had avoided his wife as much as possible, keeping himself occupied with important-looking Guild business, trying not to let her see how deeply disturbed he was. Qrista still picked up on his emotional state, but mercifully she didn't press him, since she was busy with Landholders Council duties of her own.

Qrista had been sleeping fitfully when he left their quarters in the middle of the night, made his way up to the bridge deck, and sealed himself in his ready room. There, in darkness, he had gazed at the city lights spread out like a jumble of fireflies around the anchor point. As if in a trance, he sat unmoving, mulling over possibilities and hoping that some brilliant solution to his moral dilemma would rise up of its own accord.

But nothing did. And as he watched the sun rise, his body stiff from so many hours spent in an uncomfortable position, he still had no answers.

The door to his ready room slid open without a knock or an entry signal. Tharion didn't turn; he didn't need to.

"So there you are," Qrista said with feigned good humor. "I take it your hard desk was more comfortable than snuggling against my soft body?"

Tharion allowed himself a brief smile and glanced at her. He could tell from her concerned expression how haggard he must look. He felt as if he had rubbed glass chips into his eyes and face.

"Tharion," she said after a pause, "why have you been avoiding me?"

He shook his head slightly. "I can't tell you. Not now."

"Since when have we started keeping secrets from each other?" she asked, putting her hands on her narrow hips. Her pale hair hung down her back, untended this early in the morning; he could see the kinks left by her braids.

"I can't talk about it, and I can't ask you for advice," he said. "At least not until I understand it better myself." When he stood, his knees cracked and his back twinged. He took her hand, hoping and trusting that she wouldn't abuse the contact to read his thoughts.

"Are you going to tell me when it's over?" Qrista said.

"I'll . . . I'll try," was the best he could say.

Qrista raised a pale eyebrow and shook her head. "Wrong answer, Tharion."

He allowed himself a brief laugh. "All right. I'll tell you—but only when it's over."

But he wondered if it would ever be over.

ii

The answers would be at Dokken Holding, Tharion knew, so he had little choice but to go there. Unannounced.

Leaving Guild Headquarters, Tharion allowed the elite guard to escort him through the streets with as little spectacle as they could manage. He dismissed them abruptly when they reached the rail station, though, and commandeered one of the Guild's private mag-lev cars.

A small magnetic/hydraulic crane picked up the vessel and set it on an outbound rail that would take him to Dokken Station. As the computer verified that the line would be clear for the duration of his trip, he climbed aboard without luggage, taking with him only his concerns.

Tharion sealed the door, reveling in his privacy. The elite guards looked alarmed at the idea of the Guild Master leaving unaccompanied. He carried no weapons, though for protection he had brought a small cartridge of the paralyzing drug *stenn* from the Guild's storehouse. It might prove useful if someone resisted his questioning.

He lay back in the padded seat and ignored the acceleration, closing his eyes against the dizzying blur of the landscape—an uncomfortable metaphorical reminder of how quickly circumstances were whipping past him.

Tharion would never dare to sneak a truth-reading on Dokken. The landholder had been "unavailable" for a few days, and in a way Tharion hoped that Dokken *wouldn't* be at his villa right now, that he had disappeared on one of his frequent private "sojourns." That would give him time to subtly interrogate the others. Schandra seemed disaffected with her lover; she might be willing to divulge the secrets Tharion needed. Or perhaps even Maximillian, though the bald manservant seemed to have his guard up as securely as did Franz Dokken himself.

When the mag-lev car docked at the glass-and-steel hub of Dokken Station, Tharion stepped out and looked around, trying to decide his next step. Five of Dokken's sol-pols were already there waiting for him. He frowned with some annoyance. The elite guard must have transmitted a warning from First Landing, which spoiled Tharion's element of surprise.

These sol-pols were part of the contingent that had been assigned to Dokken Holding for generations. Though they ostensibly reported to the Truthsayers Guild, there were times when Tharion suspected their loyalty might instead lie with the landholding they considered home.

"Greetings, Guild Master," said Captain Vanicus, Dokken's chief officer. "How may we assist you?"

Tharion spoke sharply. "You may obtain a fast methane vehicle for me. I'm going up to the villa."

"Yes, sir," the sol-pol said unruffled. "We'll arrange an escort."

"I didn't ask for an escort," Tharion said. "I asked for a vehicle. A *one-man* vehicle. That will be all."

The guards looked at each other, then Vanicus nodded toward a vehicle pool at the rear of the station building, where rovers and construction machinery sat available for work. "Very well. That's easily managed."

Before long, Tharion found himself seated in one of the ground-hugging wire-wheeled cars that bounced as its engine drove the lightweight frame along the packed gravel road that led from the station.

He drove jerkily, lurching and overcompensating until he

became accustomed to the controls. He had driven such vehicles before, but chauffeurs usually took him where he needed to go. Now, though, he had to proceed alone, whatever might happen.

The town in the foothills was small and bustling, but he didn't care about the villagers or the other colonists or anything else on Atlas at the moment. He needed only to find answers about Franz Dokken.

He followed the winding, switchback road up into the bluffs. The isolated villa looked formidable: pale stucco roofed with red tile, turrets thrust high, its satellite dish a high-tech incongruity on the medieval-style structure. Soot stained the upper lips of the chimneys, but no smoke curled up today.

As he approached the well-tended courtyard filled with mulberry bushes and bright red geraniums, Tharion could see shadowy figures moving behind the translucent panes of the silkworm greenhouse. He drove up to the flagstone patio in front of the main entrance, with its reinforced doors made of steel plate under a veneer of varnished pine. Behind the villa he saw no one in the stables or on the riding paths that led out to the desert highlands.

Tharion climbed out of his vehicle and stood before the imposing doors. He yanked the pull rope connected to a bronze bell that hung beside the door, and waited a few moments. When no one answered, he rang the bell repeatedly until finally a broad-shouldered man with cinnamon hair and deep brown eyes pulled the heavy door open a crack. He seemed surprised to see the Guild Master standing there in his white Truthsayer robes and royal blue sash.

Tharion squared his shoulders and looked at the man— Dokken's chef, Garien. "I must speak with your master," he said.

The simple request flustered the chef. "But he's not here, Master Guild Master, sir."

"Where did he go?" Tharion asked, keeping his voice calm. He pushed the door open and stepped across the threshold into the cleanly swept foyer.

Garien backed away, clearly not knowing what to do. "Master Dokken rode off two days ago with Maximillian," he said. "I'm sure he intends to be gone for some time. We're never told where he goes on his sojourns or when he'll be back, but we do expect Maximillian to return shortly. By tomorrow at the very latest."

"Ah," Tharion said, nodding sagely. "Very well," he said. "May I speak with Schandra? She might be able to help me."

The chef shrugged and spread his hands. "Sorry, sir, but no one has seen Lady Schandra for weeks. She's gone."

"What do you mean, she's gone?" Tharion asked.

Garien looked embarrassed. "It's not my place to inquire of such things, sir." Tharion wondered if Dokken had dismissed Schandra, finally losing patience with her demands and dissatisfactions.

He moved closer to the chef. No one was around. The villa seemed otherwise empty and abandoned. "I really must speak with Franz," Tharion said, intentionally using the familiar name. "Do you have any idea how I could contact him?" He reached out to touch the chef on his sweaty neck. The man nearly lost his balance, but Tharion held him up. "Can you think of anyplace I might look?"

Before he could ponder the implications, Tharion dipped into Garien's mind, rummaging around. He had already compromised his ideals once by reading Dieter Pan, and this was far more trivial. Tharion discarded the irrelevant and uninteresting thoughts the man had about meals he wanted to prepare, ingredients he lacked, ideas for different ways to serve desserts—until finally he found an image of Dokken and Maximillian riding off on two horses, the path they had taken, the direction they had gone.

"I . . . I don't know, sir," the chef said, not realizing what hints he held in his own mind.

"Thank you," Tharion said, releasing his touch and stepping back through the doorway. "You've been a great help."

The chef blinked, unable to understand what Tharion meant. The Guild Master turned around and hurried back to his vehicle.

iii

Just as he departed, another contingent of Dokken's loyal solpols hurried up to the villa, no doubt to "assist" him. Tharion had no wish to talk to them, though. Dust and grit showered up in a plume behind the wire-wheeled vehicle as he moved the accelerator to its highest level. Tearing up the smooth landscape, he sped away into the wastelands.

The single trail of side-by-side hoofprints in the clay desert was easy to follow, even after the road petered out and the two riders had set off overland. Tharion rolled along at a reckless speed. Though the two men had a day's head start, he still hoped to catch up. His vehicle could travel much faster—and he knew that Franz Dokken was rarely in any sort of hurry.

His white robe was spattered and stained with the ochre dust thrown up by his passage through the desert. Grit got into his mouth and eyes, but still Tharion stared fixedly ahead, intent on his goal. It both exhilarated and intimidated him to think about confronting Dokken out here alone, far from watching eyes, free of masks and secrets—where they could be honest with each other and come to some sort of agreement. Here, the two of them would be without rules—and also without protection. He fingered the *stenn* ampoule in the pocket of his robes. Everything was up for grabs.

Then he saw the figure on horseback, trotting beside a second, riderless horse.

Tharion's vehicle must have been visible across the flatland for kilometers, and so the rider had certainly seen him by now. The figure halted, looking directly at the approaching methane car. Tharion drove toward him without hesitation.

It was Maximillian with a riderless horse and without Franz Dokken.

Tharion had become impatient, afraid and confused and wanting answers. He knew that Maximillian would resist any inquiry about his master, dodging questions Tharion *needed* to have answered.

The tall manservant was the Guild Master's physical superior, and as he pulled the methane vehicle to a halt at the edge of a ravine, Tharion realized just how alone and defenseless he was here, so far out in the desert.

Maximillian dismounted and crossed the gully, taking long strides toward him. He looked down at the Guild Master with an expressionless mask as Tharion sat brushing clouds of dust from his white robes. Maximillian's forehead wrinkled. "Guild Master Tharion, this is most unusual. What may I do for you?"

As Tharion struggled to climb out of the vehicle, he made up his mind. He could always apologize later if Maximillian knew nothing, but he knew from his reading of Dieter Pan that both Dokken and his manservant were deeply involved. Too involved. Too many secrets.

"First off, you can help me out of this car," he said, extending his hand.

Maximillian instinctively reached out to pull him up—and Tharion jabbed with the small *stenn* needle cupped in his palm.

The manservant blinked in surprise. His face froze in a ridiculous expression as the sudden paralysis hit him. This minor dose would last only a few minutes, but as the craggy man collapsed beside the horses, Tharion went to work with a vengeance.

"I need to know what you know," he said. Maximillian could not move his eyes or focus, but Tharion thought he saw a shudder of alarm go through the man, dismay at having been tricked so easily.

Tharion knelt in the dust and wrapped his hands around the sides of Maximillian's bald head, pressing with his fingertips. "I need to know your secrets," he whispered, deeply regretting the ethical gulf he had already crossed. But he pushed aside those thoughts for now.

Maximillian resisted, trying to muddle his thoughts, but Tharion had taken an additional dose of Veritas, a higher concentration than he had ever used before. He brought his full mental strength to bear, battering down the barriers of thought as if they were no more than gauze veils.

Maximillian twitched one of his arms, and Tharion dug deeper into the manservant's mind, hoping the *stenn* wouldn't wear off too soon.

Inside the labyrinth of protected memories, he saw that Maximillian had killed Cialben, dumping the body so that someone else was bound to find it in the holding warehouse. He saw that Cialben, though involved in the drug smuggling, had been only an incidental player. A diversion. Troy Boren's unfortunate finding of the body had been nothing more than coincidence.

Everything had been done under the orders of Franz Dokken.

He saw glimpses of Maximillian's work to incite the Pilgrims, to sabotage the Bondalar/Carsus rail link. But Tharion had burning questions about Dokken himself: Why was he doing this? What else did the landholder have in store? So Tharion plowed inward with no finesse, no care, seeking information, ransacking the manservant's mind.

Maximillian's feet began to jitter against the dry ground, his booted heels tapping up and down in a rapid rhythm as he struggled to regain control of his body. Tharion didn't let him.

Inside the manservant's memories, Tharion found more dark and compelling images: how Dokken had murdered Schandra as they camped by a drying lakebed, how Maximillian had helped dispose of her body, telling no one. Getting away with murder.

Maximillian's mind was a maze filled with trapdoors and land mines, appalling secrets at every corner. There was more . . . so much more. Tharion breathed quickly, fascinated and unable to withdraw. Not yet.

His predecessor, former Guild Master Klaryus, had indeed been poisoned, a deliberate act conceived by Dokken and implemented by Dieter Pan on OrbLab 2. A very special capsule of Veritas had been manufactured, designated for Klaryus. It had all been done to make Tharion the next Guild Master, herding him relentlessly toward the leadership position. Dokken had meant this for Tharion all his life. He had been an unwitting part of the plan.

*But why?* A strangled, gurgling cry came from deep within the manservant's throat. Tharion plunged inward, guided to the most important information by his victim's increasing attempts to resist. He found one sealed-away nugget of information—and Maximillian seemed willing to die before he would give it up. . . .

Ruthless, Tharion battered down the locked door in the manservant's mind—and reeled backward with the final revelation, jerking his hands away from the bald scalp. His mouth was dry, hanging open, his eyes wide. Tharion's heart pounded in outrage and disbelief—but the fact had been incontrovertible in Maximillian's mind.

Franz Dokken, Tharion's lifelong mentor—the supposedly childless landholder who had worked for so many years on his various schemes, setting people in motion like windup soldiers—*was Tharion's father.*

Dokken had somehow insinuated his own secret son into the Guild nursery tanks. Dokken had been preparing Tharion all his life, hoping that the young man would rise to the very position of power he now held, Master of the Truthsayers Guild. Dokken had taken great care to ensure that he could manipulate his offspring.

And it had worked perfectly. Tharion had trusted him. He had played right into the landholder's hands.

Until now.

Biting back an outcry of rage, Tharion grabbed Maximillian's head again and squeezed, glaring down with clenched teeth. "Tell me more, dammit!" he said and dug into the manservant's mind like a sharp plow blade.

There was indeed more, but Maximillian resisted one last time, destroying all that remained. Savagely, Tharion tore the strands free and felt something snap in Maximillian's mind, a brutal collapse where the shield of his persona lost its integrity and crumbled. All the remaining secrets scattered apart like random perceptions, unconnected memories, incoherent thoughts. Nothing.

By the time Tharion realized he would recover no more information from this treacherous man's mind, Maximillian lay convulsing on the ground.

Tharion stood, holding his hands like claws in front of him as he looked down. Maximillian writhed helplessly. Drool spilled from his lips. His eyes were open, but empty, comprehending nothing.

Like a broken machine, Maximillian hauled himself to his knees, then to his feet, as if some atavistic instinct to flee still sent relentless signals to his ruined brain. The gaunt man fell flat on his face in the dust, but got up one more time, lurched to his feet, and stood swaying. He staggered away and tumbled over the edge of the ravine, bringing a shower of mud and clods of dirt around him.

Tharion went to the edge, wondering what he should do now: if he should help the man, or put him out of his misery. The gaunt manservant crawled to his knees on the rocky bottom of the ravine, splashing in a few brownish puddles. He groped his way along the floor of the gully, bumping into walls, feeling with his fingers as if he couldn't see the rock around him.

"Guilty," Tharion whispered, but the manservant did not hear his judgment.

Tharion watched Maximillian for a long time, coldly vengeful, thinking of all the information the manservant had harbored, the vital secrets he had kept from Tharion. Finally, Tharion clapped his hands and shouted to send the two horses galloping into the distance. The animals would find their way back to the stables, or wander into one of the outlying agricultural fields. He didn't care.

Tharion paused beside his methane car, still reeling from the information that seemed to be exploding within him. He clenched his fists and seethed into the fading afternoon.

His entire life had been planned by Dokken, from the moment his embryo was placed in the Guild infirmary. Now Tharion had to question everything he had ever done. He was just a pawn.

Tharion didn't know how long he stood there; he felt already dead and empty as he climbed back into the seat of his methane vehicle and rode back toward the village and the mag-lev station. He felt as if he were following in the footsteps of his father, with schemes of his own.

He began to make plans as to how he could arrange for a new manservant to be delivered to his "mentor."

# EXILES

They didn't have many options.

# CHAPTER

# 36

i

The dark, wood-smelling cargo pod hurtled through the night. Troy and Kalliana tried to make themselves comfortable as they sat shivering in the sawdust, smelling the warm scent of pine. They couldn't see each other in the shadows but sat within touching distance, occasionally reaching out a hand just to make sure the other was still there.

"Do you have any idea where we're going yet?" Kalliana asked, her small voice sounding loud in the darkness.

Troy shook his head, realized she couldn't see him, then said, "Wherever we're going . . . at least we've made it this far."

He could barely believe it himself. Not long ago, he had been trapped on OrbLab 2, doomed to spend the rest of his life processing Veritas bacteria and working beside Eli Strone. Now Strone was probably dead, and he was back on the surface, hiding inside a mag-lev cargo pod—owing his freedom to the same Truthsayer who had falsely convicted him of murder. "Funny," he said, shaking his head.

"What?" Kalliana asked.

Troy, realizing he had spoken aloud, decided not to say any more about it. "I guess it wasn't so funny after all. Never mind."

The gentle motion of the high-velocity train was soothing, much more restful than the tense countdown of hours while hiding inside the elevator crawl space. The danger seemed to be over for the moment.

But what came next? Would Kalliana abandon him to seek her own shelter, her own friends—or was she counting on him to find solutions for both of them, now that she was as much a fugitive as he was? Or they could work together and *both* find solutions. They didn't have many options.

"Nothing is turning out the way it was planned," Kalliana said. "We can't ask for help, because there's no telling who our enemies are. . . . I'm not used to this."

Troy smiled wryly. "I'm no expert either, but I'd rather take an active role in deciding what happens to us, than let circumstances make all our choices."

"I agree," Kalliana said. "I think."

Some hours later the train decelerated rapidly, then jerked off to the side on a rail bypass, where it slowed further and finally came to a stop.

"What's going on?" Kalliana asked.

"I was hoping you could tell me," Troy said. "I never rode the mag-lev much."

"Let's take a look," she suggested.

When the mag-lev train came to a full stop, they crept to the sealed door, moving by feel. A splinter jabbed Troy in the heel of his hand, as he slid the door aside partway to show a starry evening, with curtains of the aurora swirling overhead in pale green and whitish gray—but he saw no village lights, no receiving station. Only empty agricultural fields.

He did notice a second mag-lev line not far away, parallel to their own track, and heard a quiet whine building louder and louder—another train approaching. The sound sent a shiver grating down his spine. Were they being pursued? Could this new train have been sent by the sol-pols to capture them? Then Troy realized it was coming from the opposite direction, heading back toward First Landing from the outer lands.

Beside him, Kalliana leaned forward to look around. "Ah," she said, her face lighting up with realization. "We're on a shunt spur. This cargo train has low priority on the roster. We'll have to sit aside here for a few seconds until the other train passes. Must be a passenger line."

Troy stared into the night at the shadowy cropland. They were in a developed portion of whichever landholding they had entered—but they were not yet in the village. "Maybe we should get out now," he suggested, "make our own way, so that we can enter a town on our own terms. Find the right spot and slip in. Otherwise, we'll be caught when the train reaches its destination."

He had to speak louder as the drone of the approaching mag-lev train increased until it became a scream. The high-velocity train rocketed by, and then Dopplered to a lower pitch as it proceeded through the night toward First Landing.

The cargo container jolted as their train began to move slowly, picking up speed again as magnetic repulsion created a frictionless surface on the rails and the engines at the rear car began to push. Troy looked out at the endless fields, saw no sign of civilization anywhere, and shivered. The ground began to crawl by as the train accelerated.

"All right," Kalliana said quickly. "We have to make up our minds now, and I don't want anybody to find us."

Troy grabbed her arm, and together they leaped from the cargo pod as the train continued to pick up speed. They landed on crumbly dirt, rolled to their feet, and then ran toward the shelter of dark croplands. Looking over his shoulder, Troy saw the mag-lev train streaking off into the distance, abandoning them.

In the middle of the isolated agricultural lands, the night was silent. They ducked into the fields to hide.

ii

They plunged into the cultivated acreage and suddenly entered another world. The tall plants were like skeletal soldiers three meters high, standing in rank upon rank.

Troy led Kalliana between two rows, and they jogged farther out of sight of the mag-lev rails. Once they had begun to run, they kept fleeing as if the hounds of hell were nipping at their ankles. It burned off tension and helped them clear their heads as they ran deeper and deeper—and for Troy the sheer exhilaration of being free and alive, of being *able* to run, triggered a rush of adrenaline. Finally he stumbled on a tangled root and fell to his knees.

Kalliana, who couldn't react fast enough, crashed into him, and they piled together on the ground. She gasped and shuddered, ready to cry out, but Troy began chuckling with the release of pressure. "We made it," he said gasping. "We made it."

Kalliana looked at him as if he were a fool. "Yes, but where did we make it to?" She rattled one of the stems of the wide-leaved plants. "And what are these things?"

Troy squinted, still panting from the headlong flight. The spatulate leaves were covered with a fine hair, and the trunks seemed furred as well. The scent in the air was thick and resinous. "Kenaf, I think," he said. "They raise some of it in Koman Holding, back where I used to live, in the flatlands below the Mining District. Provides fiber for canvas, particle board, and paper pulp. It's hardy, too, and grows pretty fast even in bad soil."

"Can we eat it?" Kalliana asked.

Troy sighed. "No. It figures we would run off into a field full of a crop that we can't even snack on."

Kalliana's shadowed face was severely highlighted in the eerie auroral glow. She groaned. "None of this was supposed to happen. I need more than those emergency rations we ate in the elevator. . . ." She hung her head and looked very small seated on the ground in her smudged and ragged woolen clothes, much less glamorous than her Truthsayer's robe. "You know," she said with apparent surprise, "I've never actually been hungry before." She no longer looked like a shining angel of justice, just an exhausted waif in need of a good meal. "I don't know anything about wilderness survival," she said.

"Well, I hope you weren't counting on *me*," Troy said. "My only training is as an accountant." He squared his shoulders and found inner strength. "But I suppose OrbLab 2 toughened me up a lot, because I'm not ready to give up yet."

Around them the tall kenaf plants whispered and rattled as a breeze stirred the leaves. Troy felt a primal fear caused by the spooky scratching sounds in the night. . . . The knotted kenaf plants rose like the bars of a cage around them.

Kalliana shivered. "I'm cold," she said.

He considered reminding her that she wore thick woolens, while he had only the flimsy work uniform from OrbLab 2—though he had grown used to being perpetually cold on the orbital station. He scooted closer to her. "So am I."

He moved to put his arm around her shoulders and swallowed a lump in his throat. Kalliana backed away, as if shocked he could consider such close contact after her mistake had sent him to the prison. "Aren't you afraid I might read . . . I mean, you don't know what I'll find."

He looked at her skeptically. "I think I already know what's in my mind," he said, "and if it's something I don't want to hear, don't tell me." She still pulled away from him, and he felt a twinge of exasperation. "Look, Kalliana, I'm not asking you to marry me. I just want to get a little warmer. Okay?"

Reluctantly, she slid into his arms, though he felt uneasy holding her until the warmth gradually spread between them. He wondered what the Truthsayer was reading in him now, then decided not to worry about it.

He and Kalliana sat together on the newly fertile soil of Atlas and waited for the dawn to come.

# CHAPTER

## 37

### i

Miserable. Hungry. Stiff. Cold. Exhausted. Miserable. . .

The litany plodded through Kalliana's mind as she and Troy trudged through the rustling, hairy leaves and stalks of kenaf. Morning light shone between the rows, making the cultivated ground a lattice of wavering shadows and bright splashes.

Kalliana admired Troy's energy, but even the young man's determined enthusiasm seemed to be ebbing. She could tell that he didn't have any idea where they were or where they were going. Out here in the middle of nowhere they couldn't exactly stop to ask for directions.

"I've got to rest," she said, sliding to her knees in the dirt, "again." They had already gone kilometers—hundreds, it seemed—and hadn't yet found the edge of the kenaf field. "I'm not accustomed to this sort of exertion."

Troy knelt beside her. "I'd offer you a drink of water, but I seem to be fresh out."

She stared out through the confining walls of plants. "I didn't know people used so much kenaf in the whole world."

"And this is just one crop," Troy added. After a few moments, he helped her to her feet again. "Come on, I'm sure the next field will be beans or tomatoes or peas—"

"Or broccoli, or corn, or—" Kalliana joined in. The weary game distracted her, though it didn't deceive her stomach. They walked on, parting the leaves in front of them as they went. Kalliana's pale skin was already laced with fine scratches and itching welts. Her eyes stung.

The kenaf field ended abruptly. Troy pushed through a row of hard, fibrous stems, and suddenly they stared in amazement at a long, low swath of ground-hugging plants, dark green trifoliate leaves with tiny serrated edges, and bright berries.

Strawberries.

They ate until they were sick. Pink juice stained Troy's lips and chin, and she knew she must look just as absurd.

The strawberry field was much easier to walk through than the rows of kenaf. Kalliana was relieved to be able to see where she was going. They passed white rectangular boxes that buzzed with bees flitting in and out of their hives as they dutifully pollinated the flowers. The thrum of flying insects seemed loud enough to be heard for kilometers.

Kalliana gradually fell into the rhythm of Troy's stride over the uneven ground. Her life had been spent walking the metal decks of Guild Headquarters or the cobblestoned streets in First Landing's central plaza. Now the two of them hobbled across the uneven dirt, trying not to trip on stones and careful to avoid crushing the strawberry plants.

"There must be a village out here somewhere," Troy said for the fifth time. "Somebody's got to tend all these crops."

"I don't even know which holding we're in," Kalliana said, "not that it makes any particular difference."

Beyond the grassland Troy hoped to find grazing cattle or sheep—and their requisite caretakers. Instead, the range ended in undeveloped lands, flat and rocky, splashed with color from Atlas lichens and encroaching Earth algae and mosses, tiny Terran scouts making inroads on a new landscape.

Troy looked back at the fields they had already crossed. Kalliana followed his line of sight, noting that the land seemed greener in that direction. Troy put his hands on his hips, and his face fell. "This doesn't look good," he said. "I guess we went the wrong way."

Kalliana caught a glint of movement far out in the rocky landscape ahead of them. "What's that?"

Troy's gaze followed her pointing finger. She shaded her eyes with a hand and squinted until she was certain: It was a gigantic machine lumbering in their direction.

ii

As the machine approached, the hum and roar of its grinding treads grew louder. Troy gripped Kalliana's arm hard enough that she winced. "Sorry," he said.

They stared uncertainly at the oncoming vehicle. Kalliana looked at Troy for guidance, but he had no suggestions either. "If they're hunting us, we can't outrun them," he said.

Kalliana sighed. "I don't have the energy to flee a glacier right now."

Troy gathered his courage. "Then we may as well make the best of it." He began waving his arms and shouting. "Hey, help! Over here!"

Kalliana noticed the long-range scopes and sensors mounted on the juggernaut's side. She also saw figures riding on top, small human forms who jumped up and down, waving back at Troy.

Its engine rumbling, treads clanking, the contraption grew taller and taller as it approached, nearly three times the height of a human. Its outer hull was reddish brown with streaks of metallic silver, oxidized and pitted from numerous years on the surface.

"I think it's one of the old rover vehicles," Troy said as he and Kalliana waited at the edge of the cultivated lands.

The vehicle slowed until finally its treads stopped turning. Lumps of dried dirt flaked off, and the machine settled down with a sound like a weary moan. Blue-gray exhaust curled up in a plume from a smokestack in the rear.

Four children in tattered clothes rode on the top deck, ranging in age from about eight to fourteen years, Kalliana guessed. They were all dark-skinned and long-haired, jabbering excitedly. The youngest disappeared down an unseen hatch in the roof.

Troy craned his neck up at the enormous vehicle while the remaining children looked at him agog. "Hello?"

Finally a hatch opened in the front, and an enormous woman stepped out, her hips so wide she could barely pass through the doorway. Her shoulders were broad, her skin the color of the burnt umber Troy had used in his paintings. Her short hair was a creamy, smoky gray. Her face was flat and expansive as if someone had sanded away all the rough edges; when she smiled, the grin split the bottom of her face like a ray of sun. She laughed at the two refugees in disbelief.

"Thunder in heaven!" she boomed. "Ain't no telling what we find on our patrols. We log thousands of mineral veins and land formations and unusual resource concentrations—but how are we supposed to catalog you two?" Seeing the confused looks on their faces, the big woman shook her head. "Just kidding. What were ya doin' way the diddly out here?"

Kalliana looked at Troy, hoping he had an answer. "Seemed like a . . . nice day for a long walk?" he offered.

The woman threw back her head and laughed. "Sure," she said.

Two fiftyish men emerged from the vehicle, while children scrambled out of various openings and hatches, dropping beside the tall treads. Four younger women joined them, and two more men.

The large woman came forward and extended a hand as broad as a paddle. "I'm Marriatha Bowditch, and these are the cast and crew and kids and . . . well, just call them our 'associates.'"

Kalliana warmed to the woman immediately. As she took Marriatha Bowditch's hand in a brief grip, she had to restrain herself from digging deep into the woman's mind, checking her motivations and her orders. But in a peripheral glimpse she caught no antagonism or hostility, no deception—just curiosity. "This is Troy Boren," she said, "and I'm Kalliana."

Troy flashed a surprised glance at her. She could see he was imagining teams of rover vehicles combing the landscape with orders from the Guild to track down any fugitives.

Marriatha raised her eyebrows knowingly. "Ah, so we have two runaways, eh? I can see you weren't supposed to tell me your names. Never mind," she said, dismissing their concerns. "Your agreements with your landholder make no diddly to me—and I know the grass always looks greener at another holding. Don't worry, there's plenty of work to do if you're willing. I'm sure we can find something at the next village we go to."

"Excuse me," Kalliana said, "but where are we exactly?"

This brought a gust of laughter from Marriatha's associates, even the younger children who couldn't have understood the humor. "You're lost then, ain't you? Right now you're in the lowlands of Koman Holding near the Toth border. If you have no particular preference, we'll be heading up into the mountains in the next few days. You're welcome to tag along. It won't be hard to find work in the quarries or the Mining District."

Troy frowned at the mention of the Mining District, and Kalliana recalled that his family still lived there. She couldn't tell if he was eager to see them, or so ashamed he wanted to be far away.

"Well don't just stand there," Marriatha Bowditch said. "Make up your minds. If you want to sit out here and get a suntan all day long, that's fine with me. But we have a few more grids to cover before we break for the night, so we want to keep moving."

Troy accepted with a smile. "We'll come along, if only to get off our aching feet."

The other members of the large family climbed back inside the resource rover. Marriatha Bowditch stepped aside to let Kalliana and Troy enter the stuffy, gloomy interior.

The air smelled of oil and metal and solvents and lubricants. But when Kalliana sat down on a worn bench and felt her muscles begin to melt with relief, she thought the dingy old vehicle was about as marvelous as her fine chambers back in Guild Headquarters.

iii

With Marriatha Bowditch strapped into her broad piloting seat, the rover vehicle ground across the terrain. Its huge treads and resilient struts were sufficient to engulf the rugged path, rolling over outcroppings and straddling ravines. Aboard, the entire group seemed relaxed but competent, busy with their varied duties. They worked well together as a team, the young men and women, the elders, even the children.

Troy and Kalliana took turns washing themselves in the cramped lavatory, sponging off the built-up grime and dust from the fields. Kalliana felt refreshed and presentable again. Though her dripping hair remained spiky and auburn, much of her makeup had come off. Her pale skin prickled with the angry pink of a stinging sunburn.

Kalliana watched as the two older men unrolled sheets of high-resolution satellite photos overprinted with a precise grid and kept track of the zigzagging course their rover had taken. Kalliana saw other charts pinned to the walls completely marked off with red grease pencils, a large X across every grid; she wondered how many years this rover had been cruising the landscape.

One of the coffee-colored young women sauntered up with a readout in her hand. "The outcroppings to our left have a high potash content, a solid enough concentration that someone might be interested in mining it."

"All right," Marriatha said, looking through the fingerprint-smeared front viewports. A rounded line of knobby white deposits looked as if they had been freshly exposed through harsh weathering. "Make a note of it. Anything to pump up our account when we get into the village."

The satellite photos had been taken centuries ago, upon the

arrival of the first colony ship. While the images broadly quanti-
fied the general resources of the continent, the resolution was
insufficient to pinpoint specific veins of ore or to determine the
local exploitability of metals and rocks. In addition, the surface
changed as geological processes worked the landscape, exposing
new raw materials.

Resource rovers had crisscrossed the landscape for centuries,
studying, mapping, and marking the locations of natural treasure
troves. They reported their findings, exchanging information for
the supplies they needed, but for the most part, these large gypsy-
style families valued their freedom above all, with no other desire
than to roam and look at the sights.

"So you don't work for any particular landholder?" Troy
asked.

"We work on the fringes of the lands, Mr. Troy," she said.
"Not much of anything worth having out here, and it's not like the
landholders put up fences, you know. We go where we want, and
we do what we want. Right?"

It seemed to be their family motto. Everyone within earshot
shouted "Right!" in unison.

Kalliana looked at how Marriatha Bowditch commanded all
of her 'associates.' "So are you their . . . their matriarch?"

Marriatha boomed with laughter, a deep belly laugh that was
infectious. Kalliana found herself chuckling, though she didn't
know why. The giggling kids scrambled up metal rung ladders to
ride on the roof again.

"No," Marriatha said. "I'm just the driver."

iv

The resource rover stopped at twilight after Marriatha found
an appropriately level campsite. With the engine shut down and
all the hatches opened, the associates boiled out, scrambling to
finish their nightly round of duties in as little time as possible.

Within twenty minutes the rover vehicle had been transformed into a sprawling encampment. The men worked to erect
a colorfully striped awning that rested on scratched aluminum
poles with spike ends. The young women went outside to build
a fire out of stunted mesquite and sage they had taken from the
wastelands around the cultivated areas, where hardy desert scrub
had been scatter-planted as a first step toward taming the land.

Kalliana found the campfire a treat, since electrical heaters and environment-control systems were so easily had in First Landing. The children set to work preparing rations in the galley.

"Is there anything we can do to help?" Kalliana suggested.

Marriatha Bowditch shook her head. "Just stay here and keep me company. Sometimes it's enough of an effort just to watch the others goof around, and I've been driving all day."

The fourteen-year-old boy ran to fetch water from a nearby stream; they would pump it through filtration systems and then use it for tea later in the evening. One of the women set up a grill and placed heavily seasoned meat on the rack. The meat sizzled and smoked and smelled absolutely delicious.

"We caught a bunch of jackrabbits yesterday," Marriatha said. "It's a delicacy."

"A jackrabbit?" Kalliana said. "Where do we have rabbits running free?"

"We were over in the northern portion of Dokken Holding, the part that used to belong to Van Petersden." Marriatha nodded in the general direction.

"A long time ago Van Petersden had a bright idea without thinking it through. Turned loose a bunch of jackrabbits in his scrubland, then he had to bring down some hawk embryos and coyote embryos from the Platform. Then he made some pigeons, but Van Petersden didn't understand the predator/prey pyramid—just how many rabbits and pigeons it takes to provide sufficient food for the community of predators he had unleashed. So the hawks and the coyotes died out shortly after they ate all the pigeons. But a few jackrabbits survived—and now they've realized that the real crops taste better than the scrub grass . . . and so we hunt the rabbits."

The group ate a marvelous meal of the savory meat, though Kalliana's stomach was cramped from the gluttonous amount of strawberries they had eaten earlier.

"Tastes a little gamy," Marriatha said, licking her fingers, "but you get used to it. You just have to learn to expect different tastes."

Troy helped himself to another piece while Kalliana drank more filtered water. "It's delicious," she said. "Thank you for sharing it with us."

Troy raised his eyes to look at the large woman. "And thank you for not reporting us."

"I don't care diddly about your secrets," Marriatha told them.

"There's nothing I want so badly I'm willing to do crazy things to get it. I have no idea what you did or what your motivations are or where you think you're going. That's up to you."

Kalliana looked at her somewhat warily. "But I thought resource rover crews were supposed to report all the information they find."

They spoke in low voices as the children began to play a game of tossing small pebbles into a circular target they had drawn in the dirt. The others moved about to clean up after the meal, adding more wood to the fire, making the tea and preparing to settle in for the night. Marriatha sat back in her canvas chair like a queen at court.

"Let me tell you something," she said. "I used to believe in the free exchange of information, share and share alike. I figured the resources here were for everybody. We're all colonists. We're all in this together. We've got to make a go at this planet—right? But I was pretty naive."

"No," Kalliana said. "I don't think so at all. The truth is the truth. If everyone knows it, how could it be to anyone's advantage?"

"I'll tell you how," Marriatha said. "Abraham Van Petersden was a good, honest landholder and satisfied with what he had. His holding was fairly small but it had a decent share of resources. He didn't play power games like the other landholders did. He just wanted to keep his own house and his own lands and trade what he had for what he didn't have."

She leaned forward. The canvas chair groaned under her weight. Kalliana could see that the seat had been handmade, specially constructed to accommodate her wide hips. "This was, oh, fifteen or twenty years ago, I can't remember. On one of our runs in the rover, we discovered a pure vein of silica sand, fine and white and clean and just perfect for glassmaking. It was close to the surface on stable rock, would have been a breeze to mine it. Right nearby we also found some rocks rich with deposits of essential additives. A whole rainbow of metal oxides."

"Additives for what?" Kalliana asked.

The woman driver raised her helpless gaze up to the darkening sky. "Thunder in heaven, for making stained glass!" she said. "That's how you get all those pretty colors. Iron oxide for red, cobalt oxide for blue, antimony oxide for a bright buttery yellow, manganese oxide for purple."

Kalliana nodded wisely, thinking of the shards inlaid in the windows of Guild Headquarters. "But Van Petersden never had much of a glass industry," she said. "Dokken Holding produces most of the glass we use—"

"Exactly!" Marriatha Bowditch said, holding up a ham-sized hand as if to scold her two listeners. "My rover discovered the resources for Van Petersden, and we were very excited when we made our report. Van Petersden was a little slow to exploit it. No hurry, he thought.

"But Franz Dokken was not quite as patient, and so he staged a bloody takeover. Abraham didn't know what hit him. So now Dokken Holding has a flourishing glass business . . . and Van Petersden Holding no longer exists."

Marriatha's humor-filled face now seemed weary and saddened. "Glass!" she said. "Can you believe all those lives lost, all that blood spilled—because we found some *sand*?"

One of the young women brought them each a cup of spicy tea brewed from a fresh pot. Marriatha sipped but said nothing for a long moment. "Now you see why I let you keep certain information to yourselves? It's just not worth the price."

The large family gathered in the darkness and began to sing around the fire. Kalliana knew none of the words, and she wondered if Marriatha and her associates had made up the music, or if these were old songs from Earth. Troy tried to stumble along with the words, mimicking the chorus whenever he could decipher it.

They finally left the campfire burning low and returned to the resource rover. One of the young boys showed Kalliana and Troy to empty bunks. All the family members slept out in the open, snoring and stirring and paying no heed to the lack of privacy. Kalliana didn't notice either, and fell into a deep, oblivious sleep, oddly comfortable—as if she had found a new home.

# 38

i

The cell on OrbLab 2 seemed cold and empty and hollow ...
just the way Eli Strone preferred it. His former cellmate Troy
Boren had seemed fuzzy and insubstantial somehow. And now the
young man was gone, making Strone wonder if it had all been
some kind of illusion.

Much of Strone's existence seemed like a dream, especially
since the Truthsayer had tricked the world into thinking of him
as a criminal who had dispensed justice to those who had not
deserved it ... but Strone knew the truth. Truthsayers lied. They
betrayed their own. They had poisoned their Guild Master
Klaryus, then covered it up.

Eli Strone knew how to punish those who were dishonest ...
those who had wronged him. What the Truthsayer had done
didn't make sense, especially after knowing his reasons—but he
was certain that one day the Guild would find its honor again and
rectify everything. One day.

The universe was becoming a more and more incomprehensible place. His carefully ordered existence seemed to be eroding,
dissolved away by ill-thinking human beings who put their own
needs and wishes ahead of the purity of justice. Guilty. Innocent.
Right. Wrong. There *was* a difference.

Strone had carefully cleaned Troy's side of the cell, not
hesitating for a moment to use solvent and a damp rag to obliterate
the lush painted landscape, the imaginary future Troy had drawn
on the white wall. He had made his cellmate's bunk more neatly
than Troy had left it when he had ... vanished. Escaped?

The opposite side of the room now sparkled, fresh and
untouched, and Strone could disregard it. That wasn't his portion

of the cell. It didn't belong to him. He had left it clean and new; the prospect of another cellmate didn't trouble him. Strone would simply disregard any newcomer and hope the other person would vanish, as Troy Boren had.

Strone had been able to see Troy's guilty conscience, the aftershadow of his sins—but the surprise of his escape attempt amazed Strone. He couldn't believe he had misjudged his cellmate so badly. The possibility of voluntarily leaving OrbLab 2 had never occurred to Strone until Troy's action had proved it to be possible. Almost possible.

The concept appalled Strone's sense of justice. Troy Boren had been found guilty by a Truthsayer and sentenced to his punishment. Escaping from a justly pronounced punishment was . . . wrong. Others might have found the thought ludicrous that, after slaughtering twenty-three victims, Eli Strone might refuse to do something because it was "wrong." But Strone had had plenty of reasons for his killings, and he had no legitimate reason for escaping from his legal—if unjust—punishment . . . until recently.

Dieter Pan had meant to kill him by blowing out the airlock in the bacterial separation lab. Strone knew without a doubt that they had faked the loss of an entire shipment of Veritas, and he had been an expendable bystander in their scheme.

Who watches the watchmen?

Dieter had come to his cell, raging, hovering in the air like an angry wasp. "I know you've been receiving secret messages from someone, Strone! Messages, my boy! How can a convicted criminal on an isolated laboratory be receiving messages without me knowing about it? You're a smart one, you bastard, but I know something's up. You tell me who it is!"

Strone merely sat and blinked at him, not answering, letting the station exec feel like an idiot as time passed.

"Don't think I'm not watching you!" Dieter had said, finally giving up, and flitted out of Strone's cell.

Strone saw that he could never really trust those in control. The people on OrbLab 2 who had been given the task of overseeing punishments were themselves criminals—and that skewed the entire system. *Trial and error*, he thought. OrbLab 2 was wrong. The Truthsayers were wrong. Everyone was wrong— and it was time to do some housecleaning.

Yes, he had received help from his mysterious guardian angel. He didn't know the identity of the person who had recently sent him secret notes explaining what to do, how Strone could make things right, how he could be free again to distribute his personal justice.

Strone felt warm inside. It was a mission he would be proud to accomplish.

He lay back on his cot and stared at the smashed intercom on the wall, the ruined speaker that would have summoned him to his daily round of work. Strone's hands were bruised and would have been sore if he had allowed himself to feel them. He squeezed his hands, flexing the stiff knuckles.

He should have reported for morning duty several minutes ago, so the next step depended on Dieter Pan's impatience. Since the loss of Troy Boren, Strone judged that the station exec would be all the more anxious to get Veritas production back on track. Dieter Pan would immediately come to check any delays, full of bluster and insults. Small men had big mouths.

Strone let his eyes fall closed. He breathed deeply, humming a long monotonous note that was a close approximation to the tone from his single-stringed instrument. He hummed again. . . .

He didn't have long to wait. The door whisked open, and Dieter Pan floated outside with two guards, drifting gradually to the deck, then hopping back up to maintain his illusion of flying. "Strone, where have you been, naughty boy?"

"Here," Strone said, sitting up slowly on his bunk. He curled the toes on his bare feet and, moving with methodical precision, swiveled himself off the bed.

"You were supposed to report twenty minutes ago. Didn't you hear the intercom?"

Strone looked meaningfully at the crater hammered into the wall. "No."

The sol-pols looked at the damage. One whistled. Dieter Pan scowled. "A little bit of a temper tantrum there, eh boy?" he said. "Couldn't you soothe yourself by playing your little instrument?"

"It's broken too," Strone said. On the floor beside his bunk lay the smashed instrument, its body and neck shattered in a jumbled pile.

Dieter Pan looked at the wreckage and made a low growling sound in his throat. "Well, you're not getting another one," he snapped. "You'll just have to learn to whistle or something."

"I'll manage," Strone said calmly.

"Damned right." Dieter clapped his hands. "Enough of this.

Come on, there's work to do. It's time to go."

Eli Strone agreed fully. It was indeed time to go.

ii

As they led him up to the second level and toward the sterile chambers of the laboratory ring, Strone followed, biding his time, choosing the right moment, mentally replaying the instructions he had been given. He knew exactly the steps to follow, though there seemed to be room to . . . improvise and enhance the moment.

Dieter Pan flitted within arm's reach, hopping along and drifting down the corridor. The two sol-pols stomped with each step, their heavy mag-boots anchoring them to the floor for greater stability. That would be their downfall.

As the station exec bounced along like a confident idiot and the sol-pol guards walked behind him, Strone decided not to wait any longer.

While Dieter Pan had his back turned, Strone slipped a hand carefully into the front pocket of his jumpsuit. His bare feet tingled on the cold metal floor. He tensed. The sol-pol guards noticed nothing, nor could they see his hand in his pocket.

He slipped out the long wire he had taken from his wrecked string instrument, wrapping the ends around his hands to form a nearly invisible loop.

As Dieter Pan propelled himself into the air again with another hop, Strone pushed his foot hard against the floor, jumping forward and bringing his arms around. In a single fluid motion he snagged the loop of wire around the station exec's throat and crossed the ends behind his neck.

Before the sol-pols could react, Strone yanked outward with all the strength in his arms and shoulders, drawing the thin garrote straight through Dieter Pan's throat, slicing his skin, crushing his windpipe, and embedding itself deep within the larynx. Blood sprayed in a scarlet fan into the air, where it congealed into droplets that hung like slow-moving rain.

Dieter struggled and choked and gurgled. He thrashed about, but Strone kept his hands taut, the wire cutting deeper and deeper. The station exec was already dead, but his body refused to accept the fact, writhing in the low gravity and spurting blood in all directions.

Strone rode the momentum like the other half of a spinning baton.

The sol-pols finally reacted. Shouting to each other, both drew their weapons, ready to fire, but Strone weighed the balance perfectly, swinging the body of Dieter Pan directly into their line of fire. As their rifles cracked, the ceramic bullets embedded themselves in the chest, abdomen, and thigh of the station exec. Two other projectiles shattered into powder against the metal walls.

Strone got both of his feet flat against the wall and pushed off with the full strength in his legs, holding Dieter Pan's still-twitching corpse like a battering ram. He plowed into the sol-pols, knocking them down as they struggled to turn. Their magnetic boots held them in place, making them ready targets as Strone's velocity bowled them over.

One of the rifles fell to the floor and rebounded into the air. Strone continued his flight, snatching the rifle with one long arm and swinging it around. Chambering one of the shells, he shot the first sol-pol full in the face. He raised the rifle, pointing it at the other madly scrambling guard, and pulled the trigger again ... but heard only the *click* of an empty chamber.

The second guard struggled to bring up his gun and knock aside the corpse of Dieter Pan that had fallen bleeding on him, but Strone swung the empty rifle like a baseball bat. He spun around as his body flew in the opposite direction. The rifle smashed into the nose of the guard, who flailed his hands, screaming in pain.

Strone made no sound—simply yanked the other rifle from the second guard's hands. He heard the hollow snap of the man's finger bones as he twisted the trigger guard free, then he turned the weapon and shot the sol-pol twice in the chest. The ceramic bullets impacted nicely.

Strone steadied himself from the recoil and fired the rifle into several of the large plates of glass in an enclosure down the hall. On the fourth shot, the glass cracked, setting off containment alarms on the station. Moving down the corridor, he yanked down the fire emergency switch, which set another whole series of alarms going. The remaining sol-pols would be adequately confused.

Eli Strone dropped down one of the secondary hatches to the main level, heading for the primary external airlock and the docking bay. Up above, the sol-pols would be responding to the emergency. The bodies of Dieter Pan and the two guards would throw them into a frenzy.

On the way he ducked into the empty sol-pol barracks, rummaged through the lockers, and pulled free one of the dark uniforms, holding it against his big frame to make sure it would fit. He looked forward to wearing a full uniform again.

When Strone reached the main access portal to OrbLab 2, the security station looked forbidding with its own series of alarms. But there was no going back now. He punched in the access code he had memorized, and the doors let him pass—as promised.

As the air hummed in the lock, Strone paused to catch his breath, though his pulse rate hadn't increased much. Soon his respiration slowed to its steady, relentless pace.

He cycled through, knowing this was only the first step toward freedom. But he had no doubt the rest of his escape would proceed as smoothly.

# CHAPTER

# 39

i

The resource rover toiled across the bleak land for days, far from the remotest hint of civilization. Marriatha Bowditch didn't seem a bit concerned about getting lost. She had her satellite images.

Troy did what he could to make himself useful, but it was apparent that Marriatha and her associates had the routine down precisely, tasks divided up equally. Though he felt safe from pursuit and relieved at the chance to rest and gather his wits about him, Troy knew their time with the resource rover crew could only be temporary. He and Kalliana had to plan their next step.

The terrain grew more rugged as they gained in elevation. Though the markings on the satellite photographs of the area showed only a dark pebbly texture, sheer outcroppings of gray igneous rock pushed up from the layered strata, blocking any straight path.

The rover pushed forward, moving slowly as the children rode on the roof, keeping a lookout for anything interesting. Inside the vehicle the others used scanners to document mineral and metal concentrations. Grid maps, held down with paperweights, lay unrolled across a chart table.

Marriatha let the rover continue on autopilot as she bent over the grid charts. Her large frame loomed over the landscape. Troy stood next to her, fascinated by the mapping that enabled him to see huge portions of Atlas at once.

"Where are we going next?" he asked. He traced their present location from the red marks and the point of Marriatha's stubby fingertip.

She met him with her warm dark eyes and raised her eyebrows. "Well, Mr. Troy, that's up to you. You tell me."

"What do you mean? " he asked.

"Maybe we should bring Kalliana, too, so the pair of you can make your decisions."

Kalliana came from where she had been perusing the years of records the resource rover had compiled. Marriatha pointed to dotted-line boundaries across the uninhabited desert. "Time for me to decide which direction to go. We pretty much make up our own minds, you know."

"Yes, you go where you want, and you do what you want," Troy said. "Why should you want our advice?"

"We need to find a village in the next day or two to replenish our supplies and empty our data banks. So look here." She pointed down at the charts. "We can either hook west and go through these hills—there—and end up in Koman Holding. Or"—she pointed to a different portion of the satellite chart—"we could head deeper into the mountains toward the granite quarries in Toth Holding.

"We'll drop you two off at our next stopping point. I told you I wouldn't ask any questions about where you came from or why you're running . . . but I thought I'd give you the pick. Got any preference, Toth or Koman? We'll find you a job either place. What sounds like more fun to you, working in the mines, or chopping slabs of granite?"

At the mere mention of the backbreaking labor, Kalliana blanched and looked over at Troy. He knew her life had been pampered in the Guild, and she had never experienced hard work—but neither had Troy, actually, though he had spent some time working actual jobs.

The thought of returning to the Mining District brought a surge of hope to Troy. He imagined Leisa's face. By now her belly must be rounded with the new baby. Perhaps even Rissbeth had latched on to some poor unsuspecting man and gotten herself married. Perhaps they had forgotten about him by now, the shame of their family . . . the son convicted of murder.

Kalliana was with him. The Truthsayer could vouch for him, prove that he had been falsely sentenced, that he wasn't guilty after all. Troy sighed. She couldn't do that, could she? If Guild Master Tharion or the sol-pols suspected the two fugitives were still alive, Troy's family would certainly be watched. He and Kalliana risked capture if they tried anything so foolish, yet so emotionally satisfying, as to return to his family.

Besides, he had hated the short time he had worked in the mines, even in an administrative capacity.

Kalliana looked at him with narrowed eyes, and he knew she could guess what he was thinking. She bit her lip, but offered no advice. He was glad of that. His fingers fluttered over the satellite images on the table. "Granite chopping sounds like a lot of fun," he said. "I think we'll try Toth Holding . . . if it's all right with you?"

Kalliana nodded weakly, and Marriatha removed the paper-weights so she could roll up the charts. "Sounds good to me. I look forward to some fresh mountain air," she said. "Get yourself rested, though. It's a tough job and you're gonna want a good night's sleep before you start hauling a few tons of rock."

ii

When the resource rover pulled into a village nestled deep within the gray mountains, people came out to greet the arrival with enthusiasm akin to a celebration.

The young ones leaped from the vehicle onto the gravel streets and ran to play, scouting for children their own age. The older men saw to refurbishing and repairing their rover, while villagers took advantage of the opportunity to look over the awesome vehicle, an artifact of Earth technology. Marriatha's remaining associates went into the merchants' alley to see what they could barter.

Marriatha Bowditch took Troy and Kalliana under her mater-nal wing as she sought out the village leader to renew her acquaintance. She promised to pull in a few favors to secure jobs for her two outlaws, no questions asked.

The village leader, a lantern-jawed man with big eyes, heavy eyebrows, and a gentle smile, welcomed the prospect of two more laborers. He didn't seem the least bit concerned about who they were or how they had come to be with the rover crew.

Troy and Kalliana remained silent, but the village leader—Marriatha never introduced him by name—included them in his pleasantries, filling a tiny liqueur glass for each of them.

Troy sniffed the liquid and frowned at its oily perfume smell. The village leader seemed excessively proud of it. "Gin," he said. "We've cultivated a few juniper bushes, and each year we succeed in distilling two or three bottles of the finest alcohol."

Troy nodded his thanks and took a sip. His eyes watered. The pungent taste filled the back of his mouth and his sinus cavities, but he managed to swallow the entire glass in two gulps, relieved that the social ordeal was over. Next to him, Kalliana coughed, apparently having the same reaction.

The village leader gave Marriatha a rundown of recent events while Troy listened and tried to show no reaction. The village leader mentioned the "attempted prisoner escape" from Orb-Lab 2, but brushed it aside, more concerned with the overall politics of the struggles between landholders.

"The biggest news just happened two days ago," he said. "A huge explosion out at the new mag-lev station between Bondalar and Carsus. They'd just about finished that rail linking their two holdings—you know how much trouble they've had with it?" Marriatha nodded knowingly.

"Well, it seems Hektor Carsus himself was responsible for the sabotage, blew up the entire station, killed close to a hundred of Bondalar's engineers. He denies everything, of course, but they found plenty of evidence at the site. He doesn't have any explanation for it, and Janine Bondalar is convinced Carsus was behind it all along."

"Thunder in heaven!" Marriatha said, clapping a hand to her forehead. "I thought those two were lovebirds. Maybe I'll just stay out in the wilderness and not be bothered by all this diddly crud. So the marriage is off?"

"You betcha," the village leader said. "Sure seems to be a lot of turmoil in the world these days." He shook his head, then looked at Troy and Kalliana. "You two ought to be glad you're here," he said. "It's a nice place to be. If you ever get to meet Emilio Toth, you'll be impressed. He's the way a landholder should be. Kind of like a king."

Troy nodded, feeling the acrid gin dehydrating his mouth. "I hope we get a chance to," he managed to say.

After they had chatted for half an hour, the village leader took out his rosters and found assignments for his two newest workers. "If nothing else, it'll put muscles on you," he said, nodding toward the thin arms on both Troy and Kalliana.

They stepped outside into the afternoon. The village leader pointed up the slopes to where low, booming sounds rumbled through the canyons. Work teams were dark specks crawling over the sliced tiers of the mountain being excavated. Black lines of ropes and cables made a spiderweb across the pinkish white rock face. At the base of the cliff, where heavy-duty elevators lowered the slabs of rock, a mag-lev spur delivered cargo platforms that hauled the rock to another section of the village, where the granite was cut, shaped, and polished into usable pieces.

"You'll learn fast," the village leader said, noting the concern on Troy's face. "It's backbreaking work, but not too complicated. You two will do just fine."

Troy didn't feel terribly reassured.

"I'll send a crew boss to show you around today. You and . . . Kalliana, was it?—will be assigned to different jobs, but we'll find you living quarters and let you get settled in. Tomorrow morning you can both get right to work."

"See?" Marriatha said with a broad grin on her flattened face. "Told you you should have gotten a good night's sleep." Then she nodded cordially at the village leader. "I leave you two in good hands. Thanks for your company, and I wish you the best of luck."

She gathered Troy and Kalliana into a single massive hug, then strode off, weaving down the gravel street back to the resource rover.

Once again Troy felt entirely alone, cast adrift.

iii

The rest of the day crew bosses showed them around the excavations. The other workers greeted them openly and curiously. "I hope you'll feel welcome here," one of the foremen said. "We're not too glamorous, but we can always use the extra help."

Troy realized that he did feel welcome here, sensing no antagonism or hostility from people whom he had expected to be rugged roughnecks. Many of the miners who had labored with Troy's father had been broad-shouldered brutes who spent their free time grumbling to each other, but not meaning much of it.

As he and Kalliana explored the packed mountain paths, Troy breathed dust, smelled the sulfur of blasted rock powder. They got dirt on their hands and scuffs on their clothes, and they each paid attention with a numb objectivity. Troy knew this could be the rest of his life—but at least it wasn't working in a deadly bacteria laboratory beside a serial killer.

When they returned from the mountainside at dusk, they were led to a single prefabricated hut that consisted of little more than a heater, a small lavatory, and sleeping pallets. Troy found it disconcerting to learn that the quarters set aside for them had recently been occupied by two men killed in an avalanche, but the room was their own and the walls provided privacy. Troy couldn't ask for more than that. He was uncomfortable sharing quarters with Kalliana, though. He could tell she felt the same uneasiness—but they were partners, holding common secrets at least as deep as those held by lovers. And they each still needed someone they could talk to, a friend who understood.

After a warm meal of soup and bread in the communal mess hall, they retired to their hut. Both remained quiet and withdrawn as they sat on their individual sleeping pallets, until Kalliana finally broke the silence.

"This is all so ... surprising," she said. "It's very different from anything I have experienced before."

Troy raised his eyebrows in feigned surprise. "You mean you've broken people out of prison before and it didn't turn out like this?"

"No," she said, impatient with him. "I mean the people, the ... attitude. They seem so much more open, especially Marriatha and her clan. Even the people out on the granite quarries."

Troy didn't know what she meant. "How is it different?" he said.

"As a Truthsayer the only 'normal people' I ever met were those who had been brought to me for judgment. Even the innocent ones had usually done something to trap themselves in their situation."

"Like me, you mean," Troy said.

"Well ..." Kalliana smiled briefly, considering it. "You *did* do something you weren't supposed to, and you did get caught. But ... most of the people I met were truly bad. I got the impression that all citizens other than Truthsayers were warped or evil in some way—but these people seem different."

"Kalliana," Troy said seriously now, "the people working in these granite quarries, as well as most of those in the Koman Mining Districts, are descendants of settlers from the *Botany Bay*. Their forefathers were all convicted criminals, exiled to Atlas and put to work here."

"I know," she said. "That's why I don't understand it."

Troy sat up, looking at her intently now. "*I* am a descendant of those criminals. They're proudly independent and desperate to make their mark on Atlas."

Kalliana sighed, her face backlit by a growing reluctant wonder. "Then maybe this will be a healing experience for me," she said. "After all the evil I've experienced in the minds of others, it'll do me good to see the strong hearts of these children of criminals."

"You might be surprised," Troy said. They fell asleep, trying to prepare themselves for the day to come.

# CHAPTER
## 40

i

At dawn, bronze bells rang in the center of the town, clear notes rousing everyone to the first work shift. The chill air was white with smears of mist, clouds snagged in the mountains.

Troy and Kalliana stood outside bleary-eyed, breathing the clean air with a refreshing wakefulness. The other villagers moved to the central buildings where breakfast was served: a porridge flavored with cinnamon oils and a mellow hot beverage brewed from roasted chicory.

After breakfast Troy and Kalliana split up, waving good luck to each other as they went to their separate work crews. Troy followed the group of men and women trudging up to the open excavation on the granite cliffs.

Already fearing sore muscles and an aching back, Troy looked at the biceps and broad shoulders of his coworkers; with one glimpse he saw their years of hard labor, working heavy equipment and shattering off slices of stone. Each day, they wrestled granite slabs into place, then sent them down for trimming, polishing, and shipping. Fine rose granite was one of the major products of Toth Holding, along with gold extracted from quartz veins laced through the outcroppings.

Winched elevators hauled the people up in groups of three to the top ledges of raw stone, where the equipment was stored in portable shacks. The foreman opened the shed and distributed different tools and apparatus to the main workers in each team. Everyone slipped on grimy gloves made of kenaf canvas and reinforced with steel mesh.

Because of Troy's slight build, he was added to the team of tracers who laid down a path of sonic shock waves to split the rock along desired planes. He and his companions used surveying tripods to ascertain a straight line across the edge of the cliff, then laid down a thumper wire that pounded with ultralow frequency into the granite.

Other team members attached catch nets and grappling cables to the piece of stone before it could snap free of the cliffside, while the strongest workers used methane-powered jackhammers and laser cutters the size of cannon to split the rock.

Working together, the crew took half an hour to chop the first slab. It came neatly off the side of the mountain like a slice of stone bread, striking sparks from iron grains and sending up curls of dusty smoke. As the slab fell, the workers gave a heartfelt cheer. Troy yelled loudest, with a feeling of genuine accomplishment. He coughed after inhaling too large a mouthful of dust. His face and arms were smeared with powdered white rock, but he didn't mind. He had never felt half this satisfied after inputting manifest records at the elevator anchor point.

ii

Water sprayed from high-pressure jets all around the polishing area, drenching the rock as well as Kalliana and her coworkers. The late-morning sun burned down on the canyon walls, warm enough to keep her from being uncomfortable, as long as she didn't concentrate too much on the fact that she was wet and working so hard that her hands were already raw.

Farther down the line, shapers used vibrating chisels and stone saws with diamond-tipped blades to chop the slabs into standard pieces. Some of the granite was cut to specific shapes and thicknesses for ongoing construction projects, others were simply stock material to be sold in large lots.

Once the rough slabs were evened out, cut to straight edges and flat surfaces, they moved down a roller path where teams scoured and polished them with coarse corundum abrasives on rotating heads. The people around Kalliana worked without complaint, talking openly with each other, joking, even singing songs.

Her very status as a Truthsayer had kept much of the real world hidden from her. She recalled the people she had met at Sardili Shores, the brick makers and kiln firers who had come to see the unusual spectacle of a visiting Truthsayer. Though they had welcomed her warmly, and Joachim Sardili himself had shown her the greatest hospitality, this familial warmth among companions was still a new experience for her. Kalliana remained quiet, not entirely sure how to go about making friends or opening herself to companionship.

As they worked with their lubricants and abrasives, scouring the surface of the stone, the rock slab transformed into a silken panel of glossy pink granite that fairly glowed when the sunlight dappled across it. The rosy stone was speckled with dark highlights, inclusions of black mica and hornblende as well as sparkling glitters of quartz crystals.

She ran her fingers over the slick wet surface of the finished slab. Her team had polished it to a warm pinkish tan, like skin flushed with cold. Kalliana admired the granite for a moment, then hurried to join the others farther up the line to begin work on the next piece coming down.

iii

As time passed, day after day, their bodies adjusted to the heavy work. Their muscles adapted to the extra strain, settling into a weary strength. Some of the other villagers engaged in community activities, but Troy and Kalliana were both so tired they returned to their hut and rested, their bodies exhausted, though their minds remained active.

They talked. Here in the tiny prefab hut he and Kalliana had more space than Troy had ever had while living with his family. He began by telling anecdotes about how every day had been a struggle for his family in the Mining District. Shortly after her engagement, his sister Leisa had started to make a wool sweater for her husband-to-be, but she had run out of yarn and could not afford more before the wedding; the sweater had not been finished until some months afterward.

After Troy had begun the conversation, Kalliana gradually unfurled and spoke of her own life, twisting it open like a steel can and hauling out all the things she had kept trapped inside. She talked about how her friend Ysan had been able to recognize her appetite for sweets and occasionally arranged for the Guild's food-prep workers to create the very dessert Kalliana had been unconsciously craving all day. He had secretly read the craving from her mind.

Troy listened with wonder as she spoke about Guild Headquarters, how she helped train the children for their telepathic duties, how she sometimes napped next to the fountains in the arboretum decks, how quiet and clean the ship walls were. But she also pointed out that the Truthsayers were so rigid in their duties that they rarely took time to make more than a passing acquaintance with their colleagues.

Troy sat listening to her, drinking in the details by the light of a single glow square. Outside in the darkness he could hear rising and falling waves of music and laughter in the communal building. The villagers were having their weekly dance, but Troy's muscles felt so drained from the quarry work he could barely find the strength to sit up on his pallet and look at Kalliana.

She gazed off into shadows. "I was raised to be a Truthsayer," she said. "I was created for that profession, an embryo brought down from the Platform and nurtured in Guild Headquarters. I hear you talk about your parents, your family, and that means nothing to me. I can never have children. Everyone on Atlas seems to want children, lots and lots of them. Huge families are part of our culture."

"Well," Troy said shyly, "not everyone wants children. My mother used to think I was a freak because that wasn't my highest priority. Sometimes it's enough just to have your own life."

"Well, I used to have my own life." Kalliana blinked her dusty blue eyes. "I grew up being exposed to Veritas, surrounded by enhanced mental abilities. Other people's thoughts were just another set of environmental details to me, like light or sound or smell. Now, though, it's all changed." Her small hands fumbled at the waistband of her clean coverall. "Guild Master Tharion made me remove my Truthsayers' sash and sent me off on this mission to free you—and to uncover secrets about the black market smuggling of Veritas."

"I thought something like that was going on," Troy said.

"Dieter Pan was behind it all. I read it in him when I shook his hand." Kalliana suddenly sat rigid, as if jolted with an electric shock. "You didn't—you haven't got any Veritas with you? You didn't smuggle any yourself?" Her face was flushed and eager.

"No," he said, surprised at the suggestion.

Her shoulders slumped again. He wanted to comfort her. Kalliana sighed. "I'm sorry, it's just been . . . so long. I haven't taken any Veritas since I rode up on the elevator to begin my investigation. My powers are fading. It's as if I'm"—she hesitated, searching for words—"as if I'm going blind."

Troy got up and moved closer to her. Kalliana looked away. "You wouldn't understand," she said. "It's not anything you've ever experienced before."

"I've only been on the receiving end once," he said. "And I must say I'm not thrilled with all the wonders Veritas has done for my life."

She flashed him a hurt glance. "It was a mistake, Troy," she said, "and I'm sorry. I'll never make that mistake again." Her voice dropped to a whisper. "I can't. I don't have the ability. How will I ever know the truth, right or wrong? How can I believe anything now?"

Troy tried to cheer her up. "The rest of us manage to get by somehow. Look at those villagers out there. Think of Marriatha Bowditch and her associates. We find ways to cope."

She looked up at him. "Could I . . . " and she hesitated, afraid to ask, "could I try to read you again, before my powers fade completely?"

Troy froze, then brushed away the fear. What did it matter anymore? And if it made her feel better. . . "Sure," he said. "Give it your best shot." He reached out to take her small hands. They were damp with perspiration. He pressed them against the sides of his head. "Like this?"

She nodded, biting her lip, then closed her eyes. Troy shivered, tried to feel the invisible presence probing around in his thoughts. Kalliana pressed harder. He could hear her breathing grow ragged. Her eyes squeezed shut.

Finally she shuddered and flung herself away from him. "It's gone," she said. "Nothing. I couldn't get a snatch of an image. Not a single thought."

"Are you saying I've got an empty head?" Troy said, trying to lighten the mood, but she ignored the question.

"I had to surrender my sash earlier," Kalliana said, "but now I can see I'm really no longer a Truthsayer. My whole former life has been canceled. What good did I do, and how will I survive now?"

"You don't need it," Troy said. "You're doing just fine."

"I do need it!" Kalliana's eyes flashed with anger. "It's part of me, it's what I am—it's the way I know people and read people. And now here I am, thrust among all these strangers, and I've been stripped of my defenses, my means of interaction, my weapons. How can I know anything about them?"

Gently, Troy reached out to put a hand on her shoulders, and she began to sob. He remained quiet for a moment, then touched her chin with one finger and raised her face so that he stared down into her reddened eyes. Tears trailed down her cheeks.

"Kalliana," he said, "there are ways to know and understand people even without Veritas." He cupped her chin in his two hands. "Let's take you, for example. I don't have any mind powers or truthsaying abilities, but I can still see that you're a frightened young woman suddenly tossed into circumstances she never expected. You were asked to do great things, important things that you had always thought were beyond your ability. They didn't quite turn out the way you expected, but still you've managed to get through. You've *done* what you had to do.

"You keep mourning for your Guild, but it's as if you were living your whole life inside a box. Oh, it was a pretty box and a comfortable one, but a box nevertheless. Now suddenly you've been tossed out into the big, wide world. You're stuck with me—no great pillar of strength—a man you once thought capable of murder.

"You're seeing Atlas through different eyes. You're feeling overwhelmed. Society around you is filled with wonders you never knew existed. You're finally meeting people—real, honest people, not just the ones accused of crimes—and you're having to rebuild the foundations the Truthsayers Guild established for you."

He took a deep breath, surprised at his own vehemence. "Atlas isn't neat and compartmentalized, with everything in clear-cut categories as your Guild taught you. I think you're doing a remarkable job adapting to something so incredibly new. You are resilient. You're strong, Kalliana." He used the sides of his hands to brush away the tears on her cheeks.

She looked at him dubiously. "How do you know all that? How can you tell?"

Troy shrugged. "Just by observing you in our time together. You know, they say when a person goes blind the other senses increase to compensate: sharper hearing, a more delicate sense of smell. Maybe by losing your Veritas abilities you'll become an even more astute judge of human nature just by looking at people."

She gave a wan smile. "Yes, now I remember. One time at Sardili Holding . . . I had to rely on just those intuitions, and I could see things. But I'll keep watching you, Troy. You'll be my benchmark example."

In the dim light Troy flushed with deep embarrassment. Not knowing what to say, he hugged her instead.

iv

The next week, as Kalliana began to grow accustomed to her daily schedule, she got a break in the new routine. She and Troy got a chance to see their landholder, Emilio Toth, sooner than they had expected.

The bronze bell rang in midmorning, calling people from their shifts for an unscheduled break. Everyone ran back to the village square, curious and excited. When Kalliana reached the broad central street paved with crushed granite debris, she saw a methane-powered tractor driving along the mountain road.

Emilio Toth drove the tractor himself, a big man with reddish brown hair, laugh lines around his eyes, a weathered face, and a voluminous, cinnamon-colored beard. He waved at the crowd as he drove up. Sol-pol guards rode beside him, but they seemed more for show than because of any great tension Toth felt about the populace.

Work crews continued to come from farther up the mountainside, rushing to find their families. Kalliana was too short and slight to see well as the crowd thickened. She was startled when someone put a hand on her shoulder, and she turned to see Troy, smeared with rock dust, his hands still wearing the grimy canvas gloves.

"What's going on?" he asked. "Everyone's jabbering like it's a party."

"I don't know," Kalliana said, standing on her tiptoes. "I can't see."

The big metal tractor puttered up on wire mesh wheels, and stopped. Emilio Toth stood up and waved his broad hands. "It's harvest time!" he said. "My best year ever at the orchards, and we have plenty to share. I'm keeping a large portion of the harvest to press some good cider, but the rest of you are welcome to fresh apples."

He made the announcement as if it were a surprise. The people cheered. From the back bins of the tractor, doors opened up and several workers lifted metal baskets of small round apples, yellow stained with red. The crowd moved, blocking Kalliana's vision as tossed apples fell into waving hands. Troy caught one, handed it to Kalliana, then reached up to grab another.

Kalliana bit into the fruit and tart sweetness exploded in her mouth. It had been a long time since she'd had a fresh apple. "Delicious," she said.

Troy nodded, munching on his own apple. One of the other

workers stood beside them, licking her lips as she gnawed her fruit to the core. "Toth does this every year," she said. "He divides up at least half of the produce from the orchards behind his Great House."

The mood of the workers lightened further around her, and Kalliana reveled in it. The people here seemed refreshingly satisfied with their lives, pleased with the paternal attentions of their landholder.

Emilio Toth cupped his hands around his mouth as he shouted, "And since you're all gathered here, I'd like you to meet someone who has recently joined our holding. I hope you won't have too much occasion to use his services, but he's a sharp young man, and fair. I want you all to give him a great deal of respect."

The crowd shifted. Kalliana stood on tiptoe, straining to see as another man stepped up beside Toth at the front of the tractor. "He'll be undergoing some training," Toth continued, "to familiarize himself with the workings of our villages and the business of the holding—but this is our new Magistrate."

Kalliana finally got a good glimpse of the pale-haired youth who grinned at the people welcoming him. Her surge of delight and surprise was unstoppable, and she couldn't halt her outburst. "Ysan!" she cried, engulfed by the feeling of comfort and home she had lost when she left her life in the Guild.

At the sound of his name, Ysan turned to look down at her. Toth hadn't yet introduced him, and no one should have known who he was. "Do you know somebody here?" Toth asked Ysan, but the young man shook his head.

Troy gripped Kalliana's shoulder. "Oh, this is just great," he said. "I've been so careful not to ask about my family, and here *you* go jumping up and announcing yourself the first time you see a blond-haired kid."

Villagers backed away from Troy and Kalliana, looking confused and uncertain. The sol-pols singled them out and brought them forward as Toth dismounted from his tractor.

Ysan followed Toth. The young blond looked at Kalliana, studying her dust-covered face, until finally a sunrise of recognition beamed from his face.

"Kalliana!" he said. She drew back, but she could no longer hide.

# CHAPTER

## 41

### i

The lid of the deepsleep chamber slid aside. Franz Dokken awoke cold and drained, feeling used up like an old piece of paper. The tracery of frost fingernails on the inner glass surface evaporated into the warmed air of the cave.

He took a deep breath and swallowed several times. His mouth tasted foul, and he saw with some annoyance that Maximillian had not set out a fresh squeeze bottle of water beside the chamber, as he usually did. Dokken took another breath. The tip of his nose was still cold and numb.

Sensations would come back soon. Already he could smell the flavors in the air, the dust, the metal, the old damp rock. His thoughts moved sluggishly, as if they needed to chisel new paths through his brain, but his mind would sharpen soon enough as blood began pumping at full strength again, revitalizing his tissues. He would sparkle with life and energy, as if he had slept backward, knocking ten years off his age.

He rubbed his eyes. His skin tingled, burning in reaction to the penetrating cold that had preserved him during his long rest. Silence roared around him, and his ears rang. He knew from long experience that the tinnitus would fade after an hour or so.

"Maximillian," he called. His voice came out in a croak. The manservant should have been there. He looked around, but saw that the cave was empty, the lights still dimmed to maintenance level.

"Maximillian," he said again, clearing his throat. "Where are you?" No one answered.

Taking several deep breaths, still feeling disconnected from his muscles, Dokken concentrated on planting his hands on the side of the deepsleep chamber. He hauled himself upright and swung a numb leg over the side. Below the knee his calf and foot dangled like a useless piece of wood, but as circulation increased, the nerves came afire again.

He pulled his body to a standing position and steadied himself on the side of the chamber, panting. Had the timing system awakened him too soon? Maximillian was always there waiting for him.

"Maximillian!" he shouted again, wondering if the gaunt man had gone out into the canyon to tend the horses.

Dokken finally staggered over to the supply station and poured himself some lukewarm water. He gulped the first glass as his dehydrated tissues sucked up the moisture, then sipped a second cup, while he unwrapped a package of dry protein wafers and wolfed them down. Vitality crept back into his body, accelerated by his uneasy emotional state. When he felt ready to move on, he dressed by himself, pulling on his cotton underrobes, then wrestled his arms and legs into stiff riding leathers.

Finally, strong enough, he stepped outside the cave, expecting to find the horses or Maximillian. But the steep-walled gorge was empty.

Two weeks earlier, when he and Maximillian had come here, they had ridden hard down the canyon and tied up the horses, making no effort to hide their tracks. Now he saw no fresh markings whatsoever. Just the old hoofprints. . . .

Dokken waited for hours, imagining all sorts of reasons why the manservant might have been delayed, which only made him grow more impatient. The most likely scenario was that some emergency had occurred back at the villa, and because the deepsleep cave was known to no one else, Maximillian could not send a surrogate to retrieve his master.

He cracked his knuckles, pacing the small confines of the cave and hiking a short distance up and down the canyon to where he could look out across the landscape.

"Patience," he whispered to himself, reciting the advice he had so often quoted to Tharion and others—but it did not help him now. Finally he went back to one of the rear chambers of the cave and uncovered the one-man emergency vehicle, a fast all-terrain cart that would return him to his villa.

Drawing upon two and a half centuries of experience, Dokken never constructed a plan without providing for numerous contingencies and escape hatches. In the years before he had decided to trust Maximillian, he had always handled his deepsleep activities by himself, letting no one else learn the secret. He would have words with Maximillian when he got back.

Puffing, he wheeled the vehicle outside the cave and powered it up. He let the small engine idle as he went back to shut down his computer controls and switch the deepsleep systems over to standby mode. For the next time.

Finally, he drove off at top speed, the wheels kicking up canyon dust behind the low-riding vehicle. He muttered angrily to himself, hating nothing more than when a plan—even a small one—didn't work out just right.

ii

He found the villa in a state of absolute turmoil.

Dokken had never before witnessed such joy and relief on the faces of the sol-pols and his servants as when they saw he had returned. Captain Vanicus marched smartly up to him, eyes glittering and face flushed. "Master Dokken, sir, you're back!" he said. "We were greatly concerned."

"Where's Maximillian?" Dokken demanded, looking around the courtyard as if the tall bald man would appear under an archway at any moment.

"No one knows, sir. We thought you would know his whereabouts."

Dokken raised his eyebrows as the implication sank in. "What do you mean? Report."

"Sir," Vanicus said, blinking his eyes rapidly and taking a step back. Then he seemed to remember his duty and stood straight. His dark uniform had been kept neat, as Dokken required of all sol-pols assigned to his holding. "The last we saw of him, sir, was when you both rode off together two weeks ago. We assumed you had given him some sort of assignment, that he was perhaps visiting Lady Schandra."

Dokken scowled. "He sent no message?"

"None, sir. We've been operating without guidance."

Dokken clenched his fists at his side and turned in a slow circle. Garien the chef poked his shaggy head through a doorway, then dashed back to the kitchens to set about preparing a quick meal for his master.

Dokken sighed and turned back to the captain of the guard. "So what has happened since I've been gone?"

Vanicus looked from side to side, as if trying to assess various items. "We maintained our day-to-day routine as best we could," he said. "The villagers have continued their production. The terra-cotta pottery and tiles have been shipped to First Landing. The power plant at Trident Falls is functioning at normal levels again.

"Supply requisitions needed to be sent, but we had no indication of your wishes. No forms had been filled out. The chef was rather distressed to see the food supplies diminishing in the pantries. With no specific orders from you, sir, I simply sent a copy of our last requisition to First Landing. Those supplies are on their way. I hope that was appropriate."

Dokken nodded. "You did well, Captain." He was pleased to see that the systems he had set in place functioned as he'd hoped. Everyone knew what was expected of them and had continued their work even in his absence. "Any major events?"

"Not in our holding sir, but there has been quite a shake-up over at Bondalar and Carsus. It looks like a civil war."

Dokken raised his eyebrows. "I take it Janine and Hektor are no longer engaged to be married, then?"

"No, sir," Vanicus shook his head vigorously. "Their new mag-lev station was blown up—apparently sabotaged by Hektor Carsus himself!"

Dokken *tsked* in feigned surprise. "But why should he do such a thing? What would he have to gain?"

"No one knows, sir," the captain answered. "But hundreds of people were killed, most of them Bondalar natives."

"These other landholders are just amateurs with their struggles," Dokken muttered. "What about our own holding? Everything secure?"

Vanicus stood stiff and proud. "Yes, sir. No problems. Tension levels are high, but we're keeping a close eye on the citizens. Nothing is getting out of hand. You had warned us, sir, that there might be great turmoil ahead."

The main reason for the chaos had probably been their fear and confusion, Dokken realized, afraid to be without a visible leader, though for most daily events the holding ran quite comfortably by itself.

"Thank you, Captain, that will be all." The sol-pol departed, flashing a last glance over his shoulder as if to make certain Dokken was still there.

Dokken strode past the serving board and grabbed some bread and salted fish that Garien was busily arranging on glazed plates. He spoke no word to the chef, but chewed his food distractedly as he went out to the balcony. He stood beside the potted geraniums and looked down into the courtyard.

Several workers were harvesting mulberry leaves for the silk-worms. He focused on them for a moment, but then his mind wandered back to its main concern.

What had happened to Maximillian? A frown creased his brow, and he finally confronted the two possibilities, the only two likely events he could imagine.

Maximillian could have betrayed him and gone to sell his knowledge elsewhere. Any other landholder would be pleased to have a turncoat such as Dokken's manservant. A rival might even be able to overthrow him with the dangerous knowledge Maximillian held in his bald head.

But why now? Why should Maximillian turn treacherous at this point? It made no sense. What did he have to gain? Maximillian had never shown any hint of disloyalty, any suggestion that he desired personal advancement. Maximillian was not at all like Cialben, not greedy and wanting a larger piece of the action. The manservant seemed absolutely content with his place in Dokken's tapestry. If Maximillian had wanted anything, Dokken would gladly have given it to him. No, he simply could not believe that the manservant had left of his own free volition.

The other possibility chilled and enraged him. Dokken had his enemies, of course, many of them ruthless and threatening, though clumsy. Everyone knew that Maximillian was a vital link in Dokken's machinations—and the best way to strike at Dokken would be to eliminate the manservant . . . or worse yet, capture him and interrogate him. Maximillian would never divulge his information willingly, but Dokken could imagine many types of torture that even the manservant might not be able to withstand.

The more Dokken thought about it, the more certain he became. One of the rival landholders had taken his manservant for whatever nefarious purposes—but who? Could it be Bondalar or Carsus? No, Maximillian had disappeared before the great sabotage to their alliance. Emilio Toth, perhaps?

Who would dare to strike against Franz Dokken—and *why now*? He clamped his jaws together until his teeth hurt.

Gripping the rail of his balcony so hard he might have crushed the rock, Dokken swore his revenge against whoever had done this to him.

# CHAPTER

## 42

i

Ysan was so excited to see Kalliana that it took him a full two minutes of chattering before he finally got around to asking what she was doing there in the village, with dark hair. The sol-pols escorted her and Troy over to the large tractor where workers were handing out the bruised apples from the bottom of the bins.

Standing near the landholder, Kalliana saw just how tall Emilio Toth was, practically twice her size, towering over Troy and Ysan as well. His billowing red beard made his face seem immense.

"I take it you know this woman, Ysan?" he said, raising his eyebrows. His face compressed into a knowing smile. "I thought you said you didn't get out much."

"She's a Truthsayer, Emilio." Kalliana flinched at having her secret exposed, but Ysan's voice carried no dire warning. "And a very dear friend. This other man I don't recognize, but—" Then he stopped and stared wide-eyed at Troy's birdlike figure, his narrow face. "Hey, now I recognize you. Aren't you the man that—?"

"It was a mistake," Kalliana said. "And we'd rather not talk about it, not here and not now." Troy gripped her arm, and she felt the strength in his fingers. His muscles had toughened remarkably in the last week. She couldn't tell if he held her protectively, or if he sought support himself.

Ysan blinked in surprise, but Emilio Toth drew himself up taller. He lowered his voice. "A Truthsayer, you say? And in disguise, at that." He clapped a meaty hand on Ysan's bony shoulder. "Perhaps we should discuss this in private. I think we can manage for these two to get the day off from work. They'll be our guests back at the Great House."

Kalliana felt a ball of ice form in her stomach. Once again she had been buffeted by an unexpected turn of events just when life had begun to stabilize around her.

She looked helplessly at Troy, and he shrugged. "Why not?" he said. "We could both use a day's rest."

ii

The Great House of Toth Holding was tall and imposing, squared-off like a medieval fortress. Built from midnight-green granite flecked with black and gold, it had been polished to such a high luster that the afternoon sun turned the stone into a plain of reflected fire.

Emilio Toth parked the methane tractor in one of the out-buildings; the other workers jumped off and ran to their chores. Around them, the mountainsides were carpeted with pines, tall and waving in the breeze.

Two towering oaks stood like sentinels outside the front door, rising higher than the roof of the Great House. They had been planted there more than a century ago, and now stood like a defiant shout, proof of progress against the rough environment.

Emilio Toth held open the high wooden doors that were reinforced with cast-iron hinges. Inside the Great House, children swarmed around them, greeting their father like a herd of stampeding animals. Toth laughed and picked up the smallest two, supporting one on each hip as he listened to the overlapping chatter of boys and girls telling him about their day. Toth nodded and listened intently to each one.

A beefy, sunny-faced woman about Toth's age came up to greet him with a massive hug of her own, then looked curiously at the two strangers. "Guests for dinner?" she asked.

Toth swept his arm sideways. "My friends, let me introduce you to my wife, the Lady Kiarre Toth—my best friend and the manager of my estate. While I amuse myself with public relations activities in my villages, she maintains the business, making sure everything gets done."

Lady Kiarre kissed him, and he swatted her as she bustled off. "We're starving! Tell the children to help you set up the big table in the main hall."

"How many children do you have?" Kalliana asked, a polite question—though the frenzied activity of the large family frightened her. The Guild had been comparatively quiet, and even the children were not allowed to run about shouting and playing and giggling as this brood did. But then she, like all Truthsayers, was sterile from her lifelong exposure to Veritas, and so she had not bothered to think much about the mechanics of families.

"Children?" Toth boomed. "With so many you'd think I'd lose track, but I believe we have six, ranging in age from four years to twenty." Out in the pine-floored dining hall the children were spreading out an embroidered cotton cloth on a massive trestle table made of long planks. "My father lives here too. He's eighty, but he suffered a stroke ten years ago. Now he spends his days tending the orchards. He's happy as can be—meanwhile *I* get stuck being landholder and have all the headaches that come with it."

Toth took them to a withdrawing room. Ysan followed, barely able to contain his own curiosity and eagerness to talk to Kalliana.

"Now then," the landholder said, closing the door. He tossed reddish hair out of his eyes and settled into a big wooden chair with padded armrests. "Let's hear more about you two."

"As I said," Ysan answered, picking up his cue to introduce them, "this is Kalliana, one of the Truthsayers who helped raise me and teach me. The man she's with is . . . is, um, a convicted murderer. I can't remember his name."

"Troy Boren," Troy answered.

Kalliana felt weak, knowing now that they would have to tell everything. "He's innocent," she said.

Emilio Toth chuckled at this. "Usually it's the *accused* who insists on his innocence, and the Truthsayer says otherwise."

Kalliana looked at Troy, but he spread his hands. "It's your call, Kalliana," he said. "I'm making this up as I go along, too."

Kalliana sighed, but she narrowed her eyes and looked sternly at Toth, then at young Ysan. "I hope you'll forgive my reluctance to explain," she said. "I have reason to be suspicious—we've already been betrayed several times. We have been on the run, people have tried to kill us, and threats keep coming from all directions. How do I know I can trust this landholder, Ysan?"

"Of course you can trust him," Ysan said. "Truth-read him if you doubt it. Emilio means what he says."

Stung, Kalliana said, "I can't read him. My ability has been fading since before I stood at Troy's trial. And so has yours. We found out why you failed your test—because of weakened doses of Veritas, diluted by operations up at OrbLab 2." She glanced at the young man for his reaction, then continued her explanation like a relentless excavating machine. "I've been away from the Guild for weeks now, and haven't taken Veritas in all that time." She looked to Troy, remembering the sensitive "truthsaying" he had done for her without benefit of telepathic enhancement.

"Truthsayer Kalliana," Toth said, "I am very interested to hear about this treachery. I have no doubt—although *you* most assuredly have doubts—that we all share a common enemy. There is a blight at the root of our society, and I'm not the only landholder who wants it stopped."

"Words," Kalliana said cynically, still holding her ground. "I used to believe them, used to trust what others said, confident that their loyalties were clear and their motivations transparent—but I've learned that isn't the case."

Ysan reached into the pocket of his jacket and withdrew a paper-wrapped packet. "Here," he said, carefully unfolding the sheets with his finger and exposing two sky-blue capsules.

Emilio Toth's bushy cinnamon eyebrows raised up like caterpillars, and immediately Ysan became defensive. "You told me to use these only in the most important circumstances," he said. "And it's very important for Kalliana to *believe* you so we can hear their story. What she has to say may affect our plans."

Toth nodded indulgently. "I agree," he said, "but don't expect me to keep getting more Veritas on the black market. We're trying to stop this, not encourage it."

"Of course," Ysan said and extended one of the capsules toward Kalliana.

Her eyes fixed on the small pill, riveted with fascination. It was a welcome link to her past life, to the stability of the Guild. She snatched it, then hesitated, rolled the capsule between her fingertips, and looked at Ysan. "But I'm no longer a Truthsayer," she said. "Guild Master Tharion stripped me of my rank."

Ysan shrugged with a grin. "I never was a Truthsayer. I failed my test, remember? That doesn't mean I can't use Veritas. We've taken it all our lives, haven't we?"

"But our oaths to the Guild?" she whispered, still staring at the pill. Troy stood beside her, watching the tableau, but saying nothing to influence her decision.

"I took my oath in good faith," Ysan said, "and so did you— but the Guild hasn't been treating us in good faith. I had already figured out that the Veritas was weakened, because the capsules

Emilio's been able to get are much more potent than what I've used in the Guild for a long time. When I take this, my powers are sharp and clear. With the old capsules though, I was muddled, unfocused. I couldn't read the details—and I failed my test. If the Guild had given me *this* kind of Veritas before my test, I would have had no trouble reading minds."

Kalliana swallowed in a dry throat. "And I would never have judged Troy falsely," she said quietly, looking at him. Troy's face was flushed and solemn.

She popped the Veritas into her mouth and bit down, swallowing quickly, feeling the acrid rush down the back of her throat. She closed her eyes and drew a deep breath, luxuriating in the power that surged through her neurons.

Emilio Toth bowed his head as if signaling obeisance, and she snapped out of her reverie, recalled to duty. Ysan fidgeted anxiously, gesturing her to proceed. Kalliana touched her hands to the thick mane of hair around Toth's head and dropped down into his thoughts, as naturally as breathing. She felt the strength of her Veritas boost, but without the spectacle, without the armed sol-pols, without the cheering crowd. There was no accused prisoner, just a willing subject.

It took her almost no time to read the strength and whole-someness, the essential goodness inside Emilio Toth, his well-meaning bluster and his abiding love for his wife Kiarre, his six children, and his entire landholding.

Afraid to squander her powers, unwilling to become intoxicated with the sensations of reading deeply into the man's open mind, Kalliana withdrew, all of her suspicions allayed.

And so she told him everything.

### iii

"Guild Master Tharion did not betray you," Emilio Toth said. Kalliana looked at him in open disbelief. "He only did what he was told. He had no choice in the matter."

"No choice?" Kalliana said. "He is the Guild Master, the most powerful man on Atlas. No one tells him what to do."

Toth shook his massive head at her naïveté. "No, Tharion has been so carefully manipulated that he doesn't even realize what he's doing. Franz Dokken has him wrapped around his little finger. Always has."

"Dokken?" Troy said. "He's just a landholder. How does he—"

"Any way he can," Toth answered.

"But Guild Master Tharion was the one who set up our escape plan," she pointed out.

Toth raised one finger. "And he probably blabbed it to Dokken. One of the real culprits in this seems to have been Dieter Pan on OrbLab 2, but he was recently killed. However, I happen to know that Kareem Sondheim is on our side. Let's just ask him to clear up a few details, shall we?"

Kalliana froze and gripped Troy's arm. "I don't want to go back up to the Platform," she said.

"No need for that," Toth answered. "Follow me into the study."

They walked from the withdrawing room into a wood-paneled chamber, a cozy office with a desk and a computer station, as well as paper notes tacked to a wall and reminders scrawled in ink on a reusable surface. Toth flipped up a flat viewplate and worked a set of controls that Kalliana didn't recognize.

"Satellite dish," he said. "We've hidden it on one of the peaks behind the Great House among our weather recording apparatus, just in case anyone should look. Gotta keep up the image that we're backwater primitives out here." He smiled. "And we needed our own direct line of communication. We've also been monitoring signals from the inbound colony ship, the *EarthDawn*. Dokken transmits regular signals of his own, and he thinks no one else can intercept them." Toth smiled. "He's already laying plans for when the ship arrives, but we'll take care of him long before then."

Before Kalliana had a chance to ask a question, the landholder established the uplink. A communications officer on the Platform recognized Toth and acknowledged with a serious nod. "Get Sondheim," Toth said, "if you please. This is important, but it'll only take a moment."

"Yes, sir. I'll see if I can track him down. He's not . . . he's not feeling very well."

"I wouldn't be either, if I were him," Toth said. "Get him anyway."

Sondheim drifted in a few moments later, his face shriveled like crumpled paper, the patchy white frizz of his hair standing out around his head. His eyes were red, his limbs trembling. It looked as if he had been dealt a mortal wound.

"Yes, Emilio?" Sondheim said. "I've agreed to speak to the Landholders Council and I—" He froze as he saw Kalliana and

Troy standing beside the large landholder. "Oh dear!" he said, drifting back so that his image receded. "Oh dear, oh dear— you're alive."

"Yes, we're alive," Kalliana said.

Then Kareem Sondheim did an extremely odd thing: he began to weep openly, placing his spiderlike fingers across his face. His entire body racked with sobs. "And Dieter's dead, slaughtered, along with a pair of sol-pol guards on OrbLab 2. Oh, why didn't I put a halt to this earlier? I saw it all coming. I could have prevented it, if only I had acted sooner. But I couldn't think straight! Dieter. . ."

He drew a deep, shuddery breath, then spoke directly to Troy and Kalliana. "I am so sorry. I am. I won't ask how you escaped. I must only shower you with thousands of apologies and beg your forgiveness."

"Enough sniveling, Kareem," Toth said, raising his voice. "Maybe you should offer these two a few explanations instead."

Sondheim squared his shoulders, took several deep breaths. Kalliana could see even without truth-reading that this man was not pretending his sorrow. She began to realize what Troy had meant about studying human actions with heightened senses.

Sondheim explained how Dokken had blackmailed him, how Dieter Pan's acts had backed him into a corner so that Sondheim had been forced to sabotage the escape plan to protect his protégé.

"Dokken set this up—I see that now. He was pressuring Dieter to increase the shipments, to take chances. And all along he wanted me to believe it was only poor Dieter. . . ." His red-rimmed eyes stared out of the viewplate. "Do you know how long I have been Franz Dokken's friend? Sometimes I wonder how I can do this to him even now, but it has to stop. He is out of control, and he'll destroy every one of us. I think that must be what he intended all along."

He shook his frizzy white head. "Let Emilio explain our plans to you, then, when all is done, perhaps you will consider whether to forgive me. And dear Dieter."

Troy looked meaningfully at Kalliana and said, "Sometimes we make mistakes—but we have to live through them."

Toth cut the connection. Ysan hovered by them, eager but troubled, as if he suddenly found himself far out of his depth. Before they could continue their discussion, the Lady Kiarre called them all to dinner, using a commanding tone that allowed for no excuses.

iv

They ate an enormous meal of roast lamb seasoned with salt and pink peppercorns from a wildly spreading tree on the east side of the Great House. Lady Kiarre added baked potatoes and glasses of sweet apple cider.

Kalliana felt exhausted from the quantities of food and the typhoon of conversation from the children and servants and Kiarre, all asking questions, all curious, all sharing their opinions. Two teenage boys went to the large common room and built up a crackling fire against the evening's chill, and Toth took his guests to the upper veranda where they could watch the dusk gather over the mountain peaks.

"You're very important, and you must stay here as our guests . . . unless of course you'd rather go back to the granite quarries."

"No, thank you!" Troy said. Kalliana chuckled at his rapid answer.

Emilio Toth nodded. "I know, I try to make it as pleasant as possible for the workers, but it is difficult labor. However, I sense that you two have a greater role in the events now unfolding. You have a stake in this yourselves. Franz Dokken is going to fall—and you can help us."

Kalliana looked at the cleared land behind the Great House, at the rows of low apple trees. An old man moved through the orchard with painstaking slowness, inspecting the trees as if memorizing each branch, plucking apples within his reach one at a time and carefully stowing them in a basket. He applied an intense amount of concentration to his bodily movement, as if filing a separate flight plan for each step he took.

Emilio Toth looked up into the purpling sky. His breath streamed faint and white from his generous lips, curling around his ruddy beard. "You know, when I was younger I saw the shell of the original colony ship come crashing down," he said. "It was a tragedy, a terrible waste of resources, of history. Once the Platform was detached and put in place and all the supplies moved over, the engines and the remainder of the ship, not much more than a skeleton, rode in low orbit. You could see it, a huge star moving across the night sky—so bright it cut through the aurora.

"But nobody paid attention to it, and the abandoned ship gradually dropped lower and lower until finally atmospheric friction took it away from us. By the time they realized what was going to happen, no one on the Platform could send a retrieval mission. I was standing right here with my dad beside me." He unconsciously turned and shot a glance at the old man in the orchards.

"We saw that shooting star come down, a streak of flames. It was the biggest meteor I've ever seen—and it made a great impression on me. It seemed like we were burning all our bridges behind us. None of us could go back to Earth anyway—but the obvious destruction of the ship that had brought us to Atlas to set up a new world . . . it was a profound sight."

His voice had dropped lower and trembled with feeling. "We've been given this world to make the best of it that we possibly can. We have no right to destroy it for future generations. As I look at my own children, I am doubly aware that I cannot stand by and ignore the damage being caused by someone else."

Emilio Toth swept his gaze past Kalliana and Troy and Ysan, looking at the black bulwark of impenetrable granite cliffs. "See my pine forests over there? Even with the light fading completely, you can make out that half of them are brown and dying. We've already had to cut them for lumber. Franz Dokken is poisoning them.

"He introduced a potent toxin into an aquifer that fed the streams watering those trees. My lovely pines began to die, and I had to butcher them and block off the irrigation systems to save the rest. When I learned what he had done, I sent someone over to poison his fishponds—but that was a childish thing to do. It merely escalates the level of destruction. Instead, we must remove the problem at its source."

Emilio Toth shook his large head. "What kind of animal soils its own domain? We all live here on Atlas, yet Dokken seeks to destroy it. He is overconfident, though. His great failing is his pride in the complexity of his schemes. Dokken has been playing us against each other like chessmen . . . and he's been doing it for so long that he doesn't realize others can play chess as well."

# CHAPTER
## 43

i

Breathing slowly to keep his anger and dread in check, Franz Dokken rode his stallion alongside the sol-pol's methane-powered patrol vehicle that clattered across the uneven rocky ground.

"Just up here," Vanicus shouted above the putter of the engine and the trotting horse's hoofbeats. "It's amazing he was found at all this far out in the barrens, with that gray jumpsuit of his. But a few of the villagers go rock hunting, looking for semiprecious stones and fossils they can sell in First Landing. It was already much too late. . . ."

Dokken was listening, but he didn't care. The words of the guard captain roared past his ears as he stared fixedly ahead, barely feeling the chestnut stallion, noticing neither the heat nor the bitter alkali smell.

Another vehicle with two other sol-pols sat parked in the flat alluvial fan of a broad wash that looked paler than the surrounding ground. Dokken could see them from a long distance away. The guards stood straighter as the landholder and Captain Vanicus approached.

Dokken couldn't see the other figure sprawled on the ground. Not yet. At least Atlas did not have circling buzzards that feasted on the desiccated bodies left out in the desert.

Vanicus accelerated, pulling ahead of the horse. The other sol-pols stood aside as the captain ground his wire-wheeled vehicle to a halt. Dokken slowed the horse as he approached, not wanting to see, still searching for some way to deny what he knew awaited him there on the ground. But that would do no good.

Dokken slid off his saddle, unconsciously handing the stallion's reins to one of the guards who came to meet him. With leaden legs, he walked forward. Captain Vanicus hovered close behind him, speaking at his shoulder.

"We've looked, sir, but there doesn't seem to be a mark on him. No sign of murder, or foul play—but, well, we all knew Maximillian, sir. We can't come up with any other explanation."

Dokken nodded absently as he knelt beside the manservant. "It was murder, all right," he said. "There is no other explanation. Maximillian didn't make mistakes."

The gaunt man's skin was blackened in blotches, bloating and draining into the parched dirt. His gray jumpsuit had torn, and somewhere he had lost his shoes. The soles of his feet had been shredded to the bone by sharp rocks, but still Maximillian had wandered, as if not feeling the pain. A small canteen at his side was half full of water, but he had not bothered to drink it.

"His feet were bleeding heavily," Vanicus said, "and the ground is undisturbed, so we could track him a ways. He wasn't all that far from a settlement, but he didn't seem to know where he was going. You can see the kenaf fields from here"—the captain gestured to a dark green area in the middle distance—"but he wasn't heading in that direction."

Dokken raised up Maximillian's head, and the man's neck moved with a combination of sinewy stiffness and gelatinous flexibility—a wholly unnatural feeling that made Dokken's skin crawl. He closed his eyes, taking shallow breaths to drive back the smell, and the overwhelming disbelief. Maximillian was dead! He cradled the manservant's decay-darkened bald head against his lap, wanting to rage at whoever had done this.

Dokken had seen death plenty of times before, and had caused more than his share of it. He had lived for centuries, watched the lives pass of people he had known. But Maximillian had seemed a part of him, a satellite operating under Dokken's orders. Everything had worked so smoothly with Maximillian's assistance. Dokken could always count on him.

He cursed himself for being sentimental, crushing his grief with a battering ram of anger, searching for a target. A storm swept across his sea-green eyes.

Vanicus frowned, then straightened his lips into a firm line crowned by his thin mustache. "Do you think it was one of the other landholders, sir? Are they striking out at us? Is there a conflict brewing that we should know about?"

Dokken met the man's gaze. "There's always a conflict brewing."

Vanicus nodded, but didn't flinch away. "I just wanted you to know, sir, that if it comes to fighting, you can count on us. The entire garrison of sol-pols."

Dokken studied the captain, narrowing his eyes. "You swore loyalty to the Truthsayers Guild. If some war erupts, they could recall you at any time."

Vanicus looked uneasy. "Dokken Holding is our home, sir. We have been stationed here all our lives. Some of the sol-pols have never even seen Guild Headquarters."

"Do you know what you're saying, Captain?"

"I . . . think so, sir."

Dokken sighed and stood up, his vision blurred with tears he refused to shed. Looking down at Maximillian's body again, he felt his sorrow freeze. Two more deep breaths, and the manservant's death became an abstract concept. Dokken began to ponder the next step, deciding whether he could continue weaving his overall tapestry of plans. It would be very difficult without help, without someone like Maximillian.

"Take the body back with you," Dokken said. "World-shaking conflicts can wait while we bury him properly."

ii

Atop the bluffs behind the main villa, Dokken watched the sol-pols pile a cairn of rocks over Maximillian's body. It seemed so . . . primitive in a way, but fitting. A stark grave on the frontier. He wouldn't deign to place a silly, sentimental marker, some overblown epitaph. The pile of stones was sufficient. Dokken himself knew where his loyal manservant was buried, and nobody else mattered.

After hearing the news, Guild Master Tharion had promised to come out as soon as possible, but it was sunset already and Dokken had not wanted to wait. The air temperature began to drop, and the desert breezes picked up. Dokken stood alone, gazing into the molten dusk as it silhouetted the cairn, then finally turned and began to make his way back to the villa.

He encountered Tharion hurrying up the path. When Tharion saw the landholder coming, he stopped and waited, but Dokken did not pick up his pace.

"I apologize for being late," Tharion said as soon as Dokken came close enough to hear him. He hesitated, as if uneasy. "And I'm sorry for your grief."

"Is it showing?" Dokken asked, somewhat surprised.

"It radiates from your thoughts like a glow."

"Don't try to read me!" he snapped.

Tharion shook his head. "I wouldn't dream of it, Franz. But the emotion eddies around you. Nothing distinct or specific, but I can still feel it. You're not immune to sadness—somewhat to my surprise." Tharion turned, and the two walked easily down the path toward the tall house. Inside, they could see the lamps being lit for the evening.

After an awkward silence, Tharion said, "Have you learned any more about what happened to him?"

"No," Dokken said. "I know it's one of the landholders, but I haven't yet figured out who."

"Ah." Tharion looked out beyond the range of focus as he talked. "I took the liberty of finding a new manservant for you. I know how much you depended on Maximillian, and I've found a fine candidate, I think. That's why I was late. I had to run some tests."

"You're giving *me* a manservant? How do I know I can trust him?"

"Can you trust *me?*" Tharion asked innocently.

"I don't trust anybody," Dokken answered, but his words were weak. He considered. Could Tharion be trying to infiltrate a secret Truthsayer into his holding, much the way he had sent the disguised Truthsayer to the Platform? He dismissed that possibility. He knew damned well that Tharion was simply not capable of betraying him.

"I'm not suggesting you let him shave you with a straight razor, Franz," Tharion said. "Just let him serve you, take over a few of Maximillian's former duties. It'll ease your burdens." They approached the villa, and when Dokken didn't respond for a few moments, Tharion's voice took on a strained tone. "Please, Franz—let me do this for you."

"Where did you find him?" Dokken said.

"I've known about him for some time and selected him especially for you. I have truth-read him carefully, and I vouch for his trustworthiness. I know that's important to you. He's perfectly willing to be your servant. It's my gift to you, after all you've done for me." Tharion smiled.

"All right, Tharion." Dokken hesitated, feeling touched and surprised at himself for the emotion. He was getting too damned sentimental. He couldn't afford that. "It's been a long time since you've visited me out here. Will you stay for dinner?"

"I still remember my headache from your wine," Tharion said with forced humor.

"Then we'll just have tea this time," Dokken said.

Tharion sighed and agreed. "Franz, you're too kind."

Dokken saw something odd at the edge of his smile, but disregarded it. After Maximillian's disappearance, he had been seeing conspiracies everywhere. "Yes, sometimes I'm too kind," he agreed.

### iii

The following day, sol-pol guards at Dokken Holding opened the tall doors to admit a lone man, unarmed and unassuming, who asked to see landholder Franz Dokken, claiming that he was expected.

Dokken came to the foyer, harried and snappish from lack of sleep, annoyed at the gall of this unknown person who demanded to see him. He tossed his unkempt hair behind him. Already he wanted to go back to the deepsleep chamber and escape from his troubles for a while. But he couldn't—not with Maximillian gone, not with all the plans building around him to a crescendo.

"Yes? What is it?" Dokken said. The tall, bland-looking stranger had not been allowed to pass beyond the threshold of the main doors; Captain Vanicus and two other sol-pols stood at attention, watching him.

The stranger assumed an air of neither arrogance nor submission. "Master Dokken, you may call me Lor," he said. "I was sent by Guild Master Tharion. He hoped that you might consider me as a replacement for your personal manservant."

"No one can replace Maximillian," Dokken said, but he stopped himself from directing the old anger at this newcomer. He gestured for Lor to come closer. "Yes, Tharion told me you would be coming. What can you do?"

"Whatever you wish me to do," Lor said simply.

Dokken spoke lower. "And how much are you *willing* to do?"

"Whatever you wish me to do," Lor repeated.

Dokken allowed himself a tired chuckle. "You must be from Tharion, then," he said. "He's coached you."

"Part of a servant's duty is to learn everything possible about how to take care of one's master," Lor said.

"Another good answer," Dokken replied. "All right. If the Guild Master gives you a clean bill of mental health, what more could a landholder want?"

Furrowing his brow, Dokken tried to superimpose Maximillian's craggy face on this unprepossessing man who stood so calmly before him, but could not manage it. "Just don't ask too many questions, and we'll get along fine," Dokken said.

iv

Tharion brooded in his ready room long past normal working hours, losing track of time. No one disturbed him. Everyone could sense how deeply troubled the Guild Master had grown in recent weeks.

He stared through the walls, not seeing beyond the window mosaic, gazing into his thoughts, into his future. The die was cast, as the cliché said. He had judged the case and made his ruling, and it burned him to his very core—but he was a Truthsayer. *Truth Holds No Secrets.* He had sworn to live and die by those words, and now he was trapped by his own promise.

But he would abide by it, even though Franz Dokken was his father. His father! He had spent much of his time brooding in front of a mirror, noting the resemblance he had never seen before.

Tharion had been manipulated from birth, planted in the Guild by Dokken himself, like a bomb waiting to explode whenever Franz Dokken decided to use him. Tharion's life had never been his own. He had been deceived every day of his existence, and Dokken had always been there, looking over his shoulder, pretending to be his friend, setting him up. . . .

Qrista appeared at the door, unsealing it with the Guild Master's own access code. "Tharion," she said, concerned. "Come back to our suite—please. Spend some time with me. Make love to me."

"I can't," he said.

She crossed her arms over her chest and raised a pale eyebrow. "Why not? You've been avoiding me for days."

"I know." Tharion said, hanging his head, but offering no explanation. He hadn't touched her, hadn't opened himself to her, since he had learned the terrible truth about Franz Dokken. He hadn't even allowed her to brush against his skin since he himself had wreaked such unspeakable damage on Maximillian.

"Tharion, let me help you," she pleaded, approaching him with extended hands. "I want to know what's troubling you. Let me share it with you. Together we can work through it." She leaned close, nearly touching him, but he exploded backward, avoiding her with all the revulsion he felt toward himself.

"No!" He stumbled behind his metal console desk, keeping it as a barrier between them.

Qrista gazed at him in horror. Her long hair hung in neatly knotted braids with herbs twined into the strands. She wore a clean outfit. Her face was freshly washed, her body lightly perfumed. She had taken great care to make herself beautiful for him—and she *was* beautiful, so beautiful he ached to look at her.

But he could not let Qrista touch his secrets. "No," Tharion repeated, his lips pressed tightly together. "I don't know if I can ever let you walk inside my mind again." He drew in a long, cold breath. "Monsters live there now."

Looking as if he had just slapped her, Qrista left the ready room, biting back tears.

Tharion stared blankly once again at the walls that seemed to press in around him, closer and closer. . . .

# CHAPTER

## 44

### i

When Joachim Sardili brought his boat to the river delta, keeping close to the shore because of the gray morning fog, he was astonished to see such turmoil in his village.

Pilgrims had arrived in swarms—hundreds, even thousands of them—swelling the village population to ten times its normal level. Tents had sprung up on the hillsides, and the streets were crowded with hooded forms moving about. Even from this distance he could hear the susurrus of overlapping conversations.

"What in the world is happening here?" Sardili asked, still gripping the brass deck rail and turning toward his two sons, who also stood perplexed at the boat's helm. Franklin and Russell looked at each other, then at their father, and shrugged.

"We've heard nothing of this," Russell said.

Sardili stroked his peppery goatee with his right hand. "Well, we'd better see what they're up to. Take the boat in."

The air was cold and damp as a chilled rag against Sardili's face. Russell worked the wheel and brought the boat into the muddy waters of the outflowing river. As the Pilgrims saw the approaching vessel, an agitated murmur transformed the crowd into a stirred-up hornets' nest.

Franklin stood beside Russell, his dark eyes narrowed with concern. "We don't have that many Pilgrims in our entire holding," the young man said. "They must have come from other landholdings as well."

The day before, they had pulled into one of their brick-making villages to find it empty, the buildings deserted, the people vanished. Now Sardili understood that the Pilgrims must have spread the word of this gathering. Because he had heard of no great movement along the mag-lev lines, the Pilgrims must have traveled overland in bands for days or even weeks just to reach this village. But why?

"I wish I knew what was going on," Sardili said, pursing his lips. "They never made any formal request for such a big get-together. I thought they trusted me more than this."

Russell shut down the boat engines, and Franklin jumped overboard to splash in the knee-deep silty water. Sardili stood at the bow and watched as Pilgrims pushed toward the shore. He frowned, sensing an ominous mood in the air. The Pilgrims were angry, riled up about something. "What could possibly be on their minds?" he wondered aloud.

He waved his hand in greeting, but they did not respond. They muttered among themselves, but no one seemed willing to take a position as the leader for the group. Unable to identify any spokesman, Sardili swung over the brass railing and landed in the mud, then splashed to the concrete walkway at the bank of the river. The Pilgrims backed away, as if intimidated. Russell and Franklin stayed close to the boat.

"Hello, all of you! This is quite a surprise," Sardili said, raising his voice but still feeling at a loss. "Ah . . . what brings you all here?"

Several people shouted answers that blurred together, but as their words surged louder, Sardili picked out a common theme—*homeland.* They wanted a private territory for their religious order. He sighed. Not that again. He had explained the inherent difficulties over and over. The Pilgrims had already brought their case to the Landholders Council and would have to wait until appropriate land could be made available.

"I've heard your words before." Sardili held his hands out to get them to see reason. "We all have. It would be folly for you people to march off into the desert to make your own homeland. It takes years and years to develop the soil so that it will support Earth crops. What would you eat in the meantime? You'll all die if you declare an independent state. You need time to prepare."

"We want a homeland now," someone shouted. "We've earned it."

The river breeze was cold against Sardili's skin, making him numb and clammy, but his cheeks flushed with embarrassment and rising anger. "That's why we are trying to help you, one step at a time," he said. "Certainly you must know that."

He actually felt a great deal of sympathy for their concerns.

The Pilgrims were the hardest workers he had ever seen, and his holding's productivity had increased greatly since the arrival of the battered refugee ship from Earth. His father had happily taken more than his share of the immigrants forty-seven years ago, and Sardili had continued the policy of openness.

"We've worked for you long enough, landholder!" another Pilgrim shouted.

Still trying to show his good intentions, Sardili pushed his way deeper into the crowd. The Pilgrims clearly did not know what to do. "I'm disappointed that you didn't let me know about this gathering," he said. "We could have helped you organize, a regular conference so you could discuss strategies, figure out ways that would satisfy you that you're really making progress toward your goal."

"Are you saying we're not allowed to hold a meeting?" someone else shouted, a face that ducked beneath its hood and hid back in the crowd. "That we can't speak our minds in Sardili Holding? That we have no freedom of speech?"

Sardili raised his hands. "Of course not! I've always let you say what you wished. I've never tried to obliterate your culture or repress any of the things you wanted to do."

"Then why don't you let us have a homeland?" someone else said.

Sardili had to stop himself from rolling his eyes. These people weren't listening. Anger was going up by degrees. He tried to lower his voice, to be calmer, more soothing. "Look, can't we just talk about this? The best way to solve a problem is to air the issues and then reach some sort of conclusion or a compromise we can all live with. The first thing we should do is—"

"Where's Brother Adamant?" someone yelled, and this seemed to trigger the anger in the crowd.

"Who?" Sardili said.

"Brother Adamant—what have you done with him?"

Another voice shouted. "You've arrested him!"

"I've arrested no one," Sardili said. "I don't even know who you're talking about."

"Now he's trying to cover it up." The voices grew louder. "He's executed Brother Adamant in secret to stop him from rallying us."

The idea spread like wildfire through the crowd. Sardili looked behind him, and through the sea of hooded forms he noted Franklin and Russell waiting uneasily by the boat. Joachim Sardili didn't know what to do either.

"Please, let's just calm down," he said as if speaking to children
. . . which enraged the Pilgrims even more. His heart pounded,
and he looked from side to side. Sardili struggled to be heard over
the uproar. His words sounded watery and weak, and he was
disappointed in himself for not being a stronger leader, a firmer
paternal figure to help his people work through this crisis.

"Excuse me!" he cleared his throat, then yelled louder. "Maybe
we should just back off for a little bit. You can have your rally and
your meeting, but please try to come up with some concrete
suggestions. Select a leader who will confer with me and tell me
your requests. You have all your people here; discuss some
strategies. For now, I think I should leave you to your discussions—but please be constructive."

Sardili turned and tried to push back toward the muddy river.

"Stop him!" somebody yelled. "He's going to get the sol-
pols."

"No, no, don't let him get away."

Sardili flailed his hands and fought his way back toward shore.
The uproar was too loud, drowning his shouts for Franklin and
Russell to get to the safety of the boat. He pushed through the
brown-robed people, desperately trying to reach the concrete
bank.

Sardili bumped into an old woman, and as she turned on him,
a much larger man shoved him. Next somebody else pushed
Sardili, catapulting him forward until other hands grabbed at his
sleeves, yanked his hair, held his waist. He was lifted off the
ground by a hundred angry hands, and he thrashed and struggled,
finally seeing that he had reached the edge of the crowd. Sardili
slapped at the hands, at the heads of those holding him prisoner,
trying to free himself before they got to the river—but it was too
late. They threw him facedown into the muddy water, then surged
after him.

He splashed, fighting to get to his feet, his knees, as the dirty
water flowed around him. He managed to push his head above the
surface, sucking in a long choking breath of silt and mud, but more
brown-robed Pilgrims jumped into the river nearby, splashing and
converging.

He thought he heard faint shouts, his two sons yelling for their
father—then the Pilgrims closed around Sardili and shoved him
below the surface again.

ii

When the violence reached its peak, it was as if a bubble had burst for the normally calm Pilgrims. In the sudden aftermath they looked at each other like sleepers waking from a nightmare, stunned and horrified at what they had done. Joachim Sardili's bruised and muddied body drifted facedown in the brown waters, caught up against the concrete embankment.

Some Pilgrims sat cross-legged on the ground, heads buried in their hands, moaning softly. Others splashed into the water, helpless. All seemed afraid to touch the corpse, filled with revulsion.

Russell and Franklin fought past the subdued Pilgrims, wading into the river to reach their father's body. One old woman who had remained in the water reached Sardili first. Weeping gently, she wrapped her arms around Sardili's chest and rolled him over. His thin arms flopped and drifted in the gentle current. Water streamed from his mouth and nose and open staring eyes.

"What have we done?" sobbed Serenity, the old woman who had been absolved of her crime by the Truthsayer Kalliana. "What have we done? Now who will listen to our request for a homeland? Now who will treat us with respect? What have we done!"

Russell and Franklin sloshed over. Tears streamed down their faces, echoing those that trickled down the old woman's wrinkled cheeks.

Joachim Sardili's sons took his body from her. Hugging their father's lifeless form, both bowed their heads as they stood speechless in the cold waters, feeling their feet sink into the loose mud.

"Please," Serenity said. "Please." But it was unclear exactly what the old woman was asking. . . .

Hours later, Franklin and Russell both decided that they had no desire to keep their father's marvelous boat, the possession that he had valued higher than any other belonging. Franklin remembered having read something about an ancient Earth custom, a legendary ceremony called a Viking funeral, and described it to his brother.

"Father would have found it appropriate," Russell said.

"I agree," Franklin answered.

They placed Joachim Sardili's body in the captain's chair and maneuvered the boat so that it faced out to sea. Then, starting the methane engines, they lit the fabrics and set the decks on fire. Both sons leaped overboard and swam back toward the river delta before turning to watch the boat their father had loved.

The flames increased, dappling the leaden ocean with warm orange light. They treaded water as the boat headed west in the direction of the fading morning mists. The fire burned brighter and brighter, engulfing the boat as it continued toward the horizon.

Russell and Franklin swam to shore and climbed onto the concrete walkway, where they stood dripping and shivering. The Pilgrims waited around them in guilty silence. Far out to sea, they heard the sound of an explosion that was diminished to a faint *pop* by the distance. A finger of bright white flame rose from the rear of the boat.

The Pilgrims began to mutter and then point with amazement. Franklin and Russell also saw the waters stirring with turmoil, as three enormous, primeval-looking serpents rose out of the water, hissing and thrashing, slick and silvery, like wide-mouthed eels—possibly attracted by the flash of the fire or the boom of the explosion. The monsters circled the wreck of the boat and followed it like pilot fish.

Russell and Franklin agreed later that it seemed fitting somehow, as if primordial guardian spirits had appeared to escort their father on his final journey. . . .

TRUTH

# CHAPTER
# 45

i

The doors to the great Council chambers of the Truthsayers Guild had been sealed. Sol-pol elite guards stood stationed outside, weapons shouldered, allowing no one to disturb the unscheduled mediation session. None of the other Guild members knew what was taking place, but they could sense the tension thrumming through the metal walls of the ship. The Landholders Council was discussing some matter of planetary import.

Each holding representative had received a private announcement and a sol-pol escort to bring them directly to Guild Headquarters with no chance to send any messages home. The representatives would have to make their decisions alone, as they had been delegated to do.

The flustered men and women entered the chamber, voicing sentiments of confusion and annoyance. Inside, Qrista stood waiting, arms crossed over her small breasts, her Mediator's crimson sash snug and meaningful around her waist as she watched them.

The space elevator had landed less than an hour ago, bearing its most unusual cargo.

Brown-sashed workers carried in thermal urns of tea for all of them. The Council members sat at the table in the stuffy room, with ventilation systems turned up to their maximum levels. The representatives from Carsus and Bondalar sat at opposite ends, glaring venom at each other in their newly declared war, but Qrista knew that would soon change. Her heart pounded with exhilaration, now that she finally had the true culprit surrounded by traps. It was time to spring them.

Not even Tharion knew what she was doing. She would have told him, but he had sealed himself in a private, mental prison behind walls she could not breach. Qrista would act alone, and she had no doubts.

"Now that you're all here, we have important matters to discuss," she said from the podium. "Perhaps the most important matters this Council has ever taken up."

"Wait a minute," the Sardili representative said, raising a willowy arm as she looked at the others, spotting two empty seats. "What about the representatives from Dokken Holding and the Platform?"

"Dokken Holding has not been invited to this session," Qrista answered bluntly. She nodded to one of the elite sol-pols. "And the representative from the Platform will address us immediately. I have left the rest of the day for our deliberations, though I suspect we won't need it."

Other questions were muttered down the line of representatives, but all fell into a hush as the big metal cargo doors at the rear of the sealed Council chambers groaned open. A lift platform hummed, raising a heavy load to the level of the chambers, then clanked to a stop.

Muscular guards grunted as they hauled forward a massive and cumbersome shielded tank on wheels. The walls of the tank were thick plates of anodized metal riveted into a sturdy configuration, framing wide glass panes reinforced with wire mesh. Inside the tank swirled a mixture of oils and air bubbles, murky and dark.

A stunted, gnarled body could be seen floating in the viscous fluid, supported by a flexible harness that kept Kareem Sondheim's white-frizzed head raised above the fluid level, his head and neck sticking out through an opening in the tank's cover. A respirator helped him breathe in the heavy air as he floated in the neutral-buoyancy tank.

He turned his head as if it took great effort, looking around the ornate chambers with dark, fascinated eyes. He looked older than the universe itself.

Several Council members gasped in surprise to see him, but Kareem Sondheim did not seem disturbed. He drew a deep breath without the respirator, as if exhilarated by the smells. Inside the tank, his arms and legs moved sluggishly, supported by the heavy oils that buoyed his frail body against the crush of gravity.

"This is highly irregular," the representative from Bondalar said, scowling. "What is he doing here?"

"Every landholder has the right to address this Council directly," Qrista said. "Kareem Sondheim has never before descended to the surface of Atlas, but he has matters of grave import to discuss with you."

"It's not easy for me to be here," Sondheim said, his phlegmy voice sounding even rougher in the thick air. "In only the last few days, my engineers designed and constructed this tank, so that I could come down the space elevator and withstand the crush of gravity." The circulating oils in his tank gurgled.

"Staying here is difficult for me." His head, a mass of wrinkles and patchy hair, swiveled around like a disembodied mask, glancing along the line of representatives. "But it's far more difficult to tell you what I have to say."

ii

The Council members had long since stopped looking at the sealed metal doors, engrossed in the accusations and incriminating evidence now made clear to them. Weeping as he confessed Dieter Pan's involvement—and his own —Sondheim talked well past the point at which his voice became hoarse. He asked for no mercy, only that the brewing disaster be averted.

Finally, when afternoon descended toward evening, Sondheim requested to be taken from the chamber. Floating in his support tank, the ancient landholder looked up at the metal ceiling of the *SkySword*. "This place reminds me too much of the Platform. I want to go outside and look at the sky for a while longer before I return to orbit. The sky looks much different than I had expected. I'll want to repaint the ceiling in my receiving dock. . . ." Tears welled in his eyes.

The sol-pols hauled his oil-filled tank back out through the rear doors of the chamber and down the cargo lift.

The Council members reviewed the detailed information in front of them, uneasy, appalled at the magnitude of what they had heard directly from the shriveled lips of Kareem Sondheim.

The damage done by Franz Dokken's schemes was so far-reaching that no holding had remained unaffected. A few representatives looked hungry, like birds of prey circling over a herd animal that had been marked for death.

"I have no question in my mind," Qrista said, raising her voice, "nor do any of you, I believe." In truth, she had no such assurance, had not troubled to read them, but her simple statement might sway enough of them to believe the assessment . . . thereby making it effectively true.

"We must take unprecedented action. Here and now." Qrista placed her empty hands on the table, curling her fingers into fists.

Her skin was so pale it seemed translucent, even fragile, but her own charisma gave her the powers of persuasion she needed. "I believe that Council's choice in the matter is clear."

The representatives from Carsus and Bondalar holdings—who had been at war only that morning—kept slipping glances toward each other. Though still tense, they were relieved now that they knew *Dokken* had set them at each other's throats, playing upon their suspicions, planting evidence of betrayal and sabotaging their plans for an alliance. He had intentionally corroded the raw metals sent from the Koman Mining District, causing delays and damage to the new mag-lev line. The Koman representative looked indignant but vindicated.

Some of Franz Dokken's crimes were already known, or at least deeply suspected—such as the poisoning of Toth's pine forests. But the extent of the destruction wrought by a single landholder was shocking news, a surprising revelation to those who had considered Dokken just one among the many squabbling aristocrats.

As the hours ground along, the representatives carefully studied their notes of Sondheim's disclosure, how he had so fully revealed the strands of Dokken's plots. They added together the details, reconstructing the steps of how he had managed to foment a Pilgrim rebellion at Sardili Shores, how he had triggered the black market Veritas smuggling, and on and on.

Qrista drained the last of her tea, but it was bitter and lukewarm. When the discussions came full circle for the second time, she lost her last trace of patience and requested an immediate vote, as was a Mediator's right.

"Franz Dokken clearly does not have the best interests of Atlas at heart," she said. "We all heard Sondheim. There can be no question that Dokken is responsible for a great deal of damage to our society. Can we simply stand by and allow it to continue? Let us decide now what is to be done."

She saw all the members of the Council nodding. When they finally deliberated on the action to be taken, Qrista was amazed at the results of the vote.

For the first time in her entire tenure as a Mediator, the Landholders Council agreed unanimously.


iii


To the Guild workers still going about their daily routines at

Headquarters, it was business as usual. But Qrista's body language was closed and defiant, her expression stormy as she crossed the bridge deck into her husband's office, spoiling for a fight. She intentionally left the door open to Tharion's ready room as she marched in to announce the council's decision.

She didn't care if the other administrators heard their conversation. She wanted word to spread rapidly, because the decision was unstoppable now. Not even the Guild Master could veto it.

Tharion swiveled in his chair, startled out of his preoccupied musing. Self-consciously, he slid a flat object into the drawer of his desk. A mirror. He had been staring into it.

She stood in front of him, her skin flushed. "Franz Dokken is to be stripped of his lands," she said. "The Council has decided. If he resists, he will be cut off completely. No more trade, no maglev transportation, no food—nothing. He will be isolated under these sanctions until he personally surrenders his villa and a suitable appointee takes over his holding." She clamped her lips together, waiting for his response.

Tharion sat silent for a moment. She wanted him to rail at her, to shout, to tell her she had been presumptuous, to rekindle his passion somehow—but he merely nodded. His expression was sad, weary, and apathetic. He was a stranger to her. It sent a chill rippling down her back.

Qrista decided to push for his reaction. "We have incontrovertible proof of his crimes and manipulations, Tharion. Your friend Dokken has a world of blood on his hands."

Tharion looked at her with heavy-lidded eyes. "I know," he said.

She stood across the desk from him, amazed. She had expected denial, some sort of argument.

When he stood up and came around the console, Tharion took her hands in his own. His palms were cold and clammy. For a moment Qrista was too shocked to read him, then he turned away, withdrawing from her grasp. He seemed oddly relieved at the Council's verdict, which puzzled Qrista.

Tharion shook his head in resignation and turned to stare out the stained glass window. "I'll go. Let me deliver the message to him."

Then he fixed his gaze on her, a hard, cruel smile on his lips. In that moment she noticed for the first time how much her husband resembled his mentor Franz Dokken.

"I want to see the look on his face when I tell him," Tharion said.

# CHAPTER

# 46

i

Troy Boren slept in a plush bed in Emilio Toth's Great House. He smothered himself in woolen blankets and reveled in the luxury of a small fire in his own fireplace. Crackling split-pine logs fresh from the mountain forests filled the air with a hot resinous scent. He finally felt the warmth seeping all the way through to his bones, driving away the last remnants of the physical and emotional chill that had numbed him since he had first set foot on OrbLab 2.

But though his body was exhausted, Troy lay on his mattress, troubled and lonely. He and Kalliana were not lovers, but he had grown accustomed to her company, having her beside him on the descending space elevator, or just listening to her breathe on her pallet on the other side of the small prefab hut or on Marriatha Bowditch's resource rover.

The next morning he came down to breakfast well rested and famished. The younger children were already out playing, while the teenagers helped Lady Kiarre set the morning dishes on the plank table, not bothering with the embroidered cloth this time. Apparently in the Toth household people caught breakfast whenever they could.

Kalliana appeared bright-eyed, dressed in fresh clothes. Troy felt warm inside when he saw the delight on her face as she came over to greet him. He gave her a brief, awkward hug. "Did you sleep well?" he said.

"Well enough," she answered. "It's very comfortable here."

Troy came dangerously close to telling Kalliana he had missed her, but caught himself, shuffling his feet in embarrassment. His mind swam with confusion, wondering when his attitude toward this former Truthsayer had changed. They had been thrown into such turmoil and had survived terrible adversity together. Now that they had a moment of breathing space in their lives, Troy could finally allow himself to think of possibilities beyond simply suviving until the following day.

Emilio Toth thundered in from the back doorway of the house, full of bluster and shining with perspiration. "About time you got up," he said. "I'm glad you had the forethought to rest well for our great battle ahead. We have many plans to make this morning. The co-conspirators are arriving. Our lookout on the roof has spotted their car on its way already."

Troy looked to Kalliana, mouthing, "Co-conspirators?" Kalliana shrugged.

Troy could see the pale roots of her dyed-auburn hair. Somehow he couldn't remember what she looked like as the white-robed angel of justice. He saw only her narrow face, her petite body, a delicate young woman who had been born to wield a great deal of power, yet had been given no experience to understand the people she was forced to judge.

Troy served himself a plate of steaming hash made from leftover potatoes and roast lamb from the night before. Kalliana selected two honeyed pastries with glazed fruits. Before they had finished eating, Toth's sol-pols arrived at the door, throwing it open to admit two guests. The Lady Kiarre hurried in with another tray of rolls, and the children set about brewing more of the expensive chicory coffee and stoking the fire in the great room.

The woman who entered stood tall and whip thin, her features sharp and hardened like a weapon designed for hand-to-hand combat. Her face was weathered from a lifetime of concerns, worn down by mental hardships.

"Ah, Lady Victoria." Emilio Toth strode over to her with giant steps, caught her sinewy hand in his voluminous grip, and brushed it with lips haloed by a cinnamon-colored beard. "You are lovely as always."

"And you are an unabashed exaggerator, as always," the woman said with a thin but well-meaning smile.

Kiarre Toth pretended to frown and waved with her pudgy hands. "He never talks to me that way, Lady Victoria. I think I should be concerned."

A young man entered behind her, well built and handsome, with close-cropped straw-colored hair and blue-green eyes. Troy judged him to be seventeen or eighteen years old, calm of disposition, yet with an intelligent alertness to his movements.

The sol-pols remained outside, while Toth ushered his visitors in and introduced them to his other guests. "This is my fellow landholder, Victoria Koman, and her adoptive son Michel Van Petersden."

Kalliana nodded. "Yes, I recognized them."

At one time, Troy would have felt giddy upon hearing the famous names. To the common people, landholders were relegated nearly to demigod status—and here he was, having spent the night as the guest of one landholder, being introduced to two others. It still made his head spin, but not so much as the other ordeals he had been through.

Ysan came in through the back door, holding it open so that the ponderously moving grandfather could enter, cradling six perfectly formed apples. As if completing an important ceremony, the elder Toth deposited his precious apples into an empty fruit bowl on the table, stared at his work, then began the long and tedious process of turning his body around and hobbling back out to the orchards again. Ysan joined the group, flashing a boyish grin at Kalliana.

Emilio Toth explained the circumstances that had led to Troy and Kalliana becoming fugitives. "Fellow victims, then," Koman said. Her voice rang hard as a metal cymbal.

Troy extended his hand and bowed his head shyly. "I'm certain you don't remember me, Lady Koman. My father Rambra Boren paid you a fee for a job in First Landing. You secured me work at the anchor point for the space elevator. It was a fine job . . . before everything went wrong."

Kalliana gripped Troy's free arm, but he wasn't sure whether it was meant as support for him, or a guilty reflex on her part.

"We appreciate your assistance," Michel Van Petersden said. His voice was soft and well modulated. "So you've thrown your lot in with us to help with our grand design?"

"We don't exactly know what the plan is yet," Troy said. "Only that you intend to do something about Franz Dokken."

Koman's nostrils flared as she drew in a long deep breath. "Seventeen years ago Dokken grabbed the holding of Abraham Van Petersden in a bloody takeover that slaughtered the entire family. Only young Michel—who was an infant at the time—survived. I have trained him to the best of my ability, taught him everything I know and feel. The Guild Master himself recently truth-read him and proclaimed Michel to be a good young man with the strength and moral fiber necessary to make him a leader. He seems to have a genuine knack for it.

"We plan to overthrow Dokken Holding and let Michel take back the lands that were stolen from his father." Victoria Koman looked coolly at them as if daring either of the guests to question the plans.

"We've given Dokken plenty of rope," Toth said, "and he has hung himself well and truly. He's at the end of everything, and I'm not sure he even realizes it yet. He's so smug and sure about his own schemes that he can't imagine others might be aware of what he's doing."

Toth went over to the fruit bowl to select one of the new apples brought in by his father. He scrubbed it against his shirt, then took a bite, chewing loudly. "Thanks to Kareem Sondheim, the Truthsayers Guild and the Landholders Council have now been fully informed of Dokken's plans, the various and sundry ways he has caused damage, the sabotage, the feuds, the anger. It can all be traced back to him."

Victoria Koman gave a snort of disdain. "And you trust the *Council* to do the necessary radical surgery? You expect they'll do anything more than slap Dokken's hand and admonish him never to be naughty again? That's all they did when he took over Van Petersden Holding in the first place. We need to employ sterner measures."

Michel studied the pastry Kalliana held half-eaten, then walked over to the breakfast table and selected an identical one for himself.

"That's why we're taking direct action ourselves," Toth said. "But still I feel better knowing the Council has all the information. We're on record, and the proof is there." Wiping a broad forearm across his mouth to clean the apple juice away, he tossed the core into the glowing fireplace. "They won't squawk so loudly after we do what we have planned."

Troy lowered his voice and asked nervously, "Excuse me, Lady Koman—maybe this isn't the best time to ask, but could you possibly grant me a favor?" He moistened his lips and looked at Kalliana, though she had no idea what he had in mind.

"If it's within my power," Koman said, narrowing her eyes with instant suspicion. Troy realized that in her position as a landholder she must be constantly inundated with requests for favors.

"Please, madam," he said, "my family lives in the Mining District of your holding. I can give you instructions on how to find them. I would appreciate it very much if you could . . . get a message to them, let them know I'm all right."

Kalliana spoke up. "And that he's innocent—that the Truthsayer who accused him has declared him innocent. Let them know their son is not a murderer." Troy felt his throat thicken and found it impossible to speak. With eyes stinging from unshed tears, he could only nod.

Victoria Koman, the old matriarch, softened and looked at him with a genuine smile. "I think I can manage that, Troy Boren," she said. "In fact, I'll take care of it personally."

ii

After Victoria Koman and Michel Van Petersden departed, Troy and Kalliana spent the afternoon helping Toth and his workers to clear a stand of dead pine trees from the steep mountainside. The needles had fallen off many of the trees, leaving only skeletal branches, while others retained theirs, a coppery rusty brown instead of the deep green as on the trees on the far side of the granite bluffs. Dozens of workers, acting as teams, wielded heavy-duty laser cutters that were old, but still functioned well enough to slash through the thick trunks, and the trees came toppling down.

Troy and Kalliana set to work with the lighter labor of trimming off branches, cleaning up the wood, and making it usable.

"Cutting out the deadwood," Emilio Toth said, hands on his hips. He bent backward to stare up at one of his tallest trees, now brown and ready to fall. "Slicing out the blight . . . just like getting rid of Dokken."

Most of the men were strong and well muscled, with arms as thick as the branches on the trees they cut. Many were granite quarry workers. Toth's elderly father stood by himself, mumbling occasionally. The old man wept as each tree fell.

Emilio Toth came over to slap Troy on the back. He drew in a huge breath. "Isn't it invigorating? I wish everyone could just enjoy reaping the satisfaction of their own labors, rather than preying on someone else's."

Troy recovered from the back slap, then asked the question that had been troubling him. He brushed sawdust and splinters from his shirt. "Excuse me, Master Toth," he said, "but in all our discussions we've never exactly talked about *how* you intend to overthrow Dokken Holding. What weapons do we have?"

Toth grinned. "We have regiments of loyal sol-pols—my contingents as well as Koman's—plus we have plenty of our own fighters." He gestured to the lumber cutters and the granite quarry workers. "Look at the size of their muscles. Would you want to fight against them?"

"No, but—" Troy said.

"But—" Toth interrupted. "We hope a big show of force will be enough. Dokken's assigned sol-pol forces aren't any larger than ours. If we strike and hold strategic places across his lands, we can cripple his operations before he knows he's under attack."

Kalliana finished trimming the other side of the fallen trunk and stood listening to Toth's conversation. Absently, Troy reached over to brush a few dry pine needles from her hair.

Emilio Toth took no notice as he stared down the canyon, daydreaming. "Dokken used the same tactics when he went against Abraham Van Petersden, and now he doesn't believe anyone else can carry out plans as boldly as he did. He shouldn't make such foolish assumptions."

All three looked up to a chorus of shouts as another towering tree creaked and tilted, then came crashing down.

"You see?" Toth said. "That's all there is to it. We'll launch our attack tomorrow."

# CHAPTER

## 47

i

Guild Master Tharion stormed up the walkway to the villa and flung open the heavy veneered doors himself, pushing past the sol-pols who stood at attention. With one glance at the thunderous expression on his face, they backed away in fear.

He stomped his dusty feet on the tile floor of the foyer, straightened his white robe, and knotted his royal blue sash so tightly that it might never be untied. Already making an imposing figure, he drew himself up, then strode deeper into the house, shouting for Franz Dokken.

The landholder had just come in from the stables, breathless and glistening with sweat from a hard morning ride. He looked up at Tharion with surprise. "Ah, look, it's my friend the Guild Master! I haven't seen you in far too long."

In the drawing room the new manservant Lor helped Dokken remove his black leather jerkin and toweled off his master's chest, handing him a shiny sea-green silk shirt that matched the color of Dokken's eyes. Dokken tugged the billowing shirt over his head and held his arms up, looking vibrant and awake. "As you can see, your candidate Lor is proving to be an admirable helper, Tharion. He doesn't talk much—and I like that. So, what brings you here?"

Tharion glanced at the new manservant; the two flashed a knowing glance, then proceeded to ignore each other. "It's over, Franz," he said, clasping his hands in front of him.

Dokken raised his eyebrows, but Tharion continued. The words felt leaden in his mouth. "The Landholders Council and the Truthsayers Guild know everything about your plans. They've issued an edict. You are to be stripped of your holding, blocked off with sanctions, if need be. You are no longer a power on Atlas."

Dokken paled, then high color came to his face with redoubled intensity, fueled by an anger that he barely kept under control. He gave a dismissive laugh. "And so have you come to forewarn me,

Tharion—or did they send you as their pigeon bearing a message?"

He snorted, but Tharion didn't answer. Dokken paced across the room to the balcony, but it was just a distracting gesture. He returned in a moment. "They know everything, you say? How can they know everything? They couldn't possibly guess even the half of what I've been doing. They're too dim."

He sniffed and turned away, but Tharion saw the muscles in his back bunch up. Dokken froze, as if a thought had just occurred to him. He turned slowly, his eyes narrowing in comprehension. "Maximillian! The Guild took Maximillian and interrogated him."

Lor, the new manservant, continued hanging the riding leathers, trying to remain unobtrusive.

"No, not Maximillian," Tharion said. "The Guild and the Landholders Council have obtained full disclosure regarding all your schemes and how they have affected our society—but not from your manservant."

Dokken appeared relieved—and Tharion chose that moment to drive in the knife of knowledge. "But I, personally, learned more than enough from Maximillian . . . *Father*."

Dokken's head snapped up to meet Tharion's eyes. "Leave us, Lor," he said out of the corner of his mouth, "but stay nearby. I may have need of you this morning."

Tharion was pleased to see a glimmer of fear behind the landholder's stony expression. "The Guild Master and I have some things to discuss here."

ii

When the manservant had departed, Dokken carefully went to the double door and drew it closed, fastening the locking bolt. "We'll need privacy," he said and turned, rubbing his hands together. His silk shirt was creamy and verdant, contrasting with the ruddy tone of his tanned and agitation-flushed skin.

"Well, then, Tharion," Dokken said, affecting good humor, "this *is* unexpected—but what good is a plan if it isn't flexible? How did you find out? I've kept it such a close secret for all these years . . . my son." He said the last words with an ironic lilt.

"Maximillian gave me that information," Tharion said calmly.

Dokken's eyebrows shot up. "He would never have revealed—" Genuine concern washed across his face.

"I'm afraid there wasn't much left of his mind after I had ripped loose all the secrets he kept. He resisted a great deal."

Dokken's eyes widened in unfeigned astonishment; Tharion

found it extremely gratifying. "But . . . Maximillian—"

Tharion made a dismissive gesture, taking one of the padded leather seats and sitting down with an aloof manner that he calculated would further upset Dokken. He tried to imitate his father's voice and patronizing tone. "Come now, don't get so worked up about it, Father. He was just one servant. I got you another one. What difference does it make?"

Dokken rounded on him in anger, turning about with clenched fists, but Tharion continued. "You taught me much over the years, Father. Your own schemes have squashed hundreds of people who happened to be in the way. Think of the Sardili Pilgrim revolt, the explosion of the Carsus-Bondalar mag-lev station, the disposal of your own comrade Cialben—I'm still missing quite a few, right?"

Dokken hesitated in his answer, but Tharion refused to give him the satisfaction of reacting. "Forget about Maximillian. Tell me why you've been doing all this. What is your goal? I can't figure it out. You owe me that much, Father." He rolled the word around in his mouth. "*Father*. It sounds so strange. As a Truthsayer I never thought that word would pass my lips. But you've known about me all along, watching me, helping me, setting me up. Tell me why."

Dokken finally reach a decision. "All right, Tharion," he said, his eyes as cold as a storm brewing at sea. "Listen and learn. You've always been a good student, *my son*. Now hear the rest of the lesson. You seem to have some glimpse of the plans I've set in motion— so consider Atlas and what my goals might be. Think of the future."

He took the seat next to Tharion's and leaned forward, his elbows on his knees and his chin in his hands. "Power is like . . . market share. All of the players fight for a piece, and whoever has the biggest piece is the strongest. If the rest of Atlas degenerates into self-absorbed chaos, I may not be quantitatively stronger—but if everyone else is *weaker*, then I'm relatively more powerful. Do you see?"

Tharion frowned. He understood, though he still didn't comprehend what Dokken had to gain by it.

"The *EarthDawn* is on its way, Tharion. In a few more years it will arrive, as large as our original ship 231 years ago, filled with colonists and resources and all the technology Earth has developed over the last several centuries. It's going to throw Atlas into greater turmoil than we have ever known.

"The *EarthDawn* is not just carrying a batch of exiled criminals or fleeing religious fanatics or a military invasion. This ship contains a user's kit for opening up a new world, advanced technology we never had. In ten years Atlas will be an entirely different place.

"Before that time, before the *EarthDawn* arrives, I expect to have laid the old system to rest, ground the other landholders to dust . . . and still have enough time to consolidate my power. When Captain Psalme steps out onto this world, I will be *the* power on Atlas. All of their dealings will have to go through me, and I can be assured of being in a position to reap the benefits of this new turmoil, rather than be steamrolled by it."

"A nice idea, I suppose, *Father*," Tharion said, taking every opportunity to use the word, "but the Council has stripped you of your holding. You won't have anything left to consolidate."

Dokken made a rude noise. "Bah! Landholders Council—they're nothing more than a puppet democracy. They can't do a thing."

Tharion sat up, curious. "How can you stop them?"

"Trust me," Dokken said with a smile.

"*Trust?* Who needs trust when we have truth? Tell me everything."

Dokken stood up from the chair, went to the tiled hearth, and picked up a leather-bound book on the mantel. "All right, my son," he said. "If you are ever to take on the responsibilities as my true heir, you must indeed know everything." He opened the back cover of the book, and with his fingernail split the endpapers, ripping open the beautiful spine. "Everything. Take it all."

Tharion sat up. The landholder dug in the book's binding until he pulled out a single sky-blue capsule. "You know how much I've clamped down on Veritas in my own holding—but that doesn't mean I won't make exceptions. This is one of the old, full-strength capsules. Undiluted truth such as you haven't felt in years."

Dokken held it up so that the light from the narrow windows illuminated it in his hand. "I'm proud of you for coming this far, my son. But you have only part of the story. You need all the pieces."

He pulled Tharion's hand toward him, placing the capsule in his palm. "Here, take your Veritas—and read what you must know directly from my mind. See it . . . see it all."

Tharion locked eyes with his father. Dokken could talk, and he could lie—but with Veritas he would be able to keep no secrets. Tharion would know the full truth. Without looking away, he placed the capsule in his mouth, bit down, and swallowed the bitter drug without tasting it.

Dokken grabbed both of Tharion's hands and placed them at the sides of his shaggy blond head. "Partial knowledge is dangerous," he said. "Here—take it all. Know everything that I know."

Tharion felt the mental rush of strength. Thoughts tingling across his scalp, he dipped into Franz Dokken's mind. Inside, he studied the well-organized thoughts, layer upon layer.

He saw it all: the landholder manipulations, even more plots than the Council had known about. The old civil war between Hong and Ramirez Holdings, Dokken's own overthrow of Van Petersden's lands so that he could take over the major glass industry on the planet. The Pilgrim uprising that was intended to cripple Sardili Holding, the destruction of Toth's pine forests, and the major ballet of the interholding railway between Bondalar and Carsus, built with tainted raw materials intended to destroy the credibility of the Koman suppliers . . . while Dokken engineered his masterstroke of a civil war between the two landholders.

Tharion saw the full details of how the illicit Veritas was smuggled down from OrbLab 2 via the Platform, how much Dieter Pan had enjoyed mucking up the business; Dieter Pan and Dokken had made their own alliance, bypassing muddled old Kareem Sondheim, who gave his own cooperation reluctantly, and only because he was blinded by love for his protégé.

But Franz Dokken was not so blinded.

More and more Veritas spilled out into the other holdings, disgracing the Guild, diluting the Truthsayers' doses and weakening their powers. It caused unrest among the populace—everywhere but in Dokken Holding.

The interlocked Atlas society was a tinderbox, ready to be ignited.

This labyrinth formed only the surface, and Tharion penetrated *deeper* into thoughts that continued to unfold and unfold, finally allowing him access to the information Dokken really wanted him to have: How he had planted the infant Tharion in the Guild Headquarters. How he had carefully observed the boy's progress over the years, keeping a light touch but acting as Tharion's champion and advisor when no one else had singled him out. How Dokken had become his mentor, driven him through his life, molding Tharion in his own image. How he had planned for Tharion to become the Guild Master all along. . . .

*Deeper, deeper . . .*

Then Tharion saw how Dokken had extended his own life span for centuries with endless alternating cycles of hibernation in the hidden deepsleep chamber . . . and how it had made him sterile. Sterile. Franz Dokken could not have children, had never been able to produce a son. . . .

And how Tharion was no son at all to Dokken—but a *clone*!

An embryo created in the Platform laboratories from Dokken's genetic blueprint and intentionally placed there by Franz Dokken himself. Reconstructive surgeries had altered Dokken's appearance to keep his secret of longevity well hidden, but Tharion was identical to Franz Dokken down to his very cells. Not a son. A clone!

In shock, Tharion stiffened and tried to draw away, but Dokken's clawlike hands clamped his fingers in place against his temples. "No, read more!" he said in a husky whisper. "There's more!" He didn't blink his burning eyes, and Tharion went even *deeper*, beyond the secret of his own heritage.

Until he learned that Dokken had *many clones*, not just Tharion, but more than a dozen copies of himself, of varying ages, that he had infiltrated into society. Some were businessmen, others were ranking officers in the sol-pol guards. Some had failed, or died young—but his crowning achievement was the seventeen-year-old boy known as Michel Van Petersden.

During the takeover of the weaker landholding those many years ago, Dokken had indeed slaughtered the entire Van Petersden family and replaced the true infant Michel with another of his clones. He had allowed Victoria Koman to raise the baby as her ward, though the iron-hard woman never suspected she was actually nurturing another potential Franz Dokken!

Inside his mind, Dokken's laughter echoed and rang, as if in an empty stone chamber, but Tharion couldn't pull away. Too many secrets still remained. Digging *deeper*, he came to the awful realization that because of those other clones and all of their possibilities, Dokken now considered Guild Master Tharion to be absolutely expendable. Too much of a threat.

The last thing he read, a nugget of obsidian in the landholder's thoughts that Dokken had kept shielded away, saving it for the final surprise—was that the capsule of Veritas he had given Tharion was also impregnated with a modified toxin taken from the Mindfire mutation. Just like Klaryus.

The paralyzing poison was even now sweeping through his system. The plague organism would die off quickly, unable to spread—but it would incinerate Tharion's neurons, leaving him helpless, unable to breathe or think. Even as that thought crossed his mind, Tharion began to lose his bodily control.

"Now you know everything," Dokken said in a comforting voice. "No more secrets." Then he pulled Tharion's fingers away from his temples and released his grip on the Guild Master's hands.

Tharion's muscles had turned to water, and he could not catch himself as he tumbled to the floor, twitching.

"Truth holds no secrets," Dokken murmured, standing over him. "My son."

# CHAPTER

# 48

i

Emilio Toth and Victoria Koman gathered their forces together and traveled overland in a convoy of eleven mammoth-sized methane tractors.

Troy and Kalliana accompanied the loyal sol-pol contingents as well as seventy other strong village workers who had agreed to come fight, either for a bonus to their earnings or out of devotion to their landholder. Neither Troy nor Kalliana carried weapons, but they added their support.

Emilio Toth had promised that violence would be their last resort anyway. Victoria Koman had agreed, though she didn't seem convinced that they had any chance of succeeding through peaceful means.

The tractors ground along through the night, passing out of the mountainous region to rugged foothills. By morning they reached the mag-lev rail where the spur crossed Toth lands on its way into Dokken Holding. After parking the tractors in the crumbling, virgin dirt, all the fighters dismounted, milling around and talking with nervous excitement as they passed around jugs of water or ate small snacks. Each tried to outbluff the others with their potential bravery, drilling with unfamiliar weapons, cheering the landholders every time they passed.

During the long bumpy ride, Troy and Kalliana had huddled next to each other, attempting to snatch an hour or two of sleep. As they finally crawled out of the tractors, bleary-eyed in the dawn, Troy commented, "Not quite as nice a nap as I had the night before," he said, then smiled shyly, "but it was pleasant to be next to you again."

She smiled up at him in surprise. "I was comfortable enough with you here."

Kalliana stretched her legs and walked beside him as they went to find Emilio Toth. The big, bearded man directed several of his engineers as they knelt in the powdery clay and worked on the shining mag-lev rail, tapping into the solenoids and transformers, activating the spur's emergency braking systems.

"All set," one of the engineers said. "Ready for the next train."

The landholder nodded, planted his feet squarely apart, and looked down the line. The silver rail stretched into the distance all the way to the horizon—Dokken's horizon—shimmering in the slanted sunlight.

Emilio Toth clapped his hands and bellowed for everyone's attention. Victoria Koman and Michel Van Petersden stood next to him in a show of solidarity as Toth issued commands to the encampment.

"Listen up! Everybody's got to cooperate," he said. "An empty cargo train will be shooting through here in just a few minutes. We've triggered the brakes. It'll slow down here and stop. We all have to climb aboard and be moving again within four minutes and thirty seconds, or the alarms will sound back at First Landing and up at Dokken Station.

"Now, we don't want that to happen—so we need everybody to jump on in an orderly fashion. Divide into three groups now so we can crawl in and seal down. Two of the engineers will stay here and reset the brakes once we're all aboard. No margin for error, people! When time's up, the train moves. If you aren't aboard by then, you're going to be eating dust. And it's a long walk back home."

Even as he finished, the whine of an approaching train came from the far horizon. Troy could see a blurred speck hurtling toward them at several hundred kilometers per hour—but the emergency collision sensors responded to the activated braking systems, and the train decelerated rapidly. Screeching and thundering, three corroded cargo haulers ground to a halt and then hissed, coming to rest on the magnetic rail.

The people surged forward, not in a particularly orderly fashion, but they made up for the chaos with enthusiasm. The three landholders each took one of the cars. Troy and Kalliana—accompanied by an excitement-flushed Ysan—ran for Emilio Toth's cargo hauler. The big landholder threw open broad doors designed for loading pine logs or granite slabs, and the fighters scrambled in. Toth stood on the roof bellowing, "Hurry up! Hurry!"

The two engineers waited beneath the rails, checking their chronometers and watching nervously. "Four minutes!" one of them yelled.

"Don't hold for any stragglers!" Toth called back.

Victoria Koman added her own sharp voice. "Come on—we haven't got all day."

The sol-pols moved with more efficiency, but had greater difficulty because of the weapons slung over their shoulders. The lumberjacks and quarry workers piled pell mell into the open hold. Troy snugged his arm around Kalliana's waist, and the two of them tumbled into the car and scrambled out of the way to avoid being trampled by the others.

Kalliana heaved a heavy sigh. "How many times are you going to drag me into an empty cargo train, Troy?"

"What—you were expecting a luxury car?" he asked.

Kalliana shrugged. "I've ridden in them before."

"I haven't," Troy said.

"No more time," one of the engineers shouted in a voice muffled by the rustling of people trying to pack themselves into the cargo hauler.

"Go!" Toth hollered. "Move us out!" He swung down from the roof into the car as the mag-lev train lurched into motion again, picking up speed. Four last people sprang into the car at a run; Emilio Toth grabbed the arm of one more woman and hauled her inside. Troy saw several stragglers rushing to get in, but they could not move fast enough.

"It's all right," the big landholder told everyone. "They'll wait by the tractors. They're probably a whole lot safer than we are."

"Did we make it in time?" Troy asked.

"Sure," the bearded man answered, as if there had never been any doubt. "I padded the estimate by thirty seconds." The people in the car groaned.

The sol-pols adjusted their weapons and made certain their ammunition was conveniently at hand. Several engineering specialists slung packs off their shoulders and set them in their laps, sorting through the contents.

"The next train should be thirty-three minutes behind us," Toth said, "and that one will be loaded with granite construction materials." The landholder found a place to sit down on the dirty floor. "Let's hope we can have this whole mission wrapped up by the time that cargo arrives. Or else we'll be in a world of trouble."

***

They rode on for several hours, Troy and Kalliana sitting next to each other while Ysan tried to make conversation, bubbling with youthful excitement. "I never thought I'd see the day! What do you think will change after this?" he asked. "A reshuffling of the landholdings? A shake-up in the Guild itself, do you think?"

"Depends on if we win," Troy said.

"We'll create far-reaching ripples," Kalliana said, "no matter what happens."

Ysan kept grinning. "It's still a lot more exciting than living at Guild Headquarters and being a Truthsayer."

The mag-lev train hummed onward at high speed, but the ride was smooth, lulling them into drowsy anxiety as they approached Dokken Station. Finally, at about noon, the sound of passage suddenly changed as the braking systems engaged on the rails below, and the train shot through deceleration coils that drowned the car's momentum.

"Get ready!" Toth shouted.

Four other engineers with packs buckled across their chests scrambled to their feet and pushed toward the door. The sol-pols got out of their way while the other passengers jostled each other, not knowing what the men were up to. The train continued to slow, easing down from its velocity of hundreds of kilometers per hour.

Emilio Toth flung open the sliding steel doors. Troy blinked in the sudden bright light. Though the train slowed, sandy desolation still rushed past like a soft tan blanket. The engineers stood at the edge of the car, cradling their packs and looking uneasily at each other.

"Just land and roll," Toth said, as if it would be easy. "Go on." He took a handset control from one of the engineers and pocketed it. "Plant your charges, then make sure you stay well away from the rail. I hope I don't have to blow this thing—but be ready if it comes to that."

The engineers tumbled out of the decelerating train like paratroopers. As soon as they were gone, Emilio Toth stuck his head out, looking back to see that they had landed safely. Then he hauled the car door shut and said, "Everyone else, grit your teeth. We have less than a kilometer until the station. That's when the fun starts."

ii

The braking fields caught and held the heavy cars in a magnetic embrace, slowing them to a stop. The three battered haulers came into Dokken Station on the regular run from First Landing.

As the train came to a rest, Troy glanced around him to see the fighters, some looking anxious, others spoiling for a fight. Emilio Toth stood by the door. "All right, let's go." He shoved open the cargo door, and the troops surged out, yelling like barbarian warriors.

Toth and Koman's sol-pols had gathered at the front of the car in their dark uniforms, forming the most obvious armed front. They sprang free, rifles in hand. Troy followed, trying not to be crushed by his own comrades as they pushed forward, full of enthusiasm. He looked at Kalliana and Ysan. Everyone seemed to be wondering what they had gotten into. Kalliana squeezed his hand, then they jumped.

The fighters boiled out of the mag-lev cars, shouting at the tops of their lungs. The landholders' plan was to overwhelm and intimidate any resistance before much bloodshed could occur—but shots rang out immediately. Troy ducked as low as he could while running forward with the troops.

"No shooting!" Emilio Toth bellowed. "Not yet."

But the shots continued as about thirty of Dokken's personal sol-pols ran to barricades at the mag-lev station and began firing indiscriminately. The fighters from Toth and Koman dove for cover.

"Dokken must have been forewarned," Michel Van Petersden said. "He must have reinforced his troops. He'd never keep this many sol-pols here."

"Defend yourselves," Victoria Koman said, her harsh voice slicing through the chaos.

Troy and Kalliana followed Ysan as they slipped into a passenger waiting area with concrete benches and kiosks that sold food. The vendors had fled in the first moments of fighting, but spicy aromas still wafted upward from steaming grills.

When Toth's soldiers began firing back, the sounds of gunfire and shouts redoubled inside the steel-and-glass station. As the cargo train settled into place, creaking as it cooled, the loud metallic *spangs* of bullets ricocheted from the outer walls.

Troy saw several people down and bleeding. He froze, recalling Cialben's body sprawled in a pool of congealing blood on the concrete floor of the holding warehouse. He pushed Kalliana closer to the floor, out of harm's way. Ysan ducked beside him, his eyes filled now with fear instead of enthusiasm.

Emilio Toth, whose voice rose above all other sounds, roared, "Surrender and throw down your arms, Dokken guards! You're outgunned and outnumbered."

Rifle shots sounded in staccato cracks. Two of the big plate glass windows in the upper walls shattered, and shards fell like sharp crystal snow. The people below scattered before they were sliced to ribbons.

"We've been given orders not to surrender," one of Dokken's captains called back. "We don't negotiate with invading armies."

The firefight continued for several more minutes, but neither side made much progress. Bullets whined through the air. Toth's men and women edged toward the barricades Dokken's sol-pols had thrown up in front of the main exits.

"I think it's ultimatum time," Toth said, checking his chronometer. "Now or never."

Victoria Koman looked to Michel Van Petersden, and the blond youth nodded. The old hard-edged landholder glanced up at Toth. "Do it if you have to," she said. "Everything depends on timing. We can rebuild the station."

Toth stood, bellowing at the top of his lungs. "Listen up! Our engineers have planted explosives on the braking systems a few kilometers up the mag-lev line. We've already disconnected the auxiliary brakes. There's another cargo train coming in five minutes, fully loaded and traveling at about five hundred kilometers per hour."

He held up the control in his hand. "If I detonate those explosives, that train is not going to be able to stop—and this station is the end of the line. It'll be like a starship crashing into this building. If you all don't surrender *now*, I trigger the detonator. Throw down your arms!"

The gunfire quieted for a moment, then another shot rang out with a flat crack—and Toth was flung backward from the impact. He involuntarily clenched his fist on the buttons of the signaling apparatus.

He grabbed his left shoulder and looked down at the dark blood dribbling between his fingers. "Ah, dammit!"

More than a kilometer away, Troy heard the faint rumble of distant explosions in the mag-lev braking stations.

Ysan rushed over to Emilio Toth and pressed against the

bleeding wound on the landholder's shoulder to stop the flow. "Damn, damn!" Toth said, then looked in dismay at the transmitting set in his hand, holding up bloody fingers. "I probably shouldn't have done that."

"Too late now," Koman said as she got to her knees. She yelled to her people: "Evacuate the station immediately. That train's coming in, and no power in the universe is going to stop it now. You won't want to be here in another few minutes. Dokken's solpols can make up their own minds whether or not we were bluffing."

Some of Koman's men swung their rifles around and shot out the nearest windows that looked out onto the vehicle staging area where tractors and rovers stood parked and ready for use. The lumberjacks and quarry workers led the retreat from the mag-lev rail station, running toward the open space. Troy and Kalliana helped a wounded lumberjack limp out of the station, while Ysan hovered close to Emilio Toth. The uniformed soldiers covered their retreat, ducking down and firing back at their opponents, who couldn't seem to believe the invaders were running away.

The sudden mass exodus finally brought home the reality of the threat to Dokken's guards. The defenders waited a few more minutes behind their barricade, then left their own positions, taking their weapons and their wounded and exiting through the station's main front doors.

Upon reaching the vehicle parking area, Troy rested for a moment beside Kalliana as they listened to the high-pitched whine of the approaching cargo train. The blazing hum of the vessel's passage grew louder and louder, not decelerating as it plummeted toward the terminus of its track. It could no longer stop.

"That train's coming in like a missile," Emilio Toth gasped. His skin was clammy, the result of shock from his gunshot wound. Ysan pressed a healing pad against the landholder's shoulder to soak up the blood.

The invaders stood around Dokken's vehicles, far enough from the station to watch with growing dread as the train came on, unstoppable.

It was over in less than two seconds. The cargo train struck the bull's-eye of Dokken Station, the terminus of the mag-lev line extending from First Landing. It was moving close to five hundred kilometers per hour, carrying 117 tons of freshly quarried granite, striking the empty train first, then the building, all in an instant.

The impact was deafening. Debris shot up in a pillar of fire and smoke, as glass shards and steel girders suddenly dispersed the train's kinetic energy and threw molten debris and broken glass in all directions.

From afar, a few undirected gunshots rang out, expressions of shock and rage—but the devastation caused by the runaway train struck both armies speechless.

"That was good granite," Toth said with a pained sigh.

Victoria Koman nodded. "And a perfectly serviceable mag-lev station," she said. "The price of battle."

Michel Van Petersden stood beside them. "We can rebuild it," he said. "We'll have a lot of rebuilding to do after this is all over."

Troy and Kalliana held hands as they watched the smoke and flames roar into the sky.

iii

Leaving the wreckage of the mag-lev station behind, the forces split into two groups. Michel Van Petersden took ten of Koman's sol-pols, two engineers, and Troy Boren with him on a mission to the hydroelectric power plant, where they intended to cut off all electricity to Dokken Holding.

It seemed the least dangerous of the activities, compared to occupying the main village or storming the landholder's villa itself. Troy asked if he could take Kalliana with him, but Victoria Koman shook her head and placed sinewy hands on the shoulders of Ysan and Kalliana.

"No, the Truthsayers should stay with us in case we need them. For interrogation. Go with Michel—there's not a moment to waste."

Reluctantly, Troy followed the orders. He and Kalliana spoke a silent farewell with their eyes before Troy climbed aboard one of the overland vehicles the sol-pols had commandeered. The methane engines hummed. Michel Van Petersden jumped into the metal seat beside Troy. The others assigned to the raid started two more rovers, then the team roared across the landscape at full speed toward Trident Falls.

As the vehicles jounced overland, casting up plumes of dust behind them, Troy raised his voice to the landholder's heir. "Why did you pick me to come along?" he said. "I'm not a commando."

Michel blinked his sea-green eyes. "We're making history here, and I wanted to let you have a part of it. After I heard your story, I thought you'd earned it. You looked lost, and now we can do something together."

"Thanks," Troy said dubiously. All his life he had wanted to do his work and remain unobtrusive, but lately he seemed to be calling a great deal of attention upon himself—usually to his grief.

The packed road led up into higher elevations where the cliffs grew tall and sheer. Rivers pouring down from the north hurled themselves over the geological uplift.

Troy had seen images of Trident Falls, but he was awed by the actual sight of the thundering plumes of water, the multiple rainbows that arched through the mists, and the lush green water hyacinths in the holding ponds below. Enameled metal steps ran down the cliffside near one of the three ribbons of water. Heavy power-transmission cables extended off in all directions, supported by steel pylons. The cables traced an artificial line across the badlands, distributing electricity to other substations.

The three overland vehicles pulled to a halt at the top of the cliffs, and two engineers got out, studying the power cable and jabbering with each other. They both pointed to one set of pylons that led back in the general direction from which their party had come.

"That line leads to Dokken Holding," one of the engineers shouted. She indicated the nearest support tower. "If we find some way to take out that pylon—blow it up maybe!—we'll cut off all power to Dokken's villages."

"It'll be spectacular!" the other engineer said. "That ought to even the odds a little."

Michel Van Petersden shook his head. "We've already caused enough damage today," he said. "Try to find a more efficient way." He climbed out of the vehicle, taking the lead as he headed toward the metal steps that led to the generating rooms behind the waterfalls. "Inside."

Troy crowded in with both engineers as the sol-pols formed a protective phalanx around them, weapons ready. Michel Van Petersden trotted down the steep stairs, and the others pounded after him. Troy gripped the railing as the team descended the sheer rock. Cold spray clung to his face and hands, and made the steps treacherous.

Van Petersden halted at a heavy metal door, brown with corrosion and slick with the gray-green sheen of algae and moss.

Two of the sol-pols stood at attention while a third swung wide the hatch. The others held their rifles ready, pointing into the open darkness—but they encountered none of the resistance they had feared. Van Petersden, though, took no chances, not after the reinforcements Dokken had put in place at the mag-lev station.

"Go!" he shouted. The sol-pols ran ahead into the tunnel, following the harsh lights. Troy trotted after, trying to remain in the middle of the group.

The air smelled metallic with moisture that seeped from the rocks and dripped into shallow gutters carved in the floor. The boots of the guards pounded an odd rhythm as they hustled to the main generator stations.

The team took the power plant operators completely by surprise. The men and women operating the machinery and the power grid controls looked up at the sudden intrusion. The sol-pols marched in and took their positions, weapons ready. Without thinking, one of the soldiers fired a warning shot that ricocheted twice off the uneven rock; Troy and the others ducked in unison, then the bullet vanished into the foamy wall of water pouring down the front of the cave.

"Please surrender and save us the trouble of further threats," Michel Van Petersden said. His voice was cultured, commanding, as if he had been born to be a leader.

Dokken's hydroelectric workers glanced at each other, confused and uncertain. One young man raised his hands in a submissive gesture, and the others followed suit.

"Watch them," Van Petersden said as the sol-pols rounded up the captive workers. "We have to shut down the power from here," he shouted to the engineers. The hammering water and the roar of turning turbines made Troy's head pound. He looked at the huge whirling waterwheel. The transformers and substations extended back into the rock, where cables ascended through a crack up to the overland wires. To get away from the sound and spray, he backed over to a large grid on the wall, which displayed a system map and some simple controls.

Van Petersden's engineers scuttled around, assessing the enormous machinery, conferring with each other as to how they could best sabotage the operation. Concurring, the engineers turned to the young landholder and pointed to heavy steel rods on the wall, replacement axles for the gear shafts.

"We suggest taking those, sir," the woman engineer said. "We can toss them into the turbines, and they'll jam the gears and wreck the whole operation. In just a few seconds we can shut the power down to Dokken Holding and all of Atlas."

Van Petersden frowned. "I don't want to knock out the whole world. How long will it take to get the plant functional again?"

"A few days," they said, eyes shining with pride at their plan. "We'd need to replace the damaged gears, take the whole system off-line. Can't think of a faster way."

Helpless under guard, the hydroelectric workers stared in absolute horror at the suggestion the engineers had made. They shook their heads vigorously, but the sol-pols threatened them with rifles. Troy could tell from the expressions of the workers that they didn't believe such a disaster could ever be fixed in so short a time.

Van Petersden sighed and looked from side to side, uncomfortable. "I would rather not cause such far-reaching—"

Troy stared down at the power grid controls. "Excuse me, sir!" he shouted. "Why don't we just switch off the grid to Dokken Holding?" He pointed to the controls where a map of Atlas displayed paths of electrical cables that extended to the various holdings and substations. The power output was diagrammed onto a relatively simple allocated system. "We can just shut it down here and not affect anybody else."

The engineers scowled at Troy as if he had taken away all their fun, but Van Petersden glared at the engineers. "Yes, that'll work," Van Petersden said. "I much prefer your solution, Mr. Boren."

iv

As Van Petersden's squad rode off toward the power plant, the remainder of Toth and Koman's troops at the ruins of Dokken Station commandeered numerous tractors and rovers from the vehicle yard. They piled into the vehicles and into the foothills to occupy the main village.

Kalliana and Ysan rode next to each other in the same vehicle with the injured Emilio Toth, who insisted on joining the main thrust of the attack. His bandage was bright with blood, and Ysan replaced it with a fresh dressing. The gunshot wound seemed painful, but not terribly serious, and the bleeding had already begun to slow.

Ysan sat numb, amazed at what he had gotten himself into. Kalliana could understand the young Magistrate's feelings; she would have been as stunned herself . . . if she had not already fought her way through a dozen equally impossible circumstances just in the past few weeks.

The expeditionary force continued upward. Armed sol-pols accompanied every vehicle; the largest cluster of guards rode near the front to bear the brunt of any resistance. By now Dokken's men would be flitting about like angry wasps after seeing the obliteration of the main mag-lev station. They would probably shoot on sight.

As Toth and Koman's troops rolled toward the adobe village, Kalliana could hear the clanging of an alarm bell, people shouting. The streets were a chaos of villagers who ran for safety without bothering to put out fires in their kilns or lock down their businesses. Electric streetlights up and down the cobblestone lanes burned bright, automatically triggered by the alarm.

"Your landholder Franz Dokken has been declared a criminal and a fugitive by the Landholders Council," Victoria Koman shouted to the villagers, remaining seated in relative shelter behind her sol-pol guards. She had learned her lesson after seeing Emilio Toth get shot.

"We have now occupied this village," Koman continued. "This entire holding will be restored to Michel Van Petersden, the rightful heir to these lands that were wrongfully usurped by Franz Dokken."

The villagers ran for cover, not interested in listening to speeches.

The sol-pol garrison in the village square remained closed, its big entry doors shut and silent. The vehicles from the occupying force pulled into the center of the village and halted. The sol-pols and other fighters got out of their vehicles, wondering what to do next.

Before Koman could issue further orders, the main front doors of the garrison ratcheted open. Metal slats folded away as a group of gunners pushed two impressive weapons forward. They looked like highly intricate cannons with fire tubes, solenoids, and coolant piping wrapped around a long transparent shaft. The hum of a generator powering up filled the air as the weapons built their charge.

In a nightmarish instant Kalliana recognized the weapons by the *SkySword* military insignia marked on the side. "Get out of the way!" she shouted. "Those are plasma cannons!" She grabbed

Ysan and hauled him away from the vehicle. Victoria Koman reacted just as quickly.

"Do as she says!" Koman shouted and dove for cover. Two sol-pols yanked the injured Emilio Toth to his feet and hauled him behind the fountain in the center of the square.

A crackling blue beam lanced out. High-energy plasma vaporized three of the expeditionary vehicles as well as two soldiers who had not managed to dive out of the way in time. The rovers' methane tanks exploded. Their metal frames disintegrated into glowing metal steam. Blue fire spewed across the square, and flames erupted from where the plasma outburst touched even the dry clay bricks.

The second *SkySword* cannon fired, sending out a screaming bolt that swallowed up three more vehicles. Half the square was in flames now.

Toth's men began shooting wherever they could, but their rifles were no match for the plasma cannons. Kalliana huddled beside Ysan, wondering how they could escape. It seemed impossible to defeat the technological weapons that had once been meant to take over all of Atlas.

"Fall back!" Koman shouted. "Get to cover!"

But then, unexpectedly, the streetlights winked out. All power in the village failed, and the generating hum behind the plasma cannons died into silence, leaving only the crackle of spreading flames and the moans of burned and injured fighters.

"Attack!" Toth croaked. "The power's out, and they can't fire. Attack!"

Toth and Koman's fighters reacted instantly, bringing their rifles up to shower bullets into the garrison where Dokken's gunners frantically tried to make their powerless weapons work. The plasma cannon sagged with shattered controls and broken oscillating tubes. In a matter of moments the murderous gunners lay slaughtered.

"This is our village now," Koman said to her surviving fighters. "Let's not let it burn to the ground. Everyone—help these villagers put out the fire before it spreads!"

Kalliana looked up at the tall bluffs behind the village, where Dokken's villa stood sheltered in the crags, ominous and alone—the last bastion of their enemy's power.

# CHAPTER

## 49

### i

Captain Vanicus waited in agonized impatience in the front room of Dokken's villa. He paced back and forth, tracking dust across the tiles. His boots were normally spit-polished black, but now he didn't care about his appearance. The holding had just come under attack.

Franz Dokken had insisted that he and Guild Master Tharion not be disturbed, but Vanicus finally broke training and pounded twice on the locked drawing room door. "Master Dokken," he said, "this is an emergency! I must report."

The door flung open, and Dokken burst out of the room, his eyes stormy, like a tempest out on the ocean. He seemed shaken, as if chilled from inside, though his silk shirt clung to him with sweat. "What is it?" he demanded as he closed the door behind him.

"You put us on full alert status, sir. My soldiers were waiting down in the mag-lev station as instructed, and we were attacked, a combined force from Toth and Koman holdings. The invaders intend to make Michel Van Petersden landholder of this entire territory."

Dokken raised his eyebrows. "Young Michel to take my place? How ironic. They could have made a worse choice."

"We fought them, sir, but they outnumbered us five to one. You drilled us never to surrender. But then they . . . they destroyed the entire station."

"What?" Dokken cried. "How?"

"They removed the braking coils from the mag-lev rails a kilometer up the line. A big cargo train came in and struck the terminus at full speed. I'm afraid there's . . . nothing left of the station building. You can see the smoke from here."

"Very clever," Dokken said, clasping his hands behind his back and strutting around the foyer.

"They are well armed, sir. They have a large force of dedicated sol-pols and fighters from the citizenry, sir."

"Toth and Koman," Dokken said, shaking his head. "I knew that they were allying themselves against me. Not at all full of bluster and propaganda, like Bondalar and Carsus, you understand. You never have to worry about the ones who make a big show of everything—I *should* have realized. Toth and Koman. . ." he said again in disbelief. "I'm frankly . . . amazed that the landholders would try such a thing. I was certain they'd let the Council muck around for a few months first." But then he looked back to the closed doors of the drawing room. He hadn't expected Tharion to show a strong spine either.

"They're approaching the main village even now, sir," Vanicus continued in a low, meaningful voice. "I've already given orders that our sol-pols are to resist with all weapons available. All weapons."

Dokken nodded. "I concur." He shook his shaggy head, muttering to himself. "How could the Council have moved so quickly? Tharion only now reported that they had made a resolution against me—and armed forces arrive the same time their courier does? Very unlike the Council." He lowered his voice, talking more to himself than to Vanicus. "How could they know so much?" Tharion had sworn the Landholders Council had gotten their information from someone *other* than Maximillian. . . .

He turned his sharp gaze at Captain Vanicus. "Double the guard around my villa, just in case any of these upstarts make it all the way to the bluffs. Otherwise, have your men use all available force to stop them in the village. You have the *SkySword* weapons to obliterate all attackers."

"Yes, sir," Captain Vanicus said, turning just as Lor came gliding into the room as quietly as if he weighed nothing.

"Master Dokken, a transmission for you from the Platform," the new manservant said. "Kareem Sondheim says it's urgent."

ii

"Yes, *I* told them everything, Franz," Sondheim said, drifting in and out of the viewplate's best focal point. "I came down to the surface myself—built a special tank just for the occasion and spoke to the Landholders Council face-to-face, while breathing Atlas air. And I convinced them, Franz. I gave them the proof they needed."

Dokken stood in the highest tower just beneath his satellite dish, watching the withered landholder with his patchy snowball of hair. Sondheim grinned, obnoxiously smug about what he had done.

"You told them everything?" Dokken said, crossing his arms over his chest. "Why shouldn't I retaliate by telling them all about—"

"I've already told them, Franz. I've confessed to everything. They know about the Veritas smuggling. They know I tried to kill the two escapees from the Platform—your two scapegoats are alive, you know. They managed to escape after all."

"*What?*" Dokken said. How could he have judged so many people so poorly—Tharion, Sondheim, even Maximillian? "You're bluffing."

Sondheim fixed him with his dark-eyed stare. "Dieter's dead—what else matters? I may fall because of it, but I don't care. I've been around long enough, and I'm sick of it all. *You'll* certainly fall, and you deserve it."

Sondheim looked maddeningly complacent, pleased and lighter hearted, as if he had finally cast off a heavy weight that was too great for his centuries-old bones to endure. "I've even told them how you had your man Cialben use the Truthsayers drug to infiltrate Van Petersden's Holding seventeen years ago. How you planned your takeover to get your hands on the glass industry, and how you effected it through the use of stolen Veritas."

Sondheim took time for a long and meaningful pause, then he said in a lower voice, "One last thing, Franz. A little thing, but it has been gnawing at me for eighteen years. Did you know Abraham Van Petersden was my friend? He came up to the Platform to visit me numerous times during his tenure as landholder. He played a good game of chess. He was quite skilled. I was appalled when you slaughtered him and his family just so you could have some new merchandise to sell."

Dokken used sarcasm to deflect his rage. "Business is business."

"I despise you!" Sondheim shouted, his words exploding with such force that he reeled in the weightlessness. "I told Emilio Toth and Victoria Koman what you were up to, and they made their own plans. Then I gave a full accounting to the Landholders Council—I understand they voted to strip you of your holding? It doesn't matter whether Toth's military action will work. You're doomed one way or the other. You've stepped far out of bounds,

Franz. This mess with Janine Bondalar and Hektor Carsus was completely uncalled for. They really do love each other, you know."

"Who the fuck cares about that!" Dokken spat, losing control. "They're all amateurs, juveniles playing in the big leagues. I was consolidating my influence centuries before they even learned to walk. They haven't got the slightest notion about how to play power games."

Sondheim shook his head wearily, though he was decades younger than Franz Dokken. The ancient "landholder without land" clucked in a paternal fashion. "Franz, you are a destabilizing influence on this world, and I can no longer simply sit back and watch."

Before Sondheim could say anything else, suddenly, unexpectedly, all the power went out in the villa.

"What the hell?" Dokken shouted into the dimness. He worked the console in front of the viewplate, trying to connect to the battery backup and reestablish an uplink through the satellite antenna. He heard gunshots below in the village, but his main concern was to finish what he had begun with Kareem Sondheim.

The ancient man's image appeared again, swimming through a halo of static and finally coming into focus. "Having troubles down there, Franz?" Sondheim mocked.

"Nothing I can't handle," Dokken said.

"Enough chitchat. I just called to give you fair warning. Listen closely, because I am not bluffing. Though Abraham Van Petersden was my friend, I've known you far longer than that. I remember when I was just a deformed child on the colony ship, knowing I could never go down to the planet while you and the other captains and the colonists talked incessantly about it. But you were kind to me then, Captain Dokken—and so out of deference to our long history together, I give you a fair chance to evacuate in time."

"Evacuate?" Dokken said. "What do you mean?"

"You aren't the only one who retained *SkySword* weaponry," Sondheim said. "You kept two of their best plasma cannons, as did I—but before I sent that ship down, I also removed some of the space missile defenses."

"Missiles?" Dokken said. "All this time you've had *missiles?*"

"Yes," Sondheim said, bobbing his head vigorously, "and I've just launched two of them at your villa." He paused for Dokken's indrawn breath. "I thought you'd like to know."

Dokken found himself speechless and looked up at the ceiling as if he could already see the pinpoint javelins of death plunging through the atmosphere.

"According to my best estimates," Sondheim said, "it should take them about half an hour to cruise down and begin their final-stage burn before they target your villa. They're low-yield tactical warheads, but you can bet they'll take out your entire home and the outbuildings and leave a big smoking crater in the bluffs. It should cause no damage to your village or the rest of your holding. This is meant to strike at you and you alone, Franz.

"You've created your own problems. I'm saving your life by calling you now, so tell everyone to leave. Take a few possessions, if you must, but get out of there as fast as you can."

Dokken stared, feeling cold and betrayed. His face blanched. "But *why*, Kareem? Why are you doing this now?"

The ancient man shook his head sadly. "Living for so long up in orbit has given me a true view from a height, Franz. I look down on the whole world. And even though I can never stay down there, I still feel very paternal watching from up here. I can't let you destroy it all." Sondheim switched off the transmission before Dokken could say another word.

He stared in stunned anger at the flat gray viewplate. Around him the villa was dark and silent with its power cut off. Outside in the distance he could hear gunfire echoing between the bluff walls. He supposed the loss of power meant the invaders had somehow taken over Trident Falls.

Everything was falling apart. All his plans tumbled down around him. . . he knew what he had to do. Franz Dokken would get the last word, make them remember him, no matter what else happened. He had always intended to bring it all down, though this was more drastic than anything he had ever planned.

He would still be around, though he might have to lie low for a while. He could take the time to pick up the pieces, no matter how much damage he caused. He was *Franz Dokken*. He could be flexible. He had changed the records a dozen times in the past, and now he would create a whole new life for himself, a fresh and challenging new identity . . . once he managed to wipe the slate clean.

Looking grimly down at the keyboard in front of the transmission uplink, Dokken switched on the battery backup again and entered a command string, adding his password and deploying his last surprise for Kareem Sondheim. He had hoped never to have to use this, though he had seen the necessity to put it in as a fail-safe over a century earlier. Now he had no choice but to activate it.

He hesitated for a long moment, again surprised at himself for being sentimental. Then he punched the "Commit" button.

Turning his back on decisions already made and striding off into what would be a new life for him, Dokken left the tall tower and called for his new manservant Lor. He could use the man one last time.

They had many preparations to make.

### iii

The space elevator rode along its glistening diamond-fiber cable, rising up to the Platform on its daily journey.

The elevator was only fifteen minutes from docking when Dokken activated the systems he had long ago hidden in the intricate maze of superstructures on the elevator's roof. During routine maintenance, his own men had made the modifications.

Franz Dokken, more than anyone else, had time on his hands, time to make contingency plans, to insinuate secret surprises, and to become paranoid about unlikely possibilities. If one lived long enough, unlikely possibilities grew more and more probable with each passing century. It was simply a matter of statistics.

The space elevator finally docked into its collar below the Platform. Contacts were made . . . triggers activated—and half a metric ton of explosives detonated.

The blast was stupendous. The acoustic shock wave rang through the entire station as if a god had smashed it with a cosmic sledgehammer.

The overpressure ripped bulkhead walls apart and ruptured every deck. The explosive shock front crushed skulls and rib cages like eggshells. Flames tore through the ventilation systems.

The outer armored walls were shredded, and the remaining air rushed outward with a high-pitched frosty sigh. Gaps in the outer hull showed views of stars like great patches of night shining through the idealistic clouds painted on the ceiling of the docking bay.

The flames from the blast, already starved for oxygen as atmosphere rushed out into vacuum, burned the painted dream of "Atlas, a new dawn."

# CHAPTER

## 50

i

Franz Dokken strode through his villa, yelling for everyone to flee as fast as they could. "We are under attack from the sky," he shouted. "Get to safety, or the roof will come down on your head."

Servants ran around grabbing belongings. Others simply gaped in shock. Captain Vanicus stood at attention, but didn't seem to know what to do. "Master Dokken, sir," he said, "are we surrendering?"

"There's no way we can fight this attack now. Go!" Dokken said.

"But—but what about you, sir? We must rush you to safety!" The captain's face was flushed with alarm.

Dokken fixed him with his most sincere stare. He had to do this part of the act precisely, because it would make the next few years much easier for him. Even under fire, Dokken could not stop planning ahead.

"Everything I have is here, Captain," he said. "I will not leave my beloved villa to the barbarians. I would rather see it destroyed, and myself with it. But I have no wish for anyone else to die here with me. I choose to face this alone."

Vanicus stared at him in horror. "Master Dokken! You can't—"

"That is an order!" he snapped. "Now do as I ask! Get these people to safety—and remember me." He fixed the captain of the guard with a brave gaze, and he knew that Vanicus would remember that moment for the rest of his days.

As soon as the captain rushed off, Dokken called for Lor. He found the manservant by the fireplace inside the unlocked drawing room, where Tharion's body still lay twitching on the floor. The white Truthsayers' robe pooled around the Guild Master as his glassy gaze looked off into nowhere.

Lor's eyes were round, with an odd unfocused expression. He gazed at the body with deep, unreadable interest.

"Something wrong?" Dokken asked mildly. He had to play this carefully as well. He needed the manservant's assistance, at least for a short while.

Lor shook his head, seemingly uninterested in Tharion. "No," he answered. "I've seen dead bodies before."

"Good," Dokken said, standing up straighter and using his take-charge-we're-in-a-hurry voice. "The Guild Master promised that I could count on you, even before this unfortunate accident. Now I have no choice but to trust you in this time of our greatest need. You and I have some difficult duties to attend to. Go out to the stables and saddle up my chestnut stallion and the gray mare for yourself. Then turn the other horses loose. We'll need to ride out and disappear for a while. Let some of this dust settle."

"Yes, Master Dokken," the manservant answered, and marched briskly out the double doors.

ii

As the manservant looked down helplessly, paralyzed at the sight of the Guild Master's body on the floor, he thought of how Tharion had been one of the few truly *good* members of the Truthsayers Guild. He had always admired Tharion, had known the Guild Master would not desert him in the end.

And now Eli Strone had failed him.

During the darkest hours up on OrbLab 2, Guild Master Tharion had contacted him in secret, offering Strone a new life, a new chance to *make things right*. After all this time, Tharion had finally understood what had driven Strone away from the Guild, the sacrilege of Klaryus's murder.

"I know who poisoned the Veritas," Tharion had told him. "And this man has done more than a simple murder, much more—he struck out against the Guild system itself, tried to bring us down, disgrace us."

Hearing that, Strone had gotten very angry.

"I will give him to you," Tharion had promised. "You must help me, and in the end justice will be served."

Tharion had provided Strone with the precise access codes that had already been used in Troy Boren's escape. After Strone had killed the guards and taken special joy in the death of the loathsome man Dieter Pan, he had escaped into the main docking bay, shucking his blood-soaked prison clothes and slipping into the crisp sol-pol uniform he had stolen from the barracks. Fully uniformed again, Strone had climbed into one of the spare spacesuits, leaving his prison outfit lying loose on the floor plates.

He secured himself to the wall and blew the airlock, dumping everything into space, including his discarded clothes. Then, in vacuum, he hauled his body hand over hand to a small equipment closet and locked himself inside.

For a long time he stood motionless, conserving his air, waiting, waiting. . . . Patience wasn't hard for him.

Further chaos entered OrbLab 2 when mobs of sol-pols arrived from the Platform, summoned by the emergency alarms. With Dieter Pan dead, however, nobody quite knew what to do. When at last they returned to the Platform in disorganized teams, Strone casually slipped in among them, wearing his crisp, clean uniform inside the bulky spacesuit. He enjoyed being among his old sol-pol comrades again.

Once they had finally met in secret, Tharion explained Franz Dokken's schemes. Strone listened with bitter revulsion, and the rage that boiled up inside of him constricted his chest.

"But I can't trust those sol-pols to arrest Dokken. I can't trust them to listen to me, or to the Council," Tharion said. "I have seen evidence that their loyalty may lie elsewhere. They may fight for the holding they call home, rather than for the Guild. And of course Dokken himself will resist any attempt to strip him of his power.

"Thus, I have reached a conclusion that chills me to my core." He had leaned closer to Strone, speaking in a hoarse whisper. "In order to deal with this properly, and guarantee that justice is done, I must work *outside the law*." The Guild Master turned away. Strone waited, silently and patiently, for him to continue.

"I have found the root of the evil that so inflames you, Eli Strone," Tharion finally said. "But I require your vow that once this is finished you will no longer take justice into your own hands. With Dokken removed, the Truthsayers Guild can heal. Justice is once again *our* responsibility, not yours." Tharion's eyes were cold, and strong. Impressive. Strone shuddered, feeling again the awe that Truthsayers were *supposed* to evoke.

"You have my vow, Guild Master."

Tharion nodded. "We must first follow the law, but in this instance I believe the law will fail us. The Landholders Council intends to deal with Dokken. They may not be effective. That is why you are so important, my friend. I will send you in disguised as a new manservant, complete with a false name. I need to have somebody inside that I can trust," he said, "in case all else fails."

"I will be there," Strone had promised.

*In case all else fails.*

But now Guild Master Tharion was dead by the hand of the monster Franz Dokken. Strone hadn't acted soon enough, and he barely restrained himself from going off on a rampage.

"Something wrong?" Dokken had asked.

No. He would be patient. He would strike at the right time. He had missed his first chance and would only make things worse if he acted rashly now. Clenching his big fists in an attempt to diffuse the scarlet anger blazing behind his eyes, Strone made his way out of the villa to the stables.

He would take great care to arrange a fine, private—and oh so satisfying—death for Franz Dokken. Justice would be served.

iii

Dokken looked around him quickly, at the fireplace, at the balcony, the bright geraniums and the mulberry bushes in the courtyard. The silkworms inside their glassed-in greenhouse continued to munch contentedly, though the workers scrambled to grab their own meager belongings and run down the winding gravel road away from the bluffs.

Time was running out.

Dokken had built this place over the centuries, through several identities—but it had always been *his*, growing stronger, more powerful . . . and now it was galling to have to abandon it all. But the missiles were on their way, streaking down through the atmosphere. There was no way to stop them, and he had no reason to doubt the word of Kareem Sondheim.

The *SkySword*'s high-tech weapons were devastating. Dokken had used some of them himself, and he knew his villa was doomed. He stared at the homey possessions, the little touches that Schandra had added during her ten years of living with him. He realized that anything he could salvage in just a few moments would be a poor effort at best.

He looked down at Tharion lying on the floor, cold and unaware of his fading surroundings. "This is all your doing, my son," Dokken said. "If you'd only followed along and let me keep training you, none of this would have happened. You could have been my equal."

He sighed and looked back to the mantelpiece, seeing the leather bound book in which he had hidden the poisoned Veritas capsule. Its torn binding would have to be repaired, but this was the one item he would take with him. "Machiavelli." Some things just could not be replaced.

iv

Dokken and Lor rode away from the outbuildings after turning all the other horses loose and chasing them down the bluff road. Not only would it save them from the explosion, but it would also cover the fact that two of the mounts were missing.

He and the manservant trotted their horses into the highlands and looked back toward the villa, which shone a creamy beige in the midday sun. They sat in their saddles, watching for the missiles to come.

In only a few minutes Dokken heard the sonic booms as daggers of fire screamed down, glowing a blinding white as they traced a blazing slash across the sky directly toward Dokken's fortress.

Only three seconds passed from the moment they first saw the bright specks high in the sky to the instant the missiles targeted in, one immediately after the other, striking the villa and throwing out a sun-hot ball that erased the beautiful home in an instant, turning the surrounding rock to slag. A second later the roar of the explosion reached them, its sound squelched by distance.

"Sondheim, you're a bastard," Dokken muttered.

Most people would assume that Franz Dokken had died in the detonation, and Captain Vanicus would unwittingly help in that charade—which would make it easier for Dokken to lie low. Angry tears stung his eyes, but he blinked them away, drawing a deep breath of the sharp Atlas air.

There was time. He had patience. Everything could be manipulated into place again like the pieces of a puzzle that had just been tossed to the winds.

The holocaust continued to blaze as Dokken wheeled his chestnut stallion about and urged the horse to a trot, heading into the badlands.

The plan had already crystallized in his mind, and it seemed the best he could do. The more he thought about it, the more he looked forward to the challenge of fighting his way back to the top again. It might take another century or so—but it was only a matter of time after all, and he had long ago made his peace with time. It would make life interesting.

The new manservant knew none of Dokken's secrets, but the two of them would go out to the hidden cave in the canyons, and Lor would help him set up the deepsleep chamber for a long slumber. Dokken had enough supplies stashed in the cave that by alternating cycles of hibernation and wakefulness, he could stay away for at least a year or so, and the generator was rated for centuries. He could sleep, eat, plan, sleep again . . . and remain out of sight for a good, long while.

That should be enough time for him to figure out what to do, to make new plans.

The manservant turned to gaze back over his shoulder at the smoldering conflagration in the bluffs. The tall man with big hands seemed to hold a barely contained violence within him. In another time and place Dokken might have been able to make effective use of him—but now, once they had reached the cave and the deepsleep chamber, Dokken would have to kill him, make a clean break with the past.

"Come on," Dokken said. "If you're willing to go with me, we have a long ride ahead of us."

The manservant nodded, as if happy to do his bidding. "I will enjoy taking care of you, Master Dokken," said Eli Strone with a smile.

The two men rode off into the wilderness.

# CHAPTER
# 51

i

In the aftermath they met at the Great House of Toth Holding: Troy and Kalliana and Ysan, along with Victoria Koman. Emilio Toth was recovering from the bullet wound in his shoulder. Lady Kiarre Toth took the opportunity to care for her husband, nursing him with draconian protectiveness, making him feel miserable and loved at the same time.

Lady Kiarre shooed Ysan away as she wrapped a bandage tighter, and Toth smothered a grunt of pain. She patted her husband's chest. "We've received a message from young Michel Van Petersden, Emilio," she said, "and he sends his regrets that he can't join us for the celebration. Don't fret about it."

Toth nodded. "Can you blame him for wanting to spend time on his reclaimed lands? He's got a lot of work to settle into his new holding. He's even opened negotiations with some of the Pilgrim representatives to see about setting up part of the holding for them to begin their own homeland."

Victoria Koman smiled. "And he'll earn their loyalty for all time. Michel seems a natural-born leader, brilliant and enthusiastic. He reminds me of Dokken himself in some ways, but my boy has a good heart, not a twisted one. That'll make all the difference as a landholder."

After another enormous meal fixed by Toth's wife and served by the rambunctious children, they moved out to the balcony to watch the skies. According to predictions made by Koman's overzealous engineers, the orbital Platform would crash this evening.

Kalliana kept close to Troy as the two of them stood on the edge of the balcony. Emilio Toth lowered his bulk into one of the chairs, in deference to Lady Kiarre's insistence that he not overexert himself.

Toth's ancient father moved slowly but with great determination, as if he had focused his stroke-damaged mind on a single quest and would not relax until he had followed through. The old man shuffled over to his son, patting Toth on the unhurt shoulder, squeezing it in silent support. Then the old man turned and, with immense care, drifted back out again, heading toward his orchards.

"There it is," Ysan cried, pointing upward as a bright dot moved swiftly across the nightscape, a brilliant flash cutting through the auroral curtains.

The wrecked Platform burned overhead, a meteor streaking down in flames. Behind it, accompanying the crackling sound of its passage, screamed a line of ionized air as the severed diamond-fiber cable whipped across the sky.

After the elevator explosion the transmitted shock front had traveled down the long cable with the speed of sound, resonating as it struck the ground with enough force to uproot the anchor point buildings. The fiber had trailed a swath of damage across First Landing, dragging its massive anchor blocks along with it until it finally rebounded into the sky again with the recoil of its reckless passage. Troy wondered what his old boss Cren had been doing at the time. How would he keep track of inventory now?

The explosion had tossed the Platform out of its stable geosynchronous orbit. It dipped deeper into the atmosphere with each perigee, to burn up six days later. No one remained alive on the station anyway.

The handful of survivors on OrbLab 2 had made radio contact immediately, broadcasting to the Guild receivers in First Landing as well as Toth's own satellite uplink. The sol-pols and prisoners on the free-floating laboratory pleaded for help and rescue, knowing that their food and water and air would run out soon. But the colonists were just as stranded on the surface of Atlas as the survivors were in orbit. Troy's heart went out to those isolated and condemned prisoners up on the station, but no one on Atlas could do anything to save them. They would have no way to reach orbit again until the *EarthDawn* arrived.

As the companions watched from Toth's balcony, the Platform ripped across the sky—a ball of slag and wreckage blazing with friction from the atmosphere. It would crash far out in the ocean an hour from now.

Tentatively, Troy touched Kalliana's shoulder. She moved closer to him.

Emilio Toth sat back in his chair and stared at the shooting star with tears in his eyes. "Reminds me of the crash of the original colony ship," he said. He sighed and rubbed his hands through his bushy cinnamon beard. "But this is much more than a symbolic loss."

Before long, the bright trail of the Platform vanished over the horizon.

ii

The Truthsayers Guild Headquarters opened its great ship doors and announced that the combined session of the Guild and the Landholders Council would welcome the public to join the discussions. The Council and the Guild had many changes to propose and effect.

Qrista presided, looking much aged and devastated by the loss of her husband Tharion, in addition to everything else that had changed. Grim and determined, she wore the royal blue sash at her waist with evident discomfort. But she had been chosen as the best candidate to manage the healing between the Guild and the public, the Truthsayers and the Mediators, the landholders and the workers.

When Qrista spoke, her amplified voice was loud and taut with inner strength, and people listened to her. "The only benefit that comes of such disasters," she began, "is what we learn from them."

The Council members had gathered at the long table. Beside her in honored guest chairs sat Troy Boren, Ysan, and Kalliana, each of whom had earned a place in these discussions by being involved at the core of the turmoil that had necessitated the reshaping of Atlas society. Both Kalliana and Ysan would have prominent positions in the reorganized Guild, each receiving a new green sash. It was time to admit mistakes, Qrista had said, and to live with them.

Troy remained amazed at finding himself in the middle of planet-shaking politics, playing a role of some importance. He himself would work with the new Guild and the Council, since he had been wronged by the system. Qrista had asked him to spearhead a team that would develop a series of protective measures and appeals.

In her preamble Qrista described what had gone wrong, admitting the misplaced assumptions and the mistakes made by Truthsayers as well as landholders.

"The whole concept of justice on Atlas has been based on an infallible pronouncement of guilt or innocence—but mistakes were indeed made, and we cannot excuse ourselves by claiming good intentions." She placed her hands in front of her on the table and looked out at the audience gallery.

"No system of justice is ever perfect. Here in the Guild our arrogance was in assuming that our way *was* perfect, so we allowed for no checks and balances." She drew a deep breath. "It was as if we all wore blindfolds, still believing we could see."

In an open discussion the other Guild members raised questions of how everything would change, now that they knew there would be no new shipments of Veritas, and the stockpile in the armory vault wouldn't last forever. Some suggested that new manufacturing centers be set up in isolated domes out in the dry seabeds where the Veritas progenitor thrived. This, though, held its own inherent dangers, particularly with the possible spread of the Mindfire mutation. Many people—even some Truthsayers—were unwilling to take that risk.

With or without restored Veritas production, Qrista pointed out, it would still be some time before they would be back on solid footing again.

When it came their turn to speak, Kalliana and Ysan both advocated that Truthsayers not be so isolated from other citizens. "Truthsayers must remain in touch with the people they are called upon to judge," Kalliana said. "Or we lose all right to hand down pronouncements to our peers." She glanced at Troy.

The auburn coloring had been bleached out of her hair again, and she wore a white robe that symbolized her position in the Guild, along with the bright green sash, though it was questionable whether she would ever want to perform a truthsaying again. To Troy, she looked like a distant angel once more, shining and pure—but his fondest thoughts of her were the times they had spent in the granite-quarrying village at Toth Holding.

Troy looked over to the audience gallery inside the meeting chamber and saw his family there, still exuberant from having moved to new quarters in First Landing. His mother noted his attention and waved, embarrassing him. She sat content and beaming beside his father, finally resigned to the fact that it wasn't likely her son intended to give her grandchildren . . . though the possibility of romance seemed not out of the question.

### iii

The biggest surprise came weeks later, with a new transmission from the *EarthDawn* colony ship: Captain Omar Psalme announced that they had increased speed after reassessing their power reserves. The additional acceleration would allow them to arrive in two years instead of five. Their ship was much more efficient than the original colony vessels sent out centuries before, and the new colonists had been able to shave some time off the long interstellar passage.

This placed enormous pressure on the people in First Landing. Troy and Kalliana and Ysan worked with the other landholders to prepare the way. Regular updates were transmitted and disseminated to the public at large.

The *EarthDawn* was finally close enough that the transmission lag allowed an actual dialogue. The citizens in First Landing got to know Captain Psalme and his prominent crew members by sight. The landholders and Guild members discussed plans for the important new arrival. . . .

Troy stood in the central plaza and looked across the city of First Landing. He saw the people bustling with a frantic edge to their movements, but he was content. Kalliana stepped out of Guild Headquarters and walked over to meet him, smiling.

Busy times were ahead, and Troy's heart skipped a beat as he thought of how Atlas would prepare for such enormous changes as another colony ship approached their world.